Praise for *The New York Times* bestseller
Home to Holly Springs

"Lovely . . . This is Karon's most emotionally complex novel."
—*USA Today*

"I have learned a lot about how to pray and how to deal with both my passions and my enemies from Karon's novels. . . . *Home to Holly Springs* drinks deeply from the wells of forgiveness and reconciliation."
—*Christianity Today*

"Karon's deft interweaving of past and present infuses the Mitford saga with new energy."
—*Kirkus Reviews*

"Mitford fans, rejoice! . . . Father Tim answers the summons—and learns that you can go home again."
—*The Washington Post*

Jan Karon is the author of nine Mitford novels: *At Home in Mitford*; *A Light in the Window*; *These High, Green Hills*; *Out to Canaan*; *A New Song*; *A Common Life*; *In This Mountain*; *Shepherds Abiding*; and *Light from Heaven*, all available from Penguin.

Ms. Karon is also the author of *The Mitford Bedside Companion*; *Jan Karon's Mitford Cookbook & Kitchen Reader*; *A Continual Feast*; *Patches of Godlight*; *The Mitford Snowmen*; *A Christmas Story*; *Esther's Gift*; and *The Trellis and the Seed*. Her children's books include *Miss Fannie's Hat*; *Jeremy: The Tale of an Honest Bunny*; *Violet Comes to Stay*; and *Violet Goes to the Country*.

The Father Tim Series

JAN KARON

Home to Holly Springs

PENGUIN BOOKS

PENGUIN BOOKS
Published by the Penguin Group
Penguin Group (USA) Inc., 375 Hudson Street, New York, New York 10014, U.S.A.
Penguin Group (Canada), 90 Eglinton Avenue East, Suite 700, Toronto,
Ontario, Canada M4P 2Y3 (a division of Pearson Penguin Canada Inc.)
Penguin Books Ltd, 80 Strand, London WC2R 0RL, England
Penguin Ireland, 25 St Stephen's Green, Dublin 2, Ireland
(a division of Penguin Books Ltd)
Penguin Group (Australia), 250 Camberwell Road, Camberwell,
Victoria 3124, Australia (a division of Pearson Australia Group Pty Ltd)
Penguin Books India Pvt Ltd, 11 Community Centre,
Panchsheel Park, New Delhi – 110 017, India
Penguin Group (NZ), 67 Apollo Drive, Rosedale, North Shore 0632,
New Zealand (a division of Pearson New Zealand Ltd)
Penguin Books (South Africa) (Pty) Ltd, 24 Sturdee Avenue,
Rosebank, Johannesburg 2196, South Africa

Penguin Books Ltd, Registered Offices:
80 Strand, London WC2R 0RL, England

First published in the United States of America by Viking Penguin,
a member of Penguin Group (USA) Inc. 2007
Published in Penguin Books 2008

1 3 5 7 9 10 8 6 4 2

PUBLISHER'S NOTE
This is a work of fiction. Names, characters, places, and incidents are either the product
of the author's imagination or are used fictitiously, and any resemblance to actual persons,
living or dead, business establishments, events, or locales is entirely coincidental.

THE LIBRARY OF CONGRESS HAS CATALOGED THE HARDCOVER EDITION AS FOLLOWS:
Karon, Jan.
Home to Holly Springs : the first of the Father Tim novels / Jan Karon.
p.   cm.
ISBN 978-0-670-01825-3 (hc.)
ISBN 978-0-14-311439-0 (pbk.)
1. Episcopalians—Fiction.   2. Clergy—Fiction.   3. Holly Springs (Miss.)—Fiction.   I. Title.
PS3561.A678H66   2007
813'.54—dc22   2007029976

Printed in the United States of America
Set in Goudy Oldstyle

Acknowledgments

Warmest thanks to Dr. Daniel P. Jordan, Jr.; Lou Jordan; Judge Dan Jordan, Christy Jones, Blanton Jones, Jean Ann Jones, Mary Ann Connell; Quentell Gipson; Annie Moffitt of the popular Annie's Restaurant in Holly Springs; Dorothy Warren; Ruthie Bowlin; Russell Whitehead; Cary Whitehead; Mike Moore; Betty McGeorge; Lois Swanee; Jorja Lynn; John Peaches; Dr. Ben Martin; David B. Person; Chelius Carter; Frances Gresham; Steve Gresham; Olga Reed Pruitt; Carol Hill; The Very Reverend Dr. Paul Zahl; Jim Boone; Tony Bowers; Billy Jones; Melba Darras; the late Tommie Darras; Ann Barnes; Sara Lee Barnes; Earl Scott; Polly Hawkes; Reverend Marshall Edwards; Jim Shank; Albert Ernest; Rodger Belew; Marvin Gormours; Jeff Heitzenrater; Nancy Briggs; Betty Moore; Jean Coors; Wendall Winn, Jr.; Cathie Lillis; Winston K. Barham; Wayne Dowdy; Frank S. Brown; Bill Hargrove; Larry Dean Richardson; Mike Thacker (my hunting and firearms authority); Beki Thacker; Ollie Thacker; Joyce Thacker; Judy Grigg; Reverend Edwin Pippin; Darlene Rush; Ed and Dean Rush; my sister, Brenda Furman; my daughter, Candace Freeland; Dr. David M. Heilbronner; Dr. Robert Gibson; Tom Mangold; Kevin Whiteley; Mary Minor; Major Tom Pike; Bob Maurino; Rt. Reverend William A. Jones, Jr.; and in recognition of the contributions by

Elizabeth Blanton Jones (1868–1949) to the cultural welfare of Holly Springs and beyond.

Boundless thanks to Reverend Bruce McMillan; Dr. Paul Klas; Dr. Kevin McConnell; Dr. Emanuel Cirenza; Dr. John J. Densmore; and to Dr. Thomas R. Spitzer, Director of the Bone Marrow Transplant Program at Massachusetts General Hospital, Boston.

Dedication

When I began writing the Mitford series more than a decade ago, I needed to know where my main character, Father Timothy Andrew Kavanagh, had been born and raised. He was decidedly southern in his speech, behavior, and personal affinities, but what part of the south had shaped and influenced him?

I spread a map of America on the floor of my writing room, and proceeded to eliminate every southern state but Mississippi (which I had never visited). Then my gaze roved its towns and cities for a place name with music in it. When I found Holly Springs, the decision was immediate: Tim Kavanagh was from Holly Springs, Mississippi, population 8,000, and the burying place of so many illustrious war dead that the town cemetery is also known as Little Arlington.

I never dreamed I'd actually visit this gem of the Deep South. Then, nine novels and more than a decade later, I knew I must set a book in my character's birthplace—and find the missing pieces of his early life.

In Holly Springs, I not only found the missing pieces, but something rare and wondrous. I found people who value their deep connections and shared history, and are willing to forgive each other their trespasses. Without exception, they're proud of their town and its more than sixty antebellum homes; proud of Rust College, their

century-old institution of learning; and proud of the beauty that
surrounds them on every side. Beauty is important in this fragile
life, and Holly Springs has no lack of it. Nor was there any lack of
warmth and generosity in the welcome I received.

Indeed, I am able to say, as Paige Benton Brown has said, "Mississippi isn't a state, it's a family."

If that sounds overly sentimental, so be it. I found it true.

Though this novel is set in a real town, no actual Holly Springs
personalities make their appearance in these pages. However, some
of the places mentioned herein are quite real. I chose to cast Tyson
Drug, Booker Hardware, and Phillips Grocery because all are familiar landmarks in Holly Springs today, as well as an important part of
the culture in Father Tim's youth. Other actual landmarks referenced in *Home to Holly Springs* include Airliewood, Fant Place,
Christ Church, First Baptist, First Presbyterian, the Utley Building,
the train station, Hill Crest Cemetery, Stafford's, the birthplace of
Ida Wells, and the impressive brick and limestone Greek Revival
courthouse which anchors the town square. The Peabody Hotel in
Memphis is yet another actual landmark appearing in this work.
However, even when a real place appears, the events portrayed are
fictitious.

I hope my friends in Holly Springs will forgive any blunders, historical or otherwise, contained in this work, and know that it is
dedicated with profound regard to all who call Holly Springs home.

Jan Karon
October 2007

ONE

A preacher with a lead foot, driving a red Mustang convertible with the top down, could make a state patrolman pretty testy.

He checked the rearview mirror. Though he was the only car on the highway, he slowed to fifty-five.

It was nearly fourteen years since he'd been nailed for speeding, though he had, in the meantime, been given a warning. Of course, the warning had been delivered while he was still driving his primeval Buick. Not only had the decrepitude of his car inclined the officer's compassion toward clergy in general, but he'd looked pretty astounded that the vehicle could even do seventy in a fifty-five mile zone.

He glanced toward the passenger seat. His travel companion, now occasionally known as the Old Gentleman, was obviously enjoying the wind in his face.

Perhaps he should feel guilty about making this trip with his best friend instead of his wife. But hadn't she practically booted him out the door?

'Go!' she said, hobbling about in her ankle cast. 'Go, and be as the butterfly!'

He had tested her a couple of times, to make certain he could bust out of there for five or six days and remain within the loose confines of her good will.

'What about food supplies, since you can't drive?'

'Darling, this is Mitford. They will swarm to bring covered dishes to the wife of their all-time favorite priest.'

'Swarm, will they? Just to be safe, I'll lay in victuals.'

'Don't, please. Just go. Go and be as—'

'You already said that.'

'Well, and I mean it. Butterflies have a very short life span. If they're ever going back to Mississippi to settle certain issues of the heart, they have to hop to it. And enjoy the trip while they're at it, of course.'

His wife was a children's book author and illustrator and had her own way of looking at things.

'What about the trash?'

'Sammy or Kenny will carry it out, they're right next door. Or even Harley will do it. I can't even make enough trash for all those fellows to carry out.'

'What if you get, you know, scared or something?'

'Scared or something? Have you ever known me to be scared or something?'

He had, actually, but they'd been lost in a wild cave at the time.

She'd given him that grin of hers, and blasted him with the cornflower blue of her eyes. And here he was.

Kudzu.

Everywhere.

He didn't remember such vast stretches of his old terrain being carpeted with the stuff.

It was seldom seen in the mountains of North Carolina. Too cold, he supposed, for the flowering perennial vine from the Orient; it was the boiling summers and mild winters of Mississippi that worked the charm. What the government had planted in the thirties to prevent erosion had done its job, and then some.

He turned the radio on and roamed the dial, looking for a country station. This wasn't a Mozart kind of trip.

". . . I'm goin' to Jackson, and that's a fact, yeah, we're goin' to Jackson, ain't ever comin' back . . ."

Johnny Cash and June Carter were going to Jackson, he was going to Holly Springs.

He hung a right at the first exit to his hometown, relieved that he hadn't felt it yet—the surge of sorrow or dread or even cold disinterest that he'd feared since the note arrived and he'd decided to make this journey. As they drove out of Mitford yesterday morning, he'd steeled himself for the appearance of some long-suppressed emotion that would overtake him straight out of the box. But it hadn't happened.

It might have assailed him last night in the motel room, more than five hundred miles from his wife, as he crawled, unwilling, beneath a blanket reeking of stale tobacco smoke.

There had also been a window of opportunity this morning when, downing an egg biscuit on the south side of Memphis, he'd felt suddenly panicked—ready to get behind the wheel and head back the way he'd come. But he'd caught such feelings red-handed and refused to give in to them. What he was doing had to be done, even if it produced despair, which was probable, or grief, which was likely, or anger, which was almost certain.

A few stores. Acres of kudzu.

"Brigadier General Samuel Benton," he said, speaking to his dog. It would be a miracle if he could remember the names of all the generals buried in Hill Crest Cemetery in Holly Springs.

"Brigadier General Winfield S. Featherston, Brigadier General Christopher . . ."

Brigadier General Christopher . . .

Zero. He'd have to recall this particular surname before the long, solemn train of names could move forward as they'd done in his fifth-grade recitation of Hill Crest's illustrious dead. The recitation had won five gold stars and, to his amazement, the momentary deference of his father.

He didn't recognize this road, which was a modern translation of the old 78. But then, after an absence of thirty-eight years and four months, he hadn't expected to recognize this or any other road leading into his hometown.

He touched his shirt pocket, making certain he'd remembered to bring his cell phone, and heard the sharp crackle of the envelope stuffed behind the phone. Finding the envelope in the mailbox a couple of weeks ago had literally knocked the wind out of him, like a punch in the solar plexus.

He showed it to Cynthia, along with the lined sheet of paper it contained.

She Who Loves a Mystery studied them both. She did that odd thing with her mouth that she often did when thinking, then leaned her head to one side as if listening to some inner informant.

'The handwriting appears to come from another era,' she said, giving her final verdict on the two-word epistle. 'It seems somehow . . . genteel.'

Genteel. He had always credited his wife with knowing stuff that others, himself included, couldn't know. For a couple of days, they attempted reasonable conclusions, finally deciding there were no reasonable conclusions. Ultimately, the whole thing veered down a bank into the bushes.

'It's from Peggy Cramer,' said Cynthia, 'your old girlfriend with the turquoise convertible. Perhaps her poor husband has croaked, and she'd like to see you again.

'Or it's from Jessica Raney, the one who adored you when you raised rabbits. She never married, and because signing up with eHarmony requires a computer, which she doesn't have and never will, she sent this note.'

'You're nuts.'

'You told me you kept her card in your sock drawer until you went away to college.'

He regretted his nauseating habit of telling his wife everything.

'And here's another distinct possibility.'

'More fodder from the deep wells of unconscious cerebration!'

'It could have come from your first movie date. You said you felt terrible that her parents had to sit across the street drinking coffee for two hours. The movie was . . . wait, don't tell me. *Flying Tigers.*'

He was amazed, and oddly pleased, that she remembered such hogwash.

'If we had nothing else to do,' she said, 'we could make a whole book out of what lies behind these two little words.'

Again and again, he examined the envelope and the careful inscription of his name and address. The postmark partially covering the stamp was blurred but readable. It was definitely Holly Springs, though it might have come from Jupiter or Mars, for all its cryptic content.

He compared the handwriting of the note with that on the envelope. The same.

In the address, the sender had used the title Reverend, so this fact of his life was known by at least someone in Holly Springs. But why had he or she chosen not to sign the note? At times, he found the absence of a signature menacing, a type of dark threat. At other times, the bare simplicity of the two words, without salutation or signature, seemed to implore him with a profound and even moving passion, as if anything more would have been too much.

The lined white sheet had been torn from a notebook pad and was the sort he used at his own desk. Nothing unusual there.

He smelled the paper, a veritable bloodhound searching for clues. Nothing unusual there, either.

He had walked around for several days, shaking his head as if to clear it.

Was there anyone left in Holly Springs whom he'd remember?

Except for his cousin Walter in New Jersey, his kin were dead and gone—to St. Peter's in Oxford, to Elmwood in Memphis, to Hill Crest in Holly Springs. As for Tommy Noles, whom he'd once called his best friend, he had no idea where he might be, or if he was still living. One weekend he'd come home from his parish in Arkansas, and heard around the square that Tommy had left Holly Springs. For good reason, he hadn't popped up the road to ask Tommy's mother and father about their son's so-called disappearance.

After years of refusing to think of his hometown, he now focused on it with increasing intensity. His wife had grown weary of his excessive noodling and passed on to more fulfilling pursuits, like making a trellis out of twigs for her clematis plants.

He went to the living room and lifted the sterling picture frame from the library table by the window, and studied the sepia photograph of his mother and himself at the age of four. He looked first into her eyes, and then into his own. What were they telling him, if anything? He caressed the worn frame with his thumbs, noting that his mother appeared sad, but beautiful. He appeared happy, if perplexed.

His gaze searched her strong gardener's hand, and the wedding band which Cynthia now wore. More vividly than he remembered the studio session, he remembered the day the large photograph arrived in the mail. He'd been enthralled with the image of the two of them, it was the first magic he'd ever witnessed.

He opened the drawer of the table which he'd taken from Whitefield after his mother's death, and looked at another sterling frame, lying face down in the drawer with an odd scramble of family pictures. Over the years, he'd played a confessedly neurotic game—for long periods, this picture of his father would be displayed next to the one he was holding, then put away again when some random despair struck and he couldn't bear to see his father's cold, though handsome countenance. It had been lying face down for several years.

He closed the drawer and stood looking out the window.

Did people still park around the square and spend Saturday in the stores?

Did the cavernous train station still cast its shadow over a network of rusting tracks, or had it been demolished, or rehabbed for some other use? And what about the old compress where he'd gone with Louis on the final run of his father's cotton trucks? He'd been tempted more than once to Google the town name and find answers, but he'd never followed through.

In the end, what he really wondered about was the house and the land at Whitefield, where he'd grown up. His mother had died there, just five years after his father's death, both of them too young, everyone said, for dying. He'd driven from Arkansas, from the small country parish he was serving as curate, to be with her in her last days.

Later, after her estate was settled, and her good rugs sold along with the tall case clock and the walnut wardrobe in which she'd hidden her secret Christmas gifts—after all that was gone, and even the smell of her driven out by Clorox and Bon Ami, he determined never to come back. What could possibly be left to come back to?

He geared down to second, gawking.

Strung along the crest of the hill to his right were the immense Gothic buildings of Mississippi Industrial, apparently abandoned years before and left standing in ruin. He was shaken by the sight of their brooding silhouette, and the legions of windows with broken panes that stared blankly at Rust College across the street.

He looked left to the replica of Independence Hall, the centerpiece of the college, and its impressive clock tower. The memory of

the ravaging fire that destroyed the original hall was vivid still;
Peggy, who had been like a second mother, had held him as they
watched it burn.

He remembered feeling trapped by the heavy clothes he wore
against the frigid cold, and Peggy's arms, which were squeezing the
liver out of him.

'Let me *down!*'

'You cain't git down, baby, I ain't losin' you in this crowd.'
Peggy's nose was running, the tears wet on her face.

'I ain't a baby, I'm five!' He'd been furious at being held in her
arms like an infant. But his heart was moved by her tears; he loved
their Peggy. He had stopped kicking and patted her face.

'Why you cryin'?'

'My mama wanted to go to that school, she say it were th' hope
of th' coloreds.'

When he was older, he was told how the multitudes collected
almost instantly to watch the inferno, arriving by wagons, pickups,
dilapidated cars. Black children and white were dismissed from
school, presumably to see what they would never see again, and to
watch history unfold in flames that blew mullions from windows
and collapsed five stories into rubble. He remembered his father saying that the smoke had been seen forty miles away. Others spoke of
how the fire had smoldered for weeks; the scarlet glow along the rim
of the hilltop appeared to be the setting of a January sun.

Brigadier General Christopher *Mott!* That was it. Christopher
H. Mott, to be precise. Yours truly may have turned seventy day before yesterday, but his brain wasn't fried yet, hallelujah.

He saw it then, looming above the horizon like an enormous
onion. It was definitely more impressive than the great icon of his
childhood, though lacking the nuance and character of the original.

He and Tommy had plotted the fiendish thing for two years.

Living in the country, as they both did, they couldn't just pop to
town whenever the notion hit. Two things had to happen. They

had to have a better than good reason to be in town for a whole night. And since any connection with Tommy was forbidden, they'd be forced to get there by separate means.

It had all come together pretty quickly.

He found Tommy's note in the rabbit hutch on Thursday. On Friday, Tommy would be taken to town by his father, to spend the night with his aunt and uncle and mow their grass on Saturday. Scarcely ten minutes after he found Tommy's note, his mother asked if he'd like to spend Friday and Saturday nights with his grandmother, and they'd all go to church at First Baptist on Sunday.

Trembling with excitement, raw with fear, he met Tommy at the hutch at feed-up time on Friday morning. "We can't tell *nobody*," he said.

"Deal."

They did their secret handshake: right thumbs meeting twice, pinkies hooked together two beats, palms flat and slapped together two times, right fists touching twice.

In unison, they said the secret word.

There was no turning back . . .

Unlike some donkey brains, he hadn't wanted to write anything up there, like CLASS OF whatever or GO TIGERS, and for darn sure not the word that somebody had painted on all four sides of the tank one Saturday night, to greet the frozen stares of churchgoers on Sunday morning.

He just wanted to be up there. With the stars above, and the lights of the town below.

He hadn't counted on being terrified.

The fear set into his gut the minute he climbed out Nanny Howard's window on Salem Street; as his feet hit the ground, he broke into a cold sweat. He stood behind the holly bushes a moment, queasy and stupefied.

Then he slipped across the yard and down the bank, and raced along the silent, moonlit street like a field hare. Something small and glowing, perhaps the tip of a lighted cigarette, arced through the air as he blew by the darkened houses. His heart hammered, but he saw no one and didn't hang back.

Two dogs barked. The flashlight he carried in the pocket of his shorts banged against his leg; he took it from his pocket and held it tight. If a dog came after him, he would knock it in the head; if he was bitten, he would cross that bridge when he came to it.

He arrived at the tank, drenched with sweat and scared out of his mind that Tommy would suddenly appear from the bushes, causing him to lose it right there.

In the light of the three-quarter moon, he saw Tommy; his face was as white as death.

'I'm scared,' said Tommy.

'Don' worry, ain't nobody gon' see us.' He was shaking so badly he dropped the flashlight, and had to fumble in the parched grass to find it.

'Look up yonder, we cain't even see th' top.'

'We got t' take it one rung at a time. Stop an' rest if we have to.'

'We stop t' rest, we'll be climbin' 'til daylight. Then th' police'll be on us.'

'If we get up a ways an' don' like it, we can come back down. Shut up bawlin'.'

'I ain't bawlin'.'

He placed his flashlight at the foot of the ladder; the moon was light enough.

'Come on, then.'

'You first,' said Tommy. 'An' don' be fallin' on m' head, neither.'

'Don' turn yeller on me.'

'I ain't turnin' yeller on nobody.'

Something like an electrical current shot through him when he touched the metal rung of the ladder. He drew back, then touched it again.

The jolt hadn't come from special wiring to keep people from climbing to the top and writing that word; it had come from an excitement like he'd never known.

He grabbed on to an upper rung with both hands. He could do this thing.

They climbed like maniacs for what seemed a long time, then stopped and leaned into the ladder, desperately exhausted, their hearts pounding.

'I'm about t' puke up m' gizzard,' said Tommy. 'Ever' time I look down, it hits me.'

'Don' look down, keep y'r eyes straight ahead.'

'Ain't nothin' t' see straight ahead.'

'It's puke or look straight ahead, take y'r pick.'

Tommy puked.

'Good,' he said. 'Let's go.'

They went.

They were feeling the wind now—the higher they climbed, the stronger it blew; his shirttail billowed like a sail. What if they got sucked off this thing and somebody found them splattered like toads on Van Dorn Avenue? He hadn't counted on wind. He hadn't counted on the locked gate between the ladder and the platform, either.

'We'll have t' climb over it,' he hollered above the bluster of wind.

Tommy yelled the word that had been painted on the tank.

His hands were sweating; he wiped one hand, then the other, on his pants and grabbed hold again.

'Let's go back down!' Tommy shouted.

He was glad Tommy had said it, and not him. He thought of his mother sleeping four miles away, unknowing; of his rabbits feeding on beet tops in their hutch beneath the moon. For a moment, he couldn't believe what he was doing; he was dumbfounded to find himself up here, flapping around in a smoking-hot wind as heavy as the velvet curtains in Miz Lula's parlor.

Lord, he said to himself, trying to work up a prayer. There was only one problem with praying—since he wasn't supposed to be doing this, there was no way God was going to hear anything he had to say.

The locked gate gleamed in the moonlight.

'I'm goin' over!' he yelled. 'If I die, you can have m' marbles an' slingshot. There's five quarters in a snuff can on th' shelf under th' hutch. An' m' funny books . . .' No, not that. Even if he was dead as a doornail, he didn't want to lose his funny books; they'd just have to rot under his bed.

He hesitated for a moment, then clenched his jaw.

'Tell Miz Phillips I did m' whole readin' list for summer!'

He hooked the toe of his left high-top into the wide mesh of the gate and pulled himself up and dropped down on the other side, his weight resounding on the metal platform. Tommy dropped down after him.

They leaned against the tank, panting with exertion.

The platinum moon was sailing so close he might jump up and touch it. It changed the look of everything; his shirt was silver, his hands and arms were silver, Tommy was silver.

'I can smell th' beach!' he hollered. 'All th' way from Pass Christian!' He nosed the air like a terrier, and discovered a deep vein of fragrance, something like honeysuckle and salt.

'Where's our houses at?' yelled Tommy.

He didn't want to think about their houses; he wanted to think about being free, lifted from the earth above everything he'd ever known. Already he was longing to tell somebody that they'd made it to the top, that out here beneath the moonlight was the whole state of Mississippi and maybe even Alabama and Tennessee—but of course, they couldn't tell anybody. If their fathers found out, they'd both be dead. But he, Timmy Kavanagh, would be deader.

In his gut, he knew he wouldn't keep his word to Tommy. He would have to tell Peggy. But that was okay. Since Peggy would

never, ever rat on him, telling Peggy was the same as not telling
anybody . . .

A car horn blared.

Startled, he waved an apology and moved ahead in traffic.

His heart felt strangely moved by the memory of that night, and
of Tommy pulling his knife from his pocket before they made the
long trek down the ladder.

'We done it,' Tommy had said. 'We done what we said we was
goin' t' do. Let's mix blood an' be blood brothers.'

All his life, every minute, he had wanted a brother. He'd been
pretty queasy when Tommy drew out the blade he kept so carefully
sharpened.

Maybe the feeling in his chest—some trace of sorrow or longing,
he wasn't sure which—was a precursor to what he'd been waiting
for. But the feeling passed quickly.

He gave a thumbs-up to the water tank.

The landscape was recognizable at last; they were headed toward
the town square. In the strip mall on his right, two black men in
shirts and ties washed a funeral home hearse; suds sparkled on the
baking asphalt.

During the trip from Mitford, he'd pondered the order of his vis-
itations, then rearranged the order again and again.

In the end, the square was the logical place to begin, it was
where everything began in Holly Springs. Nearly the whole of his
early life could be read in a drive around the courthouse square.
He'd be surprised if Tyson's Drugstore had made it into the twenty-
first century, and surely Booker Hardware with its oscillating nail
bins would be long gone.

Maybe a bite of lunch on the square. And next, he'd drive to the
cemetery. That made sense.

"Flowers," he said to his dog. He'd want to take flowers.

He also wanted to see Tate Place, and a few of the more than sixty antebellum houses of which Holly Springs had always been proud. He'd visited many of those homes; put his feet under many of those tables.

He loosened his tab collar and wiped his face with his handkerchief. Too blasted hot; he was a mountain man now.

He'd leave the church 'til last, and as they headed back to the motel, they'd drive four miles east to the homeplace.

He reflected on this plan.

"Not a good idea." He looked at his travel companion, who was currently sleeping. "Entirely too much to do in one day."

He was as tender as a greenhouse plant; he needed time to harden up before he was set out in the red dirt of his native ground. Besides, he had allowed four days to puzzle out the note—if it could be puzzled out—before heading back to Mitford.

As they reached the post office, he pulled into a parking space and cranked up the rag top. Bottom line, it didn't seem right to return to his birthplace after so many years, to circle the square in a red convertible with the top down. Definitely a tad on the cocky side.

He locked the top in place and poured water into the metal bowl and watched Barnabas drink, then took a few swigs from the jug himself. He pulled down the sun visor and squinted into the mirror and licked his salty fingertips and smoothed his wind-tossed hair. Then he took the envelope from his pocket and blew into the open end and removed the note and read the words once more.

Come home.

A truck roared past, and a few cars. He scratched his dog behind the ear and gazed, without seeing, at the post office. The clock ticked on the dashboard.

"Here goes, Lord."

He put the note in the envelope, stuck it in the glove compartment, and turned the key in the ignition as his cell phone rang in his shirt pocket.

Who could read the ID on these blasted things? New glasses soon. He'd roll the dice that it was his wife.

"Hey, sweetheart."

"Hey, yourself. Where are you?"

"Just coming to the square. Parked a minute to put the top up."

"Are you okay?"

"I am. How's your ankle?"

"Better by the hour. The swelling is going down."

"Still painful?"

"Definitely, but I'm staying off it, as prescribed, so we can reschedule our Ireland trip for August. I'll do anything to get this hideous moon boot removed."

"Are you needing anything?"

"I'm happy as a clam. No little book to slave over, instead I'm bingeing on other people's books. And I don't have to turn a hand to take nourishment. Puny's dropping by at noon with her fabulous chicken soup, and Dooley and Sammy and Kenny are coming over with pizza at six. Oh, and Timothy, you won't believe this—the boys are all saying 'yes, ma'am' to me."

"You never know what perks you might score with a fractured ankle."

"Kenny's so much like Dooley. And so good for Sammy. Seeing these boys together is a blessing to everyone in town. And none of it could have happened without you."

"I miss you, Kavanagh."

"I miss you back."

"Thanks for letting me go."

"I didn't let you go, I made you go. You'll be glad you did this, I promise. Are you really okay?"

"So far, so good. I'll be fine."

He was edgy, his mouth as dry as cotton.

He eased the Mustang out of the parking space and moved forward with the traffic.

"How's Barnabas?"

There it was, straight ahead.

"Great," he said. "We've both got a little sunburn, but nothing serious."

His father's office over the bank. The prewar metal stairs ascending the side of the building. Martin Houck had tumbled down those stairs, head over heels, as legend had it. He'd never been able to completely reconcile whether he'd actually seen Houck fall, or only heard about it so often he thought he'd been there.

"I'll call you tonight," he said.

Memories were pouring in now, the dam had broken.

His father's voice had been sharp outside his bedroom door.

'Do you realize that what he's done carries a five-hundred-dollar fine and a six-month jail sentence?'

'He's a minor, Matthew. Surely not . . .'

'Disobeying me yet again by carousing with that Noles ruffian, willfully defying the law and everything it stands for, everything I stand for. Move away from the door, Madelaine.'

'You've already said enough to cause any suffering he may deserve.'

'Stand aside.'

'Don't hurt him, Matthew.'

'Don't hurt him? What's the good of discipline if there's no hurt in it? Read your Baptist Bible, Madelaine.'

His father's brutal punishment on the Sunday after he climbed the tank had taught him a fact he would remember the whole of his life: No matter where his father might be, and without regard for the time of day or night, Matthew Kavanagh had eyes and ears everywhere.

He'd later asked his grandmother how his father had known.

Nanny Howard patted his arm. 'There's no tellin' about your daddy. You'll learn the answer when you get to heaven. And then it won't matter' . . .

"There's Father's office," he said to Barnabas. "It looks . . ."—he couldn't speak for a moment—"the same. Amazing. And the bank . . ."

He pulled to the curb and saw behind the iron fence the small brick storage building where he'd hidden the things he couldn't take home. He marveled at the sight. Still there.

No, he thought, still *here*.

He had done what the note commanded. He was here now. He had come home to Holly Springs.

TWO

Stafford's was closed, of course.

He had hoped it wouldn't be, but that was the way of things. Stafford's was where everyone had gone for lunch; walking into the clamor of Stafford's had nearly always given him a kind of thrill. Here were the lawyers and bankers and cotton brokers and merchants, the people who built and shaped and drove their town.

He'd been proud to look around the crowded room and see among these important men his father's finely chiseled face and mane of prematurely silver hair, and to test, always to test, whether his father would look up and see him and acknowledge his presence in the room, though he wouldn't have been welcome at his father's table in the corner.

Stafford's was where he'd tasted his first grilled cheese sandwich, mashed flat and crisp beneath the heavy lid of the grill; and where he'd slurped down his first fountain Coke, surely among the most exhilarating experiences of his early life. The fizz had entered his nasal passages and gone straight to his cerebrum, where it shivered and danced and burst like a Roman candle in his brain.

The brick and limestone courthouse, with its double portico and central cupola, looked much the same. Certainly a dash more decked out, possibly by new paint on the trim and the maturity of the trees on the square. He'd always heard that the buildings of one's childhood looked smaller and less important when viewed through the lens of years. But the rather finely wrought courthouse still looked important to him—it had been the epicenter of his, and everyone else's, life. He remembered the rhythm of his father's footsteps, the way his heel taps sounded as they walked along the hall to the courtroom. The taps on the shoe of his good leg rang sharply on the pine boards, the taps on the shoe of his bad leg gave off a hollow, dragging sound.

He checked his watch. The courthouse clock was right on the money, which gave him an unexpected sense of security.

First Presbyterian . . . the Utley Building . . .

He was cruising the square, gawking like a tourist. A car horn sounded behind him; he made a left off Memphis onto Van Dorn.

He looked farther up Van Dorn, where the spire of Christ Episcopal soared above the solid, earthbound brick of First Baptist. The Battle of the Churches, Nanny Howard had called it—his father hauling him to the rail of the Episcopalians, his mother's family warming him at the hearth of the Baptists.

'So, which side won?' he'd been asked as a young curate.

'Both,' he felt obliged to say. Years later, he realized he'd answered well.

Tyson Drug was still Tyson Drug. An amazement if ever there was one.

By the time the Main Street Grill had closed in Mitford, Percy Mosely had chalked up forty-odd years of doing business in the same spot, which was no mean accomplishment. But Tyson's had been here when he was a little kid, for Pete's sake, and who knew how long before that? He felt a swell of something like civic pride as he rolled into a parking space.

"Okay, buddyroe." He snapped the red leash on his dog's collar. "Time to meet and greet."

He didn't know about the squirrel population in Holly Springs;

he would hate to be dragged across the square in front of God and everybody. Of course, at the ripe age of twelve years, his mixed-breed Bouvier didn't do a lot of squirrel-chasing these days.

He'd been uncertain about bringing a dog on such a trip, especially a dog the size of an early Buick town car. But he was glad he'd done it; he'd talked to Barnabas from Mitford to Memphis, and, as always, his good dog actually listened.

Tyson's was the same. Albeit totally different, of course—the soda fountain had gone the way of straw boaters.

"How do you do?" he asked the young woman behind the counter.

She eyed Barnabas. "Is that . . . a dog?"

He laughed. "Barks, wags his tail, likes a good pig's ear now and then."

"I never," she said in disbelief. She leaned over the counter and let Barnabas sniff the back of her hand. "How can I help y'all?"

"We're mostly just visiting around. I used to live here."

"Right here in Holly *Springs?*"

"Yes. I haven't been back in a long time."

"Well," she said, looking him over and smiling. "I'm Amy McPherson. We're glad to have you back."

He thought it wonderful that she appeared to mean it. "Tim Kavanagh, Amy. I'm looking for some old friends." The only problem was, he had socks older than Amy McPherson. Young people wouldn't know anything about the folks he hoped to find. He peered around.

"Anybody here who's, you know, older?"

"The boss is really old, but he stepped down to the bank. He's forty-somethin'."

"So how's business?"

"Real good. Court's in session today. It's always good when court's in session."

"Nice to know that some things never change. Any postcards of the courthouse?"

"We've got th' 1900 photo—it's with th' cotton wagons, people like th' cotton wagons—or th' 2004, it's got th' gazebos."

"Two of each," he said, digging out his wallet.

He'd spent good times in this place. "Any newspapers around?"

"We carry th' *South Reporter*, that's th' Holly Springs paper, an' th' *Commercial Appeal*, that's th' Memphis paper, plus *USA Today*. Th' rack's at th' door."

"Good. Great. I'll take a *South Reporter*, and see you again to-morrow."

"Bring your dog," she said.

He stopped at the painted stone column outside Tyson's double doors, where he and Tommy had once hoped to immortalize their existence on the planet . . .

The day was blazing hot, their sweat-drenched shirts stuck to them like another skin. Only a few people moved about the square; it would be a perfect time to do what others had done before them. They pulled out their pocketknives and wiped the blades on the seats of their jeans, and claimed their spot on the column.

W I L, he scratched into the paint.

'Who's Wil?' asked Tommy.

'You'll see.' He liked the way the green paint gave way to white plaster beneath, making the letters stand out. L I A M.

'That ain't yo' name, cootie head.'

'Is now, pig brain.'

'Who's William?'

'You wouldn't know.'

'Not if you don' tell me.'

'A poet,' he said.

'A *poet*?'

' "Come forth, and bring with you a heart that watches and receives." '

'Huh?'

'Miz Babcock made us learn poetry,' he said, etching the surname.

'I'm glad I didn't git Miz Babcock, I don' want t' be no sissy.'

If men wrote poetry, why was it sissy for boys to read it? He could not understand this.

Learning scripture had given him a particular fondness for memorization, and maybe for his newfound interest in poetry—the two seemed linked as one. In a drawing in his English book, Mr. Wordsworth sported a white beard as big as a cloud, which made him look a lot like God. His eyes seemed knowing and kind, as if you could actually talk to him, if he wasn't dead.

'I'm puttin' m' *own* name on,' said Tommy. 'Someday, I'll come back t' Holly Springs and it'll still be right here.' Tommy's tongue poked out the corner of his mouth as he engraved his last name.

'Are you leavin'?' He felt suddenly anxious; people never talked about leaving Holly Springs.

'Ain't that what you do after you git out of school?'

'I guess.'

'Are you ever leavin'?' asked Tommy.

'I don' know," he said. "Maybe.'

'Where would you go?'

He knew Treasure Island wasn't real. Maybe Mount Everest; he knew that was real. Or Spain. Or India. He shrugged. 'Most anywhere would prob'ly be okay. 'Cept Africa.' He had never liked the notion of being mauled and eaten alive by lions.

'Africa's where Louis an' Sally an' all their young 'uns come from,' said Tommy. 'Yo' Peggy come from there, our Sam come from there, lots of niggers come from there.'

He'd never thought about it before, that Peggy had come from anywhere other than the little house down the lane from his big house.

'You can go anywhere you want to,' said Tommy, 'but I sho cain't.'

'How come you cain't?'

' 'Cause I'm poor—but you're rich.'

He didn't like the accusation of being rich. Of course, he knew he wasn't poor—his father was counsel to the bank, they had a car with tires on the fenders, they had a two-story house, and over six hundred acres with fifty-six in cotton—but he didn't think they were rich. Boss Tate was rich.

'You always sayin' you're poor. You ain't poor.' He said ain't as often as possible when he wasn't at home or in school or in church. "You got a house an' a barn an' a car. An' a cow. You got a cow, we don't have a cow.'

Tommy shrugged.

'An' yo' daddy's a history teacher. Teachers make lots of money." Sometimes people told his father that he'd been seen with Tommy Noles; he'd taken more than a few lickings for it, each time worse than the last, and all because his father said Jack Noles was not only an *unequipped* teacher of history, but a jackleg *drunk* whose farm machinery was allowed to *rust* in the *fields*.

If Tommy's daddy would just mow his yard and paint his house and put his farm machinery under a shed, they could probably play together, but he couldn't say that. He shut up the blade and put his knife in his pocket.

'Yo' daddy won' be likin' this, Timothy.'

Wearing a straw hat and yellow bow tie, the Colonel came up behind them, blowing from his trek along Van Dorn.

'Won' be likin' what, sir?' If the Colonel ratted on him for hanging out with Tommy, he was sunk.

'Writin' yo' name on private property! That ain't legal.' The Colonel drew out a handkerchief and mopped his red face.

'I didn't write my name,' he said.

The Colonel leaned down and squinted at the painted column, adjusting his glasses to peer at the repository of local signatures.

'From down th' street, look like I seen yo' knife out.'

'My knife's in m' pocket, sir.' He patted his pocket to give witness to the fact.

'Y'all boys don' need t' be gittin' in any trouble.'

'Nossir, we don't.'

The Colonel stuck his face closer to the column. 'William Wordsworth,' he read aloud. 'Who in th' nation's *that*?'

The Colonel straightened up and gave them the once-over. 'Y'all boys behave y'rself,' he said, opening the door to Tyson's and slamming it behind him.

He asked her the next day.

'Peggy, where were you born at?'

Peggy was sweeping the porch, wearing the red head rag. She always wore the red rag. One day he would ask if something was wrong with her head, maybe warts.

Peggy swept harder. 'Say where you *born*. Period. You can't end *nothin*' you say wit' *at*.'

He sat with his back against a porch column. 'Where were you born, then?'

'Th' piney woods.' Peggy was definitely aggravated; she swept the pollen off the side of the porch with unusual vigor and moved down to sweep the steps.

'Tommy says you come from Africa.'

'Africa, my foot! I never laid eyes on no Africa.'

'Where, then?'

'You th' aggravatin'est little weasel I ever seen.'

This was going nowhere. 'If you ever left, where would you live at?'

Peggy glared at him from the porch step. 'What I jus' tell you 'bout *at*? Say it ag'in.'

He was fed up with this. 'If you was ever to leave,' he hollered, 'where would you go-o-o-o?'

'Not back to where I started from, thass fo' sho.'

This was his chance and he was taking it. 'So where did you start from?'

Peggy shook the broom at him, looking fierce. 'This broom be tellin' you where I started from if you aks me ag'in.'

He decided he wouldn't ask her again. Not soon, anyway . . .

Hog heaven. According to the sign up ahead, Booker Hardware was still Booker Hardware.

He'd never grown tired of hanging around Booker's; and for several summers, they'd let him work there—helping customers, ringing a sale, sitting on the stool behind the counter. Even sitting down, he'd felt ten feet tall on that stool.

Booker's was where he smoked his first Lucky Strike, heard his first official dirty joke—he'd been so dumbfounded, he could still remember the darned thing—and where he'd learned a few words he'd never heard before, even in the cotton field. Booker's was one of the best memories he'd carried away from Holly Springs.

They crossed Van Dorn at a trot and entered the cavernous, wood-floored hardware store. The bell on the door jingled.

"Whoa," said the man behind the counter. "That a dog, or a coal car jumped offa th' track?"

"A mere dog. Won't bite or beg for food, and enjoys the romantic poets. Tim Kavanagh." They shook hands.

"Red Lowery." Red eyed his tab collar. "You th' new man down at th' Frozen Chosen?"

"Nope, just an old dog myself, come back to Holly Springs after nearly forty years."

"Born here?"

"I was. I have to tell you, Booker's was one of my favorite boyhood haunts, I worked here for three summers. It's a miracle it's still in business."

"Dern right it's a miracle. What with th' gov'ment gougin' th' small b'inessman every time he turns around, it don't hardly pay t' open your door of a mornin'."

"I hear you, Red, I do." He looked to his right and there they were. He hurried along the aisle and smoked over the metal nail bins, soldered to a center pole that swung around like a lazy Susan. He felt like hugging the blasted things. If he had any place to put it, he'd offer to buy this setup. Hey, Kavanagh, he'd say, I'm bringing home a nice set of nail bins, back your car out of the garage and park it on the street.

He slowly turned the bins and inspected the impressive variety of their contents, mesmerized. How often had he done this as a boy, listening to the squawk as the bins circled on their pole? He chose a nail and hiked up the aisle.

"I'll take it," he told Red.

"Jus' one?"

"Just one. For a souvenir." He drew out his wallet.

"On th' house."

"Come on. A nickel? A dime? What do nails go for these days?"

"That one's free. You ever go t' build a house, I'll be lookin' for your nail b'iness."

"Deal. Thanks."

The bell jingled; three men in camouflage scattered through the store.

"That's m' groundhog hunters," said Red.

"Folks wear camouflage to hunt groundhogs?"

"These boys do. You got family here?"

"Only at Hill Crest."

"You plannin' t' move back?"

"Can't move back. I'm dug in like a turnip in North Carolina."

"Lot of red dirt up there, I been there."

"Do you know the name Tommy Noles, by any chance?"

"Tommy Noles, Tommy Noles." Red looked blank.

"How about a black man a few years older than myself, named Willie? Or maybe he'd be called Will or William now."

"Right yonder's y'r black man named Will." Red jerked his thumb toward the front window. "Will! Here's th' IRS lookin' for you."

His heart rate kicked up; this could be the moment he'd prayed for, however randomly, since he was a kid.

"Will don't like dogs."

"Can I leave him here? He's harmless."

"Hitch 'im t' this stool right here."

As he walked toward the front window, Will came to meet him, grinning. He was a big man, wearing overalls.

"Will—Tim Kavanagh." He felt a knot rise in his throat.

They shook hands.

"Will Pruitt. I sho hope Mr. Red 's jokin' wit' me."

He noted that Will's right hand was as big as a smoked ham; his left hand was stuck down the throat of a man's street shoe.

"He was definitely joking; I'm a preacher who never got the knack of wringing money out of folks. I'm looking for someone they called Willie when he was a boy, someone I knew many years ago." He stood there, as bare-faced as he knew how, hoping Will would recognize him.

"They used t' call me Willie—now Will's m' name, an' half-solin's m' game."

"Half-soling?"

"Boots, shoes. I keep th' soles goin' 'til th' tops give out."

"A high calling, if you ask me. Would you be the Willie who worked at Tate Place when you were a boy?" Please.

"Don' b'lieve I ever worked at Tate Place."

Will removed the shoe from his left hand.

It wasn't Willie.

"You new in Holly Springs?"

"Old and new. Born here, lived here 'til I went away to school. Back for a visit. How about you?"

"Born an' raised right here. Retired las' year from maintenance at th' college, an' hang aroun' wit' Mr. Red doin' m' half-sole b'iness. Keeps me out of trouble."

"I'm retired, myself."

"I guess yo' collar do pretty good t' keep you out of trouble."

"Trouble don't dodge a collar," he said, lapsing into the vernacular. He was loving the soft, slow speech of his youth; it was like poured chocolate. He removed one of his loafers and turned it over. "Just as I thought, Will. Look here."

"Goin' down, all right. Specially 'long th' side there, you mus' walk a little slew-footed."

"The heels look all right to you?"

"Look like they can git by a good while yet."

"Can you do a couple of half-soles while I wait?"

" 'While you wait' is my slogan. You want taps?"

He hadn't had taps in decades. "Taps all the way."

Nearby, one of the hunters mowed through a display of shoelaces.

"I hear y'all are goin' groundhog huntin'," he said, standing on the hardwood floor in his sock feet.

"If we ever git out of town. These boys want t' shop more'n hunt. I'm Merle."

"Tim Kavanagh."

"That's a dog an' a half you got up front."

"He is that. You hunt groundhog for sport?"

"Me, I mostly hunt for my neighbor, he has eight kids, but I been known to eat it if it's cooked right. Clyde, he don't touch groundhog; he leaves 'em f'r th' buzzards—it's got t' where they know Clyde s' good, they follow 'is truck. But you take Smokey—he'll eat what he hunts. His idea of a seven-course meal is a groundhog an' a six-pack."

"How in the world would you cook groundhog?"

"Skin it. Quarter it. Flour it. Fry it."

One of Merle's buddies appeared with an armload of packaged snacks. "You forgot parboil. Have t' parboil th' sucker fo' 'bout a hour." He shook his hand. "Smokey Davis."

"Tim Kavanagh. Pleased to meet you."

"Okay, here you go," said Merle. "Quarter it. *Parboil* it. Flour it. Fry it."

"Hot oil," said Smokey.

"Hot," said Merle.

" 'Til brown."

"What does it taste like?"

"Chicken."

He'd like to have a nickel for every arcane flesh, including coyote and armadillo, said to taste like chicken.

"Tough?" he asked.

"Not too bad," said Merle. "Shoot, I lef' out somethin'."

"Right," said Smokey. "You forgot t' marinate it."

"What about th' sweat glan's?" Clyde walked up with a package of work socks and a pouch of Red Man. "You tell 'im 'bout th' sweat glan's?"

Merle heaved a sigh. "Oay, here you go. Th' whole nine yards. Skin it. Take out th' sweat glan's, they're right about here . . ." He raised an arm and pointed to the spot. "Quarter it. *Marinate* it. *Parboil* it. Flour it. Fry it. Eat it."

"Got it." He was sorry he'd asked.

"It's a job of work."

"I was just thinking that."

"Where you from?" asked Smokey.

"Right here."

Smokey eyed him. "I don't b'lieve I've seen you around."

"Been gone thirty-eight years plus change."

"Movin' back?"

"Can't do that."

Smokey shook his hand. "Whatever. Glad to have you. Y'ought t' try you a bite of groundhog sometime, be good for you."

He stopped by the register and collected Barnabas.

"We gon' see you 'fore you leave us again?" asked Red.

"I'll most likely pop in every day, just to chew the fat. Feels good to be in Booker's."

"Bring your dog," said Red. "He's a real conversation piece."

He liked the sound of taps on his heels. Nothing too attention-getting, merely a small reminder that he was alive, he had feet, he was walking down the street on a beautiful day. Definitely worth four bucks.

In the car, he slathered on sunscreen and gave Barnabas fresh water. Then, since he hadn't met anybody who seemed like they'd hold it against him, he put the top down again.

The heat had abated a little; cruising around the streets beneath the canopy of old trees was by no means disagreeable.

His mother had loved Holly Springs, and hated her forced move to the country as a young bride. Accustomed to the endless round of socializing which was a Holly Springs hallmark, she had struggled to forgive her husband for betraying his promise to buy them a house in town. She had struggled still more to forgive him for spending her own money, without asking, on the purchase of Whitefield.

How had he forgotten how beautiful his hometown was?

He drove along Salem Avenue, wide as a boulevard and lined with houses built by wealthy cotton planters. He remembered the French wallpaper in the enormous hallway of Fant Place, and the parties his mother and father had attended in its double parlor—he'd been invited for tea spiked with rum before he pushed off to college. And Montrose—as a child, he had played in its derelict yard, wondering if the upstairs shutters might fall on his head; now it appeared to be an image from a postcard.

He passed Airliewood, which every Holly Springs schoolchild knew as General Grant's headquarters in '62. Grant's men had stolen the silver doorknobs, shot the pickets off the iron fence, and turned the lead bathtub into bullets—but the old wounds had healed; the house looked better than ever.

His mother had taught him that nearly every house in his hometown was a living history book, including the birthplace of a slave named Ida, he couldn't recall her last name, who'd become the first civil rights worker.

Wells! There it was. Ida Wells. Facts and names he'd long ago tossed overboard were floating to the surface like so much jetsam.

He pulled to the curb and stared, swallowing hard. His grandmother's house had undergone an updo to beat the band.

He reached for his dog and buried his fingers in the thick, wiry coat. His mother had been raised here, he'd been born here. There was the very porch railing he'd tried to walk like a tightrope, resulting in a broken arm that was, to this day, not right.

"That's where I came into the world," he told Barnabas. "Dr. Jordan was going on ninety, they said, and his hand was steady as a rock."

Nanny Howard moving through the house in her blue wrapper, which she wore 'til she dressed at four in the afternoon; windows shuttered and curtains drawn against the heat of the day; her Bible lying in the seat of her favorite rocker on the sleeping porch; her daily prayer—

"Sometimes she said it at breakfast, sometimes when we walked out to the garden—'Lord, make me a blessing to someone today.'"

Barnabas looked square into his e

"She was certainly"—he cleared his throat—"a blessing to me. An island of calm in a stormy sea."

As a boy, he'd likened her smell to the fragrance of peaches in churned ice cream, and had been mildly disappointed to learn it was Coty face powder from Tyson's.

His grandfather, Yancey Howard, had been a profound influence, as well. Kindhearted, sanguine, a peacemaker—and a well-loved Baptist preacher who once risked his life to save a boy from drowning in a flooded river. He also enjoyed a type of bucolic fame for bringing twin boys into the world while making house calls to his rural congregation.

Though Grandpa Yancey had the nod of the community along with a sizable parcel of land, Nanny Howard had the money in their family, just as his own mother, Madelaine, had had a substantial amount in his. He learned that his father wouldn't accept a dime from Grandpa Kavanagh, though having made a fortune with box factories in Oxford, Jackson, and Memphis, the old man was rich by any standard. That was fine, every tub had to stand on its own bottom, but the fact that his father had used his mother's money to buy Whitefield was another matter entirely. Long before he was old enough to hear about this duplicity, he felt as if he'd been marked in the womb by something he couldn't name or understand.

From the time of his eighth birthday until he was twelve, and when no one had money to spare, Nanny Howard had given him three dollars every three months. Both his mother and father had questioned this stream of funds in war and postwar time. 'If a boy has no money to handle,' Nanny had said, 'how will he learn to handle money?'

In return for the quarterly bonanza, she expected to hear of many sacrifices made and much good done, and he'd been able to deliver—most of the time. He occasionally concealed a nickel or a dime spent shamefully, but came to relish using this treasury toward ends other than his own. Giving, he learned early on, produced as much, and sometimes more, pleasure than a Sugar Daddy, with which he'd unintentionally yanked a bad tooth clean out of his head . . .

'Twenty-five cents for funny books.'

'Yes, ma'am.'

Nanny Howard pored over his record-keeping, written with a No. 2 pencil on lined notebook paper.

'Fifty cents for socks and chewing gum for Sergeant Silverman.'

'Yes, ma'am. I put 'em in th' Care package Mama sent.'

She nodded. 'Very good. Fifty cents for shoelaces and a comb. For Sergeant Silverman, I take it.'

"No, ma'am. For Peggy. It was her birthday.'

'Very thoughtful. Thirty cents for the collection plate, for the work of the Lord in foreign lands. "The Lord loveth a cheerful . . ." ' She turned and looked at him.

' "Giver!" ' he said. 'Second Corinthians, chapter nine, verse seven.'

'Well done. Eighteen cents for postcards.'

'For Lieutenant Krepp to write home on. We sent him a USO package, an' he sent me a picture of him an' his buddies in Italy. He has two kids.'

'I hope you sent him one of the courthouse.'

'Yes, ma'am. With th' cotton wagons.'

'I don't see one red cent saved back.'

'You don't give me enough t' save somethin' back.'

'Well, now, listen to that. If I hadn't saved back, there would be nothing to give you at all. If you have only a nickel, you can save back a penny.'

He didn't like to disappoint Nanny Howard. He would do it, then. Somehow.

With a dollar and twenty-seven cents yet to be accounted, he sat through the rest of the rigmarole stiff as a board. Though worried about his decisions, he was sure of his arithmetic. At the end, she was pleased.

'You are a special boy,' she said. 'Your grandfather will be proud.' Then she talked about character, as if he weren't there and could listen only if he wanted to. ' "Character," Mr. Dwight Moody once said, "is what you are in the dark." '

There was the rub, he thought—trying to be good in the dark . . .

"Back then, there were lots of squirrels," he told his dog.

Perhaps he'd stop again and ask if he could see the house.

He drove aimlessly for a while, looking, remembering, and turned onto Gholson Avenue.

He would never forget the night at Tate Place; the memory would plague him 'til the end of his days, unless . . .

His father's laughter rose loudly above the distant murmur of voices along the gallery. He was always uneasy when his father laughed; he felt jealous that the laughter was never for him, and embarrassed that it stood out so sharply in a crowd.

He sat in the corner on a stool, watching the commotion in the steaming summer kitchen. Two cooks worked at the stove, frying chicken in huge skillets; a tall colored man named Mose handed off platters of food to a lineup of barefoot helpers outside the kitchen door. Grease popped; someone swore; yeast rolls were bundled into starched white napkins and chucked into baskets. The screen door slapped shut and was kicked open again as loaded trays and platters moved out the door and across the green lawn to the gallery.

'Y'all git across t' th' dinin' room, now, an' mind you don' spill nothin', you hear? Step along, I's comin' right behin' wit' yo' supper.'

He and a barefooted colored boy were pushed from the kitchen by a mammy in an apron.

'Willie!' somebody shouted after them. 'Make that chile eat, then y'all set on th' front porch 'til I come git you. Thass yo' job, an' I 'spec' you t' do it nice.'

They were herded across the lawn and up the steps of the house and along the hall to the small table with four chairs in the corner of Miz Lula's dining room. He'd had Sunday supper here at Easter, but there had been other children then. He had found seven dyed eggs in a grove of azalea bushes.

The mammy set the plate on the table and thumped down a knife, a fork, and a bowl of cobbler. 'You th' onliest chile at this party. Willie gon' see you eats a good supper, an' mind you 'til yo' folks gits done. You drinkin' milk?'

It couldn't hurt to ask. 'Can I please have a Co-Cola?'

'Willie, go wit' me an' bring this baby a Co-Cola. He th' onliest chile at th' party an' need a treat.'

He was furious at what she had just called him, but looked steadily into his plate, unseeing.

'Use yo' napkin!' she said, loud enough to wake the dead. He thought she looked ten feet tall.

He tucked a corner of his napkin into his starched shirt collar. He hated his stiff collar and he hated this place.

'Thass a nice baby,' she said, leaving the room with Willie.

He burned with humiliation. He didn't want a colored boy to hear him called baby. Never, ever again would he come to Miz Lula's, no matter how much people got down on their knees and begged him.

Willie returned with the Co-Cola and set the opened bottle on the table. 'What yo' name?'

Timothy sounded like a baby's name. 'Tim!' he said.

'How ol' you is?'

'Five goin' on six.'

'I's ten.'

There was a long silence. He looked at his plate, finally seeing what was on it. Fried chicken. Yes. Squash. No. Tomatoes. No. Green beans. No. In its own small dish was blueberry cobbler with thick cream. Yes. He stared at the way the berry juice had purpled the rim of the white dish.

'Y'all gon' eat all 'at?'

'I ain't much hungry.'

'I could sho eat it fo' you.'

'Guess I'll eat th' chicken. An' maybe th' cobbler.'

'Eat all you want, an' I'll clean up th' res'. But you cain't tell no-body.' Willie eyed his Co-Cola.

He picked up the drumstick and bit into the hot, savory meat. It was good, it was almost as good as Peggy's. He guessed he was hungry, after all.

'Looky here.' Willie held up his left hand; he didn't have a thumb. 'I's holdin' th' ol' hen on th' stump wit' this here han', an' th' axe comin' down in m' other han'. I done it t' m'self.'

His stomach felt funny. 'Did you cry?'

'Sho nuff I cried. Hit bled all on m'self an' th' stump, too. Cat got m' thumb an' run off t' th' barn wit' it.'

He put the drumstick down.

'I wanted that thumb, I coulda showed it aroun' an' maybe got a nickel fo' it. But th' ol' cat crawl up under th' barn an' I couldn' git it back nohow.'

'You can have m' whole supper,' he said, pushing his plate away. Willie grinned.

' 'Cept for m' Co-Cola.'

'You has to stan' lookout while I eats, else I git a whippin'.'

It was exciting to stand at the dining room door and be a look-out for somebody ten years old, even if that person was colored. He was supposed to whistle if he heard footsteps headed this way. His heart pounded, hoping the mammy would come and catch Willie eating his supper, then praying she would not.

They went out to the porch in the gathering dusk and sat on

the top step. Boss Tate's immense touring car was the only vehicle parked in the driveway; guests' cars were parked up and down Gholson.

The crickets were loud, but not as loud as at his house in the country. He wished Willie could hear his crickets, he would be impressed.

'Where d'you live at?'

'Wit' m' mama in th' winter kitchen, she th' boss cook. I he'ps Miz Lula in th' garden, she say I's natural born t' work a garden. See all 'em flower beds yonder? I weeded ever' one of 'em m' ownself.'

It was an unusually warm spell near the end of March; a small breeze carried the scent of viburnum.

'When Mose cut Miz Lula's grass, I rakes it. She save up th' scraps, I carries 'em to th' chickens. She aks me t' bring her ol' shoes, I brings 'em.'

'You a slave?'

'What you mean, a slave?' Willie threw out his chest. 'I's a freed man!'

'You ain't a man.'

'I's a freed boy!'

'Oh,' he said.

'Miz Lula, she nice, I likes doin' fo' Miz Lula. Mose say she ain't hale, she goin' down. I don' know what we do wit'out Miz Lula, nossir, I don' . . .' Willie's voice trailed off.

'Miz Lula's old an' bent over,' he said, in case Willie hadn't noticed.

'Thass her birthday party goin' on back yonder. She be ninety-eight.'

The sound of laughter and applause carried from the gallery to the front porch. Then they heard the singing.

'They be bringin' in th' cake now,' said Willie. 'You ought t' seen th' cake, hit's big as a washtub. Mr. Boss, he gon' give what he call a toas' to 'is mama.'

'Do we get a piece of cake?'

Willie shook his head. 'Colored an' you gits cobbler.'

'What kind of cake?'

'Yeller cake wit' lemon icin', thass her fav'rite an' Mr. Boss's fav'rite, too. Near 'bout ever' Sunday, Miz Lula give me a piece of yeller cake. M' mama, she won' give me yeller cake, but Miz Lula, she do.'

Peggy would give him things his mama wouldn't. Like Co-Cola. 'That ol' Co-Cola gon' rot th' teeth out yo' head,' Peggy would say. 'But I ain't lookin' at you suckin' it down, nossir, I'm lookin' how this mornin' glory vine gon' take th' place if I don' cut it back.'

When they passed from the porch to the front hall, he peered into Miz Lula's parlor and saw the piano. He had always wanted a piano, but his father didn't like noise in the house.

'I could prob'ly play that,' he told Willie.

'Does y'all know how?'

'We have a piano at our house.' The lie had slipped out so easy, it was as if someone else had said it.

'I reckon you could play a minute if you don' tell nobody. Does you play ragtime?'

'I can play most anything.' Another lie had just rolled out; he hadn't even known it was coming. People weren't supposed to lie, even to colored.

'Okay,' said Willie. 'Come on. But don' touch nothin' else, you hear?'

'I won't,' he said. And then he did.

The blue vase sat on the piano on a fringed silk shawl that draped onto the floor. As he walked to the keyboard, numb with hu-miliation at being caught in his sin, he stepped on the shawl. The shawl slid toward him, dislodging the vase; it toppled to the floor and smashed.

'Lord Jesus,' Willie whispered. 'Mr. Boss give 'er that. That was give to him for bein' th' mayor of Memphis.'

Stunned, and frozen with fear, he stared at the blue fragments scattered along the polished hardwood floor.

'Timothy.'

It seemed that the simple act of raising his head took an eternity. He saw his father in the doorway and realized that his mouth was open and he could not shut it.

His father remained in the doorway. 'I was just coming in to see about you. Who did this unholy thing?'

The silence hung in the parlor for what seemed a long time.

'I done it,' said Willie.

As the Buick navigated the rough road toward home, he lay like a stone on the backseat, sick with fear and self-loathing, pretending to sleep. When Willie took the blame, his father had grabbed Willie by the shirt and marched him out of the room—and what had he done to stop it? He'd stood there, mute, helpless, worse than a baby.

Willie had looked back at him and grinned. Yes, grinned. As if he was thrilled to death about the unmentionable act that would happen sure as fire. He couldn't get that grin out of his mind, the thought of it chilled him. If his mother knew he'd allowed Willie to be dragged away for a crime which her son had committed . . . But he could never tell her, he could never tell anybody, not even Peggy, he was in this alone. Sometimes it was hard to believe there were so many things you could never tell anybody.

He prayed with all his might that they would give Willie a nice funeral, with a black car in the lead and curtains at the windows. If they invited him, he wouldn't be able to go, of course, because he'd be too sick to get out of bed.

'. . . since Greece surrendered to Hitler.'

'. . . Germans . . . London . . .'

'. . . shouldn't have humiliated that boy in front of the servants, Matthew.'

'. . . weary of your tiresome sentimentalities, Madelaine.'

He couldn't hear all they were saying over the roar of the motor.

But he knew they were talking about the terrible thing that had happened because of his carelessness, and the worse thing that had probably already happened because of his cowardice.

The wrapped slice of yellow cake, sent to him by Miz Lula, lay on the seat beside him; he would never put a bite of it in his mouth.

His mother came into his room the following morning and stood by his bed. He squeezed his eyes shut even tighter, praying she would go away and let him suffer. *Lord,* he prayed, silent as a tomb, *let me die and be happy again.*

'Timothy?'

He twitched his nose as he'd seen Louis do while sleeping.

'You aren't sleeping. Tell me what's troubling you.'

The thought occurred to him out of the blue. 'I have th' yeller fever.'

'Really?'

He did not open his eyes, he did not want to see her face or make eye contact with someone who was not desperately fallen like himself.

'What are your symptoms?'

He didn't know the symptoms of the deadly fever that had raged through town and left hundreds dead. Even the Catholic priest. Even seven nuns. He'd been told that bodies had been stacked up like firewood, waiting to be buried. Now they were all in the ground at Hill Crest as proof of the worst thing that ever happened in Holly Springs.

'What are your symptoms, Timothy?'

His mother had nailed him, but he couldn't quit now.

'Itchin' all over. Had t' go to th' pot a hun'erd times. Skin burnin' like fire. Feet stinkin' real bad.'

'I'll see you in the kitchen in short order. Peggy has cinnamon rolls in the oven.'

She closed the door behind her, obviously not sorry for a minute that he had yellow fever and could die and be stacked up at Hill Crest like a hickory log.

He heard his father's footsteps coming along the hall—the sharp tap, the dragging sound. His voice was muffled outside the door. 'What is it?'

'Timothy has yellow fever.'

This announcement was followed by something that shocked him to the marrow. It was his father's laughter; his father's scary, out-of-control laughter.

THREE

DICKERSON
CARPENTER
GHOLSON

He drove along a narrow lane bordered by pear trees, reading the names chiseled into the headstones.

SORRELL

CLAYTON

AIRLIE

MACKIE

Here and there, the iron fences enclosing family plots nearly disappeared beneath masses of climbing roses. Cedars, magnolias, and blackjack oaks grown to what seemed enormous size cast islands of shade on mown grass. The hill seemed smaller than he remembered, but greener and more beautiful.

He had followed the hearse to Hill Crest for his Aunt Lily, Uncle Clarence, Uncle Chester, Grandpa Yancey, and then, only months later, Nanny. Far too soon after that, they'd driven up with the urn for his father's memorial service, and finally, he'd ridden in the black, chauffeured town car, known as the family car, behind his mother's hearse. He'd realized that he had no family to ride with him, as his first cousin, Walter, was in Europe at the time. He'd spoken with the funeral director about what he intended to do. There had been some raised eyebrows among funeral home staff when he and Louis, recently widowed and now doubly bereaved, climbed in the backseat together and off they went.

He parked in the lane now and retrieved the roses from the trunk. Then he let his dog out the passenger side and they walked west toward the oldest blackjack oak on the grounds. The age of the oak had been a matter of pride to his grandfather and even to his parents. Back then, owning plots near this oak, which was older than the 1851 cemetery in which it grew, had been loosely akin to owning a house on Salem Avenue.

His eyes roamed his old playground. There ought to be a law against plastic flowers, poinsettias in particular. No, a stiff tax would be better; that would get the job done. In the years he'd visited Hill Crest with his mother, there had been no such abomination . . .

He liked going to town with his mother on Saturday, which was the only day she could have the car. His Aunt Lily never went to town on Saturday, she said Saturday was for the negroes, but his mother enjoyed Saturdays in town as much as he did.

She always dressed up, and put on perfume and a hat and sometimes gloves, and always a little rouge, which she rubbed on her cheeks with her fingers. In spring and summer, they cut flowers from the garden and went to the cemetery every month to decorate the Howard family graves. He liked riding into town with the smell of lilacs or peonies or tulips or roses, and going to the cemetery, which was cool in summer because of the big trees. He was allowed to run up and down the lane, but not at all in the cemetery, because whatever he did, he must never step on a grave. That was fine with him, he didn't want to step on a grave and be hainted for the rest of his life.

Before he could read, his mother read the headstones to him.

'Lieutenant George Anderson said, and this is worth remembering, Timothy: "He longest lives who most to others gives, himself forgetting." '

She told him that Lieutenant Anderson, whose plane went down at the South Pole, lived up to those words every day, according to a letter that Admiral Byrd wrote to the Anderson family.

Fifteen-year-old Robert Walter McGuirk, Jr., was buried at Hill Crest with a letter to his dad dated December 20, 1906. Everybody seemed to know what the letter said, including his Sunday School teacher at Walnut Grove, who learned to recite it by heart as a lesson on the spirit of giving.

> Dear Pap,
>   . . . You know I want to give Mother a comb, brush and mirror and I want you to send me $10 or $20 maybe. When you send me the money please address the letter to me for I want it to be a surprise to Mother and I have to get a lot of other presents so I will be obliged to you if you come across with about 15 bucks. All are well. Your loving son, Walter. P.S. Don't be afraid that the money will be spent foolishly for I am an old head.

There were also ancestors of his mother buried here, who had died with the yellow fever.

In some ways, he thought the cemetery almost as good as a movie because you could imagine the people and their lives, and see the plane going down over the frozen South Pole, and wonder if the boy named Robert ever got his mother the comb and brush and mirror; he really wanted Mrs. McGuirk to have gotten at least the comb. In one way, Hill Crest was maybe even better than the movies, because you could go back to the cemetery again and again, and movies always left town.

Sometimes Peggy came with them and they ate lunch under a

shade tree, then went shopping, and sometimes they visited his mother's friends who had kids his age, or they would go see his grandmother and have chicken salad on a pineapple ring with a hot roll, or maybe when they shopped on the square they would get a grilled cheese at Stafford's. Plus his mother always gave him a dime, which he spent at Tyson's.

'Thank you for your business,' they said at Tyson's, which made him feel as if a dime to them was as important as a dime to him.

When he rode to town with his father, it was different. His father hardly ever spoke, and also kept his eyes glued to the road because of his bad leg, which had nerve damage and made driving a hard thing to do.

He asked a lot of questions so his father would talk to him.

'What makes big holes in the road?'

'Rain.'

'How long do butterflies live?'

'Not long.'

'Why do we have to die?' He really wanted to know the answer to this.

A muscle twitched in his father's jaw, and he didn't reply.

He often asked questions he'd asked before, just in case the answers would be different this time.

'Can I ever have a dog?'

'No.'

'Why?'

'For God's sake, the place is swarming with dogs. Rufe, Louis, everybody has a mongrel dog. Play with their dogs.'

Tommy had a dog, too, his name was Jeff; he helped teach Jeff to catch sticks in midair, and even heel and sit. But he didn't want to play with other people's dogs, he wanted his own. Why his father couldn't understand something so simple made him crave to roll down the window and holler 'til his eyes bugged out.

'Why can't I go swimmin' in th' pond, just once?'

'Water moccasins.'

'Everybody goes swimmin' in th' pond.'

No answer.

'Can I go fishin' in th' river?'

'Absolutely not.'

He would be quiet for a time, to give his father a break from so many questions.

Before he asked the next question, he always prayed. *God, let him say yes. Amen.*

'Can I ever, ever play with Tommy?'

'No.'

'Not even once?'

'Don't ask again.'

He was playing with Tommy, anyway; he and Tommy were making a dam at the creek. But it would help a lot if he had permission, it just would.

He didn't see why Tommy's daddy being a 'secret drunk' had anything to do with why he couldn't play with Tommy. Besides, if his daddy's drinking was such a big secret, how did people know about it? Plus, Tommy's daddy was a schoolteacher, and school-teachers couldn't get drunk or else they couldn't teach, and since Mr. Noles was teaching every day, then the talk about him staying liquored up must not be true.

There was something even more important that he wanted to ask, but he never did. He wanted to ask, Why do you hate me? . . .

The family plot was contained by an ornate iron fence, bought nearly a century ago in Memphis and heavily tangled with climbing roses whose canes were as large as his forefinger. The plot had been mowed, but weeds grew thick around the head- and foot-stones. He had pruning shears in the trunk, and a spade and fertilizer; he'd take care of what needed to be done before he headed back to Mitford.

Mildly detached and fully prepared, he might have been walking into a vestry meeting as he lifted the latch on the creaking iron gate and stepped inside.

REVEREND YANCEY PINCKNEY HOWARD
Safe in
the Arms
of Jesus

Grandpa Yancey had died at age seventy—the same birthday he'd celebrated only two days ago with Cynthia, Dooley, and Dooley's siblings. As for himself—with the exception of his blasted diabetes—he thought he was in pretty decent shape for seventy. But then, Grandpa Yancey had thought the same thing—he'd been chopping wood when he keeled over with a heart attack.

No pain, no lingering illness, just *taken*.

Two funeral celebrations had marked Yancey Howard's passing—one at Walnut Grove, the small country church he had pastored in his early years, and another at First Baptist in town, where he had preached for nearly two decades. First Baptist had been packed; the overflow crowded the churchyard and lined the sidewalk, as if a head of state lay in the open casket beyond the double front doors. His mother and grandmother had been deeply moved, as had he, by the legions of men who, unable to find a seat in the pews, stood outside on a frigid January morning, holding their hats over their hearts in a stinging west wind.

A knot rose in his throat and he felt at once the shame he had so long denied, the shame of being inexcusably late to stand here and pay respects that could never be fully paid.

ELIZABETH JANE MELROSE HOWARD
Her Soul Is
Christ's Abode

"Nanny," he said. The sound of her name, so long unspoken, produced a rush of feeling like he hadn't known in years.

Barnabas sat by his feet, gazing up at him as he mopped his eyes and blew his nose.

"My grandmother," he explained. Following Grandpa Yancey's passing, Nanny had been seized with a racking cough, and died of pneumonia four months later. His mother had been devastated; he'd come home from Sewanee for ten days, wrenched with grief, but stricken even more by his mother's suffering.

He'd bought the roses this morning from a florist on the square. Did he want vases? No, he didn't need vases. Did he want green florist's paper? Not needed, thank you, and no ribbon. Just newspaper would do, something to collect the two dozen stems for the ride up to Hill Crest.

He squatted between his grandparents' graves and placed a red rose on Nanny Howard's, then turned and placed a yellow rose on his grandpa's mound.

"In the name of the Father and of the Son and of the Holy Spirit," he said, making the sign of the cross. "Thank you for loving me. Thank you for the model you set for me, though I was often too blind to see it."

His heart was leaden as he stood and tore the petals from several roses and scattered them over the mounds of earth, giving thanks. Then he wiped his eyes and gazed at the green space to the far right of his grandparents' graves.

That green space was reserved for him.

Turning seventy had given him something to think about, all right. In terms of landmarks, it was right up there with turning forty, when he'd recognized that life would probably always be difficult, and also that it wouldn't go on forever.

At forty, he'd been pathetically overweight. To paraphrase an old saying, what he lacked in being tall, he made up in being wide. Worse still, it lent him an increasing resemblance to his Grandpa

Kavanagh. The family likeness was the torment of his existence; he found it brutally ironic that he should be trapped inside a body so similar in appearance to a man he despised.

Then, to top it all, no pun intended, he was clearly on the cusp of losing his hair. As there was no pattern baldness in his bloodline that he knew of, this reality had come fully loaded with complete shock and bewilderment, feelings he couldn't talk about with anyone, including his barber. He learned the best way to handle it was to make self-deprecating jokes, and he frequently kicked himself for an overblown vanity that had nothing to do with the mind of Christ.

Those seemingly insurmountable issues had been definitely exacerbated by the feeling of isolation in a remote parish given to gray winters. Soon after his forty-third birthday—he remembered the moment vividly—he realized he was sitting with his head in hands, exactly as his father had so often done. He bolted from the chair and ran out to the small, fenced yard, panicked. What if the depression that had consumed his father was consuming him? He leaned against the fence and implored God to deliver him from the darkness that so often clouded his mind in this parish—or had it been there all along, metastasizing like a tumor?

He realized as he cowered by the fence that he had struggled for years to get it right—struggled to experience the joy, the peace, the sense of oneness with the One who was born for him, gave himself for him, and in so doing, offered Timothy Kavanagh the supernatural gift of eternal life.

He genuinely believed in this One, had even been ordained as a priest in his service, and yet, in all the long years of his faith since childhood, he had never deeply, viscerally known the warmth and protection of the divinely unconditional, even tender love about which he had heard and read so much. He had trembled to think he was a fraud.

He stood now gazing at the plot he would not occupy. In a world gone berserk with asphalt, it would be good to leave a span of green earth untrammeled.

What epitaph would he want when the time came for his farewell in Mitford? He remembered the gravestone of a woman parishioner in the churchyard at St. John's in the Grove. DEMURE AT LAST, it read. He thought that the single most definitive and amusing epitaph he'd ever come across.

He saw that his father's urn had taken on a dark patina; moss grew freely on the north side. Then he looked at his mother's headstone, and the inscription he'd chosen with such care and suffering.

No. He couldn't do this now.

Turning away, he opened the gate and walked to the oak, then sat and leaned against it, still holding the roses in their shuck of newspaper. The rough bark felt good to his back; he would pray until he received the grace to pay respects at his mother's grave and his father's urn. He should also get over to Aunt Lily and the uncles, and then to his great-great-grandparents at the north corner of the hill.

A few yards away, a young woman helped an elderly lady of considerable girth transplant a geranium from a plastic pot to the head of a grave. He watched for a time, feeling invisible in the shade of the tree. The young woman watered the fresh planting from a green can, and tamped the earth around it with her foot; the old woman leaned on her cane, giving orders.

They looked up, suddenly, and stared at him; perhaps they thought he was loitering or up to no good.

He raised his hand. "Good afternoon."

"Good afternoon!" the old woman bellowed. "Who're you visitin'?"

"My family." He felt hollow as a gourd.

He realized the young woman had sold him the postcards at Tyson's; he scrambled to his feet as they made their way toward the shade.

"Amy McPherson! Long time, no see."

"Hey," said Amy. "I thought I recognized your dog."

The old woman grasped the handle of her walking stick with both hands and leaned toward him. Given the heavy-duty bifocals that had ridden down her hooked nose, and a good deal of lipstick that had overshot the mark, he thought she looked pretty ferocious.

"I'm Luola Dabney Randolph Lewis, descendant of the Dabneys and Randolphs who came horseback from Virginia in 1834. They bought this land from th' Chickasaw Cession."

"Aha."

"My people *settled* Holly Springs," she thundered.

"Well done."

"An' this is th' girl who brings me here every week to visit my husband, General Horace Parkinson Lewis. Who're you?"

"Timothy Kavanagh, ma'am." He bowed slightly.

"What kind of dog d'you call that?"

"Bouvier with more than a touch of Irish wolfhound."

"I assume he doesn't bite."

"So far, so good."

"I see by your collar you're a priest."

"Retired."

"You live in Holly Springs?"

"No, ma'am. I'm from North Carolina, but . . ."

"I knew I'd never laid eyes on you."

". . . I was born in Holly Springs."

"What's that name again?"

"Kavanagh. Timothy Kavanagh."

"Speak up, my hearin's gone in one ear!"

"Timothy Kavanagh!" he bellowed back.

"Kavanagh. Would you be Madelaine Kavanagh's boy?"

"Yes, ma'am." He felt socked in the gut, as if being Madelaine Kavanagh's boy had been only a dream, and had suddenly become a reality.

"Your mother was a beautiful woman."

"Yes, ma'am."

"A fine Baptist, into the bargain." Mrs. Lewis adjusted her glasses and squinted at him. "You don't have her good looks."

"No, ma'am."

"Step here so I can get a better look at you."

He walked closer.

"You don't favor either one of your parents."

He eyed his car sitting in a patch of shade; he could be behind the wheel in thirty seconds, max.

"Your father was a bitter man. Awfully good-lookin' an' dressed like a peacock, but bitter. Episcopalian, of course. I see you've got Madelaine's complexion. She had a lovely complexion."

Mrs. Lewis was eyeing the very pores of his skin. He stepped back and clung to a headstone.

"It's a pity your mother and father were taken so young. Madelaine would be ninety-five if she'd lived; I'm ninety-three in August; she was two years ahead of me in school. I admit I was jealous of her figure, she had th' tiniest waist you'd ever want to see. An' popular—she was very popular. We were in garden club together, th' club met any number of times at Whitefield. Your mother worked like a dog in those gardens, with hardly a soul to help but that colored girl who ran away. To this day, I never knew what she saw in your father—an' look how he dragged her out to the country an' kept her hidden from proper society. Such an air he had, as if we were all dirt under his feet, but I always believed he was innocent."

Amy put her hand over her face; he stood, stiff and silent, astounded.

"And why did you leave us for North Carolina?"

"I went away to college and—"

"That's no excuse. None at all. That's the way young people do—run off and do their own thing, as they say, and bankrupt the economy of the town that made them who they are in the first place! What happened when the yellow fever left half of Holly Springs dead as doornails? What happened when th' damn Yankees moved in an' ate up or stole everything that wadn't nailed down?"

"Please, Miz Lewis." Amy tugged at the old woman's arm.

"What happened when th' Depression wiped us out, an' th' war took our boys off to Europe an' shipped 'em home in boxes, an' th' civil rights people swarmed in here an' yanked us all up by th' scruff of th' neck?"

Amy clapped both hands over her face.

"Our young people ran off an' left us high an' dry, that's what happened. An' what did you do when cotton pulled out an' left us boilin' up chicken bones for soup? This closed down, that closed down, our beautiful depot sittin' there like a mausoleum, an' where were the young people to help us back on our feet? Gone to greener pastures!"

"I'm sorry," he said.

"Speak up!"

"I'm *sorry!*"

"*I'm* sorry," said Amy, looking aghast.

"Too late for sorry," boomed Mrs. Lewis. "Are you visitin' th' Baptists or th' Episcopalians while you're here?"

"Some of both, perhaps. Well, a pleasure meeting you." An out-and-out lie. "And good to see you again, Amy."

Amy looked close to tears. "It's her medication."

"Make sure you leave somethin' in th' plate both places," Mrs. Lewis instructed. "Somethin' we can all be proud to talk about when you run off again."

He was pouring sweat. At the car, he took out his handkerchief and realized his hand was shaking as he wiped his face. Had that been real, or a dyspeptic dream? And how much of this heat could these people take, anyway? Not very much, if that voracious old buzzard was any indication.

He sat in the car and pretended to look at the road map until

Amy and her charge walked up the lane with the watering can and got into a vehicle that had seen better days.

Good riddance. "Okay, buddy, here we go again."

He slid from under the wheel and stood by the car, feeble as an infant. He couldn't go anywhere; he was fried.

A terrible exhaustion had been working in him since morning. A marathon drive yesterday. A rotten room last night. An hour's time difference. A full day today, with no nourishment beyond an egg biscuit and a stick of sugarless gum. And when had he last drunk water? He was parched as a stone.

Twice, he'd been in a diabetic coma, thanks to his thoroughly dim-witted ways. He needed a beeper that would sound an alarm—something to protect him from himself.

He gulped warm water from the jug, and poured the remainder into the dog bowl. What time was it, anyway? Two-thirty. He had to fly out of here and get something in his stomach. Tomorrow—he'd come back to Hill Crest tomorrow, first thing. And he'd need to stock up on water and fruit; he wanted fruit.

A car moved toward him along the lane and braked a few feet from the front bumper of the Mustang. Barnabas growled, but lay motionless on the passenger seat.

A man roughly his own age, wearing a straw hat and seersucker suit, got out of the car and flipped a cigarette into the grass. "How you?"

"Good. And you?"

"Jus' jolly. Do I know you?"

"Don't believe so; I'm visiting from North Carolina."

The man folded his arms and leaned against the grille of his car. "Jim Houck."

His heart thundered. Right here in the cemetery, he would meet his first ghost.

"Tim Kavanagh."

"Lawyer Kavanagh's boy."

"Right."

"Heard you were comin' up t' Hill Crest. Thought I'd ride up an' say hello. For ol' times' sake."

"That was kind of you. I was just leaving."

"Case you don't remember, your daddy was tried for pushin' my daddy down th' steps at th' bank."

"He was found not guilty."

"Yeah, well, you know those ol'-time judges. Man's a bigwig in town, he's off th' hook, no problemo."

He was out of breath, as if he'd run up the hill. "I'm sorry about your father."

"Water over th' dam. What's done is done. Just came up t' say I heard you were in town, wanted you t' know I noticed. That a dog?"

"It is."

"Thought it might be a sofa you're haulin' around." Jim Houck let loose with a laugh that sounded like chalk moving over a blackboard; Barnabas laid his ears back.

"Maybe we'll see you around, Jim." He dug in his pocket for the key.

"You'll definitely see me around." Jim Houck got in his car, slammed the door, gunned the motor, and backed down the lane, tires squalling.

His hand was trembling as he stuck the key in the ignition.

REST IN PEACE, he read on a headstone by the lane.

How anybody could rest in peace in this place was beyond him.

FOUR

He stood and read the chalkboard over the grill. He was in the wrong place, big time.

Whip potoatos & gravy
Country stile steak
Country stile ribs
Green beans & side meat
Collard greens
Cold slaw
Black eye peas
Mac & cheese
Cornbread or biscuits
Sweet potato pie
Blueberry cobbler

Stroke City.

The cook looked up from cleaning the grill. "How you?"

"Good, thanks. This is some menu. You do this every day?"

"Ever' day th' Lord give me breath, 'cept Sunday. That's m' Sabbath rest." He wiped his hands on his apron. "Frank King."

"Tim Kavanagh." They shook hands across the counter.

"Pleased t' meet you. You ain't from around Holly Springs."

"Born here, grew up here. Been gone a long time."

"Same deal. Born here, grew up here, gone a long time—got hungry for home."

"Speaking of hungry, I could gnaw a table leg. Got anything left?"

"They 'bout cleaned me out, but I'll find you somethin' fo' sho'."

"I'm diabetic, which means—"

"I know what that means. I got diabetes m'self. Type One."

"Type Two here. Traded up from One."

"How you like takin' them shots?"

"Not bad, I'm used to it now."

"Miss'ippi got mo' diabetes than any state in th' union."

He thought Frank seemed oddly proud of the superlative. He eyed the menu again. "This is a mighty dangerous place to work."

"I don' eat this stuff, I jus' cook it. Course, Miss Ella Moffatt, she make th' biscuits, th' cobbler, an' th' pies."

In his fervid imagination, he was wolfing down country-style ribs, mashed potatoes with gravy, and a slab of cornbread. "Let me have the collard greens, the green beans, the coleslaw, and"—he was going for it—"the cornbread."

"Thass three greens you ordered. You want three greens?"

"I've been traveling."

"Got you covered. What you drinkin'?"

"Something sugar-free. Surprise me." He didn't have an active cell left in his brain.

"You got kin here?" asked Frank.

"No kin. But looking for a few people I once knew."

"Who you lookin' fo'?"

"Tommy Noles. Small build. Sandy hair. Well, it was sandy at one time, probably gray now. My age."

"Tommy Noles. Don' know 'im."

"Roosevelt Ponder, a year or two older than me. We called him Rosie." All of Louis's and Sally's boys had been older, but maybe Rosie was still around.

"Roosevelt Ponder. Sounds familiar. But no, can't say I know 'im."

"I'd also like to find a man called Willie, maybe Will or William. A few years older than me. Missing a thumb on his left hand."

"I know somebody name' Tyrone got this finger gone." Frank held up a forefinger. "Stuck it in a horse's mouth on a bet. Who else you lookin' to find?"

"Not my high school basketball coach, that's for sure. He rode me so hard I've never shot a basket since." He'd been the shortest guy on the team; Coach Mickie was determined to make him grow three inches, do or die.

Grinning, Frank passed the plate over the counter. "Git on wit' it fo' it git cold."

He sat in a booth and got on with it, thinking of the motel room.

Beggars couldn't be choosers. It was the only place he'd found online that would let him bring his dog.

The day was about shot, as far as kicking around Holly Springs was concerned, but going back to the motel room early wasn't an option. If he could get his blood sugar out of his socks, he'd swing by the homeplace on the way to Memphis.

He'd call his wife tonight, of course, and read, that was the ticket. Stick his nose in a book, and he could leave any room far behind. He was in the books of Timothy again, as he was nearly every year on his birthday. He had always felt that St. Paul intended the letters not only for his young and eager disciple, but for him, Timothy Kavanagh, a couple millennia down the pike. He'd confessed this odd notion to his mother, his bishop, his wife, and his dog, in that order, and even his dog had seemed open to the idea.

He patted his shirt pocket, checking for the phone—he'd lost two of the darned things in three months—and remembered the note. It was a relief to have forgotten it for a while.

Frank set a dish of blueberry cobbler on the table. "There you go. On th' house."

"Whoa. Thanks a lot. But—should I eat this?"

"One time ain't gon' hurt."

He studied the way the juice purpled the rim of the white dish . . .

'I need to go to Miz Lula's,' he told his mother.

'Miss Lula died, remember? Your father and I went to her funeral. She's not at her house anymore, she's with the Lord in heaven."

'I need to go *real* bad.'

'But there's no reason, Timothy. I hear the family is packing up the house.'

'I really need to do it, Mama.'

It had been weeks since the party and the awful night of the broken vase, and he knew nothing of what had happened to Willie. For a long time, he'd been afraid to find out. Now he had to know.

'Please, please, I need to *so much*.' He didn't know what else to say—and then he remembered he could tell a lie. 'I left my best marble in th' whole wide world at Miz Lula's.'

'But you'd never find a marble in what's going on over there.'

'But I *need* to do it.' He wanted to fall on the floor and writhe around and scream, but he was too old for that, and besides, the only time he ever tried it, it didn't work.

'I suppose I could buy butter from Jane Witherspoon along the way. But with the price of gas these days . . .'

'Please, please, *please*.' He was exhausted from begging.

His mother smiled. 'Like Peggy says, you are the aggravatin'est little weasel.'

They drove into town the following Saturday, while his father worked with Louis and his boys to string fence.

On the way to Miz Lula's, he studied his mother: both hands firmly on the wheel, wearing the little hat she often wore to town, the faint trace of rouge on her cheeks. He thought she was the most beautiful lady in the whole wide world. And she was going to town just because of him, because he had begged her to do it. He wished he deserved her love.

They parked the Buick in the driveway, where Boss Tate's car had left dark circles of oil.

'Run and find Mose,' she said. 'Perhaps he's seen your marble. And don't tarry.'

While his mother talked with the mammy, he found Mose outside the summer kitchen. He was sitting on a bench, banging a cook pot with a mallet.

'What you doin'?'

'Fixin' this here dent. Ol' Lucy th'owed a pot at me f'r sayin' she was old an' ugly. Course, she ain't near as old as she is ugly.'

'Did it hit you when she throwed it?'

"Went on pas' my ol' gray head an' knocked a chunk of brick outta th' steps yonder.' Mose laughed. 'If this pot was to hit my hard head, hit'd be plumb ruint, couldn't fix it a'tall.'

He would long remember what a terrible racket could be made by hammering out a dent.

'Looky there, little mister—good as new. But m' mallet's broke.' Mose sighed. 'If hit hain't one thing, hit's two.'

'Where's Willie at?' He was terrified of the answer.

'They done took Willie off from here. Po' little chap.'

Without meaning to, he began to cry.

'Whoa, now. What that all about?'

'Did they give 'im'—he scrubbed his eyes with his fist—'a nice funeral?'

'Oh, Willie ain't dead. Nossir, not a bit. They took 'im out t' th' country t' stay wit' 'is granny.'

ThankyouGod, thankyouGod, thankyouGod. 'Is he comin' back?'

'Nossir, Willie ain't comin' back. Miz Lula dead, y'know.' Mose wiped his eyes on his sleeve. 'Things is changin' 'roun' here.'

'Mr. Boss, is he comin' back?'

'He be back now an' ag'in, I reckon. This Mr. Boss's homeplace, he born in th' room at th' head of th' steps.'

He'd heard that Boss Tate often gave children a dollar bill wrapped around a pack of Dentyne; he would like to have a dollar bill from Boss Tate; he would keep it as a souvenir and never spend it, but he would probably chew the gum.

He had another question, one he'd been meaning to ask somebody, but he kept forgetting. 'What's Mr. Boss th' boss of?'

'Less see, how I gon' say it?' Mose threw his head back, closed his eyes, jiggled his leg, grunted, 'I'm thinkin'.' Then he leaned forward and said, 'He be th' boss of ever'thing.'

He raced across the yard and around the house feeling light as air, as if he might lift from the earth like a kite and fly.

'Thass a happy boy you got,' said the mammy.

His mother beamed. 'You found your marble!'

'No, ma'am, but it's okay, I don't care.' It was a relief to tell the truth. He wished he could always tell the truth, especially to his mother.

On the way home, he stood beside her on the front seat and put his arm around her neck and held on, the way he'd often done before the vase was broken. He had never been so happy.

'There's my darling Timmy,' she said. 'He's come back. Where do you think he's been for such a long time?'

He shrugged, pretending he didn't know. But he knew. He'd been in that place he'd heard about in church—the fiery furnace of HELL . . .

He threw up his hand to Frank. "See you tomorrow. I'll try to get here before th' fried chicken runs out."

He stopped at a convenience store for a jug of water and a bag of ice, and headed east. It was nearly four o'clock, and sultry. As for the temperature, ninety-two degrees in the shade would be a safe guess. Maybe he'd put the top up and turn on the a/c. He started to pull over, but changed his mind; the air was heavy with smells he wanted to explore.

He caught a blast of honeysuckle as he crested a hill; the scent seemed to enter his bloodstream like a shot of whiskey. Honeysuckle and gardenias. That had been his first bouquet to Peggy Cramer, the summer before seminary.

He craned his neck looking over the landscape, trying, perhaps, to reclaim something he'd lost. Over there, a copse of trees had been snared like flies in a cobweb of kudzu. Farther along, a barn had disappeared in the stuff, leaving visible only a rusted tin roof to mark its place. For all he knew, his homeplace had long been covered over, leaving no trace of its columns and porticos. Since cotton had pulled out and left Holly Springs "boilin' up chicken bones," why couldn't something profitable be done with this noxious weed?

He glanced at the speedometer; he was twelve miles over the speed limit, trying to catch a breeze.

Whatever fear he'd had of coming back to Whitefield had vanished—he realized he was looking forward to it, eager, even. If nobody was living there, he would walk out to the cotton fields where he'd often been a picker, and look at the barn, if it was still standing.

He realized, then, what he wanted to do even more.

He wanted to see Peggy's house . . .

Sometime before Christmas, he noticed that his mother looked pale, older somehow; she seemed more like a stranger than herself. Then came the terrible pain.

'Run!' his father said. 'Get Peggy!'

He ran as fast as he could to the little house behind the privet hedge on the lane.

The late afternoon was dark, and freezing cold. His breath vaporized on the bitter air.

Peggy was hanging wash on a line in front of her fireplace.

'Somethin's wrong with Mama. You got to come.'

'I can't leave this fire goin',' she said, shoveling ashes on the burning log. A log had rolled out on Peggy's floor one time and burned a big place in the boards. "You're takin' too long," he shouted. "Hurry!" She blew out the flame of the lamp and threw on her coat, and hand in hand they raced up the frozen lane.

When they reached the house, the black Buick wasn't parked by the front porch.

Peggy squeezed his hand so hard it hurt. 'Yo' daddy done took 'er to Memphis.'

Memphis. Where they had the big hospital. For a long time, he stood at the window to see if his father had changed his mind and would bring his mother home and let Dr. Franklin make her well with his medicine bag. But the car didn't come.

It was almost bedtime when Peggy took him to her house and stirred up a fire. Then she fed him cornbread and milk, and a mashed sweet potato with molasses. He ate as much as he could so he wouldn't hurt her feelings, and went to bed on a pallet of quilts by the fireplace. He lay there, helpless and afraid, looking at the clothes hanging above him on the line, at the way her oldest work dress fluttered when she opened the door to bring in a stick of wood.

He thought he would never forget the way Peggy's house smelled—like ashes and cold biscuits and fried side meat; it was a smell that made him feel safe and connected. He'd never before paid attention to the smell of her house, but this time was different— somewhere a kind of door had opened in him.

When he couldn't sleep, she squatted beside the pallet and stroked his back. 'Ever'thing gon' be all right, baby, ever'thing gon' be all right.' Just this once, he would let her call him that.

Shadows cast by the flaming lamp and the flickering fire danced around the walls, and for a long time Peggy prayed, aloud and urgent, raising her hands and talking to God as if He were right there in the room.

Everything was going to be all right, she had said. But if she was telling the truth, why was she crying?

Because he loved Peggy almost as much as his mother, he believed her at last, and went to sleep . . .

Whitefield could no longer be seen from the state road. In nearly forty years, trees and shrubs mature, undergrowth thrives, and things change. His mother had liked having her home seen from the road. She'd had Louis and his minions plant acres of azaleas among the pines and oaks and maples; the driveway had run straight through the woods to the green front door.

But the drive had been rerouted; it was winding now, which cut off a direct view of the house.

"We're in Rabbit City, buddy. Stick with me, and I don't mean maybe."

Cooler in these woods. He prayed the prayer that never fails as they rounded the final bend.

His homeplace.

Not derelict or torn down. Not vanished into a vernal grave. But just as he remembered it, except better. Much better.

He sat with his foot on the brake and his hands on the wheel, forgetting to breathe.

Metal scaffolding encased the front of the two-story house. The plastered, brick-core columns and double front doors were freshly painted, as were the Greek-order pilasters flanking the doors. Shutters leaned against the house, sanded and ready for primer. This was the very sort of work his mother wanted to have done, but then her illness had come, and it was too late for mending and painting.

A shirt hung over a bar of the scaffolding; empty paint cans lay discarded on a blue tarp.

Quiet. Nothing stirring. No breeze, nothing.

He noted a primordial Volvo, and a pickup truck, its fenders a lacework of rust.

He parked beneath a pine tree and snapped the leash on his dog's collar. Barnabas sniffed the area, then zeroed in on the rear wheel of the truck and lifted his leg. Together, they walked to the house and up the steps; the double doors were open.

A tarp covered the heart-pine floor of the entrance hall that led past the stairwell to open double doors at the rear. He could see out to the lawn and into the sun-bleached field beyond.

"Hello! Anybody home?"

A fly buzzed. A crow called.

A strong odor of fresh paint, combined with the sweltering heat, unsteadied him. He would wait awhile, maybe sit on the steps 'til someone showed up. As the sun was at the rear of the house, this was the coolest place to be, anyway.

"Hello!"

Then again, forget sitting on the steps like a lizard; he wanted to explore.

He didn't sense anything left of his mother here. The woods had crept closer to the porch, and the gardens appeared to be long gone. All that remained was the allée of ancient boxwood.

Nothing familiar except the box. Nothing at all. No asters as large as dinner plates, no masses of double hollyhocks, no thriving display of hostas at the woods' edge, nor any gardenias to scent the air. The ardent sweat and labor of years had vanished as surely as the barn in kudzu.

During more than one of Holly Springs' famous Pilgrimages, hundreds of people had wandered along the paths his mother had designed through the woodland grove of four hundred azaleas, and out to the smokehouse with its peony beds and trellises of roses and purple wisteria.

It was prophesied that nobody would travel four miles from town to see a garden, especially in wartime when gas was rationed and car parts were unavailable and the mechanics had been shipped out to Europe. But his mother, who longed to share her gardens with one and all, had been of a stubborn and visionary stripe. If she could not live in town, she would bring the town to her. By dint of sheer will and bone-crushing labor, she created gardens that drew spectators not only from Holly Springs, but from towns as far away as Memphis and McComb. Someone had also turned up from Brazil, which had caused a definite stir.

He walked through the allée and saw that the washhouse was gone, though some of the stone foundation remained. He'd had many whippings, recited many scriptures, and even been de-liced with sulfur in that venerable building.

It may have taken years to realize it, but a good deal of whatever character he might have had been formed in the washhouse . . .

He burst into the kitchen to tell his mother the news.

'Louis's Ol' Damn Mule got out an' run over to Tommy's house an' Mr. Noles, he wouldn' let Louis come in th' yard an' take 'im home, an' if Mr. Noles keeps Ol' Damn Mule an' won't let 'im go, Louis says th' police gon' come.'

About the only time he saw police was when they were hanging around Tyson's scarfing up ice cream, or sitting in their cars with sunglasses on.

'What did you call the mule?'

'Louis's Ol' Damn Mule.'

He saw the little furrow appear between her eyes and over her nose. 'Go to the washhouse and wait for me.'

He sat in the washhouse on a chair with busted caning, among the laundry baskets and lye soap, and paddles that stirred farm clothes in the black iron pot outside the door.

His mother arrived, wearing her apron and looking tired. Even with Peggy helping, he thought his mother worked too hard. If she didn't work so hard, she wouldn't be so tired, and if she wasn't so tired, she might not get so mad about nothing at all. He had no idea why she'd made him come out here for what a stupid old mule had done.

'There are the dirty farm clothes,' she said, pointing to two baskets. 'Muddy, because of the rain on Sunday. Smelly, because of the cows and horses and chickens and pigs and all the sweat it takes to run a country place.'

She waited for him to say something, as he tried to figure out what she wanted him to say. 'Yes, ma'am,' he said at last.

'Over there are the clothes Peggy and I washed this morning, and brought in off the line before the rain came. Clean, sweet, smelling like sunshine.' She waited.

'Yes ma'am.'

'Which would you like to be? A basket of dirty, smelly clothes or a basket of nice, clean clothes?'

He knew the answer, but he had a question.

'What did I do bad?'

'You used a bad word.'

'I did?'

'In describing Louis's mule.'

He'd completely forgotten he wasn't supposed to say that word. But that's what Louis *called* his mule. That was his mule's *name*. He couldn't *help* it if that was the mule's *name*.

'That's th' mule's *name*, Mama. Louis *always* says Ol' Damn . . . 'scuse me.'

He was going to get his mouth washed out with soap, he could feel it coming. He cut his eyes to the glass with the toothbrush in it, sitting on the windowsill.

His mother had crossed her arms and was looking at him in an odd way. He was thankful that his mother, and not his father, had taken him to the washhouse. He'd heard her tell Peggy that his father was 'too severe,' which was why she hardly ever told on him if he messed up. More than once, his father had half killed him for doing stuff, while his mother was gentle and forgiving—at least most of the time.

He hung his head. Why didn't he just say he was sorry and get it over with?

'I'm going to overlook this, Timothy. You were repeating that word in innocence. But it won't be overlooked again, do you understand? I want you to memorize Ephesians, chapter four, verses twenty-nine and thirty.'

'Yes, ma'am.' He raised his head, suddenly bold and decisive, and met her gaze. 'An' I 'preciate it.'

His mother turned away; it looked like she was laughing. He was pretty sure she was laughing . . .

"If you live as long as that mule," he told Barnabas, "you'll probably outlive me."

When Ol' Damn Mule died, Louis declared him to be twenty-one years old. 'Votin' age!'

Louis and Sally Ponder and their four boys had lived and worked at Whitefield, and were another family to him. He had played at their house at the edge of the woods, eaten at their table, and picked cotton with them. Louis had been a type of surrogate father—wise, no-nonsense, and willing to listen when nobody else would. He wondered if he could find the mule's grave that he and Louis and his boys had dug on the other side of the pond. They'd used a cast-off wagon tongue as a marker, and Louis had cried.

He revised his earlier estimate of ninety-two degrees. It was ninety-five and climbing or he was a monkey's uncle. It was no time to go hiking around the pond.

"Okay, buddy, let's go look . . ."

What a strange thing he'd almost said. He'd almost said, *Let's go look for Peggy.*

FIVE

The privet hedge was long gone. The tin-sheathed roof had col-lapsed, cedars grew through the rotting floor of the kitchen, and honeysuckle was taking care of the rest.

Thomas Wolfe had been right, of course.

Barnabas sniffed the spot where her front door once opened off the lane—in the old days, if he'd been sitting on her stoop when a wagon passed, he'd tuck in his toes, just to be safe. The traffic through here had been especially active at cotton-picking time— his father on horseback, Louis driving the wagon team—'Hum up!'; pickers straggling in from the fields, half crazed by the killing heat; Louis's boys on one reconnaissance or another; the cotton trucks rattling by.

In the searing Mississippi summers, their farm had seemed like a small town unto itself. Cole Jenkins even knocked together a lean-to store under a walnut tree at the south end of Big Field, eager for the cotton pickers' business. Nehi Strawberry, Sugar Daddys, peanut brittle—all a nickel, and every once in a while a walnut or two hit-ting Cole's tin roof, blam, blam, blam. 'Run fo' th' woods, hit's th' law!' Cole would holler, then slap his knee, laughing.

Cole spent a lot of time trying to get on Peggy's good side. Some evenings he would walk up from the field and bring her a Coca-

Cola, but she wouldn't drink it. She wouldn't even put it in the house and save it 'til later.

'Courtin' that woman's like eatin' soup wit' a fork,' Cole complained.

'You ain't s'posed t' be courtin' that woman,' Louis said. 'You'se married.'

'I ain't married,' Cole said. 'When th' preacher had us sayin' vows, I let m' wife do all th' talkin'.'

Once when his mother sent him to shell peas with Peggy, Cole tried to tempt him with a Baby Ruth, which he never saw anymore now that the war was on. 'Ol' rats like cheese, too. Go on off an' leave me an' her by ourself, an' this here's all your'n.' Cole winked at him; his half-toothless grin was a terrifying sight.

But he wouldn't leave Peggy by herself with that old nose booger, not for a hundred dollars, much less a Baby Ruth. He sat tight and stared bullets at Cole 'til Cole got mad as fire and left.

'I gon' butter you a piece of bread wit' sugar on it for gettin' me out that mess,' Peggy said later. 'That ol' darky look like he been chewin' t'bacco an' spittin' in th' wind.'

They had laughed as loud as they wanted to.

Barnabas lay in the road, panting from the heat. Time to move on.

He saw something in the weeds by the chimney, and walked over and poked at it with the toe of his shoe; it looked like a handle. He grabbed it and worked the thing loose from the clutch of weeds and red dirt. It was a cook pot.

His mother had bought new cook pots from a traveling salesman, and sent her old ones to Peggy's house. He'd carried this very pot down to Peggy himself—how many years ago?

He tossed it into the weeds.

He remembered his grief, and how he struggled to keep it hidden, and the questions he asked himself again and again. Why would Peggy leave his mother, who loved her and taught her to cook and sew and memorize scripture and write her name and read and not say ain't, who even had Peggy's teeth fixed so she could chew?

Why would she have left the little house she loved so much and kept so clean, even with all the dust from the road—the house she said was the only real home she'd ever known? And her chickens— Peggy had been sole caretaker of the Rhode Island Reds that laid the Whitefield eggs, and later ended up on the table in a bowl of dumplings. She had loved her chickens, and staved off the cook pot as long as reason would allow.

But more than all that, why would she have left him, the one she'd called baby, the one who had saved her life, the one who she always, always said was her very best friend in the whole wide world?

And yet, one day—he'd been in fifth grade—he came home from school, and Peggy wasn't in the kitchen or in the washhouse or anywhere else. Just like that, she had gone away from them forever.

He'd searched the two rooms of her house again and again, always calling her name and expecting her to answer, bewildered that her clothes still hung on nails in the corner. She had even left her apron draped over the back of a chair, as if she would walk in the door any minute.

As far as he could tell, she hadn't taken anything with her except her Bible, the dress and shoes she often wore, and her coat the color of broom straw.

He wandered to the barn and searched the stalls, fearful that she'd been looking for bantam eggs in the loft and fallen through the rotten boards.

But there was no trace of Peggy, and his mother could answer none of his questions. She seemed as distraught as he.

He went to his father, sick with grief. 'We should tell the sheriff.'

'Absolutely not. And don't mention it again.'

'I'll find her,' he said.

His father's face was set like stone. 'Leave it be. Do you hear?'

'Yes, sir.'

'I'll find her,' he told his mother.

He went to her church on Wednesday night and stood in the road in the gathering dusk, watching the congregation assemble. But Peggy didn't come. He approached two elderly women and asked if they knew Peggy. He was dumbfounded that he couldn't tell them her last name when they asked, because he didn't know it.

He'd been forced to describe her. 'Tall,' he said, struggling to put something of her essence into words. 'Bony.' That had been her view of herself. 'Wears a red kerchief.' He didn't call it a head rag, like most people; he was trying to be respectful. They said they hadn't seen Peggy and had wondered about her themselves.

He went with Louis to the walnut tree to get a pack of peanuts, and demanded to know what Cole knew.

Cole looked at him as if he were a dog pile. 'Peggy done gone where th' sun don't shine.' Then he laughed and danced around like a fool.

'Don' pay no 'tention t' that crazy nigger,' said Louis. 'He don' know n' more 'bout Peggy than us whose hearts is broke.'

He wrestled for two days with what Cole could have meant about 'where the sun don't shine.' The sun didn't shine in a grave. The thought nearly stopped his heart, he felt faint even thinking such a thing. Maybe she had died or been killed, and put in a grave without anyone knowing.

He rode his bicycle to Tommy's house and did his bobwhite imitation from the road. 'Go with me somewhere,' he said when Tommy came out.

'Where?'

'Th' nigger graveyard.'

'I ain't goin' t' no nigger graveyard.'

'Okay, then, I'll go by myself since you're chicken.'

'I ain't chicken. Just ain't los' nothin' in no graveyard.'

He rode off, believing Tommy would follow, but he didn't. He felt betrayed. Why was he the only one looking for Peggy? Why were people doing what they always did, digging postholes, riding around on a horse, pulling weeds out of the garden, as if Peggy were in the kitchen baking biscuits? She had vanished without a trace and nobody seemed to care, except Louis, who was too busy working to look for missing people, and his mother, who now had no help with the cooking and laundry, and wouldn't know where to look, anyway. It was all up to him.

The graveyard at Peggy's church had only one tree for shade; the graves lay open to a baking sun; even the weeds looked dead. He propped his bicycle against the tree and stood there like a dunce, not knowing what else to do.

It occurred to him to cross himself—maybe that would help—as he'd learned to do at Christ Church. That's where his father was forcing him to go every Sunday, now, and his mother, too.

He felt naked without the protection of his mother's Baptist church in Walnut Grove, where he knew everybody and could even sing the hymns, and where, two years ago, he had gone forward to make a confession of faith. For a long time, his father hadn't attended church at all, then all of a sudden, out of the blue, his father had decided to go to church, but it had to be his church.

He hated the memory of being dragged out of Walnut Grove by his father like a sack of potatoes, to a place where people were different, very different. Most of the grown-ups weren't friendly at all, and some of the kids in Sunday School wouldn't speak to him. He didn't like their cookies, either. Too hard, not soft like Peggy's, plus all that kneeling and carrying on, and the sermon so boring he could gag, puke, and croak.

His eyes searched for a mound of red dirt that signified a new grave, but he saw no such thing.

Don't let Peggy be here, God.

'You're looking for somebody?'

A black man in a black suit and black shoes, carrying a black book, was walking toward the shade of the tree.

His heart hammered. Yes, he was looking for somebody, but it was nobody's business who.

'How can I help you?'

A pain shot through his head, like a nail had been hammered into his skull. 'Peggy,' he said, trying to get his breath.

'Peggy.' The man moved into the shade, smiling.

'She . . .' He suddenly wanted to cry, but did not. 'I can't find our Peggy, she's tall and bony and wears a head rag. It's red. Peggy Lambert.' That was the best he could do. He stared at his bare feet, anguished.

The man laughed. 'Peggy Lambert is a fine woman. I don't know how she'd feel about being called bony.'

'She calls herself bony.'

'Is she missing?'

He nodded. 'For about a week.'

'We didn't see Peggy at church on Sunday or at meeting on Wednesday night. That's unusual.'

He thought the man looked worried. It was a relief to see somebody look worried the same as him.

'Brother Grant.' The man held out his hand.

He took it. 'Timmy Kavanagh.' It was a comfort to shake hands like a man.

'From over at Whitefield, I believe, where Peggy lives.'

'Yes.' He'd never seen anyone so dressed up on a weekday, except sometimes when court was in session.

'Did you think you might find Peggy . . . here?'

'I guess.' He was suddenly crying, sobbing; he couldn't hold it back and he couldn't stop. He sank to his haunches, wailing. He wished he could die.

The man squatted beside him, not saying or doing anything, just squatting there. It felt good for him to be there. He cried 'til he had no tears left and his nose was running and his eyes were swollen, but he felt better, as if a crushing weight had been removed and he could breathe again.

When he got up, Brother Grant stood, too, and looked at him and nodded his head. 'It's going to be all right, Timmy,' he said, as if he could look into the future like Jeremiah. For a long time, he would remember Brother Grant's words, 'It's going to be all right.'

Back at Whitefield, he lowered his head, unable to meet his mother's gaze. 'I couldn't find 'er. I tried an' tried.'

'Has anyone spoken with Cole about where she might have gone?' She knew Cole had tormented Peggy like a sting bee.

'Cole ain't nothin' but a crazy nigger.' He burned with hatred at the thought of Cole.

'What did you just say, Timothy?'

'Nigger, nigger, *nigger!*' He knew the word was taboo, that it offended his mother, but he didn't care. 'Jack Mickie says it all th' time; *ever*'body says it.'

'You're not everybody, Timothy. You're special.'

He turned his head away, exhausted, stricken, hopeless. He'd never understood why his mother wouldn't let him say what his father said, and everybody else except Peggy.

'Please look at me, Timothy. Since you were a very little boy, I've asked you not to use that hurtful word. I know you, my son, and the last thing you'd wish to do is hurt someone.'

'Cole called me a white-ass peckerwood.' He was flinging some pretty strong language around, but he couldn't seem to care.

'Let Cole call you what he pleases. What he means by such language is between him and God.'

'Is what I just said between me an' God?'

'It is between you and God. That's the whole point. God asks us to love one another, as Christ loved us.

'The vile word you used is properly pronounced as negro, which is the Spanish word for black—that and nothing more. It's how that perfectly harmless word is used these days that makes it hurtful. Louis doesn't deserve such a word, nor do his wife and children. Not even Cole, who is blasphemous and spiteful. The mispronunciation of this word reveals a great deal about the person who uses it.

'It reveals that one is narrow of mind, mean of spirit . . .'—the color rushed to her cheeks—'and coarse.'

She was really upset; he might have to memorize a whole chapter this time.

'Is Father all those things you just said?'

She turned away; he had caught his mother in something, though he didn't know what. He had shamed her in some way, and he felt miserable for having done it.

When she faced him, he thought she looked terrible, older, not even like his mother.

'What you may say in our home and out of it, Timothy, is Negro. Or you may say that someone is colored, or a person of color. That is the rule.

'You're to memorize First Corinthians, chapter twelve, verse thirteen. We'll discuss its meaning after breakfast tomorrow.'

'Yes, ma'am.'

He walked to the door, not looking back.

'Timothy?'

'Yes, ma'am.' He didn't turn around.

'I love you, my son.'

Later, he was riding in the wagon with Louis when he saw Cole dart from the bushes at the edge of Big Field, looking over his shoulder and toting a sack.

'Ol' Cole's got gamblin' goin' on wit' the pickers, which ain't good a'tall. Mr. Matthew turn a deaf eye t' Cole's foolishness, he need t' run that bad nigger off from here.'

'Don't say nigger.'

Louis pulled back on the reins as they bounced downhill on the rough track. 'What I'm gon' say?'

'Say Negro. It's Spanish.'

It took a while, but one day he realized that thinking about Peggy didn't make him sad anymore, it made him mad. Really mad. He was furious at her for dumping him, dumping his mother, dumping Louis and Sally and everybody who cared about her. His anger was as terrible as his grief had been, and he relished it, and held on to it for a long time . . .

Up ahead, he saw two men standing where the washhouse once stood.

Towels were wrapped around their waists as if they'd just stepped from a shower stall.

Keeping a tight rein on the leash, he raised his right hand in salute. The tall white man and the shorter black man returned the gesture.

He walked up faster and called out. "Couldn't find anyone home, thought I'd walk around. No harm intended."

Barnabas wasn't barking, which was a good sign.

The taller of the duo stepped forward. "T Pruitt. An' this is my buddy, Ray Edwards."

"Tim Kavanagh."

They shook hands.

"I hope you'll forgive me for making myself at home. I was raised here."

T adjusted his towel; his wet hair was combed in a pompadour. "No problem. I recognize th' name Kavanagh from th' history of th' place. Built by Porter in 1858, sold t' Kavanagh in 1934, Kavanagh sold it t' Jamison, and ten years ago Jamison sold it t' my brother, Jess."

"History in a nutshell. Good to meet you."

"Same here. You Cath'lic?"

"Episcopal. Retired, but still wearing the collar. Sometimes it gives people a safe place to run. Y'all doing the work on the house?"

T laughed. "Doin' th' best we can. Put it that way."

"It looks wonderful. Better than ever."

"Got a ways to go. After we finished up at th' house today, we jumped in th' pond to cool off."

"The pond is still there?"

"Oh, yeah. Got a few bass, a few crappie, a good many catfish."

"Yes, but how many water moccasins?"

Ray grinned, revealing pink gums only. "We keep to our side, they keep t' theirs."

He pulled out his handkerchief and wiped his forehead. "What do you think the temperature is today? Ninety-six, ninety-seven?"

"Ninety-eight," said Ray.

"In th' shade," said T. "Come on, let's go in an' have a cold drink."

"How's yo' dog do wit' little dogs?" asked Ray.

"Not a problem. You have dogs?"

"Ol' Tater an' Tot'll be comin' in from th' woods here in a minute. Prob'ly be headin' back th' way they come when they see this brother." Ray let Barnabas sniff the back of his hand.

"I don't want to intrude, we'll get on up the road to Memphis."

"Don't run off," said T. "Me an' Ray like comp'ny. Us ol' boys get lonesome out here in th' woods."

"Sho do," said Ray. "Let me get some clothes on, we'll go set on th' porch like rich folks."

"That's good of you. Thanks. I could use a little company myself."

"Hate for comp'ny to catch me wit'out teeth. They in th' shop, so to speak." Ray cut out across the yard. "See you in ten."

"Ray lives over th' garage, we built that a while back. I guess we tore down what you remember."

"A cupola on top?"

"That's th' one. Roof caved in."

They walked to the front of the house and into the hallway. "I'm camped out upstairs," said T. "Won't take me long. Look around down here, make yourself at home. You want a beer?"

"Don't believe so, thanks."

"I been dry ten years, but Ray likes t' stock a few cold ones."

He'd never paid much attention to the bones of Whitefield, which was built during the cotton boom of the late 1850s. While he'd known it was a handsome house, he'd taken the particulars of its design for granted. It was entirely different from the house in Mitford, which appeared to have been built for Lilliputians—these ceilings were twelve feet high, with ornate cornices into the bargain. Four plastered Doric columns, now bereft of fissures and the assorted signs of old age, separated the dining room and parlor from a wide central hall.

The place was beautiful. He gawked, noting every detail and wishing for his wife. Built-in bookcases had been added on either side of the parlor fireplace; French doors led to what had been the woodshed where Louis taught him to split wood.

In the dining room, he stopped and examined a window. New muntins. New glazing. New sills. By the time he was in seminary, the old windows had been nearly impossible to open and close. He'd urged his widowed mother to move into town, into something smaller, newer, and certainly less remote, but it was too late for that—she was finally at peace with living in the country, content with solitude and the company of Louis and Sally.

No more westerly view of the washhouse from this window. Instead, his gaze was led down the old wagon track, across the overgrown Big Field, and up to the tree line.

He remembered how they'd taken the rutted track and climbed

the hill into the woods. Even with mittens on, his hands had been stiff with cold . . .

They zigzagged among the leafless trees toward the west fence; somewhere in the underbrush, turkeys gobbled.

'Yonder by th' fence post—that'n look nice.'

'It's too bent on top,' he said. 'Th' star might fall off.'

'How 'bout this'n right here, then? We 'bout t' walk right into this'n.'

The crunch of hoarfrost under their feet, the stinging cold on their faces, the feel of the sled rope in his hand—and Peggy with her head wrapped in the red kerchief. It was the best thing they'd ever done.

'I like that'n.' He pointed ahead.

'Yo' mama say don' point.'

'How'm I s'posed t' show you where it's at?'

'Don' say where it's at, say where it is. An' 'stead of pointin', say how t' reco'nize it.'

'Th' one with th' wide branches at th' bottom, an' broom sage growin' all around. Next to that stump.'

'Oh, law, that tree take two strong men t' chop it down—we jus' a bony woman an' a baby.'

He stomped his foot. 'I'm not a baby.'

'Oh, you right, I forgot you ain't a baby, an' don' stomp yo' foot at me, little man. You hear what I say?'

He frowned back, so she would know he meant business.

'When you was a baby, I'd be churnin' with both hands an' rockin' yo' cradle with my foot. You been my baby a long time, but I gon' try t' do better an' quit sayin' it. That'll be yo' Santy Claus from Peggy. Now pick yo'self another tree.'

'But that's th' best of any. Besides, Mama likes a big tree.'

'You right. She do.'

'It would make her smile.' Peggy would do anything, just like he would, to make his mother smile. He'd been afraid to ask, but now he had to. 'Will Mama get well?'

'She gettin' well ever' minute we stan' here talkin'.' Peggy grasped his shoulder; he could tell by the way she touched him that she was telling the truth. 'Sho as you born, Jesus gon' make yo' mama well.'

'So can we do it?'

'We'll get Rufe or one th' other boys t' chop it,' she said.

He looked up at the tall, slender woman who could do most anything. 'We could prob'ly do it ourself, Peggy. Jus' you an' me.'

Shivering from the cold, Peggy looked down at him.

'Jus' you an' me,' he said again. He liked her face; it was the color of Postum stirred with a drop of cream.

'You know what you is?'

He knew, but he wanted to hear her say it.

'You th' aggravatin'est little weasel I ever seen.'

They laughed as loud as they wanted to. Then Peggy steamed ahead with the axe in her hand, and he followed with the sled. Peggy's old coat was the same color as the winter gold of the broom straw, her kerchief a slash of crimson against the gray and leafless trees.

'Pick up yo' feet, now, let's see can we do this thing. Lord Jesus, you got t' he'p us, that ol' tree be a hun'erd foot tall!'

'Tall as a mountain!' he hollered into the stinging cold.

They tied its trunk to the sled and dragged it home, its greenness dark and intense in the passage through winter woods.

But the tree wasn't as tall as a mountain. Even nailed onto the wooden stand Rufe made, it was only two feet above the chair rail. Somebody had stolen their tree while they ate beans and cornbread in the kitchen; somebody had robbed the tall tree that would have touched the ceiling, and left a runt tree in its place.

But Peggy liked it. 'What it lose in bein' tall, it make up in bein' wide.'

They turned on the radio to listen to Christmas carols while they trimmed the branches, but there was nothing but talk about war on Japan, and something scary about Germany, so Peggy sang instead.

> *'Jingle bells*
> *Jingle bells*
> *Jingle all th' way . . .'*

Peggy gave him a hard look.

'I can't do all th' singin' m' ownself. What kind of Santy is this, havin' t' sing by y'r ownself?'

He sang with her, his heart heavy.

> *'Silent night*
> *Holy night*
> *All is calm*
> *All is bright . . .'*

He hung the fragile, painted globes, knowing that his mother wouldn't like this tree when she came home from the hospital tomorrow. She wouldn't smile one bit, not even a little . . .

"But she did smile," he told his dog. "She said it was the most beautiful tree we ever had. And it was."

He remained at the window for a moment, crossing himself, then walked into the kitchen.

The ancient boxwood outside the windows were gone; the room was luminous with summer afternoon light.

A far cry from the last time he'd seen this room. And a far cry from the days when Grandpa Kavanagh made his clandestine visits. His grandfather had sat at the kitchen table eating his mother's cookies and telling her, in his oddly mixed Irish/Mississippi accent,

how to run things. Meanwhile, his father was working in town, un-
aware that the old man was sitting in his kitchen at Whitefield,
sometimes even in his accustomed chair.

His grandfather had done something "bad" to his father; that's
all he knew, all anyone would tell him. From what he'd overheard,
his father had never forgiven Grandpa Kavanagh; he hadn't spoken
to him in years, and had forbidden his visits to Whitefield.

Yet, twice a year, his grandfather, who was widowed when his
second son, Matthew, was born, came up from Jackson on business,
and always when court was in session and the coast was clear at the
farm. The taboo visits disarmed his mother, it could take several
days for her to recover her spirits . . .

'This boy needs to go fishin', Madelaine. He tells me he's never
been fishin'.'

His grandfather was eating cherries very fast, and spitting the
pits in a saucer.

'His father doesn't allow Timothy to go fishing; he believes fishing promotes sloth.'

'Fishin' promotes patience, Madelaine! Patience! A boy has t'
learn he can't always have what he wants, when he wants it. Look
at th' state of th' world. Most of th' troubles t'day come from havin'
no patience. An' take perseverance, that's a absolute requirement if
a boy's gon' make anything of hisself.

'Another benefit is timin'. Fishin' teaches a boy timin'. A
mighty good thing to have in any kind of b'iness, 'specially if he
goes into law like 'is daddy.'

'I can't send him fishing behind Matthew's back.'

'Matthew gon' ruin this boy if you don't step in an' have yo' say.
Timothy's got 'is nose stuck in a book ever' time I come out here.
What's that book you readin', boy?'

There was no way to avoid the truth; the title was printed
plainly on the cover. 'The Oxford Book of English Poets.'

'English poets? Lord have mercy.' His grandfather rummaged in the pockets of his rumpled suit and brought forth a large handkerchief, something like a dinner napkin, and wiped his forehead. 'Now, what good is that gon' do a boy out in th' world tryin' to make a livin'?'

'He enjoys books,' said his mother.

'An' here's another thing to look at. Fishin' promotes enjoyment. What kind of enjoyment can you get from a book?'

'A great deal,' said his mother.

'Th' trouble with Matthew is, he never learned about enjoyment, so how can he set a model fo' th' boy? You go on an' go catfishin' with Louis, you might even catch you a eel. Now, a eel is real slipp'ry, an' wiggly, too, can't catch 'em with your hands. Have t' break you off a nice switch and tickle that ol' eel kind of gentle, like you puttin' it to sleep. First thing you know, it'll quit wigglin' an' lay there still as a mouse.'

His mother suddenly rose from the kitchen table and collected their empty glasses on a tray.

'Then you can grab it an' chop off its head an' skin it.'

'Oh!' said his mother. 'Please.'

His grandfather snatched the last cookie from the plate before it was taken away, and put it in his suit pocket. 'If I lived up here, I'd take 'im huntin'.'

'Matthew says he's not the sort of boy to go hunting.'

'That's exactly why he needs t' go. It'll *make* 'im th' sort of boy that goes huntin'. He might bring y'all a nice brace of quail or a couple of rabbits.'

His grandfather emitted a resounding belch.

'Step here a minute, boy, an' listen.'

He laid the book on the table and did as he was told; a nerve jumped in his right eye as he viewed the old man's monumental presence in his father's chair.

His grandfather bent forward as if confiding something deeply private; the sour smell of whiskey mingled with the scent of roses in a vase on the table.

'When Louis carries you over t' th' north fork of th' river, take you a broomstick an' catch you some crawlers. Jus' thump that stick down in th' mud along th' bank, like this here, makin' holes. First thing you know, crawlers'll come swarmin' out ever' whichaway. Dump 'em in a five-gallon bucket with some river mud, they'll last a good three t' fo' days.

'How will I catch 'em?'

'With yo' hands, boy, with yo' hands.'

'Father Kavanagh . . .'

'Madelaine, I know what you're gon' say, but this boy needs t' get dirty. An' what his daddy don' know won't hurt 'im.'

"I will not go against his father's wishes."

'Now, now, if you worried about what's gon' happen, ain't nothin' gon' happen. Worst thing could happen fishin' is 'e might get 'is line tangled in th' bushes. As fo' huntin', I been huntin' fifty-fo' years an' th' worst thing ever happened was Albert Pitts gettin' shot in th' butt.'

His grandfather threw his head back and hooted with laughter.

He hated it when his mother wrung her hands like that . . .

SIX

Some peckerwood kep' huntin' dogs in th' house before m' brother bought it. Neighbor said fifteen, twenty at a time."

Ray shook his head. "Mos' people would've burnt th' place down an' kep' goin'."

"Th' barn was caved in, along with a couple slave cabins in th' bottom; we cleaned that up, salvaged enough brick for these steps and that path over yonder. I guess you remember th' old washhouse."

"That was my early correctional institute."

T laughed and flicked his cigarette butt into a contractor's wheelbarrow by the steps. "We took th' washhouse down pretty soon after we came on th' job. What was it, Ray, five years ago?"

"Four years August."

"It's about th' longest I've stuck t' anything," said T, "but I wanted t' do something for my brother. He's been a big help t' me, always there when I needed 'im. Anyway, I like seein' th' old place come back."

They sat together on the front steps, in the late afternoon shade of a sycamore.

"We found a few odds an' ends when we tore th' washhouse down." said T. "An old spoon, a ladle, a few bottles, stuff like that.

You can go through th' box. How long you stayin' in Holly Springs?"

"I'm out of here Saturday, headed back to North Carolina."

"Where you stayin' at?" asked Ray.

"Silver . . . Silver something or other, this side of Memphis."

"Whoa," said Ray. "That's a drug motel."

"The black hole of Calcutta. But it's the only place that would take my dog."

"They'll take your dog, your wallet, your shave kit," said T. "I'd be showin' my dust to that sucker."

He loosened his collar against the heat. "What's done is done, I'm afraid. Do y'all know a Tommy Noles, by any chance? His folks lived about a quarter mile from here."

T thought it over. "Don't know 'im."

"Me neither," said Ray.

"Jim Houck?"

"Weirdo," said T.

"Keeps to hisself," said Ray. "Seem like I heard somebody pushed his ol' man down some steps. Ended up in a big trial or somethin', way back."

There it was. There it would always be.

"What about a man named Will or Willie, maybe William—don't know his last name—missing his left thumb?"

They didn't know him.

"Rosie Ponder? In his seventies. Used to work on this place with his family."

T shook his head.

"I'm battin' zero," said Ray.

"Speakin' of names," said T, "what do we call you? Father? Rev'rend?"

"Call me Tim."

"Good deal. I'm Theophilus, named after some dead Greek guy, but I go by T as in T-bone. Easier to spell."

"Theophilus," he said, "means loved by God."

T laughed. "No way that's gon' happen."

Barnabas lumbered up the steps, panting. "When did the little house down the road fall in?"

"It was history when we came. We got to get it cleaned up down there, maybe put in a garden. We been lookin' at that project way too long."

"That's a winter project." Ray took a long pull on his beer. "Right now it's Snake City."

"We found a few scraps down there, too." said T. "Th' head off a doll, some button, an' whatnot. Tossed 'em in the box. I like diggin' around old places, I worked on a dinosaur dig in Wyoming."

"Ol' T, he's done it all. Dived on a Spanish wreck off th' coast of Georgia, did a drivin' gig for Elvis, mostly airport an' barbecue runs . . ."

"Elvis kep' a police light in his Caddy," said T. "Liked to pop that sucker on th' roof an' pull people over if they were speedin'. Two or three months before he died, we pulled over a Corvette, it must have been doin' ninety-five, an' Elvis gave th' guy a warnin'. When th' driver seen who pulled 'im over, he fainted like a woman."

"Tell 'im 'bout th' time you were a show chicken handler fo' that rich cat."

"Showed Rose Combs," said T. "Small; about three pounds. Good-lookin' little chicken. Nice temperament."

"What exactly does a chicken handler do?"

"You manage their diet, control their fluid intake, give 'em their shots. Before a show, you wash 'em, roll 'em up in a towel like a hot-dog in a bun, finish 'em off with a blow dryer, clean their combs with a Q-tip—and bingo, you got a show chicken. Went to chicken competitions all over the country, won the Grand National three times."

"Amazing."

"Rich cat put ol' T behin' th' wheel of a air-conditioned RV wit' leather interior," said Ray. "Had five custom-built chicken cages an' a three-foot flat-screen TV."

"High cotton."

"Course, he don' eat chicken n' more," said Ray.

T lit a cigarette. "I've messed with cattle, owned a roofin' company, got my plumber an' electrician's license, you name it. But next to workin' on this place, my goin' thing is kudzu."

"Miss'ippi's best kep' secret," said Ray.

"Kudzu's got more by-products than petroleum." T took a deep drag off the cigarette and exhaled a flume of smoke. "Fact is, you can use it for fuel, prob'ly gon' be the comin' thing if th' oil crisis keeps up. You can make jelly, tea, noodles, use it for cattle fodder, put it in all kind of recipes. Ever heard of kudzu quiche?"

"Never."

"It's good, real good. Plus you can grind th' root for coffee, fry th' leaves, pickle th' flowers, even make a kind of tofu."

"My favorite."

"An' get this—kudzu cures diarrhea, dysentery, gonorrhea, smallpox, flu, skin rash—an' that's just th' short list. Plus nothin' goes to waste; you use th' seeds, th' leaves, th' flowers, an' th' root."

" 'Behold,' " he said, quoting Genesis, " 'I've given you every herb bearing seed which is upon the face of the earth. To you it shall be for meat.' "

"Th' man upstairs did a number with kudzu, all right. Plus, there's big money in it. Big money. I'm workin' on a kudzu experiment that'll make forty-five percent of th' American male population better-lookin', more self-confident, and—here's th' kicker—more popular with women."

"Sounds like some of the spam I've been getting."

"Spam?"

"Sorry. It's a computer term."

"I don't mess with computers. Outside of this place, all my time an' trouble goes into a revolutionary experiment that will *grow hair*.

Dead serious. It's got a kudzu base an' I'm makin' it in a cream—rub it on th' scalp twice a day an' in six months, you got hair. It's gon' blow th' toupee b'iness in th' ditch."

Ray nodded. "It's gon' be big."

T flicked cigarette ash into the wheelbarrow. "Th' only holdback is distribution. Kudzu products have a tough time sellin' through reg'lar channels. Me an' Ray gon' knock this house out by Christmas an' take my cream on th' road, see how it goes over."

"Any test runs?"

"Not ready for test runs outside of yours truly, but we're gettin' there."

"You have a name for it?"

"Hadn' got there yet. Any an' all ideas welcome."

"I'll be thinking about it," he said. "That your Volvo out there?"

"It is. Used t' run a little taxi service out in th' sticks, mostly people pickin' up booze or goin' after groceries."

"I hear a Volvo will go 'til the cows come home. How many miles?"

"Gainin' on four hundred thousand."

"How many engines?"

"Gainin' on three."

"You guys doing this place alone?"

"Totally."

"Plumbing, wiring, the whole nine yards?"

"Turnkey," said T. "Between Ray and me, we can do everything but heat an' air. Course with only two doin' it, it takes a few years." T's laughter was followed by a rasping cough.

"Tell us about you. How long since you been home t' Holly Springs?"

"Thirty-eight years and change."

"Thirty-eight years. Why'd you take a notion t' come back?"

"Long story short, I got a letter. Not even a letter. A note."

"From kin, I guess." T ground his cigarette butt under his heel and tossed it in the wheelbarrow.

"I don't know who sent it."

He took the envelope from his pocket and removed the lined sheet of paper and passed it to T, who looked at it and passed it to Ray.

"Don' know if this would've got me back," said Ray. "Ain't no little note could get me back t' Memphis, it'd take way more'n a little note." Ray passed the note to T, who studied it.

"With no more'n this to go on, you must've wanted t' come back."

"I guess I did. Must have been waiting for a good excuse. But I dreaded doing it."

"I hear you," said T. "I lit out from Memphis when I was seventeen. For thirty years, I was a wanderin' man like ol' Louis L'Amour. Said I'd never come back t' this part of th' country. But here I am, here you are. No idea who wrote it?"

"No idea. No living kin that I know of, except a first cousin in New Jersey."

"You lookin' for whoever wrote it?"

"Don't know where to look."

"You'd have t' whup me good t' get me back t' Memphis," said Ray.

"Come on, Ray. You drove up with me one time."

"One time is right. But only 'cause you busted yo' hard head open an' had to go to th' hospital. That'd be th' first time an' th' last time. Go ahead an' call it th' only time."

"I get th' message. I ain't pushin' you on that."

"How did y'all team up?"

"I met Ray in Memphis, turns out we were both goin' through a divorce. My brother had just asked me to come down here and pull this place out of th' hole—I figured why hire a bunch of subs who're scared t' death of hard work, when I could hire a brother who can work *and* cook. Ol' Ray, he's rough as a cob, but a pretty straight shooter."

Ray laughed. "It wadn't my cookin' he was after, it was my new set of telescopin' ladders."

T laughed, coughed hard, and spit in the wheelbarrow. "A man can rise pretty high in th' world with a good set of ladders."

" 'Bout all I had left after th' divorce lawyer worked me over."

"Ray did a long pull in th' contractin' business, then spent a few years cookin' down at th' governor's mansion in Jackson. He was th' right hand to th' main honcho."

"Cooked for presidents, first ladies, governors, Indian chiefs, guys from th' Mideast wearin' those tablecloth hat deals . . ."

"How 'bout you, Tim? Can preachers marry in your church?"

He dug in his pocket for his wallet and flipped it open. "Mrs. Kavanagh."

"Whoa," said T. "Look here, Ray."

"Nice," said Ray. "Real nice."

"Famous, too."

"What fo'?"

"Writing and illustrating children's books."

"Very cool," said T.

"And this is my boy, Dooley."

"Good-lookin' cat," said Ray. "Redheaded."

"We adopted him a few months ago. He was left on my doorstep at the age of eleven. He changed my life."

"You're a lucky man," said Ray. "A wife, a kid . . ."

"Grace," he said.

"Me an' Ray have about laid offa women."

"About laid off? I'm done. They got me three times."

"Got me twice," said T. "I'm way done."

Ray tossed his empty bottle in the wheelbarrow and stood up. "I got to git in there an' start flourin' m' catch. Tuesday's our big night aroun' here, I don' cook but once a week. You ought t' stay an' eat wit' us."

"Very kind of you. Better get up the road." He noticed for the first time the ache in his bones—Memphis seemed a thousand miles away; he wanted to sit on this porch for eternity.

"After he left th' mansion, Ray went back to Memphis an' hustled ribs at Rendezvous a few years. He's good, you ought t' stay. When my brother and his wife come down from Memphis, Ray does th' cookin'."

Ray squared back his shoulders and stretched. "T'night's menu feature is catfish, caught this mornin'. Gon' fry it extra crispy, whip up some hush puppies, then come in behin' th' hush puppies wit' coleslaw. None of that mess in a package, we gratin' a actual head."

"Sittin' in there on th' sink right now," said T. "A nice little head."

"Who's th' grater?"

"We got a division of labor goin' on. Ray fishes, I clean. I grate, he makes th' slaw—his ingredients are so secret, I have to turn m' back an' swear on th' Bible not t' look."

"You ain't gon' git no better offer," said Ray.

Though his homeplace didn't seem especially familiar, he felt at home with the kind of hospitality he'd been raised with. He crunched the last sliver of ice in his tea glass and got up from the porch step. He wouldn't mind a refill, but didn't want to trouble anybody. Leaving was the right thing to do—preachers were notorious for showing up at mealtime and wearing out their welcome.

"How about a rain check?" he asked.

"If you leavin' Saturday an' I only cook Tuesday, they ain't gon' be no rain check."

"True."

"Come back even if we're not cookin'," said T. "All us country dudes got on our calendars is, I'm makin' up a new mess of kudzu cream on Thursday, an' Ray's pickin' up his dentures."

Ray grinned. "From th' cat who do teeth fo' th' convicts."

"Must be the price point."

"You got it."

They laughed and shook hands.

"It's been a pleasure," he said. "A real pleasure. Thank you."

T scratched Barnabas behind the ear. "We get started around seven and wind down at four. When you come back, you can go through th' box."

"By the way, what happened to Tater and Tot?"

"They're prob'ly haulin' into Tupelo about now, with a squirrel in the lead."

Ray looked bemused. "B'lieve I'll put a pitcher of homemade lemonade behin' that catfish. Plenty of cracked ice, sting it wit' a little peppermint from m' patch out back . . ."

He couldn't take it anymore. Why should he be the one to redeem clergy's reputation for lurking at mealtime?

"That did it," he said. "I'm in."

They sat around the kitchen table after supper and went through the plunder of lives that had been lived at Whitefield for a hundred and fifty years. He didn't recognize the gizmo from a toy, or the plowshare or the buttons.

"Ain't it somethin', you settin' right here in th' kitchen where you was a boy?" Ray had cubed a fresh pineapple; they were eating it with their fingers and wiping up the juice with paper towels.

"Grace," he said.

"When I went back to Memphis in th' nineties, I went to see my ol' house, an' it wadn't there n' more. There was a basketball hoop and two white boys an' a black. I say, 'This is where I used t' live at.' Black boy, he 'bout fourteen, fifteen, say, 'Ain't nobody ever live here, I been here all my life an' ain't nobody live here but this hoop.' "

"Jus' gone," said T.

"Wit' th' wind," said Ray. "You a lucky man, t' come back to th' homeplace an' it still standin'."

"Still standing and looking good," he said.

Rosie's yo-yo. He took it in his hand with reverence. Pieces of rotted string sifted back into the box . . .

He had mixed his blood with Louis Ponder's youngest son, Rosie, because if it hadn't been for Rosie, he couldn't have saved Peggy's life. Rosie had wanted a yo-yo worse than anything, and since it was right to do good stuff for your blood brother, he'd paid for it with his own money and given it to Rosie at Christmas.

Not long after that, Rufe told him where real brothers come from. Before he learned this horrible truth, he had often asked for a brother, and his mother always said it depended on what God thought about it.

He couldn't imagine that God would have anything to do with giving him a brother the way Rufe said you get a brother. He asked Peggy how he might be able to get a brother without exactly requesting one from his mother.

'That's th' good Lord's business, let Him handle such as that. You cain't be jus' pressin' a button on somebody an' gettin' a brother.'

So he prayed every night for a long time.

When nothing appeared to be happening, he bucked up his courage and went to his mother, completely blanking out of his mind anything Rufe had said.

'Mama.'

She looked up and smiled. She was sewing a shirt for him; it was red and green plaid, his favorite.

'Could I please, please have a brother? I've been prayin'.'

She leaned over and kissed him on the cheek. 'Well, then, I'm sure He'll answer. It may not be the answer we're expecting, but God always answers.'

He wanted to say, *Yes, but you have to do your part, are you doing your part?* He knew that his mother and father weren't sleeping in the same room anymore, which could have something to do with the problem. He later asked Rufe if people got sisters the same way they got brothers, and learned the disturbing truth.

Feeling overwhelmed by the whole business, he did not ask again for a brother. But he kept praying . . .

His mother's old trowel.

When he took it from the box, the worn wooden handle with traces of green paint seemed comfortable in his hand, and oddly consoling. The garden had been her life's work, her confession that something lovely could be wrought from disappointment. Madelaine Kavanagh herself had lived out Roethke's premise that "deep in their roots, all flowers keep the light" . . .

When he heard how gravely ill she was, he folded his purple and white ribbon stole and put it in his duffel bag. But this was admitting the worst, so he took it out and replaced it in the bureau drawer. As he was getting in the car for the drive to Holly Springs, he turned and looked at the house a long time, then unlocked the door and went inside. He knew he would need the stole, no matter how hard he may have prayed against her dying.

There were many assurances his mother had missed in her short life, not the least of which was the assurance of her husband's innocence in the Martin Houck affair. The whole business—the tragedy, the lawsuit, the trial, and the suspicion that his father had been guilty—had eaten away at her, not to mention himself, for years.

His father's clerk had attested to an argument between Houck and his employer, which led to a brief scuffle, and to his employer walking with Houck to the door, where the argument continued. The clerk testified that his quick glance at the scuffle led him to believe Houck started the altercation, soon after which he heard a shout. Then, he said, 'Thumps racked the metal steps and were felt for a moment in the floorboards of my office.' He rushed from his office to the landing, where he saw 'the defendant, Matthew Kavanagh, standing white as a sheet and speechless, and Mr. Houck crumpled on the pavement below.' There were no other witnesses.

In the end, the only assurance he'd ever been able to offer his mother was his love. He would give anything to feel that had been enough, but it had not been enough.

His hands trembled as he put on the stole in her bedroom and poured wine into the small chalice.

She rallied a little after taking the infinitesimal crumb of bread, moistened with wine, but her eyes remained closed.

'Timmy?'

'Yes, ma'am?'

There was a long silence, then she said, 'There's someone at the door.'

He knelt and took her cold hand and held it against his cheek.

'They've come to see the gardens,' she whispered. 'Tell them . . .' She tugged at his hand, urgent.

'I'm here, Mother.'

'Tell them . . .'

He knew the sound; in the old days, it had been called the death rattle. He bent closer and listened.

'Tell them . . . I'm so sorry, but . . .'

He clasped her hand in both of his.

'. . . the garden is closed.'

He continued to kneel beside her, frozen in place, looking at the bluish shadow of her eyelids and the nearly invisible veins beneath her cheekbones. Her skin was translucent as porcelain against the pillowcase bordered with his grandmother's tatting.

He kissed her forehead. Then he released her hand—it seemed to take a long time to lay it at her side—and, still kneeling, offered the supplication he'd memorized from the 1928 prayer book.

' "Into thy hands, O merciful Saviour, we commend the soul of thy servant, now departed from the body. Acknowledge, we humbly beseech thee, a sheep of thine own fold, a lamb of thine own flock, a sinner of thine own redeeming. Receive her into the arms of thy mercy, into the blessed rest of everlasting peace, and into the glorious company of the saints in light. Amen." '

He stood up and drew the sheet over her face, and went to the kitchen, where Louis and the doctor and nurse were drinking coffee, and said, 'She's gone.'

Louis uttered an instantaneous and primordial howl that might have been his own if he would allow it.

The funeral home dispatched a hearse to Whitefield, and afterward, he had gone to his room and stood at the open window for a long time, looking out to the moon-washed garden. He had never felt such agony; it was as if he couldn't possibly go on . . .

He wiped his eyes with his handkerchief. "Better save this box for another day."

"You ought to stay with us tonight," said T.

"Yeah," said Ray. "We take dogs."

He blew his nose.

"You can have your old room; my brother uses it to bunk some of th' guys he hunts an' fishes with. Th' sheets didn't get changed since Charlie Stokes, but Charlie's pretty clean, all things considered."

"Plus, th' toilet flushes," said Ray, "an' you got a ceilin' fan."

"Thanks, fellas, but I can't do it. I'm diabetic, and my insulin's at the motel. I need a shot tonight, and again in the morning."

What he really needed was an airlift; he was completely, utterly fried.

At the end of Whitefield's winding driveway, he stopped and put the top up, and called his wife.

"Touching base," he said.

"Where are you?"

"Headed to Memphis. How's your ankle?"

"Better. How's your heart?"

"Better," he said. "I love you."

"I love you back."

"I've just been to Whitefield; I'll tell you everything in the morning."

"I'll come with you next time, no matter what."

Maybe there wouldn't be a next time.

He turned left and drove along the graveled country road until it turned to asphalt, then connected with the highway to Memphis and the motel whose roof was still decorated with Christmas lights. He slept soundly until sunrise.

By six-thirty, he had walked his dog, paid his bill, and was out of the Silver something or other with the top down, his good pants and sport coat lying flat in the trunk and his duffel bag on the back-seat.

If the person who wrote the note was going to show himself, or even possibly, though not probably, herself, he wanted to get it over with. He was amazed, still, that he'd allowed two small words to whirl him like a dervish.

He hunkered over the wheel, liking the feel of the wind in his hair—what was left of it. And another thing: What kind of mind could reasonably believe that such spare communication would bring someone running across three state lines?

"You're the one who wanted me to come back," he said aloud. "That's what this is all about. So here I am, as ready as Samuel to do whatever you want done."

From the moment the note arrived, he'd felt called, led, drawn, pulled—the whole thing was clearly in God's hands and out of his own. And since he didn't know what else to do, he'd do something completely uncharacteristic—starting now, he would, as some were fond of saying, go with the flow.

"Wouldn't mind seeing the old cotton compress," he told his

dog, "if it's still standing. Maybe somebody will let us in Nanny Howard's house." If he got to the church today, fine; if not, he had time to cover that base. "We'll definitely drive by my old school, and hey, maybe Phillips Grocery is still in the hamburger business." After Stafford's, Phillips Grocery had been his favorite food haunt.

His spirits were definitely charging. "If Phillips is still going, I'll treat you to a burger."

He looked at Barnabas, who eyed him from the passenger seat.

"But no onions," he said.

SEVEN

H e found coffee and an egg biscuit at a place on the square, and ate in the Mustang with yesterday's *South Reporter* propped on the steering wheel. After talking with Cynthia for a half hour, he was at Tyson's by nine, looking for razor blades and lip balm.

He bought a *Commercial Appeal* at the rack, and found Amy sorting change into the register.

"How are you, Amy?"

"Terrible," she whispered. "It's Miz Lewis. I had to pick her up on my way in an' bring her with me so I can take her to the doctor at eleven."

"Where is she?"

"Over behind th' card rack. She's worse than ever, our pharmacist says it's th' medication for sure. If she speaks, don't say a word back, it sets her off, okay?"

"Okay."

"Lower your voice. Where's your dog?"

"In the car. In the shade. I'll bring him in tomorrow."

"It's goin' to be ninety-nine today, with a storm this evenin'. You want your lip balm in cherry, lemon, or chocolate?"

"Can't it just be plain?" Nothing was plain anymore.

"No plain. I like th' cherry, it's our most popular. Th' chocolate feels icky."

"Cherry, then." He was whispering, too.

"Well, well, well!" boomed Mrs. Lewis, who was roaring up on his left flank. "If it isn't Father Crowley!"

Amy gave him a desperate look. "You're in for it," she said under her breath.

"Back to try and mend broken fences, I suppose! And don't bother apologizin' to me, when you ought to be beggin' forgiveness from th' whole bloomin' town!"

Keeping his mouth shut wasn't a problem; he had no idea what to say. He dug in his pocket for his wallet.

"And what, may I ask, are you doing with th' money you helped yourself to?"

He extracted a ten and he handed it to Amy.

Mrs. Lewis gasped. "Spending it, of course! Flinging it around like a heathen while children go hungry all over the world! It's no wonder your church is in a fix, you people think you can get away with every trick in the book. Makes me glad to be a Presbyterian." She frowned at Amy. "Or am I a Baptist?"

"The Gen'ral was a Presbyterian, Miz Lewis, you're a Baptist."

The old woman leaned toward him on her cane. "And proud of it!" she thundered.

He grabbed his change. "I'm out of here. I'll pray for things to go well at eleven."

"Thank you, we need it. Oh, and there's an envelope for you. Th' pharmacist said it was brought in late yesterday."

Amy rummaged beneath the counter.

"How did anyone know I'm in town?"

"Everybody knows. I told all my customers yesterday, and Red came over from th' hardware, he mentioned it, too, but he was mostly talkin' about your dog."

The cane wagged in his face. "Give poor Miz Crowley my regards, if she's still livin' after all you've put her through."

Amy handed him an envelope inscribed *Timothy Kavanagh*.

"Thanks," he said, catching his breath.

He turned to leave, but instead surprised himself by hugging Miz Lewis, who was shocked speechless. "God bless you," he said, and blew out the door. By George, if he could hug Luola Lewis, he could do anything, the world was his onion.

He sprinted across the street to the hardware for a plastic dog dish; the metal deal they were traveling with conducted heat and turned cool water to warm.

"You're gettin' to be a regular," said Red. "How's it goin'?"

"Good, real good, thanks."

"Where's y'r dog?"

"In the car. He sends his regards."

"Findin' y'r people?"

"Not so far. Any word on how the hunters did yesterday?"

"Clyde just stopped by. Said a couple buzzards followed 'is truck home."

He laughed. "Need a plastic dog bowl."

"What color?"

"What color do you have?"

"Green."

"I'll take green."

Red called to a helper unpacking work shoes. "Run get this customer a dog bowl. Extra-large."

Red opened the cash register. "Somebody left somethin' for you a few minutes ago." He removed the drawer and produced an envelope. "Pretty nice-lookin'."

"What's nice-lookin'?"

Red handed him the envelope and winked. "Th' lady that brought it in."

He sat in the car with the a/c running and looked at the two envelopes. Not the handwriting he was hoping for, not at all.

He lifted the loosely sealed flap of the envelope from Tyson's, and pulled out the sheet of cream-colored stationery monogrammed PCC.

Dear Timothy,

I've just heard that you are in town, though only for a short visit. Let me be among the first to welcome you home to Holly Springs.

Though I know I don't deserve it, I hope you will allow me the chance to apologize—I have prayed for the opportunity for many years.

I am living at Mama and Daddy's old place on Salem Avenue. Mama and Daddy left Three Oaks to me, and since my husband, Dr. Wayne Cochran, died three years ago with cancer, I've been trying my best to "doll it up." So many people have moved to Holly Springs and are buying our beautiful old houses and restoring them.

If you get this, I hope to see you today at three o'clock. If you choose not to come, I will understand, but so hope you will. And if you still like chocolate, I believe you are in for a treat and a half.

Yours truly,
Peggy Cramer Cochran

He sat for a time and gazed, unseeing, at the people passing on the sidewalk.

The second envelope was so well sealed, he tore off one end and removed the single sheet of white bond.

Dear Timmy,

I hear you are a priest, and I am so happy that you got to be what you always wanted. It is so good when people do what they

*always wanted. As for me, I was a private nurse for twenty years
in Holly Springs, then I spent twenty years working at the hospital
in Oxford which amounted to hundreds of hours in the car, many
of which I used to listen to books on tape, including the New Testament twice. Now I am retired and it is so much fun. I have a
dog named Nellie. She's a Border collie.*

    *Wouldn't it be great to talk about old times? Can you meet for
lunch at Phillips Grocery today at noon? Or any other day, I don't
know how long you will be in Holly Springs. So sorry you missed
the azaleas, this was their best year in ages.*

    I hope you can make it. I'll jot my number so you can call me.
    Your friend and neighbor from the past,
    Jessica Raney

He dialed his wife, astounded that she'd predicted something
like this.

"I've had a note from Peggy Cramer," he said. "She's inviting me
for tea. She wants to apologize." He might as well tell the whole
truth. "She's a widow."

"Do you want to go?"

"I don't know. But it might be a good thing, her heart seems . . .
differently disposed." He read the note to her.

"You should go."

"Is that what you really think?"

"Life is short, and the road to Holly Springs is long. If she
doesn't behave herself, I'll come and scratch her eyes out." The
sound of his wife's laughter soothed him. "How's that?"

"Deal," he said.

"Beware of the chocolate thingamajig."

"I will." He'd been in two deep comas from gambling with his diabetes. "One more thing. Jessica Raney, of the card-in-the-sock-
drawer business, has invited me to have lunch."

"Oh, good grief. You see, Timothy? What did I tell you?"

"She left a note at Booker Hardware."

"In there buying a drill bit, I suppose."

"She wants to meet at Phillips Grocery for a hamburger. I confess I'd like to see her—it would be great to talk with someone I knew in the old days."

Silence.

Early on, they'd agreed to tell each other everything. He'd failed to do that more than once, and disaster had followed.

"Kavanagh? Are you there?"

"Hush," she said, "I'm praying."

"Excuse me."

"Of course, I can't absolutely, positively tell you what to do. As your wife, however, I can make a suggestion."

"Fire away."

"Have a hamburger, darling."

"Thanks."

"With onions."

He called the number Jessica had given him and got her answering machine.

"Hey, this is Jessica, I hope you're havin' a good day. Leave me a message and I'll call you back. Bye-bye."

He cleared his throat in preparation for the end of a long beep.

"Hello, Jessica, this is Timothy Kavanagh." He regretted sounding pompous, and tried sounding more upbeat. "Thanks for your kind invitation to meet for lunch, I've been wondering if Phillips is still in the hamburger business. I have my dog with me, since my wife couldn't come." That didn't sound right. "It'll be great to see you. Noon today, then, at—" The beep cut him off.

He rinsed the new dog bowl and tossed the water on the roots of a tree. He poured another round and set the bowl on the asphalt.

Barnabas sniffed the new bowl, drank, and looked up at him, expectant.

"The cemetery. We're off to the *cemetery*. The hamburger comes later."

He took his ringing cell phone from his pocket and flipped it open. Morning light illuminated the ID: *Dooley Barlowe*.

"Hey," he said, grinning.

"Hey, yourself."

"What's up, buddyroe?" He would probably never get over the thrill of hearing his son's voice.

"Remember Edith, the ewe that stomped her foot at Cynthia?"

"I remember."

"Triplets."

"Who vetted?"

"Me. Had to do a C-section. One of the triplets was malformed and stillborn. I wish you could have been there, I've never seen anything like it and don't want to again."

"You handled the whole thing?"

"Blake was over at the cow barn when she went into labor. I saw she couldn't deliver, so I reached in there and felt around, and I knew we had real problems. I yelled for somebody to get Blake. I managed to hold her 'til Blake brought the kit and handed me the knife. I've watched Hal and Blake, but I'd never done a C. I was scared. Really scared."

"I'm scared just hearing about it."

"Except for when Barnabas got hit by a car, it was the worst thing I ever had to do. I thought we were going to lose her. Slicing into her belly was really tough, I didn't know if I could do it, but she was pretty calm through the whole business. I have a lot of admiration for what she could handle."

"How is she?"

"Good. Strong."

"Are you bottle-feeding?"

"Nope. We gave 'em a bottle right after, but she was nursing a few hours later."

"Well done, son. It's interesting that Blake turned it over to you."

"Ever since I confronted him, he's been different. It's like he knew it was true."

"So it's a good summer."

"How's it goin' for you? Is it weird to be back in the place you were born?"

"Weird. Good. Hard. Important."

"I'll go out there with you someday. You can show me that water tank you climbed."

He laughed. "How's Kenny?"

"Great. I think he might want to go to college."

"Terrific. Let's talk about that when I get home. How's Sammy?"

"Hardheaded. But okay. Clowns around too much. It's like shooting pool is the only thing that really keeps him centered."

"And how's Lace doing?"

"Gotta go, Dad."

"Later, alligator. Love you."

"Love you back."

So things weren't so good with Lace Harper, who, like his boy, had been a thrown-away mountain kid with everything against her.

The temperature was climbing. He chugged a pint of water.

No flowers today.

They drove through the gate and up the hill and found their spot. He pulled the Mustang onto the grass, beneath what would soon be the shade of an oak, and got out of the car.

He hadn't allowed himself to think about it much, but he had to wonder why Jim Houck had followed him up here yesterday. He'd never really known Jim, but remembered he'd been a surly kid, a loner, and the only son of the cotton broker Martin Houck, who was infamous for his hostility and aggression in business dealings.

Houck had been severely crippled in the fall down the steps from the law office, and confined to a wheelchair for the rest of his life.

In his gut, he'd always feared that his father might have pushed Houck—the possibility had disturbed his sleep for years. The assurance he sought, as did his mother and all those at Whitefield, was that it had been winter, and with any trace of ice on the steps, it would be easy to slip and fall. Indeed, his father's clerk usually cautioned visitors to be careful when going up or down the steps in winter. One of the points made by Houck's attorney was that the temperature on the day of Houck's fall had been four degrees above freezing.

What Jim Houck said yesterday was true—men with status in the community had often gotten off scot-free when facing charges, even very crucial charges. His Grandfather Kavanagh, in one of his legendary fits of anger, had shot a Holly Springs black man who accidentally backed into his automobile on the square. The shooting incident, which was serious but not fatal, had been brushed off with an informal hearing. God help a man who had no prominence in Holly Springs in the years he'd grown up here; he didn't even want to think about some of the stories that had come from the courthouse.

He walked to the oak and sat in the same spot he'd occupied yesterday, his dog beside him. He would pick up where he left off.

He leaned back and closed his eyes, relishing the light breeze and the peace.

Tea with Peggy Cramer. Of all things.

He could remember the time, not so long ago, when he would never have considered such a meeting. Had he really forgiven her? During the years in seminary, he'd certainly prayed for the grace to forgive her, and on the surface, at least, he was certain he had.

It had been the first blow to his manhood, not to mention his social pride. He'd probably been more humiliated by Peggy Cramer than anyone else in his seven decades.

His bishop, Stuart Cullen, had run into her a few years ago. 'She's still a beautiful woman, Timothy, but good heavens—boring as bathwater. Never appropriated the depth of feeling you'd be needing in a mate.'

He'd always thought himself essentially boring until Cynthia convinced him otherwise—he would be eternally grateful to his wife for that.

"Don't fear whatever God lays before you today," she'd said this morning.

Before he went sticking his fork in whatever chocolate business Peggy was setting out, he wanted to get his act together . . .

Peggy Cramer had the whitest teeth he'd ever seen.

Sure, he knew what the other guys were looking at, he looked there, too. But more than anything, he was mesmerized by her teeth.

He'd never spoken to her, and as far as he knew, she had never noticed him. Then, one day after school, they were seniors, she brushed against him at the foot of the front steps and looked at him and smiled.

His knees did an H_2O.

'Hey,' he said. His voice didn't sound like his own.

'Hey.'

He wanted her to keep walking like nothing had happened, but she just stood there, looking at him. He tried to step back, but was shackled at the ankles and couldn't move.

"Why do you have such great teeth?" He didn't mean to say that.

"Milk."

She pronounced the word as *mee-ulk*. It had a sound as ravishing as Henry James's favorite phrase, summer afternoon.

'I drank milk when I was little,' she said, 'an' never had a Co-Cola, not one time.'

He was incredulous. 'You never had a Co-Cola?'

'Not one time. My daddy says a worm will disappear jus' like that in a bottle of Co-Cola.' She snapped her fingers, her charm bracelet jangled; he found it the most extraordinary physical gesture he'd ever witnessed. 'Not to mention a nail, so just think what it does to your insides.'

People walked around them.

'Have you ever watched a nail disappear in a Co-Cola?' he asked. Why couldn't he at least step back from her? He could feel her breath as his own.

'Why take th' trouble if Daddy already did it?'

Her daddy was the richest man in Marshall County. Whatever Ed Cramer said, went—with everybody. Just standing next to somebody so rich was scary. But her sweater was pink, and his heart was hammering.

She ran her fingers through her blond hair, her eyes locked with his. 'I'm Peggy Cramer.'

'Tim. Kavanagh.'

'Your daddy an' my daddy know each other. You write poetry.'

'No. I just read it. Memorize it, sometimes.'

'I can't understand poetry. Not at all. Except, "I think that I shall never see a poem lovely as a tree" is really pretty.'

He would pay cash money for someone to pull him away from her by force.

'You're a big track star,' she said.

Not really, but why argue? He shrugged.

'Do you smoke?'

He'd had serious bad luck with smoking.

'No. But I could.'

'So, do you want to go smoke?'

She was wearing pearls; she smelled good; he couldn't bear this another minute.

'I'll meet you at th' cemetery at four o'clock,' she said. 'At the big angel, under the holly.'

She was gone before he could speak.

He was scared out of his mind by the stupid things he'd just said, stupid from start to finish. He didn't want to meet her at the cemetery—or anywhere else—plus he had practice in fifteen minutes. Why had she even talked to him? She'd never once looked his way before. She could have anybody she wanted, she had at least four guys on the string, including Jack Sutton, and any one of them could easily break his neck. But no, he thought, Peggy Cramer herself would do the breaking—in some way he couldn't imagine.

He didn't meet her at the cemetery that day.

Not that day . . .

"Are you Timmy Kavanagh?"

Startled, he opened his eyes and looked up. A woman in tan pants and a red blouse was peering down at him.

"I'm Jessica. Jessica Raney. I got your message just before I left to bring flowers to Mama and Daddy, an' I looked over here an' saw this nice man sittin' under a tree, an' I knew you looked sort of familiar, an' you were wearin' your collar an' all, so . . ."

He scrambled to his feet and shook her hand.

"Jessica! I declare."

". . . so I knew it must be you!"

"It's me, all right. Good gracious, you haven't changed."

She laughed. "Preachers aren't supposed to tell lies."

"No lie at all. You look wonderful."

"Well, thanks. I really 'preciate it, 'cause I'm a whole year older than you."

"Nobody's older than me, I've decided. And this is my dog, Barnabas."

Barnabas stood, also, wagging his tail.

"Oh, my gosh. He's big as a haymow."

"I like your pastoral view of things."

"My Nellie would have a heart attack."

"He's good with other dogs, wouldn't harm a fly."

"How old is he?"

"Eighty-four in dog years. We occasionally call him the Old Gentleman. I'd offer you a seat, but . . ."

She proceeded to thump down in the grass and settle an enormous handbag in her lap. "I'll just plop down with you. Hope I can get up again!"

He sat beside her, bones creaking. "Fancy meeting you here, Jessica."

"I like to visit Mama and Daddy at least once a week, an' sometimes th' graves of my old patients, but only th' nice ones."

"When did you lose your parents?"

"Mama passed ten years ago. I lost Daddy two years ago, he was ninety-four."

"I remember Lloyd Raney as very robust and hardworking. What became of your dairy farm?"

"I sold it when he passed. It has a golf course and fourteen houses on it now. I hate they tore the springhouse down, I always loved the springhouse."

"I rode my bike over to your place one day to take your mother some jam, it was hot as blazes. You took me in the springhouse and gave me a Coke you said you'd been saving for a special occasion. It was ice-cold, I felt like a heel for drinking it."

"Right there is proof that old age doesn't mean you lose your memory! That is very sweet of you to remember." She dug into her canvas handbag and removed a large envelope. "When I got your message, I was so excited, I just grabbed every ol' picture I could find. I have no idea where my yearbook is, or I would've brought that, too."

He glanced at his watch. "Don't you want to look over those at lunch?"

She beamed. "If we look at some now, we'll have more time at lunch to talk about th' good ol' days."

"There's a thought. But were they really the good old days, do you think?"

She pondered this. "Well, yes, I think they were. Nobody talkin' about bird flu goin' to kill us. About nuclear winters. About subways bein' flooded by terrorists. About California sinkin' in th' ocean. About polio and TB and yellow fever comin' back. About ice floes meltin'—"

"You've definitely got a point."

She opened the envelope and sorted through several pictures, clearly happy. She was prettier now than he remembered. She chose a photo and looked at it a moment without revealing the image to him.

"Want to see your handsome self at age fourteen?"

"How do you know I was fourteen?"

"I know you were fourteen because I was fifteen."

"How on earth do you remember such things?"

"Mama said good memory is a gift. A blessin' and a curse is what I call it, since I also remember things I don't want to. When I was gettin' dressed this mornin' I remembered when your daddy died. It was October twelfth."

"Correct. Amazing."

"I was at the hospital that day, I'd gone in to take a birthday card to Ellie Johnson, one of the nurses, she was so good-hearted—and they were all sayin' you'd left to go back to school because the doctor thought your daddy would be all right, and then he died right after that."

"Yes."

She turned the photo around. "Ta-dahhhh!"

Was that him? Or a complete stranger? It was him, all right. He was grinning, as if he knew something no one else knew. All that showed was his head, which was fully covered by hair. Overall, a pretty nice-looking guy. Why had he always thought he was ugly as a mud fence?

"Margaret Nelson took it with my camera so I could have a picture with th' Holly High track team, then I took hers. That's me way over on th' left," she said. "Th' one with th' stringy hair and th' horse face."

"That's no horse face. Why would you say that?"

"Mama always said I had a horse face."

He felt a stab of something like anger. "Jessica, we're in our eighth decade. We must stop listening to voices from the past—and we must stop immediately. What do you say?"

Tears brimmed in her eyes. "You are so right, Timmy. You are so right. I just knew it would be great to see you again, you always had so much common sense."

"I'm afraid it's my wife who has the common sense in our family."

"I'm glad to know you're married; I always wondered. I never married. Are you happy?"

"I am. God's grace has been boundless in my life."

"It's been hard to keep up with you, since you never came home after your mama died and you settled everything. I sure am sorry I couldn't nurse her when she was sick, but I was nursin' Mr. Houck full-time."

"It's all right," he said. "Everything worked out. By the way, thanks for the card you sent when my rabbits died, it meant a great deal."

"Oh, gosh, I sent you a card?"

"You did."

"Isn't it funny, th' different things people remember?"

She shuffled through the large photos and chose one; he noticed the color rising in her cheeks as if she were blushing. "I didn't know if you'd want to see this. I took it that night at th' Peabody, I hope it's all right to bring it."

"I'd like to see anything you have."

He and Peggy Cramer stood in front of the duck fountain at the Peabody Hotel, holding hands and dressed to kill. Peggy wore a strapless gown with a gardenia corsage pinned to the wrist of an elbow-length white glove, and held aloft in her other hand, as if it were some rare prize, the pack of Lucky Strikes he'd bought her from the tray of the cigarette girl. He wore a white dress shirt with French cuffs, navy trousers, bow tie, and a white jacket with the two-carat engagement ring in the breast pocket.

He felt color suffuse his own face. Peggy was looking at him like he hung the moon; he was looking at her—he remembered the torrent of his feelings even now—with a mixture of gut-wrenching trepidation and the full menu of 1 John 2:16. It was his first year in seminary.

"Back then," she said, "it seemed like people could hardly get engaged without runnin' up to Memphis; we just swarmed up there like house flies."

"Diamond rings burning holes in our pockets," he said.

"Doin' th' foxtrot an' th' Memphis Shuffle. About to faint 'cause we'd nearly starved ourselves to death to get in our dresses."

"Smelling up the place with aftershave."

"An' 'Evenin' in Paris,' " she said. "Don't forget 'Evenin' in Paris.' "

He laughed. "Who could forget 'Evening in Paris'?"

"I was sorry things didn't work out," said Jessica.

He handed her the photograph. "Don't be."

It was th' same night Harold Wilson and I got engaged."

"Should I be sorry things didn't work out?"

"No," she said, laughing. "Definitely not. Mama an' Daddy were scared to death I'd be an old maid, so when Harold asked me, I said yes. Oh, gosh, then two weeks later, I told him I couldn't go through with it, but not to take it personally. To tell th' truth, I think he was awful relieved. He married Beth Snyder and has a whole gang of kids an' grandkids."

A light breeze moved in the branches above them; shadows trembled in their laps.

"I was thinkin'," she said, "as I went through my pictures that th' whole Holly Springs crowd that night had been off to college an' had jobs an' all, an' they still hadn't gotten engaged or married. It seemed like we were, I don't know, th' last of th' breed or some-thin'."

Deep down, he'd wanted to remain one of that breed.

"Remember how Patty Franklin turned Tommy down flat, so Tommy was roamin' around tryin' to make out with everybody else's girlfriend?"

"That was Tommy, all right." He'd been wounded by the fact that Tommy never contacted him after he disappeared from Holly Springs. Tommy had simply vanished, and all he could learn was that Tommy had broken up with his fiancée and threatened to join the Marines. For a long time, he'd been angry that he'd mixed his blood with someone who chose to do his own thing without giving a rip for how others felt about it. "Any idea where he is now?"

"Not th' faintest. Gosh, I hadn't thought about Tommy in years. I remember he wore wax lips that night an' put a whoopee cushion in Patty's chair. But he was a great dancer, an' so popular with everybody. Course, he got awful bad to drink, did you know that?"

"I knew he was drinking pretty heavily back then, but so were a lot of other people."

"Maybe it was because he couldn't find a good job after college. Course, even his mama was an alcoholic, not to mention his daddy. I never saw Miz Noles but maybe once or twice, they say she hardly ever left th' house. Anyway, she passed a long time ago, I can't remember exactly when, an' his little sister married th' brother of her college roommate an' moved to Cincinnati."

"His father?"

"Died about fifteen years ago. I went to th' funeral out of respect because he was my history teacher an' I always liked him, but Tommy didn't come."

"Tommy used to say, 'Die young and make a good-lookin' corpse.' I hope that's not the answer to his whereabouts. Otherwise, people don't just vanish off the face of the earth."

"You did," she said.

"So what else have you got there? This is the most entertainment I've had since crossing the state line."

She sorted through the photographs and handed him one.

Louis and Ol' Damn Mule! He had an impulse to kiss the fading image. Louis in his overalls, wearing his primordial felt hat, grinning, and showing the gold tooth which was his most prized possession after Ol' Damn Mule and his Remington pump.

He shook his head with wonder. There was no way he could keep his eyes dry.

"You can have that. I took it myself."

"This is a very powerful portrait," he said. "You're another Eudora Welty."

"Thank you, that's a huge compliment. I love Miss Welty's pictures, I guess I understand her pictures better than her books. Did you ever read her?"

"Not in years."

"I'm fixin' to read her again. I had a professor who said that under all those cotton dresses with a smocked bodice, Miss Welty was dancin' naked to a piped tune. I hope you don't mind my sayin' that. If Miss Welty could come back as anything she wanted to, I think she would be a unicorn—livin' on th' old Trace."

"Do you have the negative? I won't take it if . . ."

"Oh, mercy, I have boxes and boxes of negatives. I was just wild with a camera, I even made a darkroom in my closet so Daddy wouldn't have to foot the bill at the drugstore. Here's that family who lived on your farm."

Louis and Sally. And Rufe and Washington and Lincoln and Rosie. In the wagon, posing as if in a studio. Solemn, respectful of the camera. Sally seated on a bench with her husband. The light soft on their faces, on their innocence, their wonder.

He leaned his head against the tree and closed his eyes.

Jessica was quiet. The temperature was rising.

"Okay," he said after a moment. "I'm back."

She smiled and shuffled through the photographs. "I thought I might have one of your other Peggy. But I guess I don't. I know you thought th' world of her. Do you remember all those years ago when you an' your mama an' daddy came to our house for a covered-dish? It was before th' war was over. Oh, gosh, I know exactly when it was, it was the day we got th' news that Glenn Miller's plane went down, my mother was just devastated, she loved Glenn Miller, we had all his records. Anyway, I was ten, which would make you nine. So many people showed up, we must have invited th' whole county. Your mama brought Peggy to help out, and we ate at a long table under the cherry trees."

He hated that he didn't remember.

"I thought your Peggy was nice, and really pretty, too. I could swear on th' Bible I took her picture with my Kodak, or maybe then it would have been my Brownie. Anyway, Daddy nearly had a fit that I wasted money takin' pictures of colored people, it cost so much for film and developin' and nobody had two nickels to rub together durin' th' war."

He dug into his pants pocket. He was wearing out his handkerchiefs, and this was only his second day in town.

"I'm sorry this is makin' you sad. Should I show you any more?"

"I want to see everything. It's just that it's hard . . . to come home."

"I never left, so I don't know. I wanted to leave, but I was too scared."

They looked out to the stones, silent for a time.

"Let me show you some pictures." He pulled out his wallet and flipped it open to the face of his son.

"My son, Dooley. Adopted at the age of twenty-one."

"He is so handsome! I dearly love freckles."

"Sophomore at the University of Georgia, he's going to be a vet. And this is Mrs. Kavanagh." He liked saying that.

"Oh, my gosh, she's beautiful. Just beautiful."

"Yes. She is. Her name is Cynthia."

"I'm so glad you have each other, Timmy. I had a crush on you, did you ever know that?"

"I had no idea. And I can't imagine why."

"You were different. Really different. Do you remember reciting Wordsworth to me one day? You were twelve, I was thirteen."

"I'm sorry I don't remember. I'm sure girls didn't want to hear Wordsworth, but I never really knew what girls wanted to hear."

"It was the Lucy poems. You had the most beautiful voice I ever heard, th' words just rolled out—not like you were reciting, but like you were livin' in those poems. I don't know how to explain it, exactly."

"Thank you. You're kind."

"I remember you always wanted a brother, and I always wanted a sister." She was pensive for a moment. "But you know what?"

"What?"

"I think th' whole point of life is to know God, and be able to accept the way things turn out."

"I agree absolutely. And you, Jessica? Why didn't you marry?"

"I never had th' courage."

"It does take courage, I'll grant you that."

"Sometimes I hate it because I let myself miss so much in life. Too scared to do this, too scared to do that. But I really did give my nursin' everything I had. I loved my patients better than anything in the world. I saw so much sufferin', and I really feel like I helped a little."

"I believe that helping even a little can be enough," he said. "Yet I'm sure you helped much. Very much."

"Somewhere at home I have a picture of your track team taken by a real photographer. You were such a big track star at Holly High, you just ran like th' wind. I even remember your number."

"No way," he said.

"Seven"

"You're amazing."

"I'll look for th' picture—you were sixteen, I was seventeen."

"Why don't we head off to Phillips, we'll beat the crowd? My bones can't endure this hard ground another minute." Barnabas stood and shook himself, eager to move on.

"Oh, mercy," said Jessica, "it'll take a crane to get me up from here."

He stood and gave her a hand up, and she brushed herself off and dug into her purse and pulled out a camera and looked at him, beaming.

"Would you mind if I take your picture?" she said.

EIGHT

S he was still beautiful.

"Timothy." She held out her hand and he took it. "Thank you for coming."

"Thank you for having me." The palm of her hand was cool; she wore a suit the color of the blue parlor walls.

"I didn't know whether you'd come."

"I wasn't so sure about it myself." He'd changed pants in the stockroom at Booker's, put on his linen sport coat, and left Barnabas with Red.

"Please," she said. "Let's sit in the window."

The room wasn't greatly changed from his visits many years ago, though the overall spirit of it was brighter. They sat in high-backed velvet chairs in the bay window, at a table furnished with a silver tea service and a vase of roses. Three petals had fallen onto the white cloth; a small cake, ornamented with a curl of shaved chocolate, was displayed on a crystal stand.

"After I wrote the note, I was sorry to have used chocolate as a bribe." She smiled a little and took up the cake knife.

"And I'm sorry to confess that diabetes is my thorn. I must plead a very small portion."

She deftly laid his thin slice on a plate and cut another for herself. "Betsy, the one who let you in—this is her famous dark chocolate mousse cake with raspberry-lemon filling. The chocolate is what food writers call 'intense.' I scarcely ever allow it in the house except for special guests." She poured an amber-colored tea into his cup. "And you are a very special guest."

Something pounded in his skull like hoofbeats, once, twice, three times. This had happened to him in the pulpit on occasion, while wrestling with an especially daunting topic. He shouldn't have done this.

"Lemon? Sugar? Cream?"

"I take it as it comes from the pot, thanks. The house looks wonderful."

"I did all the things Mama wanted to do but couldn't, with Daddy being sick all those years." She filled her own cup. "I drove out to Whitefield a few weeks ago and saw the work that's going on. Whitefield will again be a star in our crown. Have you seen it?"

"I have. And couldn't like it better."

As she lifted her cup, her teaspoon clattered to the table. "Excuse me! Oh, my goodness."

She appeared to be trembling a little. "It's just that I'm . . . so nervous."

He managed a smile. "Join the crowd."

"I've waited all these years to apologize to you, and I'm not terribly good at small talk."

"Please don't stand on ceremony with me."

"Thank you. So if you don't mind, I think I should just . . ." She seemed uncertain.

"Get it over with?"

"Yes." She clasped her hands together in her lap. "Before you came, I asked that God's will be done."

"That's the prayer that never fails."

"I hardly know where to begin."

He couldn't be any help there. He took a sip of tea—strong, fragrant, just the ticket.

"Before I go on, I'd like you to know . . . that I cared for you. I know you can't believe it"—she caught her breath—"but it's true."

He shouldn't have done this . . .

She sat on the garden bench with her legs crossed, smoking. The Pall Mall bore a crimson band of lipstick which he knew to be Cherries in the Snow.

He liked seeing his great-grandmother's ring on her finger, it made him feel more confident about the future. Several weeks before the night at the Peabody, on a break from his first year in seminary, Nanny had offered him her mother's platinum two-carat engagement ring.

'Do you love her?' she had asked.

'Yes, ma'am.' He had felt miserable saying it, because he wasn't absolutely certain.

'Her father is a very rich man. I'm sure her family will approve of Mother's lovely old ring.'

'Are you sure you want to do this, Nanny?'

'Of course I'm sure. And heaven forbid, if things don't work out, she'll give it back to you and no harm done.'

She had handed him the ring in its original box from the Jackson jeweler, saying, 'Be careful, dear child, but not afraid.' He hadn't known, and didn't ask, why she had said that.

Peggy gave him a chilling look. 'Why are you goin' to that ol' seminary, anyway?'

'Because.'

'Because why?'

He had never understood it himself, not completely. 'Because I have to.'

'Why do you have to?'

Because he wanted to do something for God for a change, not for himself.

Because he knew he'd never make it as a lawyer.

Because loving poetry and literature and being pretty good at track and excelling academically wouldn't cut it as a profession.

Because he believed it might please his father, and even reveal to Matthew Kavanagh some truth that would free him from the cold anguish he suffered and caused others to suffer.

And finally, because nothing else promised the ineffable mystery and joy that he hoped, that he prayed, would be his if he placed himself in God's service.

'I don't know.' He felt miserable. 'I just have to.' She wanted answers, he wanted answers. There were no answers.

She was jiggling her right foot, something she did when she was sour and impatient. 'Daddy says the cotton business is *not* dead or dyin', there's still plenty of money to make in th' cotton business if you know what you're doin'. Besides, Daddy is diversifyin', which is what all smart people learn to do in hard times.'

He paced the brick path by the bench, he'd heard this before.

In a while she said, 'You sure could kiss me.' She was staring at the garden wall, avoiding his gaze.

'Why?'

She turned to him, incensed. 'I can't believe you said that! I know boys who would never ask such a stupid question, why!'

He asked why all the time, he couldn't help himself, but he'd spoken too soon. He was nuts to pass up kissing Peggy Cramer, who was beautiful, who was actually wonderful to kiss.

But she was like nettles, and he drew back . . .

"I remember the time in assembly that you recited *Hiawatha*—the whole thing. It was so amazing, I wondered how in the world anyone could do that."

"Today, I'd wonder, too. But it wasn't the whole poem, it was only Part Five."

"I remember the rhythm of your voice—it was like the beating of an Indian drum."

"It was written in that meter. Quite thrilling to a boy, of course, once I got the hang of it."

"So when we ran into each other our senior year, I knew who you were. I thought you would be happy to meet me for a cigarette." She colored a little. "I never told you that I was happy you didn't, because I didn't think I'd know how to talk to you."

No news there. She had never known how to talk to him.

"I spent all my time back then feeling stupid and inferior," she said, "but it came out as haughty and mean, as if I were better than other people. It didn't help that Daddy had me driven to school in that big car." She looked at him, imploring, as if he might forgive her that.

"I understand."

"With all my heart, I wanted to walk to school like everybody else."

She was obviously trying to find a way into what she needed to tell him.

"I hated the thought of going to college, I never liked school, really. School was awfully hard for me, and the girls always despised me. I hoped Jack would ask me to marry him and I wouldn't have to go away to Ole Miss. But of course . . ."

"Of course?"

"He didn't marry me, he went off to med school at Duke."

He and Peggy had finished college and come home to Holly Springs the summer before he returned to Sewanee and entered seminary. Jack Sutton had come home that summer, too . . .

He had no idea why, but Peggy Cramer suddenly decided that he, Timothy Kavanagh, was interesting. That's what she said, anyway. 'You're so interesting.'

He knew better. He wasn't interesting at all, though he ardently wished to believe her.

She was going to work for her father in the fall, and had the whole golden summer, as she called it, at her disposal, not to mention a custom-painted turquoise Thunderbird convertible with wire wheels.

She drove out to Whitefield one afternoon; he was dumbfounded to see the grille of the car that was turning heads all over Holly Springs coming up his driveway. Cumulus clouds of dust billowed in her wake, she was flying.

He was wearing dirty shorts and a torn T-shirt and sneakers, and had stepped around to the front porch to fetch the bucket of his mother's gardening tools. His heart thundered; he wanted nothing more than to run, but she had already seen him and was waving.

'God help me,' he said under his breath. He had no idea why he had uttered such a petition . . .

"I remember driving out to your house that day." She pulled a handkerchief from the sleeve of her jacket. Something told him she'd finally gotten a grip on how this thing should go.

"If only we could erase that day," she said.

But he had willfully gone with her; there was no one to blame but himself. He felt his face suffuse with color; if he had a fan, he'd use it like a dowager at a church picnic.

That day had been the first of many days. Indeed, he had experienced his own "golden summer," and at the end of it, he was not only convinced that he was interesting, but he was going steady with Peggy Cramer and Jack Sutton was hating his guts . . .

'We don't have to get married for ages and ages,' she said. 'I just want the feelin' of your ring on my finger.'

They had gone steady only a few months when Peggy insisted on getting engaged. He gave her his high school ring, but she gave it back with a look he hadn't seen before. 'Not that ring.'

'It's not the time for an engagement,' his mother said. He knew she was right; it was the middle of his first year in seminary.

'This is ridiculous,' said his father. 'You'll be a laughingstock. I hope you don't expect a priest to earn the sort of income that could satisfy Ed Cramer's daughter.'

Louis pressed his lips together and shook his head. 'I ain't sayin' nothin'. It ain't none my b'iness *a'tall*.'

'Jack Sutton gon' kick yo' ass,' said Tommy, who thought the whole thing a terrific idea. All that money, a Thunderbird convertible with a stick, and Peggy Cramer, too.

'I don't know who said it, Cousin, but, "It is characteristic of wisdom not to do desperate things." ' His Oxford cousin, Walter Kavanagh, had certainly done a few desperate things in his time, but far be it from him to go over the list.

'Don't do it,' said Stuart Cullen. Stuart had been on the track team with him in college and was his best friend at seminary. He knew Stuart to be a profound believer, far more earnest in his faith than he. Stuart, who had met Peggy during a spring break, ended his counsel by saying, 'I beg you.'

He struggled to put those three words out of his mind. But Peggy was determined, and in the end, so was he. All that was left to do was convince his rector, Father Polk, who would call the dean at Sewanee, who would call the Kavanaghs' diocesan bishop, who would call his postulant, Timothy Kavanagh. They would all suggest he wait until he was out of seminary, and he would have his argument ready, which ran thus: The formal declaration of their engagement was just that, a formality. They had every intention of waiting to marry until he was out of seminary. It would please his fiancée very much, and he would be grateful for their blessing.

He had been frankly astonished when Nanny Howard offered

him the ring, and alarmed by the tumult that followed its presentation at the Peabody. His remembered his parents' cold dislike of mingling with the Cramers, who were known for their generous, albeit grudging, hospitality; but even worse was the social blitz that followed. He wanted to bolt like a rabbit into a hole.

At the engagement party at the Fant place, Heloise Griffin had dosed him liberally with her poisonous tongue. 'Nobody thinks you two will make it, but any excuse for a party.'

Seminary was different from college, but he was glad to be there. Courses were tough, breaks were few and far between, and summers promised to be internships in far-flung parishes. It was months before he went home to Holly Springs at Easter, and found that Peggy was in Philadelphia with her parents. He was surprised, then miffed, and finally, relieved.

They wrote each other, he writing more often than she, who professed to hate writing.

Dear Timmy,

Heloise gave me the most adorable apron, I think you will just love it on me but I don't have any idea what to cook. Daddy says Pauline can come live with us as I have never even boiled water, ha ha! I just want to sit on your lap and look into your eyes, phooey on dusting and running the Hoover! Don't you agree?

Must run. I am wild about the picture you sent in your track uniform. Number 72! I just love anything 7.

Loads of love and kisses from your Peg-Peg.

Dear Timmy,

I am so bored with Holly Springs, it is just party, party, party, as if there's nothing else to do in this whole wide world. All I want to do is get married and settle down. Everybody says you will make the cutest husband. Well, I'd better go now. Loads of love and kisses from your Peg-Peg.

Married. Everybody says. What had happened on those summer days in Peggy's convertible was eclipsed by what he could honestly define as panic . . .

"There are so many things to ask your forgiveness for," she said. "First, I want to apologize for losing the ring. I know it hurt you very much and made your grandmother sad. That carelessness haunts me to this day. I'm so sorry."

"You're forgiven. Long ago."

"And I deeply regret using you to make Jack Sutton jealous." She pressed the handkerchief to her eyes. "I hope you can find it in your heart to forgive me."

"You're forgiven. Again, long ago." For nearly a half century, he'd wanted to ask her a particular question. Life is short, his wife had said, and the road to Holly Springs is long. "I'd like to ask you something."

The prospect seemed to cheer her.

"Why did you pick me to make Jack Sutton jealous?" Male vanity was a terrible thing.

"Because I felt safe with you."

He was touched by this confession, though in his opinion it didn't really answer the question.

"Most of all, please forgive me for telling everyone that the child was yours, and trying to make you believe it, too."

"I was always pretty good at math," he said.

"I know how everyone made fun of you when they learned the truth, and what that must have felt like. I know how it humiliated your family." She closed her eyes for a moment.

He remembered the horrific conflict between his father and Ed Cramer. Ed Cramer wanted to buy Matthew Kavanagh's son, it was that simple. Fifteen thousand—a huge sum—together with a house, a car, and a vice presidency in the Cramer empire was how the attempted deal fell out. The idea of buying off a Kavanagh to cover the treachery of a Sutton was infuriating to his father, who not only refused the offer but forbade for all time the speaking of the Cramer name in his household.

Immediately afterward, Ed Cramer went straight to the source. *Timothy Kavanagh* was scrawled across the face of the envelope in what his mother called 'a racing hand,' and delivered to Whitefield by a driver who appeared embarrassed by his mission. Peggy's father wanted to meet with him in his office at three o'clock the following day, stating cryptically, *You will not regret it*.

He was totally intimidated by Ed Cramer, but he showed up and stood his ground. There was no way he could do what her father demanded. Mr. Cramer gave him five days to think it over, though he didn't want five days or five hours or even five minutes.

Yet there were moments when he felt compelled to go through with it; it would be an honorable thing to do. Indeed, it would save her face and possibly even his, but no, he could not. At times he felt very tenderly toward her—he was always aroused by her—but it wasn't right, of course; it had never been right. He wouldn't forget the day she fell to her knees and begged him to marry her, which may have been the profoundest embarrassment of the whole nightmarish business.

For moral support, he called Stuart, who was never one to mince words. 'You don't love her, the child isn't yours, her father is a tyrant, you would hate the cotton business. Come on, Timothy, don't try to be a hero.'

Though his father wanted the refusal delivered to Ed Cramer via the Kavanagh family attorney, he, Timothy, did the deed himself. He wanted to suffer, he deserved to suffer.

Wearing his school jacket and feeling as stiff as an undertaker, he shook hands with Ed Cramer, who stood firmly planted behind his desk, a terrible look of triumph on his face.

'Mr. Cramer,' he said, 'I must decline your offer.' While he had legs to do it, he fled the office. On the way home, he was forced to pull the car off the road and heave what little nourishment he'd managed to swallow down.

He confessed the whole excruciating business to Father Polk, who believed him at once and claimed himself 'ill-disposed to esteem Jack Sutton's character.' Polk then called Sewanee's dean, who called the Kavanaghs' diocesan bishop, who would call his postulant, Timothy Kavanagh.

When he knew the call was coming, he raced to the toilet with the heaves that were now part of the package. The breaking of the engagement, the rumors that would go with it—he would likely be required to meet with the bishop and, depending on the outcome, be sent to another seminary or asked to take a year off from Sewanee. Worst case, he wouldn't be allowed to return at all. It was nothing less than a cataclysm.

When the call came, the bishop said merely that he would be allowed to remain in seminary, but wanted to see a letter of apology written in his postulant's own hand and make it snappy.

The bishop followed this astonishing news with a warning: Abstain completely from further romantic involvements while at Sewanee. Given the foolish and impetuous thinking of one Timothy Kavanagh, the bishop stated further, it may be wise to abstain from the aforesaid for all eternity.

The Kavanaghs and Howards had escaped with their dignity.

He heard that Jack Sutton didn't receive the same offer, or any offer at all, as far as he knew. Rumor had it that Ed Cramer vowed to put a bullet in any Sutton who stepped foot on Cramer property.

"It was so long ago," Peggy said, "and yet seeing you again makes it seem . . . almost like yesterday."

"The child," he said.

"You know that Mother took me to New York. And you may have heard it was a little girl—she was adopted by a couple in the city. She still lives there—her name is Amanda."

Again, she pressed the handkerchief to her eyes, which was

something he'd recently had to do a few times himself. He set his cup and saucer on the table and waited.

"Everyone in Holly Springs knows, of course. I gave a tea for Amanda when she visited with the children a few years ago, and everyone came. It was terribly uncomfortable and hard for me, but I had given my heart to Jesus, and so it was easier than I had any right to hope. We all felt better for having it out in the open where things always belong in the end."

"That was a very courageous thing to do."

"I see my daughter as often as I can, she's given me three wonderful grandchildren. With my four grans in Jackson, that makes seven."

"God's number," he said, smiling. The tea had accomplished its appointed labor—the tension was gone from him. "And Wayne?"

"Wayne was the dearest man in the world to me, and a lovely father—not only to our two sons, but also to Amanda. I never deserved Wayne." She looked at him steadily for a moment. "I never deserved you, Timothy."

He had no idea what to say.

"I hear you're married. I'm so glad."

He was Pavlov's dog; he pulled out his wallet and leaned across the table to show her his family. With some feeling, she said all the things he never tired of hearing.

He slipped the wallet into his pocket and folded his napkin and placed it on the table. "Well, then," he said. He tried to avoid looking at the cake, which, from the beginning, had lured him as shamelessly as the Three Sirens. "My compliments to Betsy."

They stood in the foyer for several minutes and talked—of the success of the most recent annual spring Pilgrimage, of the entrance hall's elaborate French wallpaper mural, of the heat.

"Thank you for apologizing, Peggy; it means a great deal." He took her hand. "It occurs to me to apologize to you, as well. When you drove out to the house that day, I acted of my own accord. My actions were heedless, and entirely without regard for you. I'm sorry."

"We were young," she said.

"I hope you know that God has forgiven us both."

Her smile was ironic. "I do know that God has forgiven me, but I can't seem to forgive myself."

"That," he said, "is the hard part. May I pray for you?"

She gripped his hand. "Please."

He took a deep breath. "Father, thank you for arranging this time together, and for the presence of your Holy Spirit within us. Thank you in advance for blessing your child, Peggy, with the courage to forgive herself as you have so freely and utterly forgiven her. Thank you for Amanda and the three grandchildren, for Peggy's two sons and the Jackson grandchildren, and for your mighty protection of their hearts, minds, souls, and bodies. Thank you, Father, for faithfully using the hard things in our lives for great good, and for your tender and loving redemption of Peggy's soul for all eternity, through Jesus Christ our Lord. Amen."

They stood together for a moment, silent. "Thank you," she said. "Thank you."

He was backing out of Three Oaks' driveway when it came to him as if a spigot had been opened.

" 'You shall hear how Hiawatha prayed and fasted in the forest, not for greater skill in hunting, not for greater craft in fishing, not for triumphs in the battle, and renown among the warriors, but for profit of the people, for advantage of the nations . . .' "

He soldiered on, mangling most of it.

" 'Till at length a small green feather from the earth shot slowly upward, then another and another, and before the Summer ended, stood the maize in all its beauty, with its shining robes about it . . .' "

Today, it might be said, a feather had shot upward.

NINE

He couldn't believe he hadn't thought of it earlier.

At four-thirty, he blew into Tyson's, asked for the phone book, and opened it to Residential.

Pintner.

Poindexter.

Ponder.

Ponder, Roosevelt.

"Catch you later," he said to Amy.

"They changed her medication!" she called after him.

It was a small white house with shutters and cement steps painted green, a fenced garden shimmering with pie tins, house numbers on a post, an older-model truck in the driveway, a birdbath.

For someone who didn't like surprises, he was pretty deft at handing them out.

He heard barking inside, from what was definitely a small dog. A tall black man with a gray beard opened the door and peered at him. He was holding a newspaper and looking like Louis. But it was Rosie.

Rosie took off his glasses, stared at him, and rubbed his eyes. "Tim? That ain't you, is it?"

He nodded, unable to speak. Rosie dropped the newspaper and they threw their arms around each other.

"Oh, law!" Rosie said, weeping.

They were both weeping, both clapping each other on the back.

"I thought you mus' be gone to glory."

"Not yet."

"This th' mos' su'prised I been since Santy Claus showed up at Sunday School."

They stood back and looked at one another, marveling. "You haven't aged a day, and that's the gospel truth." Rosie Ponder was the most beautiful sight he'd seen since coming home.

"Get in out of th' heat, an' set down where it's cool. Sylvie, run see who th' Lord done brought, praise God!"

"I have a dog in the car." He hated to say that.

"We got Zippy shut up in th' kitchen, bring yo' dog on in. It too blame hot t' set in th' car."

They walked to the road together.

"You a sight for these ol' eyes."

"Forgive me," he said, "for taking so long to get here."

"Didn't know if I'd ever see you ag'in on this side."

He reached through the open window and clipped on the leash and opened the door. Barnabas bounded out and gave Rosie a good sniffing.

"Hoo-boy. My Sylvie gon' be headin' fo' th' county line when she see this booger."

But Sylvie Ponder didn't head for the county line. Barnabas lay at her feet as the three of them sat in the living room and drank iced tea and talked over the hum of the window unit and Zippy's occasional outbursts from the kitchen. He hadn't known such peace in a long time.

"How old you be, now?"

"Seventy. On the money. You?"

"Seventy-fo'. Three kids, two went t' Rus' College, one went out on 'is own, got a nice brick b'iness . . ."

"Eleven grans an' three great-grans," said Sylvie. Sylvie was tall and slender, with white hair. She wore a red cotton dress and quietly tapped her foot as if to some inner music. He thought her elegant, like royalty. "They all live right aroun' here, close by."

Close by. Hardly any families lived close by anymore.

"An' Rosie, he went back t' school awhile, went t' Rus' College his ownself."

"Went to night class an' took religion an' American hist'ry . I learned a lot, yes, I did. People say, 'Rosie, what you gon' do with all that learnin'?' I say, 'Enjoy it, thass what!' "

He loved Rosie's laugh, it was Louis's laugh into the bargain. In his youngest son, Louis Ponder had been immortalized, a two-in-one deal of a rare sort. "You're your dad made over. I loved Louis, he was like a father to me."

"He was a good one, all right. I still got 'is ol' gun. That's it up yonder."

The Remington hung by a strap on the wall above the bookcase.

"I been wantin' th' *Antique Road Show* t' come tell me what kind of value t' put on it."

But, of course, a value couldn't be put on Louis Ponder's sixteen-gauge shotgun. It was priceless . . .

Tommy was in town with his aunt and uncle, and he'd taken Rosie down to the fort he and Tommy built along the creek. Just fifteen yards from what had been a Chickasaw trading path, the fort was a masterpiece, pure and simple. It was the single greatest accomplishment of his entire life.

He and Tommy had cut four young beeches from the woods by the creek, and with a hatchet hacked a six-foot-long pole from each, reserving the brush. Even with the hatchet, it was slow going. They hauled the poles to an old beech and leaned them against the trunk at a forty-five-degree angle, one at the north, one at the south, one at the east, one at the west. They stood on boards laid across his Radio Flyer, and using cow rope lashed the tops of the poles to the tree.

'Where on earth have you been?' His mother examined the welts left by chigger and spider bites; between the two of them, he and Tommy sported one hundred and thirty-seven bites. 'And these clothes. Good heavens! What have you been doing?'

He shrugged, as if to say he didn't really remember or think it worth discussing, and because she was busy, she didn't ask again.

Everything they did to the fort had to be perfect, because what if he got polio like Albert Hadley and had to live forever in an iron lung? He wanted to leave something behind that was wonderful, that people would discover and be amazed at. The thought of getting polio and living in an iron lung made him crazy, but Tommy didn't seem to care if he got polio or even died.

They thatched the openings between the poles with pine and beech brush, knowing the beech leaves would cling on through winter and provide cover. Three of the openings were so thickly thatched, the dim woods light scarcely penetrated. The fourth opening led out to a deep trench, engineered to trap any outlaws and Indians who tried to take the fort. The trench was concealed with brush, and looked so natural they'd once fallen in it themselves.

Though the trench was dug only three feet deep, it took days to shovel out the black alluvial soil, which they hauled upstream in his wagon. At a spot with a small waterfall, they dumped the dirt down the bank and made themselves a beach. He named the beach Pass Christian in honor of the real thing, even though the dirt was too dark to be convincing.

They spent several more days covering their muddy tracks and the ruts his beat-up Radio Flyer had made, so their fort would be harder to locate by scouting Indians.

Then, suddenly, the whole exhausting and exhilarating business was finished. He had wanted it to go on and on forever, even while dreaming of the wondrous result. The summer had passed without his knowing it.

On the first day of school, he was oddly jubilant, knowing that the fort was waiting and belonged only to him and to Tommy. He felt bigger, taller, stronger, smarter. He blew past the creeps who picked on him last year about reciting poetry, and in his mind dared anybody to mess with him.

It was a huge honor for Rosie to be allowed at the fort, and Rosie knew it.

They were huddled inside, in a solemn darkness that smelled of limestone and water, leaf mold and sweat.

'You th' only one b'sides me an' Tommy that ever gets to be in this fort.'

Rosie's eyes were big, very big. He thought he should remind Rosie of the rules.

'You know you cain't ever tell nobody this fort's down here.'

'I ain't tellin' nobody.'

'You might think you could get away with tellin', but you cain't. If you tell'—he made the scariest face he could imagine—'somethin' awful gon' happen.' It was mean to threaten Rosie, but it had to be done.

'Even if somebody chop m' head off, I ain't tellin'.'

'Cross y'r heart, hope t' die.'

'Cross m' heart, but I ain't hopin' t' die.'

Rosie wasn't like Tommy. Tommy would do anything, say anything, Tommy totally got it.

'Okay, here's th' deal. T'day you get t' do somethin' you ain't never done b'fore.' He chewed his bubble gum really hard. 'You git t' kill Indians.'

Rosie froze.

'I gon' climb that big tree out yonder an' look fo' th' Chickasaw warriors. You know they still roam all over this place.'

'They does?'

'All th' time, everywhere. On spotted horses, wantin' their land back.' Cold chills broke out on his legs; his scalp felt electrified.

'Yeah, but what happen when they come an' you up a tree an' me down here?'

'I can look out over th' whole state, an' soon as I see 'em, I'm gon' holler they're comin', then I gon' come down here an' help you shoot. We'll poke th' guns th'ough th' brush toward th' path out yonder, that's th' warpath they'll be ridin' in on.'

'Don' see no guns t' poke nowhere.'

'Look around,' he snapped. 'We got guns all over th' place. Use that muzzle-loader yonder, there's th' powder. Let 'em have it.' He could see the powder horn plain as day, and the rifle standing on its stock against the tree trunk. He wanted to say don't shoot the horses, but when he said that to Tommy the other day, Tommy called him a fairy.

'How 'bout if I climb th' tree an' you does th' shootin'?'

'I always climb th' tree, I'm th' lookout. It's *official*.' It was obvious that Rosie didn't get it.

'This tree sho take up a lot of room in here,' said Rosie. 'You chop it down, y'all have mo' room.'

Rosie didn't get it at all.

He slapped his rear pocket to make sure his slingshot was still there. 'Cover me,' he said to Rosie.

Halfway up the beech, behind a full curtain of leaves, he leaned back on the branch he always leaned on; it was his certified station. He could see beyond the woods that bordered the creek, and across the field to the tree line where wild turkeys often appeared.

He could see out, but nobody could see in. It was his favorite place.

Every time he climbed the tree, he expected Indians. He would always expect Indians; it was the right thing to do, to believe with all your heart they were still out there.

His mother said there were no Indians anymore. His Grandpa Yancey said the same. Miz Conroy said all the Indians had been converted and were living in trailers with radios and curtains. He didn't believe this. How could a red Indian riding a spotted horse and carrying a bow and arrow go live in a trailer with curtains? It would be shameful.

The scream was like ice in his blood.

Indians could scream like that, he'd seen it in movies. His heart thundered as he reached for his slingshot.

"Rosie!" he shouted. This was the real thing, and the guns in the fort existed only in dreams.

The scream came again, and yet again. It was moving through the woods along the other side of the creek, a kind of running scream.

And then he saw them in the clearing—two men, one fat and one scrawny, and a dark woman racing ahead of them as if everything under heaven depended on it, the screams not stopping.

The dark woman in a torn dress was running for her life, and the woman was Peggy . . .

Sylvie was in the kitchen; something smelled good, smelled like home.

"Have you seen what's going on at Whitefield?" he asked.

"Oh, my, ain't it beautiful!"

"I don't think I ever knew it was such a wonderful house. It was just where we lived."

"Always had plenty to eat, worked a big garden, had butter an' milk an' cream, right on th'ough th' war. We saw some hard times out at Whitefield, what with things bein' rationed an' all, but I don' recall ever feelin' pore."

"The war was a scary time," he said. "I was thinking the other day about your daddy, how all during those years he kept looking up at the sky, looking for enemy planes. I remember I started doing it, too. Long after the war ended, I'd catch myself looking up. You remember Rufe singing, 'The biscuits that they give you, they say they're mighty fine'?"

" 'One roll' off th' table an' kill a pal of mine!' Rufe could sing, all right. Had a good voice. An' he sho wanted t' go off an' fight. I remember he went to th' courthouse t' sign up, but you know he was blind in one eye, they wouldn' take 'im. Daddy killed four or five squirrels—to celebrate, I guess you'd say. Mama made squirrel dumplin's, you remember her squirrel dumplin's?"

"I do!"

"An' us settin' there spittin' out buckshot?"

"Yessir! I'd give anything for a bowl of those dumplings, buckshot and all."

"Ever now an' again, I dream about that little house at th' edge of th' field—Mama tryin' to keep us boys in line, Ol' Damn Mule bustin' th'ough th' gate an' runnin' off." Rosie smiled and nodded, then looked sober. "An' sometimes I think about that day you aks me down to yo' fort. I was a kid when I went down t' shoot Indians, but seem like I come back t' th' house a man."

"Yes."

"You done as a good a job that day as any man ever done."

"Grace," he said . . .

'Rosie!'

'Who that screamin'?'

'It's Peggy! Git yo' daddy's gun an' bring it quick, God A'mighty, hurry!'

He saw Rosie break from the fort and streak like a rabbit toward the house in the upper field. Louis and his boys were working at the far side of Big Field, his father was in town at the law office, it was just him and Rosie.

He was trembling so hard he could scarcely breathe; a crushing pain jarred his chest. Peggy was still running, and the men were catching up. She slid down the creek bank, splashed into the water, fell, and scrambled up the bank on the fort side. He found the stones in his pocket, he never carried his slingshot without stones, and tried to load one in, but it plummeted to the ground. Peggy was streaking his way, not screaming now but saving her breath, and one of the men caught her and knocked her down and fell on top of her.

He loaded the slingshot again and pulled the strap back with all his might, and without thinking yelled, 'God help me an' help Peggy,' and let the stone go and saw the man roll off Peggy, clutching his head, and she tried to get up, but the fat one forced her down and was tearing at her dress. He loaded the last stone and fumbled it into the branches below.

His legs were water, yet he shimmied down the tree, desperate to run home to the safety of his mother, but he wouldn't leave Peggy, he couldn't leave Peggy. He screamed silently for Rosie to hurry and an eternity passed before Rosie was racing down the hill and he ran to meet him. Gasping for breath, Rosie shoved the sixteen-gauge shotgun into his hands.

'Mama say it loaded.'

He'd had two short lessons from Louis on his old Remington pump, one on how to hold it, one on how to fire it. He'd fired only four shots in his life, and the blast had kicked him so bad he landed on his butt every time, but now he had to do it right and he prayed again, begging God for help as he crept closer to the place where the hideous thing was happening. Still in the cover of the summer woods, he dropped to his knees at a fallen tree and sighted the thrashing head of the man on top of Peggy and knew that if he missed his mark, Peggy would be a goner and he and Rosie would have to run for their lives. The one holding her down would be a closer shot, and maybe he could get some pellets in the scrawny one at the same time. Anticipating the kick, he tensed his body so he could shoot straight and true and knocked off the safety and steadied the gun against his right shoulder and fixed the bead on his target, and fired, praying the shot would be directed by God and no pellets would hit Peggy. He was knocked onto his back and was up in an instant, seeing the fat man clutch his left arm, howling. The men had leaped up startled, and he pumped in a second shot and fired again as they turned and broke for the creek, one holding his arm and bleeding, the other one trying to yank up his britches as he ran. Now that he had the hang of it, he pumped in a third shot, aimed at the one yanking up his britches, and pulled the trigger.

Peggy lay in the stubbled field naked and weeping, he had no idea what to do about Peggy being naked, he was burning with shame and fear, his heart pounding in his throat. Still clutching the shotgun as he ran toward Peggy, he heard the blast and felt the searing burn on his right foot. He saw the hole in the ground and how the right side of his high-top was blown away. Then everything went black . . .

"What about Rufe?" he asked Rosie.

"Rufe was nine years older'n me, he went out huntin' turkey one Christmas an' stepped in a hole, broke 'is leg. He laid out there in th' cold for two, three days 'fore they found 'im. He was goin' on seventy-some when it happened."

"I'm sorry."

"Lef' a nice wife, three kids, nine grans, an' five great-grans. Washin'ton, some fool hit 'im when he was walkin' along th' road. They never found who done it." Rosie wiped his eyes on his shirt-sleeve. "We lost Link to alcohol, alcohol got 'im 'bout fifteen years ago. Th' Lord lef' jus' me, th' baby, with no brothers a'tall."

"I'm your brother. Just not a very good one. Do you remember?"

Rosie rubbed his eyes with the heels of his hands and grinned. "Law, I was scared t' death of that ol' knife you cut my finger with, that knife you carried wouldn' hardly cut butter. You was bound an' determined we gon' be brothers. Then you went an' done it with Tommy Noles. Daddy say, 'That boy be brothers with half of Miss'ippi.'"

They laughed, and Sylvie joined them. Their laughter was profoundly moving to him, he wanted it to go on and on . . .

'You th' luckiest little weasel I ever seen,' Peggy said. Her face was bruised and swollen, greenish in places; there was a bad cut on her arm that his mother had bandaged, and a gash hidden by her head rag.

'Show me th' place on your head,' he begged.

'I ain't showin' you no such thing.'

Tears welled in her eyes as she swabbed Mercurochrome on his foot. 'You my angel from heaven, thass what. I gon' make you apple pie, ham biscuits, an' lemonade 'til you old an' gray.'

His own close call had drawn blood, but nothing serious. He wanted to wear the shell-blasted high-top everywhere he went, but he couldn't, because word might get around to the criminals and they'd know who did it. Every night, he took off his shirt and looked in the mirror at the bruise in the cup of his right shoulder, the sore place where the butt of the shotgun had kicked him—it was constantly changing color. He thought it beautiful and wished it would never go away.

Louis brought the news from the square. Somebody at Whitefield had shot a man in the arm and put a wound on another man's head. Some speculated they were the tramps living at the railroad tracks, and it was too bad the people at Whitefield hadn't finished the job and fed them to the hogs.

A rumor circulated that the duo had turned up at the door of old

Doc Jamison, who, though he was said to be going on a hundred and hadn't used a scalpel in years, obliged the fat man by gouging pellets out of his hide with a kitchen knife.

Everyone found this hilariously funny, but he did not.

'What if they come back?' he asked Louis. 'What if they come looking for who did the shooting?'

'They ain't gon' be lookin' fo' you 'cause they never seen who done it. You was hid in th' woods. You take it from ol' Louis, them low-down, badass peckerwoods ain't never comin' back here.'

His father mentioned in his distracted way that Rosie had done a good job of routing the trespassers.

It wasn't Rosie, he longed to say. *It was me, Timothy.* But he said nothing, for he wasn't allowed to use guns, nor would his father have believed him capable of doing what had been done.

Otherwise, he was a hero at Whitefield. To Peggy. To his mother. To Louis and Sally and Rufe and Washington and Link and Rosie and, of course, to Tommy. But that didn't make the nightmares stop. Again and again, the men saw him in town and jumped out of a truck and grabbed him off the street and took him to the woods, where, right before he woke up, they were about to do what he'd done to them.

His brain burned with a thousand questions, but none of them could be put to his mother or father. 'How come Father won't take 'em to court?' he asked Louis. He was accustomed to people being taken to court when they did something bad.

'It ain't took as rape if it be a white man doin' it to a colored woman.' Louis looked him in the eye. 'Thass th' way it is.'

Rape. He looked it up in the dictionary. It was a plant, you could cook it and eat it. It was an act of forced sexual intercourse.

He felt violently ill. If what Rufe told him was right, it was sexual intercourse that made people have babies. Deeply distressed, he went to Louis.

'Peggy, she fought 'em like a wildcat,' Louis said, 'then our little man here whup 'em good an' run 'em off 'fore anything happen.'

He had racked his brain about what he wanted to be when he grew up. Now he knew. He would be a lawyer. But unlike his father, he would be a lawyer who would prosecute white people for hurting colored people without any reason at all . . .

They stood at the front door and talked. No, Rosie didn't know of a Will or Willie with a thumb missing, nor did he have any idea of Tommy's whereabouts.

"I wish you'd stay an' eat with us," said Rosie. "Sylvie, she th' best cook of anybody."

"I'll see you before I leave," he said. He would give Jessica's photo to Rosie on the next visit, when they had time to relish the surprise together.

"If Rosie was still huntin'," said Sylvie, "I'd make you some dumplin's."

He took both her hands in his. "Thanks. Just hearing you say it is a blessing."

"Where you stayin' at?"

"You won't believe this. Looks like I'll be staying in my old room at Whitefield. A couple of good fellows are out there fixing the place up, I believe they'll let me in."

"You come on back here if they don't."

Sylvie slipped her arm around her husband. "We got a nice roast in th' oven, makin' its own gravy. Got potatoes boilin'. Got green beans cookin' with a little ham. You ought t' stay."

But he had to get to Whitefield and nail down his room reservation, and feed Barnabas and call his wife and put something in his growling stomach and fall into bed, he was sinking.

"Y'all come an' go with me," he said. It's what everyone said when he was growing up, and what no one ever said anymore.

Rosie grinned. "We better sit tight right here, stick wit' what th' good Lord give us."

Rosie got it. Actually, Rosie had always gotten it.

It was after six o'clock when he headed to the country, then turned around and went to Frank King's place and bought two chicken dinners.

"Fresh an' smokin' hot. Mashed p'tatoes? Gravy?"

"Th' whole nine yards." He'd eaten pretty carefully today, had actually shucked the bun off his burger and made up for the lack with double coleslaw. Now he needed something to stick to his ribs.

"And give me a country-style steak with lima beans, mashed potatoes, gravy, coleslaw, and cornbread." T Pruitt would definitely let him spend a couple of nights in his old room.

Frank filled the Styrofoam boxes. "Find any yo' people yet?"

"Thanks for asking. I did, I found my blood brother, Rosie Ponder. I guess the reason you don't know him is, his wife can cook like a house afire."

"I hope you round 'em all up fo' it's over."

He put the take-out dinners on the floor behind the driver's seat, feeling as fried as the chicken.

"Hey, Tim!"

Frank King came through the door waving something.

"I forgot somebody lef' this t'day."

"How'd anybody know to leave it here?"

"I tol' people 'bout th' white brother come home lookin' fo' 'is people, told 'em you was comin' back t' see me."

"Thanks, Frank. Catch you later."

He stared at the envelope, forgetting to breathe. It was the same handwriting. *Reverend Timothy Kavanagh*.

At last.

Something would be required of him—he could sense it. And whatever it might be, he didn't know whether he'd have the strength for it. He got in the car and sat looking at the envelope for several minutes. He didn't really want to open it.

But he opened it.

Dear Reverend Kavanagh,
   I will greatly appreciate it if you will call me at the following number at your earliest convenience.
   It is a matter of utmost and extreme importance.
   Very sincerely yours,
   Henry Winchester

He felt suddenly feeble, as he had all those years ago when Louis told him the news . . .

'They done hauled one of 'em off to th' chain gang. An' you really gon' like this—that other peckerwood got hisself killed.'

His whole being turned to jelly; he would hate to faint in front of Louis.

Louis grabbed him and gave him a big hug and a slap on the back.

It was the best news he'd had in his whole life.

TEN

H e sniffed the air.

Yeast rolls baking, coffee perking.

It was definitely Sunday.

Without opening his eyes, he knew it was still dark; his mother and Peggy were up before sunrise, cooking and baking so the Howards could come to Whitefield after church.

Like lots of ladies in Holly Springs, his mother would be serving Boss Tate's favorite Sunday dinner. Used to, Mr. Boss would drive his touring car all the way from the mayor's house in Memphis to Miz Lula's house on Gholson Avenue, and every single Sunday Miz Lula served the very same dinner, it was a tradition. Since Miz Lula died, Mr. Boss hardly ever came to town anymore, but the menu, right down to dessert, had caught on in Holly Springs.

Mr. Boss's favorite Sunday dinner included butter beans, so most everybody in Holly Springs would be having butter beans today. There would also be rice and gravy, and a million biscuits with plenty of peach jam. There were only three things they never had at White-field that Boss Tate liked. One was biscuits, because the Howards and Kavanaghs liked yeast rolls—soft and hot, with butter melting inside. One was sherry for the pound cake, because the Howards were

Baptists. The other thing was spinach, because at Whitefield, not even his mother would eat spinach.

Mr. Boss was crazy about fried chicken, too, but only if fried real crispy. Hardly anybody could get the hang of frying their chicken crispy. Peggy said three ladies had the gall to ask for his mother's recipe, which was famous for crispy, but it was a really big secret. Peggy was the only other person in the whole wide world who knew the secret, but she had sworn not to tell. All he could find out was that it had something to do with buttermilk. He hated buttermilk, and chose to believe this particular information was a dodge to throw people off the track.

He thought about going down the hall to the bathroom, but decided to wait. He would rather see how long it took his bladder to bust from drinking a quart of lemonade before bedtime.

They almost never had the whole Howard 'clan,' as his father called them. Which, considering his goony cousins, was fine by him. Abigail ate her boogers, and as for Ferdy, Ferdy was a goofball who blew his nose on his shirttail and broke wind whenever he wanted to.

Peggy said if she ever caught him doing some of the stuff his cousins did, she would kill him on the spot.

He imagined the lemon pie and the pound cake sitting on the sideboard under glass domes, and the bowls and platters being passed around the table.

His eyes followed the chicken platter. Nanny Howard liked breast meat at her house, but at Whitefield she always took a back, saying the oysters were the most delicious 'morsels' on any chicken; Uncle Clarence would make jokes about the part that goes over the fence last, fork a breast, and look for the liver, which was always left for him because he'd fought in the war and had to walk with a crutch he'd made himself. Aunt Lily would take a wing.

'Peggy and I fried two of our very best hens,' his mother would say. 'Please take something more substantial, sister.' Once or twice, he prayed that Aunt Lily would take something more substantial and please his mother, but she never did.

'We *love* the wing,' Aunt Lily would say.

He found that remark stupid. It might be possible to like a wing, but it would be impossible to love a wing. Besides, Pastor Simon said people were not supposed to love things, only humans. Uncle Chester would take white meat—and plenty of it, because he was a bachelor with nobody to cook for him; Grandpa Yancey would take a drumstick and a thigh, and he, Timothy, would have the same as his grandpa. Later, while everybody was eating cake and pie, his mother was going to ask him to recite the thirteenth chapter of First Corinthians, which he had practiced for two weeks.

He hoped his father would stay at the table to hear him recite. He hadn't stayed the last time, he'd gone to his office in the basement to work on the farm ledger. The time before that, he had gone to the field to do something with Louis.

His mouth formed the words. *Though I speak with the tongues of men and of angels, and have not charity.*

He opened his eyes and looked around the darkened room.

Dear God!

He sat up, dazed. He was no farm boy on his cot, he was an old man dreaming.

The Howards were at Hill Crest—except for himself and Ferdy, every soul who sat at the table so many years ago was on the hill near the blackjack oak. Abigail, who was four years his senior, had married a man from Hattiesburg and later died in a train wreck, but he had no idea what had become of Ferdy; as far as he knew, Timothy Kavanagh was the last of the Holly Springs clan.

He swung his legs over the side of the bed. The last of the clan. He had never felt it as sorely as now. But of course somebody had to be last, just as somebody had been first.

He realized that the furniture, what there was of it, was placed as it had been when this room was his own. The head of the bed on the east wall, the chest of drawers on the south wall. Strange. And now the second note, and whatever strangeness might await when he called Henry Winchester.

A moth slammed against the window screen; he switched on the lamp and looked at his watch. Four o'clock.

He switched off the lamp and walked to the open window. Stars. Bright and shimmering in a cloudless sky. The air cool and clean after the rain that still sounded in the gutters. He stood there for a long time, gazing out, half dreaming and half sentient.

An awareness was dawning in him, an awareness of the close presence of the land whose boundaries once enclosed six hundred and fifty-four acres in which he'd sweated and yearned and dreamed and swam naked in spite of the water moccasins. He realized he'd never experienced this familiar connection to the land anywhere else—not in his twenty years in North Carolina, nor in his long exile in Arkansas or any other place in which he'd served. This connection, which he'd thought forever lost, was in him still, as ingrained and natural as the impulse to breathe.

"Major General Edward C. Walthall."

Out of nowhere, the train was suddenly moving again. "Brigadier General Absalom West. Brigadier General Daniel C., maybe D., Govan. Ha!"

At the sound of his voice, his good dog got up from the rug by the bed, and stretched, and came and lay at his feet.

All things work together for good to those who love God . . .

A motley collection of nonsense and wisdom often swam into his sleep-drugged consciousness.

. . . to those who are the called according to His purpose.

The smell of yeast rolls baking had been so real. So real.

"All things," he whispered into the dark . . .

As usual, his father hadn't gone with them to Walnut Grove, and now he was late to dinner, also as usual.

They sat through the awkward mess of waiting. Grandpa Yancey pulled out his pocket watch and stared at it. The grown-ups talked about dumb things that didn't matter. His mother made excuses for his father. He hated this for his mother's sake, but what could he do, he was starving.

'I'm starving,' he said.

'You are not starving,' said Aunt Lily. 'The children in France are starving, thanks to the Germans. The children of Berlin are starving, thanks to the Russians.'

'And thanks to Madelaine and Peggy,' said Nanny, 'we have all come together at a board laden with the fruits of His mercy and grace.'

'Amen!' said Grandpa Yancey. 'Why don't we thank the good Lord for His provisions before they're cold as a stone? I'm sure Matthew will understand.'

They were joining hands when they heard his father approaching the dining room. As he entered through the archway, something fell—the sound was sharp, like the report of a pistol—and clattered on the hardwood floor. Looking startled, his father appeared to lie back as if in a swoon, and then, in slow motion, he was falling.

Because he sat on the opposite side of the table, he saw his father simply disappear from view, followed by a jolt to the floor that rattled the ice in their tea glasses.

'Matthew.' His mother rose from her chair.

He was stunned, then humiliated, by his father's fall.

'Stand back, Madelaine.' His father struggled to his feet, holding Uncle Clarence's crutch; his face was white beneath the silver hair.

When it happened, there was the instant recognition that this moment would be too awful to ever think about again. His father gripped the crutch at either end, drew up his good knee, and lowered it with full force onto the crutch, snapping the wood in half. Then he tossed the pieces to the floor.

No one moved.

His father looked at Uncle Clarence, who sat with his mouth open.

'Cripple,' said his father.

They heard the hard tap of his right foot and the dragging of his left as he walked from the room. Then the screen door slammed.

And still no one moved.

After Uncle Clarence's homemade crutch fell from its leaning post against the archway and tripped his father, he started hearing things he'd never heard before—his grandmother talking to his mother, his mother whispering to Peggy, Peggy whispering to Louis, his grandfather talking to his grandmother. Over and over again, he was banished from the room or ordered into the yard to play, but still he heard things.

'In my time, it was melancholia,' said Nanny. Her knitting needles clicked very fast. 'They call it depression now.'

'Forgiveness, my dear, forgiveness,' said his grandpa, 'or we'll all be taken down by depression.'

'It's hard to imagine ever going there again.'

'Of course we'll go again, we're her family, we can't abandon our own child. And what about Timmy? Of course we'll go again.'

'Clarence and Lily will never step foot in that house again, nor will Chester. And what a shame. A child needs aunts and uncles, too.'

'Don't let it trouble you so, my girl.'

'How I wish we'd known before they married what a terrible relationship he had with his father. God help that dreadful old reprobate! And Matthew so angry over it all, he wouldn't take the money his father offered as a wedding present. It would have paid for everything, surely Matthew would never have used Madelaine's money to buy Whitefield if he had money of his own.'

'Your blood pressure won't take kindly to this, Betsy.'

'For the life of me, I can't think why Madelaine lets the old blasphemer in her house, it makes no sense.'

'He forces those visits, of course. She's trying not to make more trouble, and believes some good could come of it, some healing.'

'Without the grace of the Savior,' Nanny said, 'there can be no healing between two such stubborn and godless men.'

'Amen and amen. That's why we must continue to forgive—and continue to pray.'

'I'm trying, Yancey. But look what happened because the innocence and trust of one motherless boy was defiled—one whole family is left suffering for it. And look at Matthew's poor brother and how their father has sullied even that relationship. On and on the suffering goes, into the next generation and, God forbid, even into the next unless Matthew comes to his senses. We're all held hostage by his rage.'

He heard the striking of a match on the hearthstone; then came the scent of tobacco, sweet as cherries.

When Louis and Peggy were pulling onions, he hunkered behind the board fence and listened.

'His Gran'paw Kav'nagh goan burn in hell fo' what he done t' Mr. Matthew,' Louis said.

'Yes,' said Peggy. 'He will.'

'Course, a person can't keep blamin' ever'thing on what happen' a long time back, we got t' git up an' *go on*.'

'Yes. We do.'

He was consumed by wanting to ask what Grandpa Kavanagh had done to his father. But he was terrified of the answer.

On Friday afternoons in spring and summer, he often went with Grandpa Yancey to Indian Camp, the Howard homeplace where his grandpa was born and raised.

The two-story house stood unpainted in a cow pasture and was empty save for a furnished room on the upper floor, which was the room his grandpa had been born in. It had an iron bedstead with a corn-shuck mattress, a table, a kerosene lamp, a chair, a chamber pot under the bed, a pair of overalls hanging on a nail, and a calendar dated 1932. That was it, except for a flashlight, a fly swatter, a glass to hold his grandpa's teeth at night, and a pouch of pipe tobacco stuffed in a tin box.

The whole place smelled ancient—of fireplace ashes and old biscuits, of rancid grease and pine boards, all of it laced with pipe smoke and the permeating scent of horse liniment which his grandpa rubbed on his legs when they cramped.

Sometimes he was scared of the house and its haunting loneliness—his voice ricocheted off the bare walls even when he whispered, and there were cow patties everywhere, right up to the front door. Plus if he went outside at night to pee, he was always looking over his shoulder for foxes and bears, not to mention bats. Sometimes a bat got in the house and went crazy beating itself against the walls. He hated bats, you couldn't see a bat's eyes; you didn't know when they were looking at you or what disgusting things they were thinking. But worse than bats was the black snake which his grandpa called his rat catcher. It lived in the attic, and twice he saw it crawling out on a tree limb that overhung the roof, where it sunned itself like it owned the place.

'Huge!' he told Tommy, spreading his arms as wide as he could. 'Eight foot, maybe ten, an' lives in th' dern attic right over where we sleep.' He realized he was bragging about the stupid thing which Louis would have chopped up with a hoe before you could even spit.

Each time he was invited, he plotted an excuse not to go. Then, at the last minute, he wanted to go more than anything in the whole world—he would rather die than miss smelling the liniment and the kerosene and the pipe smoke, and gobbling up cookies and sitting on the steps at night listening to his grandpa talk in his soft, happy voice. After a while, he even got to liking the corn-shuck mattress.

'Grandpa, wake up,' he once said.

'What is it, boy?'

'There's somethin' in th' mattress.'

'Like what?'

'Like somethin' chewin'.'

'Bugs have to eat, too. Go back to sleep.'

He brought books from the town library or his grandfather's shelves, unfailingly gripped by curiosity over what he might learn or feel persuaded by the author to imagine. Grandpa Yancey brought a notebook, the Bible he used in the pulpit at First Baptist, and his favorite pipe, along with a vast picnic basket packed by Nanny Howard's cook, Mitsy.

There were always chocolate cookies in a round tin with a picture of Santa Claus on the lid. And his grandpa would always grin really big and wiggle his eyebrows as he dug around in the basket for the tin. 'Ho ho ho, Timothy!' he always said when he pulled it out. Then they'd take the lid off and say a blessing and eat the cookies before they ate the other stuff. Always.

This evening before dark, he had helped his grandpa toss hay off the truck bed to his twenty-one steers, then they'd straggled to the house and foraged in the basket and shook the cookie crumbs from the tin into their hands.

'Father, make us ever thankful for crumbs as well as banquets, in the name of our Lord, Jesus Christ.'

'Amen!' they said, and licked the crumbs from their salty palms without washing up first.

It was May, and a whippoorwill called as they sat together on the porch step. His grandfather lit his pipe as the bird spoke its name again and again into the deep of the dusky wood.

'Twenty-eight times,' he told his grandpa. A waxing moon lit the porch and yard and silvered his grandfather's face. 'That's th' most yet.'

'You still have a ways to go to beat my count, little buddy.'

When his grandpa was a boy, he had counted a chain of forty-two calls from a single bird. He, Timothy, was determined to hear forty-three if it was the last thing he ever did. He'd even prayed about God letting him hear forty-three calls, though he wondered how it would feel to beat his grandpa, who might not like being beaten.

His grandpa puffed his pipe, thoughtful. 'Just think how all this good land around us was home to the Chickasaw nation.'

Thinking about that nearly always made the hair stand up on his arms.

'Think about the Indian princess whose summer camp was right behind those trees yonder and down that little hill where the springs bubble up. Several times over the years, I know I heard their horses whinnyin' and their children laughin'. Shoot, one time I even smelled their meat roastin' on th' spit. It was wild boar hog, sure as you're born.'

'Do you think you really did hear th' horses an' all?'

'Seemed real to me, but maybe it was th' product of an over-active imagination—like somebody I know whose name begins with T.'

"I wish I could have lived back then.'

'It was a peaceful time before we rode in here an' tore up jack. I hate we did that.'

'Yes, sir.'

'Some say those springs over yonder are the true holly springs the town was named after, but I never thought so.'

'How come you never?'

'Not big enough to have a whole town named after 'em, not even big enough to swim a horse. No, sir, you got to be a spring and a half to get a town named after you.'

'There's no holly bushes down there, neither.'

'Not a one. That settles it.'

His Grandpa Yancey's voice was different from Grandpa Kavanagh, who hollered when he talked and still had a weird Irish accent after living in Mississippi for practically his entire life.

He heard the long sucking-in of breath; amber light flamed in the bowl of the pipe; the air was sweet with the scent of mown hay and cherries and the residue of their hard sweat from feeding up.

'Tell what happened when the Chickasaw ceded th' land to the government, Gandpa.' In this particular story, his part would come up pretty fast; he knew it as good as he knew his own name.

'Soon after the government half stole th' land from th' Chickasaw and did that terrible thing of movin' them west, here comes Virginia and the Carolinas troopin' in—foundin' towns, settin' up shop, buildin' mansions. Here comes doctors, lawyers, bankers, clergymen, th' whole shebang. As you recall, it wasn't long after that, that your great-great-grandma, Mary Jane, lit out to Mississippi with her brother James—had th' tools of his trade in a wood box nailed to th' wagon bed. Mary Jane was seventeen years old, and pretty as a speckled pup. James was twenty-four. Where'd they come from?'

'Th' mountains of Tennessee. They took th' Wilderness Road that passes through the Cumberland Gap.'

'Why were they comin' to Mississippi?'

'Land was really cheap, so a whole lot of people were movin' here, an' lots of 'em needed hats.'

'Where did they take on fresh supplies?'

'Nashville, Tennessee.'

'After they took on supplies in Nashville, they turned their ox team onto th' Andrew Jackson Military Road and headed to Colbert Ferry on the Tennessee River. They'd sold up th' homestead an' its contents after their mama an' daddy died of fever, an' had all their belongin's on that homemade covered wagon. Think of that. If we could put all our belongin's on a wagon today, we'd be better

off. Crossed th' Tennessee River on a ferry an' picked up th' Old
Natchez Trace to Jackson. We don't know why they decided to use
th' Trace, as better roads were available by then, but they must have
known what they were doin'. Why were they headed to Jackson?'

'Uncle James knew somebody in Jackson.' His mother and
Nanny Howard had taken him to Jackson to shop at Kennington's
and get their silk stockings mended. Tommy had never been to
Jackson or hardly even Oxford or Yazoo or anywhere.

'So here they come in that wagon, can you see 'em comin'?' His
grandpa spit in the yard.

'Yes, sir, I can.' He spit, too.

'Sometimes they're ridin', but mostly they're walkin', because
those old wagons didn't have any suspension system—they'd beat
you to death. Whenever they could, they walked barefooted to save
shoe leather, which I can tell you right now I wouldn't have th'
courage to do, with all those copperheads slitherin' every whichaway.'

He hated that he could see the copperheads plain as day, moving
through leaf mold and shimmering along creek beds.

'Well, sir, here they come with a team of oxen down that
crooked ol' Trace overhung with vines, and pocked with mud holes
deep enough to sink your wagon to th' axle. There was a lot for a
young man and a young woman to look out for in th' wilderness, but
some say th' worst thing was Indians. Not all th' Chickasaw had
cottoned to th' cession idea, which I wouldn't, either, if I was an Indian. Some stayed on th' land and not a few liked makin' trouble for
whoever came along th' Trace. Then there was th' next worst thing,
don't you know.'

'Th' weather.'

'Yes, sir. Th' weather. They got held back by hard rains that
didn't let up for three weeks, and it was three weeks more before th'
ground dried up so they could press ahead. Most of their flour went

bad with weevils and damp. No hot biscuits or hoe cakes, no dumplin's in th' soup pot. An' pretty soon their jerked venison was runnin' low an' they were givin' out of coffee. So what kind of rations did the good Lord provide?'

'Berries, lots of berries. An' bird eggs an' rabbit an' squirrel an' a turkey gobbler. An' for tea, they boiled up sassafras root, an' chickory root for coffee.'

'Just think about that good smell of turkey stewin' under that tarp they set up to keep th' rain out, an' th' Ol' Trace still troubled with th' next worst thing . . .'

'Robbers an' murderers.'

'Yessir. Th' Trace was still haunted by th' memory of men like th' Harpes, who butchered travelers and homesteaders all along the way. An' now that th' traffic had died down a good bit because of better roads, criminals were usin' th' Trace as a hidey-hole. Just ponder how those good cookin' smells might be th' very ticket to draw out th' lowlife.'

He imagined how a robber could have crouched in a tree right over his great-great-grandmother's head—she could have been sitting right under the branches shelling pecans, not knowing he was up there biding his time 'til the turkey got done.

'So what did Uncle James and Mary Jane do to keep safe from th' perils of a fallen world?'

'They prayed mornin' an' evenin' an' all times in between,' he said.

'Does it seem foolish to think somethin' as simple as prayer could do even a mite of good against wild beasts, mad Indians, an' murderers?'

'No, sir. Psalm Seventy-two says, "He shall deliver th' needy when he crieth; the poor also, and him that hath no helper." '

'Amen! And what happened?'

'It turned out other people goin' toward Jackson got stopped by th' rain, and they all connected up 'til pretty soon there was a whole bunch of people that formed a camp that wouldn't anybody try to rob.'

'God's grace on th' Ol' Trace. There's many stories about that. So James an' Mary Jane, they're back in th' wagon now, headed south. Th' weather's faired off an' th' wildflowers are bloomin' an' they're on their way. You see 'em comin'?' His grandpa spit.

He spit, too. 'Yessir!'

They had stopped to water the oxen, and his great-great-grandma was sitting in the wagon on a pile of blankets, writing the story of their journey in the back of a big Bible. It had engravings of all the Old and New Testament stories, including Jesus preaching in the temple, an image which he had the honor to see anytime he wanted, as the very same Bible lay open to this picture in his grandpa's glass-front bookcase. His imagination never let him see his great-great-grandma's face, but she was wearing a brown dress, and the stock of a Springfield muzzle-loader poked out from under the quilts.

'They're comin' on down to around where Tupelo is now, it was Harrisburg back then, and James, he pulls th' wagon over in th' bushes in case anybody wants to pass, an' he walks back a little ways an' steps behind a big rock. Then he pulls his britches down an' he's doin' what a man has to do, when . . .'

It was his cue to tell the best part of the story. 'When he looks up an' a big ol' black bear is standin' at the edge of the woods.'

'What did Miss Mary Jane say th' bear was doin'?'

'Studyin' Uncle James.'

'How close was th' bear to her brother?'

'Five yards.'

'How tall was th' bear?'

'Better than six foot.'

'Does James get up an' run?'

'No, sir, he didn't move. He says in a normal voice, "Mary Jane, take care of this bear." '

His grandpa laughed at the mimic. 'Say on!'

'She was seein' all this from th' back end of th' wagon, where the rifle was lyin' under th' quilts. Quick as a flash, she grabbed up th' rifle, which they kept loaded at all times, and sighted th' bear. Then, before she got off a shot, th' team shied an' she kind of lost her balance and the ball went over th' bear's head. Th' bear looked at th' wagon like he was changin' his plan, an' she knew she didn't have time to load again. So she stepped back and grabbed their muzzle-loadin' pistol, which was lyin' next to her Bible on th' work box.' The hair stood up on his neck.

'What'd she say?' asked his grandpa.

'She cocked th' hammer an' said, "Lord, You got to do this thing, amen." By now th' bear was comin' for th' wagon. He was gettin' so close she could smell 'im when she fired th' pistol.'

'What did she say he smelled like?'

'Leaf mold. Wet dirt. Berries an' skunk.'

'Where'd she shoot 'im?'

'Right between th' eyes with a fifty-caliber ball.'

'Good shot.'

'But he kept on comin'.'

'Lord have mercy.'

' 'Til he got right up to the wagon.' Though he knew the story like a book, his heart was beating faster. 'Then he sort of just crumpled over and fell down. Dead as a doornail.' Right here, he could never keep from feeling kind of sad.

'If your great-great-grandma hadn't pulled th' trigger on that bear, you and I wouldn't be sittin' here tonight. Nossir, we wouldn't even have been a *twinkle* in somebody's eye.

'An' just look how many ways th' good Lord was workin' in this. He gave her th' gumption and th' wherewithal to kill that poor

beast, which saved at least one life an' maybe two—an' on top of
that, he threw in another portion of mercy and grace.'

'Yessir, because they got to eat th' bear,' he said. 'An' what was
left fed two more wagonloads.'

His grandpa shook his head, marveling. 'Knee-deep in manna
and quail! What comes next?'

'Pretty soon after they shot th' bear, they had a change of heart
about where they were goin'. A man on th' Trace told 'em Jackson
already had two hatmakers . . .'

'Competition!'

'. . . and said he knew a good place that didn't have any hatmakers at all.'

'So what'd they do?'

'They turned off th' Trace an' cut th' team northwest to Holly
Springs.'

'Hot dog! Now you're talkin'.'

His grandpa knocked the ashes from his pipe. 'They pulled into
Holly Springs on September th' fourteenth, th' year of our Lord
eighteen hundred an' thirty-six, at three o'clock in the afternoon.
They got busy buyin' this land we're sittin' on, an' buildin' a dogtrot
cabin down by th' springs. Then James bought a little patch about
where th' square is now, and put up a shop an' started makin' hats
with Mary Jane helpin'. Beaver hats, they were—warm, waterproof,
an' economical! Uncle James got his hides from th' Chickasaw and
some from th' Choctaw. An' all th' time, people just swarmin' into
town like ants, nailin' and hammerin', diggin' and hoein', lawyerin'
and bankin', midwifin' and doctorin'.'

The dry summer grass was loud with crickets. His grandpa spit
toward the grass to see if he could hit it. 'You remember, now, not to
spit in town.'

'Yes, sir.'

'Spittin's for th' country.'

'Yes, sir. My turn again?'

"Your turn."

' 'Til one day my Great-Great-Granddaddy Pinckney walked in th' shop an' took off his old beaver hat and said, "Ma'am, can you patch these holes? I was comin' along the Trace on my little mare a while back when a rogue rifle ball passed clean through my hat—which I happened to be wearin' at th' time. As I heard it, a lady had fired two shots at a bear and this was th' shot that missed."

'My double-great-grandma said, "Was that late August a year ago, by any chance?" And he said, "Yes, ma'am, I believe it was." And she said, "Around about Harrisburg?" An' he said "Yes, ma'am, it sure was." An' she said, "You got off a good deal better than th' bear." '

They laughed at this every time, out of respect.

'Sometime before Christmas of 1837'—his grandpa liked to handle what he called the finale—'Miss Mary Jane Bush, who by then had turned eighteen, gave Mr. Adam Pinckney Howard a gift crafted by her own hand. It was a fine, brand-new silk hat to make up for the damage she'd done—silk was startin' to come in fashion and beaver was startin' to go out—and he wore it, don't you know . . .'—his grandpa held on to the last words of the story—'to his nuptials.'

They always clapped at this, and whooped a little. A dog barked in the distance.

'And . . .' He nudged his grandpa with his elbow and wiggled his eyebrows.

'And here we are!' they shouted.

'You've got this story down pat, son. When you come out again, we'll start on the next installment. There's a whole passel of fascinatin' ancestors in that round, includin' one who freed all his slaves. Then, on th' next pass or two, we'll include a young fella named Timothy Andrew Kavanagh. How would you like that?'

'I'd like it.'

'One of the verses your great-great-grandmother scribed in the back of her Bible was Deuteronomy, chapter four, verse nine.

' "Be careful not to forget the things you have seen God do for you. Keep reminding yourself and tell your children and grandchildren, too." Because she left us a record, one day you can do th' tellin' to your children and grandchildren.'

He couldn't see how he would ever have children, much less grandchildren. Mostly because he would never get married in a hundred years.

A cloud covered the moon, his grandfather vanished. A match scraped across the surface of the step, flamed up, was carried to the bowl of the pipe—and there again was his grandfather's face. 'I'll have one more sneak of tobacco, then we best fly up to roost.'

He realized that something had gnawed at him all through the story. As the wagon came down the Trace, the gnawing had hidden beneath the rumble of wheels and bed boards; it had hidden between the lines his double-great-grandmother was scribing in the Bible; he had recognized it again in the eyes of the bear.

'What did my other grandpa do to my father?'

He hadn't known he was going to ask the question that had exploded in his head for weeks. His sudden trembling was hard and uncontrollable, his teeth chattered.

Grandpa Yancey's arm went around his shoulders and held him tight for a long time until some of the trembling stopped.

'When your daddy was sixteen years old, his father gave him a beating, what you might call a horsewhippin'. It was . . . brutal. I'm sorry to say it, son, it's hard to tell you this. Are you all right?'

'Yes, sir.' His teeth chattered like windup joke teeth.

'It happened at a cattle auction in Jackson. The way your mother tells it, your grandpa got mad at a little colored boy who was hangin' around the place and told your daddy to shut the boy up in a hot truck—th' temperature was boilin'—an' give him no water. I don't know if your daddy handled it the best way, but I believe he did th' right thing—he refused to obey those orders.

'It was your grandpa's auction at one of his barns, and he was up on a kind of a platform, don't you know, with the auctioneer—an' your daddy was up there, too. When Matthew wouldn't do what he was told, your grandpa took a horsewhip that was hangin' on the wall of the barn, an' grabbed your daddy and told th' auctioneer to hold 'im while . . .'

Grandpa Yancey cleared his throat. 'I'm sorry, son, I'm sorry. Your mother told me I should tell you if you ever asked. She could never do it, because it hurts her and she knew it would hurt you. Best to hear it from someone who loves you before you hear it someplace else.'

He had never before suffered like this. As clearly as if he'd been there, he saw his young father on the platform, and the look on his face while the auctioneer held him.

'That terrible whippin' was bad enough. But the next worst thing is, it happened in public, in front of a whole crowd of people. Think how that kind of humiliation made him feel, I'm sure people remembered that awful sight for years to come. That's a lot for a young person to handle.'

'Yes, sir.' Tears and snot were all over the place.

'You can blow your nose on your shirttail, I won't tell anybody.'

The trembling continued to come in waves he couldn't control. *Is there a next worst thing?* he wanted to ask. *Please don't let there be a next worst thing.*

'Grandpa Kavanagh's rage was what I'd call unquenchable. After that vicious sideshow he put on for Satan himself, he shoved your daddy off the platform, and his leg was broken in several places. It's a low-down shame about th' doctor they took him to—some quack who, as far as I can tell, didn't know a bloomin' thing about settin' bones.'

In the black wood, the whippoorwill called and called, but he knew that counting didn't matter anymore. He stood up suddenly, wanting to run and never stop running, but he had lost his breath and was suffocating.

'Come on, son, let's walk. We'll go to the stump and back. Everything will be all right, it's all gon' be all right.'

His grandfather was practically dragging him across the yard, but he flung off his hand and ran as hard as he could across the moonlit field. He would run 'til he dropped somewhere, he didn't care where. But what he really wanted to do was get in Louis's truck and drive to Jackson and stab his other grandpa a hundred million times—in the eyes, in the heart, in his hideous face.

He would never tell his mother about this conversation. It was time he knew something secret and terrible like everyone else, it gave him power he wouldn't otherwise have had. If anyone knew that he knew, they would realize that power belonged also to him, and try to take it from him.

Later, he asked his grandpa two questions.

'Grandpa, did you tell Mama you told me?'

'Not yet. Should I?'

'Nossir. And Grandpa, when we get to th' part of th' story that has me in it, do we have to tell th' part about what happened to my father?'

Grandpa Yancey's eyes looked misty. 'Only if you want to, son. Only if you want to.'

ELEVEN

"Come get you some breakfast."

"The coffee sure smells good."

"Ol' T was a Sanka fien' when we started out. I said, 'Man, you can't be drinkin' no powdered coffee on this high-class job, we doin' this gig with whole beans an' a grinder.' Cream an' sugar right there."

"Just black, thanks." He took the steaming mug from Ray and eyed the breakfast buffet: sardines in a tin, saltines, and a saucer of cheddar cheese cut into cubes. "Believe I'll catch something over town. How 'bout that rain?"

"Good rain. An' how 'bout that Tater an' Tot?"

They laughed. Last night's unexpected arrival had been easier than he imagined. Tater and Tot, whose breed mix was arcane, to say the least, sniffed Barnabas; Barnabas sniffed Tater and Tot. No baring of teeth, no flying of fur. After a decent meal and a dried beef tendon, all three had claimed a spot and lapsed into a drugged sleep.

"We'll be waitin' to hear how things go wit' th' phone call," said Ray.

"Haven't called him yet. Don't know exactly when I'll get back here, but I'll pick up something for us at Frank's."

"Don't do it. I'm itchin' to cook t'night. You won't be around much longer, I'm gon' give you Mississippi Catfish Magic with Sauce Jacques."

"Whoa."

"Chef invented that down at th' mansion fo' th' Southern Gov-'nors' Association. Had th' first lady of Virginia, first lady of Tennessee, first lady of Arkansas, governor of South Ca'lina, you name it. Out in th' mansion's historic garden."

"I'd be honored. But isn't this the night you're picking up your dentures?"

"I'll pick 'em up after supper."

"If you're sure."

"Won't heat th' skillet 'til I see you comin'. T says we gave you catfish las' time—doin' it t'night might be too much. I said ain't no such thing as too much catfish."

"Amen. What can I bring?"

"A stick of butter."

"Consider it done."

"Unsalted," said Ray.

"Got it."

He walked out to the front porch, where T stirred a can of stain. "Goin' after th' basement steps today. You sleep all right in your old room?"

"Can't complain. I appreciate it more than you know."

"Hope everything goes okay with your phone call. We'll keep an eye on 'im so he don't ramble with our boys."

He'd fed and walked his dog, who would be spending the day at Whitefield. "I appreciate it," he said again. "I appreciate everything."

"Don't mention it. You hear tonight's menu?"

"Sauce *Jacques*?"

T laughed. "High-rollin' out here in th' piney woods."

"Hope I'm not interfering too much with your kudzu project."

T flipped his cigarette into the wheelbarrow. "Can't hardly figure out what t' do next. I'm lookin' for interference."

He braked the Mustang at the end of the driveway and checked his watch. Seven-forty. He fiddled with the radio dial. Noise and babblement.

George Macdonald had said what he needed to heed: *You have a disagreeable duty to do at twelve o'clock. Do not blacken nine and ten and eleven, and all between, with the color of twelve.*

He looked at the note and punched in the numbers.

"Hello?"

His heart pounded. "Is this Henry Winchester?"

"This is he."

"Tim Kavanagh. I received your note asking me to call. Hope I'm not calling too early."

"Not at all. Thank you, Reverend. I was hoping we could meet today." Winchester's voice was quiet, restrained. "It's a matter of extreme importance."

"Can you tell me more?"

"There's someone who would like very much to see you. I don't believe I should say more at this time."

"You wrote to me in Mitford a few weeks ago?"

"Yes, sir, I did."

"The message was certainly brief."

"I wrote it just as it was dictated."

"Do I know you?"

"No, sir. You don't."

"This is all quite peculiar, to say the least. You sent a total stranger an unsigned message of just two words, but what's even more peculiar is, I let it talk me into driving more than six hundred miles."

"Please be assured that great prayer was lifted over the contents of that simple message. We didn't know whether you would come, but we fully believed you would. We're deeply grateful, Reverend."

"I believe you can understand, Mr. Winchester, why I feel uncertain."

"If you're certain of nothing else, Reverend Kavanagh, you can be certain that the Lord is in this."

Parish counseling had given him some insight, after all, into character. The man sounded well-meaning, and fish or cut bait, it had to be done.

"Then I'm in it, too."

"Thank you." The relief in Winchester's voice was obvious. "I heard you would be in Holly Springs only a short time, which is another reason for our urgency. If it would suit, we could meet at Frank King's place today at one o'clock, and drive from there. I wish we could meet earlier, but I have . . . something important to take care of in Memphis."

"Where are we going?" he asked.

"Out to the country about fifteen miles."

"Well, then. One o'clock. Frank's place."

"I'll be driving a blue Buick," said Henry.

He pondered the conversation as he drove into town. His stomach was in an uproar—not enough sleep, no breakfast, too much caffeine, and a blasted long wait 'til he met Henry Winchester at Frank's. On the upside, his sugar was stable.

He wheeled into a parking space near Tyson's, and sat looking at the steeple of Christ Church. Now? No. Tomorrow.

A newspaper, that was the ticket. Just holding one of the blasted things in his hands offered an odd comfort. Then he had to take nourishment.

He walked to the courthouse and looked around until Tyson's opened.

"How's the new medication doing?" he asked Amy. "Any word yet?"

"It'll take a while to work, but when I stopped by this mornin', she was sleepin' like a baby. Just layin' there with her hands folded across her chest like she was in a coffin, it like to scared me to death. But I wish you could have seen her, she was so peaceful."

"She was breathing?"

"Oh, yessir, I made sure to look an' see if her chest was goin' up an' down. I decided not to wake her up, I mean, she's been through an awful lot lately an' I'm sure you know how hard it is to sleep good when you're old.

"I should prob'ly call an' make sure she's awake—if she sleeps half th' day she'll never sleep a wink tonight. Stand right there, don't move, I won't be a sec." She punched in a number and listened.

"It's ringin'."

Amy looked at him. "Still ringin'. I bet she's not wearin' her hearin' aids. I don't blame her, they make an awful screechin' sound.

"Still ringin'. I wonder if I should go over there an' check." She punched the off button.

"I'm curious about something. Why do you care so much about Mrs. Lewis?"

Amy looked surprised. "I don't know. I guess because she cares about me."

"Aha."

"I know she's an awful pill, but speakin' of pills, she's been takin' fourteen a day. Fourteen! But since th' doctor changed things around yesterday, she's only takin' ten, that is such a blessin'. Richard says she's practically kept th' roof on this place."

"Amy."

"Yes, sir?"

"You're a wonderful person."

"Really?" Amy blushed. "I mean, thanks. I don't think so, necessarily."

The phone rang.

"Tyson's Drug, this is Amy. Yes, ma'am, it was me. What were you doin', I was worried to death."

Amy gave him a wide-eyed look. "Goin' through *boxes*? What in th' world . . . Yes, ma'am, I've seen him. He's standin' right here lookin' at me.

"I don't know if he could do that. I mean, do you want him to come to your house?"

Amy put her hand over the mouthpiece. "She has somethin' to show you. Can you go over there?"

The very thought made his heart fibrillate. "What could she possibly have to show me?"

"What could you possibly have to show him? he says. Really? That is truly amazing. It is such a small world!"

"What?" he said.

"She found some pictures of your mother."

"Put your hand over the mouthpiece," he whispered. "Does she still think I'm Father Crowley?" He had no need of pictures of the elder Mrs. Crowley.

"When she asked if I'd seen you, she said Madelaine Kavanagh's boy."

"Oh."

"She thinks you should come."

"Could she just give them to you and you could give them to me? I don't want to go over there, I really don't." He heard the miserable whine in his voice. How could he walk into that woman's house alone and unprotected, much less engage in civil conversation? End of discussion, he wasn't going.

"She really thinks you should come."

It was obvious that Amy thought so, too.

"He's thinkin' about it," said Amy.

He motioned for her to put her hand over the mouthpiece. "I'll do it. But only if you'll go with me."

"I'd better not, Father, but I'll ask her to stick 'em in the door."

"Brilliant."

"Miz Lewis, could you stick th' pictures in th' door? Yes, ma'am, I think he must have a lot to do, bein' here only a short time.

"She says you have to be sure an' return the pictures. They're promised to the historical society."

"I'll return them tomorrow morning, first thing."

"They're really valuable, she says. They're goin' to maybe do a display."

"Got it."

"She says you can *not* lose a single one."

"Of course."

A couple of blocks from Nanny Howard's, he pulled into the driveway of a galleried brick house that had seen better times, and walked to the porch along an allée of boxwood troubled by mites.

The sight of Luola Dabney Randolph Lewis clutching a manila envelope and filling the doorway jamb to jamb literally took his breath. Dressed in a wrapper and gown, and wearing on her feet what appeared to be the hides of two enormous pink rabbits, she was the definitive "sight for sore eyes."

"I saw you pull in. Don't mind my looks, I was up half th' night goin' through boxes to find these prints of Madelaine's gardens."

"Thank you, that was more than good of you."

"From 1940 to 1952, I covered th' Pilgrimage with nothin' but a Kodak. Twelve years of buyin' film an' orderin' prints, all out of my own pocket an' no thanks from anybody far as I recall. I took these in 1941—it was th' only year I ordered eight-by-tens, which was a high compliment to what Madelaine scratched out of th' dirt down at Whitefield." She wagged her cane at him. "You have to promise to wash your hands before you look, so you don't leave fingerprints."

"I promise."

"You what?" she shouted.

"I promise!"

"These are valuable historical documents, an' human skin has oil in it. Old as you are, Father, you might forget to wash first. Do you cross your heart an' hope to die?"

He crossed his heart.

She yanked a handkerchief from her pocket and blew her nose with force. "I kicked up enough dust to sink a ship lookin' for these bloomin' things." She thrust the packet into his hands. "I hope you appreciate th' trouble I went to."

"I do. Thank you very much."

She cupped her hand to her ear. "What's that?"

"Thank you very much!"

"There are fourteen prints in there. Because of th' dust, I didn't look at every one, but there's descriptions on th' back. Lucy Gilchrest documented every picture I took—we were fixin' to do a book to raise money for th' garden club, but Lucy moved to Philadelphia to nurse her mother. Th' Whitefield azalea groves are in there, an' th' hosta garden, an' th' fish pond, an' I don't know what all. Madelaine had the most beautiful gardens of th' whole Pilgrimage whenever she showed. These are th' first year, I don't have time or patience to rummage around for th' other years."

He was walking backward. "Certainly not."

"People were jealous, mind you, because your mother had fine gardens and was beautiful into th' bargain. I hate speakin' ill of th' dead, but people like Louise Grant despised her for it and didn't mind sayin' so behind her back. I couldn't stand th' sight of Louise Grant, do you remember Louise?"

"No, ma'am." Picking up speed.

"If my hair was combed out, I'd ask you in for cheese wafers, it's a secret family recipe that came horseback from Virginia."

"Bless you. No, thanks."

"There's gummy bears in th' bread box if you'd care to have a handful."

"I greatly appreciate it." Off the porch and down the steps.

"In case I'm not up when you get here, stick 'em in th' door an' ring th' bell."

"I will. And thank you again."

"If you're not where you can wash your hands," she shouted, "wipe 'em on your pants first, you hear?"

"Yes, ma'am!"

"If I'm up, I'll show you th' oil portrait of th' General, he was a wonderful husband, never complained. His people settled Kentucky, they produced four senators, a congressman, seven preachers, five medical doctors . . ."

He vanished into the boxwood.

". . . an' a first cousin on his mother's side invented th' door-to-door diaper service."

He dived into the Mustang, gunned the engine, and roared out of her driveway in reverse. A wrench in his gut reminded him he had to put something in his stomach pronto, he was ravenous.

He was driving by the courthouse when he saw Jim Houck standing at the gazebo as if waiting for someone. Before he could look away, they made eye contact. He instinctively threw up his hand in an awkward combination of a military salute and a wave from a parade car; Houck shot up his arm in response.

Though he was in a moving vehicle, the eye contact seemed to last a long time, long enough for him to see the expression on Houck's face—longing, perhaps, or desperation. It was as if he'd been surprised in some raw feeling, and not quick enough to mask it.

He puzzled over the fleeting exchange as he circled the square for another look at the brick storage building next to his father's office. The Shed, as they'd called it, was where he'd hid his "mischief," as Louis liked to say.

He remembered what he'd charged for looking at the pinup calendar: four cents. 'Wipe your hands,' he told his customers. 'Four cents an' clean hands is th' deal.' He had won the calendar playing marbles with Otis Gibson, whose daddy owned a tire store and could get calendars even in wartime. That little foray into commerce had earned him close to three dollars over the course of two

summers, and when business fell off, mainly because the boys he
knew had all had their go at it, he'd torn out the pages and sold
eleven of them for a nickel each. The page with the blond lady in
the pink swimsuit standing on the wing of a B-24 Liberator he
stashed beneath the newspaper that lined his sock drawer.

With the calendar venture under his belt, he hid a pack
of Camels in the Shed, and after smoking one and throwing up
his gizzard, he sold the remaining nineteen for a dime apiece. 'A
whole pack ain't but twenty cent,' said Rufe. 'You cain't git no dime
a smoke.' But in two months, he had a dollar and ninety cents,
which was pure profit, since he'd found the unopened pack in the
grass behind Booker's. From this, he learned that people would do
crazy things on a whim, like spend a dime for something worth a
penny.

As an act of obedience, he had taken his grandmother's advice
about putting something aside, and had actually gotten to like the
idea. There was also a bonus he hadn't expected—the ladies at the
bank treated him like Boss Tate every time he made a deposit.

He parked the Mustang at the curb and looked at the iconic
building as if it were a kind of memorial.

Including the junk bicycle he'd sold for parts and the funny
books he sometimes, though rarely, recycled for four cents apiece,
his juvenile enterprises had added roughly eight dollars to his sav-
ings account. This encouraged him to project the amount he could
expect to amass by his twelfth birthday, including what he was able
to save back from Nanny Howard's allotment—fifty-five bucks
seemed likely, maybe sixty-five if he really hustled. Then he spent
hours figuring out how he would spend it. A BB gun, definitely,
though he'd have to keep it hidden, and a comb and brush set like
Robert McGuirk had desperately wanted to give his mother. Or
maybe he wouldn't touch a penny of it 'til he was fifteen and old
enough to get a driver's license—then he would buy a flathead V-8.

He didn't like to think about the cookie venture, which had been a total failure . . .

'I'll give you a whole nickel to make me two dozen cookies,' he told Peggy.

'What you want two dozen cookies fo'?'

'To sell.'

'I can't be makin' you cookies t' sell 'less you aks yo' mama.'

He asked his mother, who thought about it and finally said yes, enterprise was character-building and his idea to put the money in the bank was wise and farsighted, but only after he tithed his ten percent, of course, and he may have only one dozen, not two, given the sugar shortage.

He rode to town with his father, the paper sack between his legs. The scent of fresh-baked raisin-oatmeal cookies permeated the car, he was nearly drooling. He would not eat one if his life depended on it; he'd been invited to lick the bowl and spoon, which should be enough for anybody trying to make an honest dollar. Chances were, he could sell every single cookie at Booker's, or if he couldn't move the whole dozen there, he could count on the ladies at the bank to take what was left. They might even give him reorders. *I'll have two every Wednesday,* Miz Cox might say. *One for me and one for my husband, Bill.* Miz Cox had winked at him two different times.

'This is wartime,' said his father, who never took his eyes off the road while driving.

'Yessir.'

'Wartime is not a time to pleasure ourselves.'

He didn't understand.

'The cookies,' said his father. 'People are starving by the tens of thousands.'

'Yessir. But they're not for me, they're for sale.'

'Who made them?'

'Peggy.'

His father reached over and lifted the sack from between his knees and set it between them on the seat. Then he opened the sack, removed a cookie, and took a bite.

Two bites.

Gone.

When he reached for the bag, his father stayed his hand. 'Leave it there.'

He watched his father's hand enter the bag and exit with another cookie, which he ate as if he were as starved as all of Europe.

Almost immediately he ate yet another cookie, and another— not saying a word, but making an occasional grunting sound.

It was the first time he'd ever seen his father really like what he was eating. Once, when they were having Sunday dinner at Nanny's, his father had said with obvious pride, 'I don't live to eat, I eat to live.'

Since he'd learned what happened at the cattle auction, he had tried hard to love his father more. But pity didn't have the power he hoped it might, and all he felt was another kind of guilt for being unable to love the man who had suffered and seemed to like holding on to his suffering. He had finally figured out that what his father was doing was making everybody in his whole life pay for what had happened to him. He and his mother, especially, were the lambs in the thicket.

Crumbs on the seat.

Six whole cookies gone.

Thirty-six cents down the drain.

His father's eyes looked dreamy. He was scared by the person driving the car, who didn't act like his father at all.

When they arrived at the bank and parked on the square, the person driving the car turned and looked at him. 'Don't tell.'

'Nossir.'

Sick with something like shame, he went to the Shed and sat on an old file box and methodically withdrew the rest of the cookies,

one by one, and ate them, then upended the paper sack and sprin-
kled the crumbs on the floor for the rats . . .

At Frank's, he ordered breakfast to go from someone who wasn't
Frank—two scrambled eggs, dry whole-wheat toast, link sausage
with extra napkins to absorb the grease, and grits—and took the
carryout box to Booker's, where he sat on a wooden crate at the rear
of the storeroom and ate like a field hand.

Nine-thirty. Three and a half hours to go.

He washed up at the ancient sink in the corner and walked to
the window and tried to open it, but the sash wouldn't budge.
Sweating, he returned to the crate and shook the folds from the
bandanna he'd bought from Red. He refolded it and put the thing
around his nose and mouth and drew the ends behind his head and
tied them. Dust made his sinuses drain like taps, and this envelope
hadn't seen daylight since the pharaohs came to power.

Before he drew the prints from the envelope, he stopped and
prayed and tried to collect what seemed shattered in himself. All
morning, he'd had the sensation of being lost—floating, but not
free; he couldn't put his finger on it. He was feeling his age in
spades, but it was more than that—he wanted to bolt and run. His
personal wizard, however, had nailed it: Life is short, and the road
to Holly Springs is long. He wasn't going anywhere—not yet.

As for what this trip might really mean, maybe he'd be able to
figure it out later—on the road to North Carolina, back home in
Mitford, or even hiking in Sligo in August with his living wife and
alive-and-breathing travel companions, Walter and Katherine.
Dear God, it helped to remember that the grave had not triumphed,
he had a family—he would call Cynthia as soon as he got to the car,
where he'd left his cell phone, and Walter—he'd call Walter, too,
who would like to know his cousin was back in their old stomping
grounds, that he'd seen Peggy Cramer, that Whitefield was getting a
face-lift. Though Matthew Kavanagh had had an uneasy alliance

with his brother, Walter's father, both men had tolerated their boys spending time together, though the occasions were rare. Walter had twice spent a week at Whitefield, and he, Timothy, had taken the bus to Oxford for a week one summer. That was the summer they determined to be friends forever, no matter what their fathers had going on about a soured cotton deal that implicated their Grandpa Kavanagh.

He drew the prints from the envelope backside up.

April 14, 1941 Photo #12

Mrs. Matthew (Madelaine) Kavanagh, née Howard, entering her woodland azalea and dogwood grove at Whitefield, 4 mi east of courthouse. Whitefield boasts one of the most extensive private azalea gardens in Marshall County. Her frock of Irish linen is from Kennington's in Jackson. Ice tea and lemon cookies were served on the porch. The first bus ever used by the Pilgrimage hauled visitors from the square for ten cents a piece, which will go to cover expenses. 131 people signed the Whitefield guestbook today. Temp. 72°. (Note bed of *Iris sibirica* in background, a stunning tetraploid that arranges beautifully with herbaceous peonies.) Photo by Luola Dabney Randolph Lewis. All rights reserved.

He turned the photograph over.

The old photos in the drawer back home were memorized and familiar, but this—he felt he was seeing his young mother for the first time. She stood beneath a canopy of ivory blossoms, her head slightly tilted back, her eyes squinting into the sun, laughing. He had loved nothing better than his mother's laughter.

April 14, 1941 Photo #3

The fish pond at Whitefield, home of Mr. and Mrs.

Matthew Kavanagh and their son, Timothy. The pretty pond grasses were transplanted from the wild and have not been identified. The limestone statue of the boy with a billy goat was a gift to Mrs. Kavanagh from HS Garden Club member, Mrs. Robert (Mae) Wilkerson, purchased during one of her trips to Paris. Photo by Luola Dabney Randolph Lewis. All rights reserved.

The boy in the statue was 'buck-naked,' as Louis had said, a fact which distressed his mother. Mrs. Wilkerson, a particularly liberal artist and club member, had effusively bestowed the thing on his mother, who saw nothing to do but partially conceal it behind pond grasses.

He remembered tossing a rock into the pond, and the pitch hadn't gone well; he'd broken a horn off the goat.

Louis laughed. 'You could of busted off somethin' 'stead of a horn, an' yo' mama would like it mo' better.'

'Can you fix it back?'

'You got to quit runnin' t' Louis ever' time somethin' go wrong. Someday you ain't gon' have no Louis t' run to, then what you gon' do?'

Louis had made him fix the blasted thing himself. Miraculously, the horn held fast over the years. After his mother's death, he had given the statue to the garden club, along with two stone benches, a wrought-iron gate, and a pair of urns.

April 14, 1941 Photo #7

Mrs. Matthew (Madelaine) Kavanagh and her son, Timothy, soon to turn six yrs old in June, relax on their porch after Pilgrimage visitors have gone. Marge Gholson (HSGC Pres. 1937–39) brought the boy a book which he asked his mother to read aloud. She seemed very pleased to do so, though it had been a long day with 131 guests signing the register!

Young Timothy says he wants to be an Indian chief or a preacher like his grandfather, Holly Springs' beloved Rev Yancey Howard. Photo by Luola Dabney Randolph Lewis. All rights reserved.

He turned the photograph over.

He sat on his mother's lap, a rare treat, in a rocking chair on their porch. He was gazing at the open book in her hands, and clearly happy. He could see that his mother was tired, but she, too, was happy—he knew it from the way she was holding her mouth. His mother's mouth had been more expressive even than her eyes. He struggled to make some connection with the boy in the playsuit and well-shined shoes, but he could not. It seemed someone else's life entirely.

His gaze roved their faces, as if he could etch the image onto his memory and keep it forever. Then he saw Peggy at the far end of the porch—she was shaking a tablecloth over the railing. He was moved by the late afternoon light shining through the cloth, and oddly startled by her presence.

Though her strong features and expressive eyes were indistinct in the photograph, he knew she had been striking, even comely. He was certain he hadn't known that then, of course—she had just been Peggy to him. He held the fading image closer and looked at it a long time.

He turned the photograph over and read the inscription again. Peggy wasn't acknowledged.

He sat for a while with the prints in his lap, his mind as absent as his mortal flesh was present.

April 14, 1941 Photo #10

Mr. and Mrs. Matthew Kavanagh in the hosta grove at Whitefield. Mrs. Kavanagh has planted fourteen different varieties in recent years, including giant and miniature. Mrs.

Kavanagh claims to have no favorite, but admits to a special fondness for H. *plantaginea* owing to its sweet scent along a shady summer path in the woods. Photo by Luola Dabney Randolph Lewis. All rights reserved.

He was riveted by the power of the black-and-white image. His mother and father stood among the hostas, facing one another. Their presence was so palpable he felt they might at any moment live and move and have their being. A light breeze pressed his mother's dress against her slender frame; she seemed weightless, ethereal. Each of his parents was clearly magnetized by the other; the intimacy was so real he felt intrusive.

He held the print closer and adjusted his glasses. On his father's face was something he had never seen before—it was an expression of undeniable tenderness.

He stood suddenly and slid the prints back into the envelope.

"Whoa!" said Red. "This a stickup?"

"Give me your cash and make it snappy."

"You barkin' up th' wrong tree. There ain't any cash left by th' time th' government gets through with th' small b'iness owner."

He pulled the bandanna off his face and wiped his eyes and sneezed.

"Bless you," said Red, taking a canned drink from a derelict refrigerator. "You want a drink while you're here, help yourself. Honor system. Drop some change in th' jar."

"I appreciate it." He blew his nose and stuffed the bandanna into his pocket. "What do you know about Jim Houck?"

Red popped the tab. "Loner. Won't win any popularity contests."

"Married? Family?"

"Twice. Three kids, a few grandkids. Left town a good many years ago, came back; can't seem to find whatever he's lookin' for."

He walked to the car and called home.

"Hey," he said.

"Hey, yourself."

"On the way out to Whitefield last night, I stopped by Frank King's. Someone had left me a note."

"Another note? Who?"

"A man named Henry Winchester."

"Who is Henry Winchester?"

"I have no idea, except he's the one who wrote me in Mitford. I talked to him on the phone this morning, he wants to meet this afternoon at one o'clock."

"Where? And what for?"

"We'll meet at Frank's place, he says someone wants to see me, insists the whole thing is covered by prayer. We'll drive out to the country about fifteen miles."

She pondered this. "How do you feel about going off with a total stranger who lacks the courtesy to sign what he writes, much less tell you what he's up to?"

"He sounds like an agreeable fellow. There's nothing to worry about. I promise."

"Take your cell phone."

"Of course. Don't worry."

"I should have gone to Holly Springs with you, no matter what."

"No. It's as it should be. I've been in constant motion, which wouldn't be good for you right now. I'll call this afternoon as soon as we're done. Sorry I didn't call last night. I was whipped."

"So was I, I was in bed at eight-thirty. I dreamed about you, darling."

"Tell me everything."

"You were wearing an aviator's cap and sitting at the kitchen table."

"And?"

"And I came in and sat down and you kissed my hand and suddenly the table lifted up and we went through the roof and were just floating around up there, easy as you please."

"I kissed your hand? That's it?"

"That's it. It was nice to see you, sweetheart, you looked great in that cap. Oh. Breaking news: It's here. Came yesterday with four men in back braces."

"How is it?"

"Huge."

"You're a saint to let him do this."

"Otherwise it would be just another room with lamps and tables, and chairs in a fabric I could never bear to look at, anyway. Harley and Dooley hauled everything to the basement, and good riddance."

"When will the boys be over?"

"They're coming for supper. They'll use the back door, of course, so nothing will be revealed 'til after we eat. Dooley is beside himself with joy. He saw it yesterday afternoon and thinks you'll approve."

"Definitely. What are you feeding the legions?"

"Dooley asked for steak, Sammy requested pizza, Kenny wants fried chicken. So we're having burgers with oven fries."

"I'll be right there," he said.

"Are you eating properly?"

"I cannot tell a lie. I'm not. But I'll be home before real damage is done. How's Kenny?"

"Amazing. A truly amazing young man. Who would have dreamed Ed Sikes would drop Kenny off with his grandparents and he'd be raised by loving believers? I find it the most miraculous of all the miracles that brought the Barlowe family together."

"Grace, and grace alone." He still marveled at the recent upturn that reunited Dooley with all his siblings.

"Dooley has bought new clothes for himself and his brothers and little sister. He seems intent on sharing his wealth. And, of course, this wonderful surprise for Sammy will be fun for all of us." Sammy was the high school dropout whose genius had surfaced in a pool room.

"What's up with Dooley and Lace?"

"More of what's always up with them—fear. Both are terrified of loving. They're going to dinner and a movie tomorrow night. I'm praying."

"I'm praying with you," he said. "Summer is short." He would like it if Lace and Dooley could come to an understanding and stick at it—though he'd been hard-pressed to do the same when he courted Cynthia. After months of misery, the fear had simply released him, like a hawk on the wing might suddenly release a chicken from its talons.

"Rats. I was just walking up the hall to the living room and turned my ankle a funny way. I'm seeing the doctor tomorrow, this boot is driving me nuts. I've been moaning and groaning to beat the band."

"I'd be glad for a dose of your moaning and groaning. I miss you."

"I miss you back. I'm starving for your hugs and kisses. Oh, good grief."

"What?"

"I just popped in here to have another look. It's bigger than I thought. We'll have to be lowered by crane to make a shot, there's hardly room to move around the darn thing."

Dooley's gift of a billiard table to his pool-shooting brother, Sammy, had established itself in their minuscule living room. Life would definitely never be the same.

He talked a little mush, as Dooley called it, with his wife before ringing off, and thought of calling Walter. Instead, he sat with the envelope of prints beside him on the passenger seat and stared unseeing at people moving on the sidewalk.

The point was to do it all—and after that, let it all go.

He cranked the engine and drove to Van Dorn and parked at the curb, then got out of the car and stood looking at the double front doors and up to the cross on the spire. The sky was perfectly blue and cloudless . . .

He had never before heard his parents fight, he'd heard only the long, loud silences.

He sat up, straining to make sense of the words that traveled through their closed door and across the hall.

'Christ Church' and 'ignorant' and 'no more,' he heard his father say. And later, his mother's cry, 'For the love of God, Matthew!'

He was holding his breath. He should go and help her. But his legs were paralyzed like Albert Hadley. He punched his right leg and felt the blow, it was not polio. It should be polio, he deserved polio for not being able to do anything about his father. He pummeled both legs with his fists, very hard and very fast, feeling the pain.

During the break between Sunday School and church the following morning, he was sitting in the front row at Walnut Grove Baptist with his mother, waiting for the service to begin. This was the church where his mother had been baptized and grown up, the church where his Grandpa Yancey had preached until he was asked to move to First Baptist in town. Everybody at Walnut Grove said how much they hated to see Yancey Howard go, he'd been the best of the best, they said, but they got a blessing in the end—after she married, his daughter, Madelaine, moved to the country and returned her letter to Walnut Grove. Everybody thought it was because she loved her old church, but he, Timothy, knew the truth. The truth was, his father didn't like Baptists, and never let them have the car to drive into town on Sunday; they rode the half mile to Walnut Grove with the Blackburns, or sometimes they walked.

Mr. Blackburn, the organist, hammered out a last-minute rehearsal of the opening hymn; members of the choir scattered down the aisles and disappeared into the robing room. It was raining, a terrific downpour that someone said would last the day and into the night. He pretended to look at the rain lashing the windows, but cut his eyes toward his mother when he thought she wasn't looking. She had wanted him to sit by her during the break instead of playing, as he usually did, in the church hall with his friends. He hated the awful sadness in his mother, he was seeing a lot of it lately. It might be a sin for someone so beautiful and kind to be so sad.

She turned her head sharply and looked directly into his eyes; he felt as if he'd been caught in a crime. Embarrassed for them both, he tried to look away, but could not. He knew only that there was a whole book of words in her eyes—she was trying to tell him something.

'Let's open our Bibles,' she said over the roar of the organ. 'Pastor Simon is taking his message from John's Gospel, chapter three, verse three.'

He paged toward the Gospels, quick as a rabbit, wanting to beat his mother to the scripture.

'I beat you,' he said. He was looking into the sudden warmth of her smile when somebody grabbed the collar of his jacket and jerked him to his feet.

'Matthew!'

He was nearly lifted from the floor as his father hauled him into the aisle and along the worn carpet to the door. 'March,' he was told.

He choked back the scream because he understood at once this was not real, this was a nightmare and he would soon wake up.

They drove into town, wet as dishrags, silent. His father's hair was sopping, but the comb marks were still perfect, like the furrows Louis and Ol' Damn Mule made in the vegetable garden.

After parking the Buick at the curb in front of Christ Church, his father turned and looked at his mother. 'Henceforth,' he said, 'this is where the Kavanagh family will attend services.'

TWELVE

W alter . . ."

"Cousin!"

"You'll never guess where I am."

"Surely you haven't ventured beyond the Mitford town limits?"

"I have."

"This reenforces my view that miracles still happen. But you're right—I'll never guess. Where art thou?"

"I'm sitting on a bench outside Christ Church at Van Dorn and North Randolph."

"In *Holly Springs?*"

"Our old stomping grounds."

"I'm just picking myself up from the floor. Tell me everything."

"Remember Rosie? Louis and Sally's son?"

"I do. Little skinny guy. Great marble shooter."

"I went to see him yesterday. He's the spittin' image of his father, it was like paying a visit to Louis. And I'm spending a couple of nights at the old place, at Whitefield."

"Good heavens. How does it look?"

"Better than ever. Two fellows are fixing it up, top to bottom— they live there and have taken me in like family. Wish you were here. It's wonderful." He was surprised by the truth he'd just spoken—suddenly, it actually was wonderful to be in his hometown, sitting in the sun on a rain-washed summer morning, talking to his living kin. "I've seen Peggy Cramer."

"No regrets there, I presume."

"We had a good visit. A widow with seven grandchildren. A believer. Still beautiful. Asked my forgiveness, and I asked hers."

"Glad to hear it. What on earth took you out there? Is Cynthia with you?"

"Nope. Brought Barnabas. You know about her ankle, of course. Again, sorry we had to cancel Ireland. Did you get your refunds?"

"By a hair. We're on for the end of August."

"Great. As for what took me out here, I'll tell you that another time. It begs disbelief."

"I don't suppose Stafford's is still open?"

"No, but Booker's is, and Tyson's, and Phillips Grocery still makes cheeseburgers." He glanced at his watch. Noon.

"Amazing. I'm starved for a dose of something that hasn't changed in a hundred years. Makes me want to fly down and join you. Any gardens left at Whitefield?"

"Just the old boxwood, nothing more. The washhouse is gone, of course; I think Mother took you out there once and gave you what-for."

"I remember it well, which was undoubtedly her intention. I said the s-word. Just quoting, of course, what was written in plain view on the water tank."

"Ah, yes."

"She sent me to the forsythia bush after my own switch, had to strip the leaves off and present it ready to roll."

It was good to laugh. "This trip comes with a reminder that life is short. We haven't laid eyes on each other in . . . how long?"

"Since you and Cynthia tied the knot—nearly eight years."

"I'm forgetting what you look like."

"More and more like Woody Allen, I regret to say. But it'll be great to meet again in August, to go slogging through sheep meadows, visiting the family castle. Pretty spooky place, by the way, I'll take only a small portion of family castle this go-'round."

"After Ireland, maybe we could fly down here—bring Cynthia and Katherine, check out our haunts in Oxford, have a picnic in your beloved Grove. What do you think?"

"Very appealing idea," said Walter. "Very appealing."

He entered the narthex and stood for a moment in its cool shadow. Little had changed, which, in his opinion, was one of the lesser, albeit important, gifts a church building could offer—timelessness in the midst of a time-obsessed world.

The black slate shelf. And the guest book. Still here.

He took a deep breath, then walked to the shelf and picked up the pen and inscribed the fact of his being—here, now.

July 3   Fr Timothy A. Kavanagh
Mitford, North Carolina . . .

Tommy was suspicious of the ability to memorize anything, especially verses from the Bible. 'How many of 'em can you say?' asked Tommy.

A lot. But he didn't want Tommy to know it was a lot. 'Maybe eight or ten,' he said.

'Do you b'lieve all 'at mess?'

He shrugged. 'Kind of.'

'If there's a God, why can't we do stuff together without you gettin' your butt whipped?'

With all his heart, he wanted to say something to defend God, but he couldn't think of anything. 'Prob'ly God knows stuff we don't know.'

Tommy said the word that had been painted on the water tower . . .

'You've got an amazing boy, Matthew.'

The rector was talking with his father toward the rear of the nave; he sat apart on the gospel side in what had become the Kavanagh family pew, and thumbed through the hymn book.

'Amazing in what way?'

'Very learned about things of the Bible.'

'No surprise. His mother, his grandmother, his grandfather, Archibald Simon at Walnut Grove—they've all kept after him like hounds after a hare.'

'Are you aware of what he's been able to take in?'

'Not really.'

'Timothy,' said Father Polk.

'Yes, sir?'

'How many books in the Old Testament?'

He couldn't count on his voice lately, so most of the time he kept his mouth shut. Totally to his surprise, it would go baritone on him, and people would fall out laughing, even Louis. He cleared his throat.

'Thirty-nine.'

'The New Testament?'

'Twenty-seven.'

'What's the, let's see, shortest verse in the Old Testament?'

Please, God. 'First Chronicles one twenty-five.'

'Can you recite it?'

' "Eber, Peleg, Reu." '

'Did you know that, Matthew?'

'Of course not, it isn't worth knowing.'

'True in the strict sense, of course, but in a practical sense, think how it trains one's mind to commit to memory such incidentals.'

'A waste of time.'

'Timothy?'

'Yes, sir?'

'The, ah, middle verse of the Bible?'

He sucked in his gut. 'Psalm One hundred an' three, verses one and two.'

'Would you give us the pleasure of reciting those verses?'

He sighed deeply. ' "Bless the Lord, O my soul; and all that is within me, bless his holy name. Bless the Lord, O my soul, and forget not all his benefits." '

'Well done. Would you step back here, please?'

He walked up the aisle—his legs like water, his breath gone from him.

'He also knows the longest verse in the Bible,' said the rector. 'Esther eight, verse nine. Want to hear it?'

'These are ridiculous Sunday School games. For God's sake, Father.'

'You're an amazement, Timothy. Just a few more questions and we're finished. How's that?'

He nodded, suddenly dumb as a doorknob. He had never done anything like this in front of his father, except for occasional recitations at the Sunday dinner table.

'Tell us, Timothy, what is Holy Baptism?'

'It's a sacrament. It means God adopts us as His children. When this happens, we get to be members of Christ's body and inheritors of the kingdom of God.'

'Can you fill us in on the concept of prayer? What is that all about, anyway?'

'Prayer is getting into relationship with God.'

'Isn't it about asking for things we want, and letting God know what's what?'

'No, sir. He already knows what we want and what we need. Prayer is about getting to know him, and worshipping him and trusting him, and thanking him.' If he fainted in front of his father, much less his priest, he would hobo out of Holly Springs on the afternoon train and nobody would set eyes on him again.

'Well *done*. Now. What is sin? People certainly dislike hearing about it, especially from the pulpit. What do you think sin is?'

Reverend Simon had caused him to suffer many times on this particular point. He knew what sin was. 'Sin comes about because of its middle letter: *i*,' he said in his old voice. 'It's the seeking of our own will instead of the will of God,' he said in his new voice.

His father appeared impatient. The rector appeared delighted. 'Is there any hope for us, Timothy, weak and foolish as we are?'

Though his face flamed, he felt a bold strength gathering in him. 'Loving God is our only hope,' he proclaimed in the new baritone. He realized how ardently he meant it. He hadn't known he would mean it, but as he said it, he recognized the truth of it.

He sank into a pew, exhausted.

'See there, Matthew? It's obvious we've got something to learn from your boy.'

'Surely you don't believe all the drivel—like the virgin birth, for God's sake, and the resurrection?'

'I'm afraid I do believe it, and I proclaim it every Sunday in the Apostles' Creed—just as you, by the way, also do. Perhaps you'd like to meet one day and discuss the great articles of our faith.'

'That sort of thing is entirely your business.'

'Well, then. I'm also very taken with Timothy's current desire to help with the Berlin Airlift, he's proposed a wonderful project for the Sunday School. Thirteen years old, mind you! At thirteen, I was empty-headed as a chicken.'

Father Polk turned to him and extended his hand. 'So, Timothy! How would you like to be an acolyte?'

'He'd like it very much,' said his father.

He wouldn't like any such thing. He wanted to go back to Walnut Grove, where he'd been happy. He didn't want to wear a goofy robe and light candles in front of everybody. He'd been at Christ

Church long enough to know that candles don't always light, sometimes you have to try over and over while the other kids snicker and point like goons, and sometimes they won't snuff out, either, which is even worse, plus acolytes were famous for going to sleep on the bench in front of God and everybody.

He wanted to be a Baptist in honor of his grandfather, and maybe one day a Baptist preacher, though his father would never heed anything a Baptist had to say—the Baptists with their covenantal ways were anathema to Matthew Kavanagh.

But he'd been thinking. Maybe if he was a priest, he could save his father's soul. Maybe God would let him say what his father needed to hear, and everything would be different.

His heart beat dully as he took the rector's hand and they shook.

It was done. Something irreversible was done . . .

He knelt in the pew his family had so long ago occupied—on the center aisle, gospel side, five rows back, with a view of the organ loft.

His heart was a stone; his shoulders ached as if he'd been heaving bricks over a wall. Clearly, he was tensing himself against whatever the Henry Winchester business might be, and the fear of running into someone who would dredge up the Martin Houck affair and call out the dogs all over again.

He put his arms on the back of the pew before him and rested his forehead on the cushion they made. The worst thing about this trip, really, was the fear it stirred in him. In truth, he seemed to be tending what C. S. Lewis called a "nursery of fears," all of which he managed to deny very ably at home.

At home, he was the priest everybody loved, the fine fellow who made everyone feel good about themselves, when so often he felt only the misery of his own damage and derangement. He had even been called "perfect" on a couple of occasions, which had embarrassed and infuriated him.

At home, there were no Henry Winchesters—everything and everybody, give or take a few, were consistently proven factors.

At home, no one knew about or would ever allude to the trial that so effectively wounded his mother and burdened the family with shame and unknowing.

But for all that, Holly Springs was precisely where he belonged right now. He'd been journeying for seventy years to this place, this moment, this pew. It was God's plan.

Enough, then. He'd come in to pray, seeking peace from the only one who could hear his heart and not despise him for it, the only one who could see him as a worm, yes, but love him still, because he'd been so fashioned that the hard chrysalis would soon shatter and the wings unfold, and he would ascend again and soar.

Chances were, the incident surrounding the trip to the country would turn out to be innocuous. The important thing was that he had come back at last to honor the dead. He would spend time at the cemetery tomorrow, clipping grass around the stones, watering and fertilizing the roses, getting settled in himself for the trip home.

He heard the front door open and close. Someone entered the narthex and walked into the nave. Whoever it was stood at the rear of the nave for a time before moving along the carpeted aisle and sitting in a pew directly across from him. He could tell it was a man by his movements, his walk; and he was a heavy smoker—he smelled it in his clothes.

He struggled to refocus his attention, asking God for the grace to take his mind off his mewling introspection. But he couldn't focus. The close presence of the person across the aisle was agitating and unwelcome, as if some grave urgency had devoured the air. And why would anyone sit so near when the nave was as empty as the Easter tomb?

Aggravated, he raised his head and looked directly into the eyes of Jim Houck.

He had no idea what to say. He rose abruptly from the kneeler and sat in the pew as if awakened by force from sleep. *Why are you here? What do you want from me?* But he said nothing.

"Do you think your old man did it?"

He was stunned by Houck's directness. The well-worn legion of stock answers flashed through his mind, and none of them, not one, would any longer suffice. He looked at the son of Martin Houck, to whom he was, in many ways, as connected as he'd ever been to Rosie or Tommy.

"I don't know," he said. "Many times I've wondered."

"You can quit wonderin'."

"What do you mean?"

"Daddy told me th' truth before he died."

Wait, he almost said, *maybe I don't want to know the truth.*

"He hated your daddy's guts, an' when he slipped an' fell, he said he knew before he hit th' ground what he'd do—he'd nail Matthew Kavanagh for pushin' 'im."

He uttered an involuntary sound as if struck from behind; tears came on a wave of feeling that nearly overswept him. He stretched out his right hand, reaching for something, though he didn't know what, and Jim Houck took it and gripped it as if he, too, were reaching for something but didn't know what.

"My mother." He couldn't speak beyond that utterance.

Embarrassed, Jim Houck released his hand and stood in the aisle, awkward.

"I'm sorry about your mother. Sorry about your whole family. My daddy was in such rotten financial shape, he figured he had nothin' to lose by accusin' your ol' man. You prob'ly know your daddy had a few enemies his ownself; I guess my daddy thought th' judge an' jury could be persuaded.

"I've never done much of anything right, but I knew it was right for me to tell you th' truth an' I didn't see any reason to beat around th' bush. I came up to Hill Crest th' other day to tell you, but I chickened out an' ended up actin' like a hard-ass."

He was a piñata, struck and shattered, the pieces still falling.

"All these years knowin' th' truth an' knowin' how bad it was for your people. I remember your gran'daddy, he treated me like I was somebody, he didn't hold th' lawsuit against me, he said it had nothin' to do with me. He was what I wish I could be, but that ain't gon' happen."

His mother's suffering over that costly and humiliating incident had been for nothing.

Jim sat again in the pew across the aisle. "When Daddy lost th' case, I was dog crap in this town. I hated your guts an' your family's guts for years. Even after Daddy told me th' truth, I hated you because that's what I was used to doin', it took a long time to break m'self of that. I thought a lot about gettin' even. If I'd known where to find you, I'd've burnt your barn down if you had one."

"Never had one," he said, ironic.

"They say a dog returns to its vomit, an' here I am, back in th' town I said I'd never set foot in again. Tryin' to figure out my life, what th' deal is, where I fit in. Knowin' what really happened forced me to think along lines I'd never thought along, you might say. Seemed like if I could get one thing right, if I could tell you th' truth, it'd be kind of like dominoes—th' other stuff would start fallin' in place."

"Thank you for telling me." He blew his nose, using his last handkerchief. The jury had found Matthew Kavanagh innocent, but his own son, his own wife, even Louis had in their hearts found him guilty.

"Why'd you come back?" asked Jim.

"Maybe this is why." He was surprised that he felt no acrimony toward Jim Houck; they had both been imprisoned by a lie and they'd both served their time. Enough of accusation and anguish, it was done.

"I didn't know if I'd ever see you again, then you showed up in Holly Springs. I guess that's what you call coincidence."

"I don't believe in coincidence," he said.

"Whatever."

"God did this. He brought me back, and look what he had waiting: something I would never have known if I hadn't done what I dreaded most. I believe he has something for you, too." He hesitated, needing to be certain he meant what he wanted to say. "I'll pray for you, Jim."

"I could use it."

They sat for a moment, silent.

"How about right now?" he said. "Up there." He gestured toward the altar rail.

"I don' know."

"Painless," he said.

"Painless?" said Jim. "I'll take painless."

THIRTEEN

H e was at Frank's place fifteen minutes 'til one.
"Tell me about Henry Winchester."

"Nice guy. Comes in now an' again, likes meatloaf."

"Who doesn't?"

"Usually goes home with a chicken-liver takeout, side of green limas, an' coleslaw. Pretty quiet."

"That's all you know?"

"Started comin' in a while back, I can't hardly say when."

"What does he look like?"

"Black guy. Light skin, dresses good, talks educated. Keeps 'is shoes shined, you could see yo' face in 'is shoes. He one of th' people you lookin' fo'?"

"Yes, actually. A glass of tea, please. Unsweetened." He foraged in his pocket for his wallet.

"Ain't got unsweetened, ain't gon' git unsweetened. Can't sell it."

"You're holdin' on to the nation's record for the most cases of diabetes?"

Frank laughed. "We're holdin' on, thass right."

"Full bore, then. And give me a quick salad with oil and vinegar, no onions."

"Got your oil an' vinegar on th' table."

"And a piece of that lady's pie. Blackberry." Hallelujah.

"You loosenin' up out here in ol' Miss'ippi."

He grinned. "The heat." He liked being in a place where every-thing from forgetfulness to homicide might be blamed on the heat. "What does Henry Winchester do?"

"Railroad conductor. Th' boss of th' whole choo-choo. Seem like he retired a while back."

"How old?"

"Late fifties, sixty, maybe."

"You get that good rain last night?"

"My gauge said an inch and a quarter."

He sat in the first booth, gulping his food and keeping an eye on the parking lot.

Five 'til one. Henry Winchester was early, too. When the blue Buick rolled in, he felt suddenly tentative, like a child going off to first grade. He wiped his mouth and dialed his wife.

"Here I go. Love you."

"I'm praying," she said. "Love you back."

When he reached the blue Buick, Henry was standing by the passenger door. Six feet tall, on the slender side, kind eyes. He wore a sport coat and tie, as if to say this wasn't a casual thing he was doing.

"Mr. Winchester?"

"Reverend Kavanagh?"

They shook hands. Henry's grip was firm, his palm mildly damp.

"May I drive us, Reverend? Or would you like to follow me? I'll sure be glad to drive us."

He'd wondered about taking off to an unknown destination with a total stranger, but hadn't figured out what to do about it.

"You know the way," he said. "We'll give my Mustang a rest, it's hot on the heels of antiquity. How long do you think we might be?"

"I don't know exactly, but I'll be ready to bring you back anytime you say."

Henry opened the passenger door before he could do it himself. As he got in, he eyed Henry Winchester's shoes. Buffed to the max.

The Buick was old but clean, and the leather interior freshly polished; the surface of the seat squeaked as he sat down.

"The town looks good," he said, attempting small talk as they drove around the square and headed south. The air conditioner roared against the escalating temperature.

"Coming along."

"Frank tells me you're a railroad conductor."

"Yes, sir. I was."

"Retired?"

"Pretty recently. You can retire from the railroad at age sixty."

A bruise on Henry's right hand. One on the right side of his face, near the chin. He realized he was staring and averted his eyes to the highway.

"Good rain last night," he said.

"Yes, sir. Good rain."

He perceived he wasn't the only one who was going off to first grade for the first time. "Do you garden?"

"Just a little patch. I was glad to get the rain."

"What are you growing?"

"Corn. Potatoes. Bush tomatoes. Cabbage. A few salad greens. I like to wilt th' greens."

"I know wilted greens, all right. Have to have cornbread with wilted greens."

"Yessir." Henry glanced at him. "Sure do."

"My wife and I garden, but no vegetables. Not enough room unless we tear down the garage, which we've considered a time or two."

He checked the needle. Holding steady on fifty-five; Henry concentrating on the road. They drove without talking for several minutes, with only the roar of the air conditioner breaking their silence.

"So, you like the trains."

"I like th' trains, sure do. Got trains in my blood. Went to college, thought I might go into business. But th' trains . . . they'll call you."

"Frank says the conductor is the boss of the whole choo-choo."

Henry laughed a little. "Tried to be."

"I don't know much about trains. Took the *Panama Limited* to Jackson one time. I was a boy. Always meant to do it again."

"I worked the *City of New Orleans* for many years. It was a good run."

"Never got tired of the same run?"

"Suppose I should have, but no, the passengers kept things interesting for me. I always liked meeting new people, observing their attitude when they came on board, and how the trip might have changed . . . Didn't mean to go on."

"Please go on. If there's anything I like in this world, it's a story. My grandpa was a great storyteller. How the trip might have changed . . . ?"

"Changed their lives in some way."

"Ah."

"People feel affection for trains," said Henry.

"Yes, I think you're right. A link to the past, perhaps."

"Link is a good word. Trains also link people to each other. Everybody today seems hungry for a sense of connection."

"Hungry, yes." Jim Houck. T Ray. He remembered Ray's story about the basketball hoop, how the house where he grew up had vanished, all connections severed, as if it had never existed.

They were in the country now. Fields bordered the road; here and there, a house, an occasional horse grazing.

"May I ask if God called you to the priesthood?"

"I didn't feel called in the usual sense, not in the beginning. In the beginning, I thought it was about being good, doing the right things, believing the right things. And, of course, it is about all that, but it really doesn't work unless we're in relationship with him. I was in my forties before God cracked open my heart and revealed himself to me and I surrendered my life to him. That was the breakthrough. Before that, I was merely a man with an agenda. After that, I was God's man and it was his agenda. It changed everything."

In a fleeting glance his way, he saw deep feeling in Henry's eyes. "I was fourteen when I threw out my agenda and asked for his."

"Fourteen. Saved yourself a world of trouble."

Henry nodded. "I had good teachers."

They rode in silence. Flat terrain. Temperature rising. Henry's clock wasn't working; he checked his watch and loosened his collar. The knowledge of his father's innocence had rolled something away from the tomb of his chest, but the guilt of having convicted him was rolling it back. He prayed for forgiveness, and the grace to forgive himself.

They turned right at a mailbox bearing the name WINCHESTER and drove along a narrow dirt road through pine woods.

In the clearing at the end of the road stood an unpainted house, fastidiously kept and striking in appearance. Part of the yard was swept and bare; he hadn't seen a swept yard since boyhood. An enormous car with tail fins was parked by the porch.

"My sister lives down the road and has a beauty shop in her home; she parks her car here to leave space for her customers."

"Good plan."

Henry switched off the motor and dropped his hands into his lap, looking suddenly spent. Bruising also on the left hand.

"Will we be going inside?"

"Yes, sir. We will."

"Mr. Winchester, I admit I'm not one for surprises. Is there anything I should know before we go in?"

Henry slowly shifted on the seat and looked at him; the gravity of his expression was unsettling. "You'll be told something you may not want to hear, and asked to do something you may not wish to do. I'd like you to know that none of this was my idea."

"Whose idea was it?"

"My mother's."

"Who is your mother?"

"Peggy Lambert Winchester."

The feeling wasn't unlike diving off a board and striking the water on his belly.

"My mother wants to see you. It's something she's prayed about for a long time. It's the most important thing in her life now, to see you again."

Peggy. He managed, finally, to ask a civil question. "Her health?"

"Scheuermann's kyphosis."

"I've known a couple of parishioners with that form of kyphosis. Can be a good bit of pain associated with it."

"Other than the kyphosis and keeping her sugar down, she's in fine health. Mentally, she's sharp and quick, with a memory far better than mine."

"How old?"

"Gaining on ninety."

"Ah." He couldn't find anything else to say.

"My mother has sacrificed greatly for me. I would do anything for her. So when she started asking God to show us how to find you, I was bound to help in any way I could."

"Well, then." He opened the passenger door; the humidity struck him full-force.

"We didn't tell you beforehand, Reverend; she was afraid you wouldn't come."

"I see." But, of course, he didn't see.

FOURTEEN

They stepped beyond the drenching heat into the shade of a darkened room.

The windows were heavily draped; only a ribbon of light streamed across the floor. The air was sweet with the scent of coffee and cooked apples.

"Mama keeps it dark during the day. The heat."

"Yes."

"Please make yourself at home, Reverend. I'll tell Mama you're here."

Bare floorboards, bleached with wear and scrubbing, gave light to the chiaroscuro of the enormous space. There seemed a holy calm over the commonplace things of the room—a dining table and chairs; a fireplace furnished with a vase of dried flowers; a bookcase heavy with books. An oscillating fan whirred and turned, soundless beneath the high ceiling.

On a table next to an upholstered chair, a lamp illumined a Bible and several framed photographs: a dark man with a mustache; Henry in a conductor's uniform; Henry and a younger woman wearing a brooch on the lapel of her blue jacket; two young boys and a girl in school portraits.

Peggy—alive and well, and with a life other than any he'd ever imagined.

He tried to gather the explosion of feelings he'd experienced since leaving Mitford, tried to collect them into something focused and manageable, but he could not.

Lord. He found he couldn't form words for prayer, but called on him all the same, as he'd always done when mute with grief or joy or wild speculation.

There was a whispering sound, and he turned and saw her, bent nearly double and aided by a cane, moving toward him in the dim light. It was her bare feet that whispered over the pine boards.

Her hand alighted in his, like the claw of a bird with bones so brittle they might shatter beneath his breath. There was a strong impulse to kneel, but he remained standing, awkward and tremulous, foraging for his handkerchief.

She looked up at him, into his eyes. The tall woman he'd known sixty years ago appeared as small as a child.

"I aks God to send you," she said. Her voice was reedy, like the piping of a flute. "I knew he would."

"Yes, ma'am."

"Please come and sit," she said.

She led him by the hand to the chair beside the table and the lighted lamp.

"May I help you?" He was a basket case.

"Oh, no. I've got my way of sittin' down and gettin' up."

She lowered herself into the chair and stationed her cane against the arm. The osteoporosis had set her bones like the half portion of a paperclip. "You might take the footstool, most people do—pull it up close so I can get a good look at your face, the face I aks God to let me see again."

He sat on the low stool and gazed at her, forgetting to breathe. Peggy.

A light kindled in her eyes. "I prayed for you all these years."

"Yes, ma'am. Thank you." He wouldn't say that he'd stopped praying for her because, in his heart, she had died.

"I thank God for sending you, and I thank you for coming." Tears coursed along her cheeks; she took a handkerchief from her dress pocket. "You're han'some as can be."

"Your eyes are playing tricks."

"God have blessed me with second sight. You know what that is, second sight?"

"Yes, ma'am."

"I can see a chigger crawlin' on a blackberry. But he didn't leave a hair on this ol' noggin, I'm bald as a hen egg." She laid her hand for a moment on her red head scarf. "How is your health?"

"Good," he said, skipping the canned response about diabetes. "Can't complain."

"You don't look a bit like your Gran'pa Kavanagh. Some say you did as a boy, but now you look like your ownself."

"Do you mean it?"

"I do mean it." She made the slightest movement with her hand, as if to touch him, but did not. Even so, he felt the sensation of her fingertips on his cheek.

"You do got your mama's pretty eyes." She squinted at him. "An' your Gran'pa Yancey's mouth. Best thing is, you got your Gran'pa Yancey's ways."

It was a gift to believe her.

"I hope you'll excuse my bare feet, an' forgive me for treatin' you like family. If Brother Grant knew I was entertainin' a man of God barefooted, he'd be scandalized. I can't bear th' weight of shoes on my feet 'less I'm in church."

"It's good to be treated like family."

"Reverend." Henry's quiet baritone sounded from across the room. "Will you have a glass of lemonade? Homemade this morning."

"I'd like that. Many thanks." He shouldn't follow Frank's black-berry pie with another blast of sugar, but he wouldn't mention his diabetes if his life depended on it; he was sick of the very word.

"Be right up," said Henry.

"Henry is a gentleman."

"Yes, ma'am." He was reminded that he'd never before said ma'am to Peggy; in his day, white children didn't do that, it was the code.

"He's educated, and he's mingled with educated people." She turned to the table and picked up the photograph of the dark man with the mustache.

"This was my husband, Dr. Packard Winchester. He was princi-pal of a school for colored up in Memphis. He read all those books there, and more, to boot. He helped me learn things I'd always hun-gered to know. Packard Winchester was a wonderful husband, a de-voted educator, and a fine father. We lost him way too soon."

He took the framed photograph and gazed at it a moment. Kind. Benevolent. "He was good to you," he said.

"Oh, yes. He was my angel from heaven, I miss him every day. And that's our daughter, Sister, there with Henry. Sister has a beauty shop right down th' road, and does real well; she raised three lovely children out of th' beauty shop business, and has four grans. Sister helps Henry look after me."

"Doesn't look like you need much looking after."

She chuckled. "Sister claims I run 'em ragged." She touched her forehead. "I'm a little dizzy today, I didn't sleep good last night."

"I'm sorry."

"Old age. And talkin' to th' Lord about this visit."

"I didn't know what to make of the note you sent me. But some-thing powerful drew me here."

"I prayed night an' day on what to do, and th' Lord finally di-rected me to write and aks you to come. He told me clear as a bell what to say and Henry wrote it down. Henry said, 'Mama, seem like you ought to say more.' But when we tried to say more, it was too much. So we wrote what the Lord said write."

"How did you know where I was?"

"Henry found your name and address in a library book. It had a red cover and listed clergy."

"How did you know I was clergy?"

"I guess I knew it in my heart. First we tried to find you in th' Baptists, then we looked in th' Episcopalians. I expected you'd gone one way or th' other."

"Why did you want me to come?"

"I'm gon' tell you everything. Night might pass and I won't be finished tellin' you everything. Are you in a hurry?"

"I'm not in a hurry."

"That's good. People nowadays are always in a hurry."

"Yes, ma'am. Would you tell me why you didn't sign the note or say how to reach you?"

"I didn't treat you and your fam'ly right. I thought if you knew who wanted you to come, you wouldn't come. I hope you won't be sorry for comin'."

"Why would I be sorry?"

"I aks th' Lord whether to tell the truth, or let things go on like they been going on."

"He gave truth the go-ahead."

"Yes. The go-ahead."

Her eyes had no dim cloud of age; he recognized Peggy Lambert in her eyes.

"I want to ask your forgiveness for how I left you without sayin' goodbye. You meant the world to me. I guess you couldn't know it from how I acted, but you were like my own. An' look how you saved my life that bad day. I thank you again."

"It was the grace of God," he said. "I didn't know what I was doing."

"You was the smartest little somebody I ever saw. I remember how you read your schoolbooks to me, hard as you could go, like learning was a nail you could drive in my hard head.

"Your mother helped me in more ways than I could ever say, but it was you who gave me the notion to get an actual education. What I got wasn't all I needed, but I can read nearly every word in the King James, an' spell Deuteronomy slick as grease."

Thank God for laughter; some pressure went off his chest.

"But the thing that cut the deepest," she said, "is that I left your mother without a word. There was nothing else I could do. I want you to know how sorry I was and still am, about leaving her."

"I wanted to find you," he said, "as much for her as for myself. I looked for you everywhere, and worried for years about what had happened. And of course you're forgiven. Absolutely. Please know that."

"I thank you." She was silent for a time, then said, "Did she suffer at the end?"

"She passed very peacefully. I was with her."

"Have you been back to the old place?"

"Yes, ma'am. I stayed there last night. In my old room."

"You don't mean it."

"I do."

"All her pretty gardens? They gone?"

"All gone."

Peggy rested her head in her hands. She wore a slender gold band on her left hand.

"I visited Rosie yesterday," he said. "We remembered you."

She looked up. "Rosie Ponder? His people were good people. Has th' Lord given you a wife?"

"Yes, ma'am. He kept me an old bachelor 'til I was sixty-two, and then . . ." He dug out his wallet and flipped it open. "Here's what happened."

He held the wallet out to her; she studied the image closely. "Great day! That is a beautiful woman."

"Her name is Cynthia. She writes books for children."

"Books! Packard would have loved to meet her."

"In heaven," he said.

"Yes! That's right."

"And this is my son."

"A han'some boy. Han'some. But I don't see any of your people in his looks."

"Adopted. Just a few months ago. I raised him from the age of eleven."

"Eleven."

That's how old I was when you left, he nearly said.

"I'm glad you have family—someone to love you, an' even mo' better, someone to love. You always had the most love in you."

"When you went away, I thought something terrible might have happened with Cole Jenkins."

"Cole Jenkins! Law help, I hadn't thought about that ol' darky in years. No, nothin' like that."

"Reverend."

Henry had come into the room without a sound, and stood by the footstool. Two tall glasses of lemonade on a silver tray. Two white, starched napkins.

"Thank you," he said. He took a perspiring glass and a napkin and passed them to Peggy, then took the other glass for his own. "I'd appreciate it if you'd call me Tim."

Henry looked doubtful. "I don't believe I ever called a clergyman by his first name."

"If you practice," he said, "it gets easier."

A dark half-moon of perspiration stained the underarms of Henry's jacket.

"I hope that means you'll drop th' Mr. Winchester."

"Starting now. Henry."

"Y'all gettin' sociable," said Peggy. "Makes th' lemonade mo' sweeter."

Cold. And so heavy with sugar it made his molars ache. The ice clinked in the glass; it was the lemonade of his postwar boyhood. "Boy howdy. Who made this?"

"Henry made it. He can do most anything. Henry was a member of th' Brotherhood of Sleepin' Car Porters, he knows how to treat people. He was Employee of the Year two times runnin'."

"Mama likes to remember me as a porter," Henry said with obvious affection, "though the brotherhood merged with a larger union soon after I became a member. I went on to serve as a conductor for thirty-two years."

"Henry, Reverend Kavanagh says he's not in a hurry. Why don't you get a glass of lemonade and sit with us a little bit?"

"No, ma'am, I don't care for lemonade just now. I'll just stand a minute."

He could see the anxiety in Henry's face, as if he'd aged, somehow, since Frank's parking lot. Even in the dim light, he noticed the bruises again.

"Henry worked on th' *City of New Orleans*. Mr. Arlo Guthrie put out a song about that train, it runs from Chicago all the way to the city it's named after. There's a northbound and a southbound, Henry worked northbound."

Henry nodded. "A nine-hundred-and-twenty-six-mile run."

"It's a beautiful train. Henry and Sister took me on it for my eightieth. We ate Dover sole from china plates on a white tablecloth, an' the dinin' car people sang 'Happy Birthday.' They had movies on that train."

"Mr. Elvis Presley rode with us now and again," said Henry. "We once served him a barbecue sandwich for breakfast, he took it chopped. He ate it mighty fast and ordered two more; we gave him the fourth one on the house. Said it was the best barbecue he ever tasted, but said, don't quote that around Memphis, they'd run him out on a rail."

"Left Henry a hundred-dollar bill."

Henry looked uneasy. "I'd best be getting back to . . . I'm just baking a pie for . . . later. When . . . that is, if you'll have a piece." He hurried from the room.

"Henry writes poetry," said Peggy.

"Poetry!"

"He can do most anything, Reverend."

"I believe it. Will you stop calling me Reverend?"

"It might be hard callin' you Tim, it doesn't seem right."

"Timothy, then! That's what God calls me. You can't do better than that."

Her laughter was reedy, girlish.

"How were you going to know when I showed up in Holly Springs?"

"I speculated you'd go directly to Booker's. Somebody named Willie was Henry's lookout at Booker's, but before Henry heard from Willie that you'd come, Henry heard it at Frank's. Henry came home yesterday and we talked, and he wrote the note and took it to Frank."

"Only God could put that plan together."

"It was all prayed about, every jot and every tittle. I wish everybody could understand what a powerful thing prayer is." She was thoughtful for a moment. "There's some that believe in him but don't believe in prayer, did you know that?"

"Yes, ma'am."

Peggy sat forward in the chair and put her head in her hands.

The fan whirred to the left, then to the right, and back again. A deep tremor coursed through his body, and was spent as quickly as it had come. Something heavy had entered the room; he had no idea where this journey was headed.

She raised her head and looked at him.

"We're goin' to talk now," she said.

FIFTEEN

"Back in the ol' days, there was a question you always aks me—where was Peggy born, where did Peggy come from? You remember that?"

"I remember."

"I was born in a turpentine camp close by Middleton, Georgia. Do you know what that is, a turpentine camp?"

"I don't."

"They gone with th' wind now, thank th' Lord in his mercy." Something passed over her features like the shadow of a bird flying across water. "It was a camp way back in th' piney woods. We called 'em th' turpentine woods, where thirty or forty or maybe sixty people lived in rows of little jackleg shacks all spring an' summer, an' sometimes right through th' year.

"I was my young mama's first child, with four to come—Sam, Lona, Minnie, an' sweet baby Jack. When I was seven years old, they put me to mindin' babies. Cookin', cleanin', washin', I did all that like a grown-up, so my mama could go weed boxes.

"When I was eight or so, they put me out in th' trees rakin' pine. I mostly worked with my little brother Sam. He was what they call retarded, but he kep' up, bless his soul, he kep' up. What I did, Sam did in behind me 'til he got it straight in his head.

"I learned to use a boxin' axe to cut a box on th' tree, down near the ground. Th' sap would run in the box, up to a quart or more, an' that was what we called dip turpentine; it was put in barrels and hauled to market. All durin' the spring and summer when the sap was runnin', some of it would catch on the face of a boxed tree where we'd scraped it. That caught sap would harden up and flake, so scrapers would go in durin' the cold months, the off season, and gather it up in boxes and pack it in barrels and off it would go. They didn' waste a thing, they even worked gum out of dead wood lyin' on th' ground."

Peggy rested her elbows on her knees and bowed her head into her hands.

"There was a lot to workin' th' trees. Some camps had stills set up to cook gum, an' kilns to make tar, my daddy ran a tar kiln. He also dipped when he could, he could dip up to two barrels a day, better than any man in camp. But whatever we did, it was hard labor six days a week, sunup to sundown, an' all for such a mite of pay you could barely feed yourself."

"What happened if you got sick?"

"If we got sick, we doctored ourselves. Sometimes with turpentine, but you had to be careful how you used it. Mama drank it now an' again to kill parasites in her intestines—I was a grown woman before I learned that drinkin' it can kill you.

"Course, it was real good for cuts, we all used it for cuts an' scrapes. I remember a man named Toby, he was gamblin' for a pack of Camel cigarettes—a fight broke out an' somebody cut him eighteen times with a razor, they were bad cuts. He was a good worker, so they were goin' to take him to a doctor over in th' county, but he was scared of doctors, so he said, 'Bring th' turpentine an' pour it on me.' He was back in th' trees in no time, that's th' gospel truth.

"Another thing you could do—if you had a sore throat or somethin' bad goin' on in your lungs, you could fry off some fatback an' mix th' grease with turpentine an' rub it on your chest. Or you could rub it on plain to get rid of lice. Th' camps were a bad place for lice and bedbugs—an' a whole lot of other things there's no use to talk about. But I'm goin' on too long."

"Not a bit. I want to hear everything."

She raised her head and looked at him. "I beg your pardon for talkin' with my head down, it seems disrespectful, but holdin' my head up when I'm sittin' aggravates these ol' bones."

"It's okay, I understand."

"Every bite we ate and all we wore, we had to buy at the company store because it was twelve miles to town an' hardly anybody with a truck to ride in. They ran the prices at the store way up, so first thing you know, you didn't get any pay a'tall because of your debt. Then, next thing you know, you owed th' store such a big lick, you couldn't manage to ever pay it back, so you got in a cycle like that an' the rule was, you couldn't quit camp 'til you paid up th' store."

"Could anyone leave?"

"Some made it out, but you wouldn't want t' run away, no. My daddy tried. He figured if he could get away, he could go make enough money to buy Mama an' us children out. But th' woods rider got him. A camp always had a woods rider. It was a high position, he was the boss of everything. He rode th' woods on horseback, with a shotgun on one side an' a rifle on the other.

"He used th' shotgun on my daddy. Unless you were known to make trouble in camp, th' woods rider didn't shoot to kill, he didn't want to lose a worker. But th' shot got in him so bad, Daddy couldn't ever work turpentine again. One of th' buckshot ended up in his shoulder. There was a man in camp who could dig out shot, he jus' went in through th' hole in my daddy's arm with a knife and dug around 'til he got it out. They made Mama an' us children watch this brutal thing. The infection was so bad, we thought Daddy would lose his arm.

"Pretty soon, they ran us off from camp, just said, Get out an' stay out. All we had was th' clothes on our backs. It was a terrible price my daddy paid to get us free, but we were together an' God took care of us, every one. Mama used to look around at Daddy and all her children an' say, 'All us got is God an' us, an' that's enough.'

"We ended up at a farm where Daddy found a little work, he got so he couldn't use but his one good arm, an' Mama an' I cooked and cleaned in Miz Prichard's house. We were all livin' in the barn, we had quilts an' fresh hay to sleep on an' I never regretted that time. It was a lovely time—smellin' the hay, an' th' corn an' molasses they mixed in th' feed, an' havin' th' company of the cows an' horses an' chickens. We even had an old mule that made us children laugh, his name was Nelson.

"I never forgot th' sound of that barn at night when we were all layin' down to sleep; th' cows chewin' cud, th' horses breathin', th' ol' mule snortin' in his muley dreams—it seemed like God had sent his angels to watch around us and keep us safe. By then, my little sister, Lona, was lookin' after th' tots durin' the day, and in th' evenin', we sat out in the barnyard an' cooked over a little pit fire with two pots an' a skillet. I was nine years old.

"One time a fox carried off one of Miz Prichard's layin' hens; Sam ran hollerin' at th' fox 'til he dropped th' hen—its neck was broken. Sam took th' hen around to Miz Pritchard an' said, 'Here's your layin' hen th' ol' fox run off with, it's neck's broke.' Miz Pritchard looked at th' hen, said, 'Why, I believe that's your layin' hen, Sam. It sure *looks* like your layin' hen.'

"Sam came runnin' to th' barn with that hen an' we shucked off its feathers and singed the little hairs off th' skin and popped it in that big cookin' pot with a handful of wild onions, an' you never saw such a time as we had. We jus' went *all* out—made hoe cake and roasted up potatoes in th' hot coals, an' drank coffee with milk straight out of th' cow, an' after while, sucked on a honeycomb Sam found in a snag tree. It was th' best meal I ever had in all my years, an' me gainin' on ninety."

"I hear you!"

"One day Miz Prichard said she was goin' to send us all to Miss'ippi in th' back end of a truck. Th' truck was goin' out to pick up her widowed sister and her household goods an' carry 'em home to Middleton. She said there would be work for us out there, an' a place to stay."

Peggy looked up at him and smiled a little. "It was a long road to Mississippi."

"Sure enough."

Her eyes were amber, with flecks of gold. "Jackson was where we went. And th' place that took us in was right across th' road from your Grandpa Kavanagh's place."

"You never told me that."

"No use to tell you that, no use to tell about Peggy. There were too many broken parts of Peggy to talk about.

"Th' most broken part back then came from losin' baby Jack." She closed her eyes and shook her head. "All us were playin' in th' yard. Mama kept a swep' yard, it was smooth as linoleum, an' Jack was crawlin' around under that old yellow pine tree.

"Under that tree is where we set up our imaginary store. You could get anything you wanted in that store, and all for free. We hardly noticed that Ol' Man Crowder was comin' up th' road whippin' on his horse—he rode that horse in a criminal way. All of a sudden, he reined in at our place. He never reined in at our place before, it all happened so quick. Jack had crawled out in th' yard . . ."

Peggy took a handkerchief from her dress pocket and pressed it to her eyes. For the first time, he heard the ticking of a clock in the room.

"It's fresh," she said. "Eighty years gone, an' anytime I call it back, it's fresh. That ol' fool said he thought it was a little black dog in th' yard an' dogs knew how to get out th' way of a horse.

"Th' suffering made a mark that never left me and never will.

For a long time after, Mama looked around at Daddy an' her children and said, 'All us got is us.' "

She turned and took her lemonade from the table and looked at his empty glass. "Our manners are gettin' triflin'. Would you like more lemonade, Timothy? Henry made enough for a cornshuckin'."

He was glad to hear her speak his name. "No, ma'am. Thank you. How about you?"

"No, no." She drank, thirsty; beads of perspiration rolled from the glass into her lap.

"Your grandpa raised cattle, I can't remember what kind, seem like Holsteins, maybe. They were beautiful creatures to look at, movin' over th' pastures, lyin' under trees, drinkin' from th' spring. They used to say you could count a man's money by countin' his cows. My daddy said Boss Kavanagh was rich as Croesus. Did you ever hear of Croesus?"

"He minted the first gold and silver coins, and is said to have parted Midas from a few. Seems like Aunt Lily used to say that, too."

"I don't know how Daddy knew about that saying, but he used it a good bit. Now an' again, your gran'pa had a big cattle auction. People came from all over creation in fancy cars, old trucks, horseback, walkin', drivin' mule teams. Some came to buy an' some to look. At auction time, they said nearly any ol' body could go on Boss Kavanagh's property an' look his eyes full if he had a mind to.

"This day I'm tellin' you about, they said Boss Kavanagh was puttin' on a big show. Daddy would have gone, but he was sick in his chest, so Mama stayed home with him an' Minnie. She said Sam an' Lona could go with me if I'd mind 'em every minute an' stay well back from th' food.

"They put out a big feed at auction time, but no children or colored was allowed to touch anything at all, not a slice of bread, not a candy stick, nothin', that was th' rule. You ever been to a cattle auction?"

"No, ma'am. Never."

"Great big ol' heifers, an' bulls big as Sister's car out yonder. When they get in th' show ring, they get to jumpin' around, kickin' up their heels, dirt an' manure flyin' every whichaway—you better keep back. It was very exciting to us Lambert children, very thrilling, better maybe than goin' to th' circus. An' all those smells of food cookin'—it was hog meat roastin' on a spit, an' steaks fryin,' an' I don' know what all, with a whole table full of whiskey an' branch water, free to anybody with a green ticket.

"It was a hot day, th' kind of heat that burns right through to your marrow, and th' whiskey was a popular item. Even some of th' women were throwin' that whiskey down like a man, an' everybody eyein' th' hog meat an' those steaks fryin'.

"Before we left out th' house, Mama sermonized the children. She told us plain an' simple, 'Touch a bite of rations an' you'll draw back a nub.'

"Sam couldn't help from sometimes doin' what he was told not to do. He wasn't a bad boy, I declare he wasn't. It was his brain, th' way it worked. Tell him to do one thing, he was liable to up an' do th' direct opposite.

"The auction was goin' on an' people were standin' around or sittin' in chairs they'd toted, and th' auctioneer and your gran'pa were up there on a kind of stage, talkin' through a bullhorn. I saw somebody else up there, too, a handsome young white man."

"My father."

Peggy looked up. "Yes, your father."

"He was sixteen," he said.

"Yes. Sixteen. Do you know this story?"

"Grandpa Yancey told me."

"I figured somebody would tell you sometime. I'd like to tell you th' part you never heard."

"I'd like to hear it," he said. His mouth was dry as cotton.

"I tried to mind Mama and keep my eyes on th' young 'uns, but I was so caught up—it was so much to see an' smell an' hear, they even had people playin' banjos and fiddles, an' somebody blowin' cane. I think I just stood there, not even movin' for a long time, but Sam an' Lona, they went off ever' whichaway.

"In a little bit, I heard a commotion over where th' rations were cookin.' An' there went Sam streakin' through the crowd with somethin' under his shirt. Two great big white men were right in behind him.

"They caught Sam, and Sam didn't fight or kick or even holler, he just looked around for me. I was frozen to the spot, an' nothin' I could do to save him.

"Boss Kavanagh hollered in that bullhorn, said, 'Men, bring that boy over here.' They took Sam to the foot of th' stage.

"Boss Kavanagh looked down at Sam, he said, 'Boy, what's that under yo' shirt?'

"Sam said, 'Beefsteak.'

"Your gran'pa said, 'Is it yo' beef steak?'

"Sam said, 'Is now.'

"The crowd laughed, an' your gran'pa colored red as a beet. He turned to your daddy an', still usin' th' bullhorn, said, 'Matthew, go shut that nigger boy up in J.C.'s truck. Lock 'im in good an' roll up th' windows, an' let that be a lesson to anybody else who needs it.'

"Your daddy said, 'I won't do it.'

"So you see, there was a little colored boy back-talkin' him, an' his own son back-talkin' him—two in a row, right in front of everybody.

"Your gran'pa said, 'Did you hear me?' And your daddy said, 'I won't do it, let him go.'

"Did your Gran'pa Yancey tell what happened then?"

"Yes. He did."

"After your daddy was pushed off th' stage an' broke his leg, he couldn't get up. Those same white men came with an old door they'd been usin' as a tabletop over two sawhorses. They laid him up on it. His leg was so broken, it flapped like th' limb of a creek willow.

"When they carried him out to th' truck on that door, th' crowd parted in such a way that I was standin' where they passed; I saw th' blood soakin' his shirt where he'd been whipped.

"As they went by, he looked straight in my eyes. Not many people look in the eyes of a barefooted ten-year-old pickaninny, but he did. And I knew that he saw me as a human being who had also known suffering.

"The power of that look and the depth of that feeling will be with me for the rest of my days; it shook me to my soul. It was as if God himself was in that look, and the whole of God's grief for our brutality towards one another.

"I thought you should know that."

He took Peggy's hand and waited until he could speak. "What about Sam?"

"While all th' commotion was goin' on, Sam got away. When Lona an' I tailed in home, there he was, happy an' innocent as could be. He never really understood that he'd done something wrong; he just smelled meat cookin' an' couldn't hold back.

"Somehow, he'd managed to hold on to that beefsteak. What he did was cut th' meat in seven pieces, countin' one for Jack, and put them on Mama's best plate. We were so thankful your daddy hadn't let him be shut up in that truck. When he passed th' plate around for everybody to have their piece, not a word was spoken. It was my first Holy Communion."

The splinter of light across the bare floor grew brighter. He sat holding her hand, their pulses beating strong in their palms.

"I'm glad to know that he defended Sam." He had known this, after a fashion, from his grandpa's story. But this version told him that and more. It was as if another piece of the jigsaw puzzle had slid into place, and a new, though as yet unidentifiable, image was emerging.

"Now I feel disrespectful," he said, "but I must ask about the . . . facilities."

"Down the hall, first door on your right. It's Henry's quarters. You can see your face in th' floorboards."

And he could.

When he returned to the living room, Peggy was standing by her chair.

"May I hold on to you?"

"Yes, ma'am. You bet."

"My center of gravity done slipped forward. One these days, I'm gon' tip over on my ol' bald head."

"Don't even say it."

She linked her arm in his, and led him to the south-facing window.

"Us can't sit too long without stretchin' good, we might get a blood clot." She drew the draperies back and they looked out to the garden, a neat rectangle of potatoes, onions, gourd vines, beet tops, cabbage. The sunlight was nearly blinding.

"Off to th' back, there's Henry's collard patch," she said with obvious pride.

"Can't get enough collards!"

"You never liked collards when you were little."

It was good to be in the company of someone who'd known him as a child, who knew he hadn't liked collards then.

"What did I like?"

Peggy chuckled. "You were crazy about fried chicken, an' you sho liked cornbread—you could eat half a cake. Then there was baked beans an' fried catfish and chocolate pie."

"Oh, yes."

"An' hominy grits. You th' only child I ever knew who liked hominy grits."

"Yes," he said, "but only with butter and lots of sugar. I sure did miss you, Peggy. And I have to tell you something. After you left, I was sad for a long time. And then I got mad. Plenty mad. I stayed mad a good while, but I got over it."

She looked up at him and smiled. "I'm glad you got mad; it was good to get mad. And it was good to get over it."

"Why did you leave?"

"Have we shook down that blood clot?"

"Yes, ma'am."

"Let's go sit, then. The good Lord aks me to tell you everything."

She drew the draperies against the afternoon light; the room was dark again, and cool.

"That footstool must be gettin' mighty hard. You could draw up that armchair right there. That's it, pull it up close to me, an' get that nice little pillow off th' sofa—it'll feel good to your back."

He did her bidding; she was right.

"My daddy passed when I was fourteen. He's buried on th' farm across from your gran'pa's old place."

"I'm sorry."

"He was a good man, I sho loved my daddy, we all did. Mama an' us stayed on th' farm a month or two, then they changed hands, so we moved to town. We had a dresser, a mirror, three chairs, and two bedsteads with corn-shuck mattresses to set up housekeepin'."

"Did you ever see my father again before you moved?"

"I never did. Many times I looked for him to pass on the road, but I never saw him again. I heard he went off to what they call prep school, an' then to Ole Miss. People said he lived at school an' didn't come home anymore."

Like most people he'd known at Holly High, he'd wanted to go to Ole Miss, too, but early on he made the decision for Sewanee. He didn't wish to go where his father had gone, he didn't want to do anything that might, in some dangerous way, fashion his soul in the image of his father's. Sewanee had been the right choice, and one that Father Polk, a Sewanee alumnus, eagerly supported. With Nanny Howard's financial assistance and Father Polk's enthusiasm on his side, his father had relented, though he bitterly disliked the notion of a Tennessee school.

"What was it like living in the big city of Jackson?"

"Oh, it was good in th' beginnin'; it was th' best thing we ever did. Lona and Minnie went to a school for colored, they could walk there every mornin' with their lunch buckets, but with Sam th' way he was, he couldn't be in school. So he helped Mama an' me take up th' caterin' business. We'd never heard of caterin', we just knew people have to eat, and since they couldn't come to us, we'd go to them.

"What I wanted to do worse than anything was go to school. I could write my name and do simple sums, but I couldn't read. Oh, how I wanted to read like you used to read to me, just boundin' along like a rabbit across an open field; but Mama couldn't pull that big load all by herself.

"We got up way before daylight, Sam, too, an' started makin' sandwiches. Sam would put th' mustard on, or th' mayonnaise, we used Duke's, an' Mama would add in th' ham an' cheese, th' lettuce an' tomato, th' peanut butter an' jelly, an' th' baloney—we used two slices of baloney for good measure—pressed down an' runnin' over, like th' Bible says. Then I wrapped everything good an' tight an' stacked 'em in a box an' started off about seven o'clock, walkin' two miles barefooted to save shoe leather.

"I went around to Kennington's Department Store, an' right there I could sell nearly all we made, just standin' by the back door where the help went in. Those were some hungry people worked at Kennington's! I'd sell out an' walk home, an' Mama an' Sam would have another batch ready an' back I'd go two miles to a big hole in th' ground where they were fixin' to put up a bank. Th' men workin' that job would buy me out an' toss pennies an' nickels in my box.

"I saw a lot of ladies go in Kennington's, help as well as customers. They all dressed like they were glad to be somebody. So I started savin' for a down payment on a second dress. I'd never bought a dress, Mama made our clothes out of feed sacks an' th' cast-off goods of people we stayed with.

"What with rent an' rations an' all, it took nearly a year to get my dress out of layaway. An' when I got it, I didn't even wear it. Don't it beat all, that I wouldn't wear that pretty dress, green with pink rickrack at th' neck an' pink-covered buttons down th' front?

"I just kep' wearin' my ol' dress—wash it, hang it up to dry, stick an iron to it, an' go.

"One day, I finally figured out why I didn't wear my new dress."

"Let's hear it."

"It was too beautiful to wear."

"Ah."

"But I kept it hangin' out where I could look at it."

"Good idea."

"I guess I didn't know I was savin' it—to wear th' day I turned seventeen, an' knocked on your grandmother's door in Holly Springs."

SIXTEEN

I said, Is Miz Howard home?

"She said, I'm Miz Howard, an' who are you?

"I was tremblin' like a leaf, I thought somebody my color would come to th' back door. I said, Peggy Lambert, please, ma'am. I'm lookin' for work if you have some.

"She said, What kind of work are you looking for? An' I said, Any kind you have. Th' sweat was rollin' off me, I was so nervous. I remember standin' with my arms stuck out at my sides, so I wouldn't sweat on that pretty dress with th' rickrack. I must've looked like a rooster gettin' ready to crow.

"They tol' me Miz Howard was good to colored, so it was th' first place I knocked. But I was ready to knock all over town if I had to. Th' Great Depression was goin' on an' work was hard to find. Hard to find.

"She said, Do you iron, Peggy? I said, Yes, ma'am. Do you cook? Yes, ma'am, I said, I'm a good, *clean* cook. Do you do floors and laundry? Oh, yes, ma'am, I does laundry, I does floors, I does it all. She said, You *do* it all. I said, Yes, ma'am, I does it all. She laughed. I didn't know then what tickled her so. She had a nice, ringin' little laugh.

"She said, When did you last eat, Peggy? I said, Yesterday

mornin'. She said, An' here it is two o'clock th' next day. Step in and get you a bite.

"It was potato salad an' a slice of fried yellow squash, I'll never forget it; with a yeast roll an' a nice glass of sweet tea. Th' lady who was with your gran'ma for twenty-five years had passed two months back; your gran'ma had been prayin' for God to send just th' right one to take her place."

"So Nanny prayed you to Holly Springs."

She nodded. "That's what she did. Surely did.

"In Jackson, they robbed me of my sandwich money three times. Th' last time they beat me so bad, Mama was fixin' to send me to th' hospital, but I knew we couldn't pay a hospital. So I said, Bring me some turpentine. Mama an' the children had to hold me down. It burned so terribly from my head to my feet, I felt like my flesh was fryin' in an iron skillet. I said, How'm I gon' stand this, Mama?

"Mama said, Keep yo' eyes on God. So I did. In all that agony, my eyes were opened in a very strange, new way, an' I saw Jesus. He was hangin' on th' cross. He didn't see me, but I could see him, plain as day. His suffering was so great that my own grew sweeter, an' not too long after that, all th' cuts an' hurt places healed.

"These many years later, I can still see him on th' cross, plain as day. Everything that has happened in my life has been a gift; I believe he has allowed me to share in his suffering.

"Mama said, We got to get you out this town, yo' work keep you on th' street, you need to be workin' for a nice fam'ly in a nice house. I said, Where I'm gon' go? She said, North. I said, No, ma'am, I'm scared of th' North. She said, I mean north Miss'ippi.

"She heard of a place would take in colored girls to train for housekeepin' work. They wanted a hundred dollars for that, an' to boot, they would get you a job.

"You done trained me, I said. She said, No, ma'am, you are not trained, you was raised in a turpentine camp.

"Mama was makin' hats by then, pretty hats, a lot of people

came to her for their hats, an' she said she could run things without me. I didn't want to leave Sam an' Lona an' Minnie, they were bawlin' an' hangin' on to me for dear life, but Mama said, Go on out this place, an' come home when you can. I was sho scared, but I got on th' bus with a change of clothes in my grip an' a hundred an' five dollars sewed in my jacket, an' went up around Tupelo."

Peggy raised her head and looked at him. "Right away, I saw th' place was worse than a turpentine camp. But they already had my hundred dollars, they took it at th' door. Mama would never have let me go if she'd known what it was. Maybe you can figure th' kind of place it was; it wasn't anything to do with housekeepin', I can tell you that."

"What did you do?"

"I ran out of there before they stole my five dollars an' change of clothes. One of th' girls said, Go to Holly Springs, they got big pretty houses over there. Look for Miz Howard on Salem Avenue. She said, I been meanin' to go my ownself, but it's too late.

"Too late, she said. An' she was only fifteen!

"One time Sister said to me when I was talkin' about somethin', she said, Mama, this is more than I need to know. Is this more than you need to know?"

"I've waited years to know," he said. "I want to hear everything God asked you to tell me."

"Could you use a little bite of somethin'? What did you have for your dinner?"

"Salad and a piece of pie."

"Salad don't last long. We have pie if you can eat another piece."

"Tell you what. You keep talking—and when you're through, I'll have the pie. How's that?"

"That's good."

"How are you holding up?"

She smiled a little. "I'm gettin' my second wind."

"Me, too."

"Where was I?"

"One of the so-called training school crowd sent you to Holly Springs, to Nanny's house."

"Your grandmother invited me into her beautiful home; I'd taken off my jacket so she could see my new dress, an' left my grip in th' privet hedge. I ate that nice dinner she gave me in little tiny bites, so she wouldn' see me with my mouth full, an' so I could answer if she aks me another question.

"She said, Peggy, you are a lovely girl with a wise heart, when can you begin? I said, Would right now be too soon, please, ma'am? I was afraid she might aks me to start th' next day or th' next week, an' I wouldn't have any place to stay. She said, Not a minute too soon, I'll show you to your quarters.

"I was so happy, it like to scared me to death. A lovely girl with a wise heart—I had never heard such beautiful talk. I followed her along th' gallery doin' a little skip dance in my imagination.

"She made up a room at th' back of th' house, it was that old room off th' porch, and gave me that bad little dog named Rooster to guard my door at night. She wanted me to feel safe in a new place. I had never met a white lady like her before. I thanked God for a nice, clean bed and a chest of drawers to put my things in. I didn't feel I deserved it all—me, Peggy Lambert, born an' raised in a turpentine camp.

"I was with your wonderful grandma a year and three months when your mother came to stay with your grandma an' grandpa, because you were soon to be born. We were all excited about a little baby comin' to be with us. Your mama never looked more beautiful, an' she was already th' prettiest woman in Holly Springs."

"My father," he said. "How did he feel about having a child?"

"He was proud, that's what. An' when he saw it was a boy, that did it. He was about to bust."

"Honestly?"

"Honestly. You know your daddy picked out your Christian name."

"Yes. After St. Paul's boon companion."

"And your mother picked out Andrew for your middle name. That was from a saint, too."

"Teamwork."

Maybe he had missed something. Maybe there had been good times, and he'd been blind to them. *Why did he hate me?* he wanted to ask, but he couldn't say it.

"Your mama and daddy were sleepin' in th' front bedroom when th' pains woke her up about one o'clock. She called for me, an' when your daddy left to get Dr. Jordan, th' whole house got out of bed an' put on a pot of coffee an' stirred around in their night-clothes, prayin' for your mama an' for a healthy baby.

"You were born at five o'clock sharp, we heard th' clock strike as you came into th' world, an' let me tell you, you made a *racket*. Yo' gran'pa said right off, Pulpit lungs! I thought that was some kind of disease."

It was as if he'd come unplugged years ago, and he was getting plugged in again. His grandparents in their nightclothes, the smell of coffee percolating on the old range, the windows open to the June night—he'd never heard this part of the story before. The images it evoked were sharp and real to him.

"Your mama stayed at th' house four weeks—your daddy came back and forth from Whitefield. Well, no use to hide it—I was plain crazy about you, yes, I was. You was my baby, too! You got th' colic so bad, didn't anybody get a wink of sleep for I don't know how long. Your mama let me rock you all th' way to th' moon an' back. Night after night, it was just you an' me in that ol' rockin' chair, travelin' around in my imagination to places I wanted to see: St. Louis, New Orleans, th' Atlantic Ocean, th' inside of Rust College.

"When th' time started comin' for you to go home to Whitefield,

I was cryin' every day an' tryin' to hide it. Then I heard your Nanny say to your daddy, Matthew, you can't take a new mother an' baby out to Whitefield with no help. Whitefield is a farm, and farms are hard work.

"Next thing you know, we were in that big black Buick—your daddy an' mama in th' front an' me ridin' in th' back holdin' you. You wore a little blue cap an' slept all th' way home over that rough country road."

He'd never known this; he'd heard only that Peggy had once worked for Nanny.

"She turned me over to your mother, an' paid my first year's wages because your daddy was still gettin' his law practice up an' runnin'."

"What did Nanny do for help?"

"She said she started prayin' for God to send her some, an' right off, Mitsy turned up."

He smiled at that. "She was a saint in every sense of the word. Sacrifice was second nature to her."

"She was a fine lady. Very fine."

"When you met my father at Nanny's, did you recognize each other from the cattle auction?"

She raised her head and looked at him. "Yes. We did."

"Perhaps you looked much the same at seventeen."

"Taller," she said.

"Small world," he said.

"Yes. Very small."

"Were you happy with us, Peggy?"

"Yes. I was happy."

"I remember Mother going with you to hear the a cappella choir at Rust College. You talked about it for a long time afterward."

"It was one of th' best things I ever did in my life, hearin' that choir."

"You liked your little house down the lane?"

"It was my first true home."

"Several people tried to court you, Mother said."

"They did. But livin' in camp let me see how men could be with women, so I stayed back from all that. As best I could."

"You devoted yourself to us."

"Yes, I did."

"What about your mother, your family? Did you see them when you lived with us?"

"My mama married again an' he wasn't a good man. No. He was a bad man. I couldn't go home."

"Sam and Minnie and Lona?"

"Minnie married an' had two children, she passed ten years ago in New Orleans. When Mama passed, Lona took over th' hat business; she lives out in Chicago, she's eighty-six, an' Sam . . ."

She closed her eyes and shook her head. He probably didn't want to hear the answer, but he had to know. "Sam?"

"Sam played in th' street a good bit, even when he got up in age. He was like a child all his life. I'd been with your mother about five years when he ran out chasin' a ball; they say he didn' see th' truck."

"I'm sorry."

"So many things not to talk about when you used to aks me," she said.

"Peggy." He took her right hand in both of his; her palm was as smooth as the hide of an acorn. "Why did you leave without saying goodbye?"

She raised her head and looked at him directly; the lamplight on the red bandanna was a flame in the darkened room.

"I was carrying a child.

"I knew I would have to leave Whitefield. Not a living soul knew th' truth, but your mother guessed. I was straightenin' up th' bedclothes in th' hall closet when she came an' found me. She was very calm. She said, You're going to have a child.

"I said, Yes, ma'am. I never lied to your mother an' I could not do it then.

"I covered my face with my hands for my shame, my terrible shame, but that was not enough covering. I sat on th' closet floor and pulled a blanket over my head and wept. I wept for her, mostly, mostly for her, an' for you. Your mother sat on the little stool that stayed in th' closet an' kept watch with me. She didn't move, and she never said a word.

"I could tell, somehow, that she knew it was your father's child."

He felt as if he'd been injected with a paralyzing drug; he could not move his mouth nor avert his gaze from hers. He stared into her eyes as if looking down an interminably long corridor in which he might wander, lost, for all time.

"Your mother never said this to me, and I would not have said it to her." She hesitated, sensing his feelings, letting him gather himself.

He'd spent seventy years journeying to the pew at Christ Church this morning. Now he'd arrived in this place—not a moment too soon or too late—only to find the shattered pieces falling again.

"The next morning, I left the little house I loved, an' you, who I loved better than anything on earth, an' your mother, the kindest woman I'd ever known. No one knew where I was goin', an' except for your mother, no one knew why I left. I took the clothes on my back an' the Bible your mother gave me at Christmas.

"In all the days of my long life, I never hurt so deep as I hurt then, for the suffering I would bring to people who had been kind an' loving to me."

She appeared suddenly worn beyond telling, though her gaze was steady and certain. "I'm sorry to tell you this, so sorry to tell you this."

He could feel himself running, see himself running.

"Are you sure?" he asked. "Absolutely sure?"

"Yes. I'm sure."

"You said only Mother knew why you left."

"Yes. Your father didn't know."

What was he to do with what she was telling him? Where was he to go with this? *Lord*, he prayed.

"Why are you telling me now, Peggy? Why tell me after all these years? Did you have the child? What happened to the child?"

He looked up as Henry came quietly into the room and stood beside Peggy. He had taken off his jacket and rolled up the sleeves of his white shirt; there were dark bruises on his arms.

"Henry is your father's son," she said.

SEVENTEEN

Henry's face was gray. "I'm sorry. Truly sorry."

"Henry didn't want to do this," said Peggy. "But it had to be done. I prayed that God would help you find it in your heart to understand."

She looked at him intently; a weight pressed upon his brain. He was inclined to shake his head and somehow clear it, but he couldn't.

"As a little boy, you often prayed for a brother," said Peggy. "God in his wisdom answered your prayer, but in a hard way, I know."

From somewhere above, he was gazing down on the room—at the top of the red bandanna, at Henry's head and his shoulders sloping beneath it, at his own head with its balding patch—the three of them forming a kind of triangle in the lamplit room. The sense that he had somehow risen beyond himself lasted only a moment, yet it seemed to absorb his attention for a long time.

"Why are you telling me this?" he asked.

"My son cares for me when I'm ailin', loves me when I'm unlovable, an' made this old place like new—all that an' more. Henry has done everything for me. An' I'm willin' to do anything for Henry.

"He has a disease I can't pronounce an' can't spell, but it's slowly killin' him."

Henry continued to stand, his coloring ashen.

"Please sit down," he said to Henry. For God's sake, sit down. He couldn't bear to look for another moment at someone who was obviously exerting an effort to remain upright on his feet.

"I will, thank you." Henry pulled a chair away from the dining table and sat, briefly closing his eyes.

"For a good while, Henry's been weak as pond water, runnin' fevers, feelin' bad, not himself a'tall. He went up to Memphis in May, to a good doctor. They did tests."

"What did they find?" he asked Henry.

"Acute myelogenous leukemia. There's a lack of new red blood cells, and the white blood cell and platelet counts are very low." Henry pushed a rolled-up sleeve above his elbow. "That's the reason for the bruising. Essentially, my bone marrow isn't producing enough new blood cells."

"Some of his blood cells have cancer," said Peggy. "They're takin' over his healthy cells. Th' outcome of that is, Henry will die . . . if we don't do somethin'."

Henry looked at his mother, seemingly agonized.

"Henry needs a stem cell transplant." Peggy was calm, even cool. "They used to call it a bone marrow transplant, but now they got a new way of doin' it."

The fan moved the air, the clock ticked. He was in a kind of free fall.

"Best thing is to have a brother or sister donate th' stem cells," she said. Peggy Lambert Winchester was a locomotive hurtling along the track, not stopping at the stations. She looked at him, her eyes wide, her breath short. "Sister can't do it, too much heart problems, an' anemic since she was a child."

"You're sure about the diagnosis?" he asked Henry.

"They drilled into my pelvis and pulled out bone marrow with a syringe. They're sure."

"What happens if you don't get the transplant?"

"They say I could live for some months. A lot of transfusions and antibiotics. Chemo would help, but not for long."

"What happens if you do get the transplant?"

"Rejection and infection can be serious problems," said Henry, "along with the possibility of liver or kidney failure. And yet, there's also the possibility that God would grant me a few more years, that I could live a normal life. Any way you look at it, there's no guarantee of success. But I would take that. I would take it gladly."

"You want me to donate the stem cells."

"Yes," said Peggy. "We do." Tears spilled along her cheeks.

"When Mama began praying about this, I was completely against getting in touch with you. I tried to put myself in your shoes, and knew it was too much to ask. But God and Mama are a force to be reckoned with.

"I guess I never really believed you'd come, and that would be all right. I've lived a full life—I've met a lot of good people, seen beautiful places, and I know where I'm going when I pass.

"Then we heard you were in Holly Springs, and I knew God had answered a selfish prayer. I admit that, for the first time, I began to hope.

"I don't want to leave Mama at this late stage, though Sister would do all she could to help. But I want you to know that I'm not expecting anything, I have no right to expect anything. It's enough to meet you, Tim, to see you face to face. I've heard about you all my life, it was a comfort to know you were out there somewhere. You've always been . . ."—Henry paused, moved—"a brother to me."

He was overwhelmed to think he'd been counted a brother to someone all these years, that God had used such a fragile scrap for binding.

"Would you be willin' to talk to Henry's doctor?" asked Peggy.

"I have diabetes," he said. "Type Two. And I have a wife and son." With or without a medical problem, he had no idea what the consequences could be. He had never heard of a stem cell transplant, only bone marrow transplants.

Peggy leaned toward him. "Would you be willin'?"

"I don't know." All he knew for certain was that he didn't have time for a crisis; he was headed home to Mitford day after tomorrow. "I need time."

Peggy pressed her fingers to her forehead. "An' I need to lie down a little bit. I'm sorry for all this; we'd give anything if it could be some other way. Help me up, please, Henry."

Henry helped his mother from the chair; she seemed even smaller than she had looked when they arrived hours, days, years ago.

"Excuse us," said Henry. "I'll be right back."

"Take your time."

He heard the ticking of the clock, and stared, unseeing, at the pool of light cast by the lamp onto the empty chair.

"We could walk outside if that would be all right." Henry came back to the room, appearing eager to leave it again. "There's a bench."

They walked across the yard to the shade of an immense oak, passing beneath the drip line of the branches into a zone of cool, sweet air, and sat on the bench. The wire fence behind them was massed with honeysuckle and humming with bees.

"I can take you to Frank's anytime you need to go."

"I'll wait 'til she gets up," he said. "I couldn't leave now."

"This has worn on her," said Henry. "And on you, too. I'm sorry."

"No need to apologize. No need. It's going to take time; it's a great deal to take in."

"Yes," said Henry. "I've been taking in the fact that I had a half brother over a period of years, so I don't feel the brunt of it as you do. But having you here in the flesh, and not in a dream or a story, that's a great deal to take in for me.

"If you hadn't come, this would be just another day, but Mama would have tried and that would have helped her, somehow. Of course, I didn't know you when we sent that letter, and I couldn't realize . . . I never really carried it forward to think how it would be painful for you—and even for me, though I have no right to say so. No one is taking anything from me, or asking anything of me. But it's hard to be the cause of another's suffering."

"Did she love him?"

"Yes. She did."

"A lot of questions come to mind. Did it go on a long time?"

"A few months, she said. She knew it was wrong, and had the potential to hurt a lot of people. She loved him, I think, because he was wounded—as she was. Perhaps the principal thing is that he wasn't afraid of her."

"Was he afraid of my mother?" He felt a stab of anger, and deep humiliation that a stranger might know more about his father than he had known.

"I think he may have been afraid of most everybody."

Afraid. That wasn't one of the words he'd use to define Matthew Kavanagh, though it suddenly seemed right. "Did he love your mother?"

"She thinks he felt safe with her. She said he used to come to her house at Whitefield and sit and cry like a baby. He never said why, he just sat there and wept. Then he'd get up and wash his face and hands and go home.

"He always told her he couldn't stay long, because her house smelled like a nigger cabin and the smell would get in his clothes. She didn't like that, as you can imagine, and made him explain himself. He said the smell he was talking about was of cold biscuits and stale ashes and ham grease and wood smoke. She said to me not long ago, How can you change the smell of wood smoke if you cook with wood? How can you change the smell of biscuits if that's what you bake, and ham if that's what you fry? That incident has stood out in her memory all these years.

"In the end, she believes he felt safe with her because she believed him when no one else seemed to."

He meant the Houck trial. The truth was like a knife.

"Maybe he never let anyone see again the compassionate side that spared Sam his punishment," said Henry. "Mama also loved him for what he did for Sam."

He didn't have to sit here asking these naked questions. He put one hand over his face and sat speechless and unmoving amid the humming of the bees.

"I'm thanking God for you, Tim, and asking him to give you strength and wisdom."

He could not move his hand from his face—the touch, even of his own hand on his brow, was a kind of comfort. "I'm angry," he said at last, "and sad, yes—that my father may have shown love and even tenderness to someone else." His mother had longed for it, needed it, deserved it.

"He loved your mother."

"How can you say that?" he snapped.

"I only know what Mama told me." Henry's voice was calm. "He loved your mother very much. He was proud of her, too, but he was afraid of her strong faith. He could never understand it; he could only see that it made her more whole than he felt he could ever be."

"She also had the money in the family," he told Henry. "God help us." He saw his mother and father standing among the hostas, and the open, surrendered look on his father's face. For a time, if only when the shutter exposed them in that fleeting and vulnerable moment, they had been happy.

He looked beyond the shade of the tree to the sun-bleached garden. "Did you ever see him?"

"I never did. When Mama left your family, she went down to Batesville to stay with people she'd known in camp. She met Packard Winchester there. Thank God for him; he was a wonderful father to me, the best of the best. We called him Papa. Mama probably told you he was principal of an academy for black children. After teaching and administrating all day, he made house calls to parents, helping them learn to read and write. Then he'd come home to Mama and Sister and me, and help us with our homework—we all had homework from Papa.

"He taught me a good bit of Latin. Of course, I've forgotten a good bit more."

"They probably don't use much Latin on the choo-choo," he said.

Henry chuckled. "Not much, that's right. Papa was careful to have me read the poets, too, including the black poets, though their work wasn't easy to come by then. But no matter how hard Sister and I labored at our studies, he called Mama his favorite pupil.

"All this time, Mama was out working, doing whatever she could find, and saving to put me through college. Sister never wanted to go to college; she said they'd have to catch her first.

"When Papa died twenty years ago, we moved here; it was an old property of the Winchester family that needed a lot of work. Sister's husband had left a long time back, so she came with us and made a new life down the road there."

"When did you know about your biological father?"

"I was pretty young, maybe ten or twelve. Papa thought I should know the truth. He believed in the truth."

"Did you ever want to find him?"

"Not really," said Henry. "It would have embarrassed him and hurt me, so I never could see the use of it. May I ask how it was with the two of you?"

"His pain was agony to me. More than anything, I wanted him

to know the love of Christ, to know it deeply and truly. It would have transformed him. But as far as I'm aware, he died without that assurance.

"I spent a long time at his bedside at the hospital, desperately hoping to persuade him of God's love. I left to drive back to seminary, and he died only an hour or two later. I won't know until heaven what the Holy Spirit did with any of that.

"Even knowing what an ungodly act it is to carry guilt, I've nonetheless carried a lot of it over the years. A good deal of it was because I tried to persuade my father before I was persuaded myself.

"It was years later before I surrendered my life to Christ. In the meantime, I had the words right, the outward behavior right, but my soul was lost. That simple."

Henry nodded.

"Down deep, I think I loved him very much. But I spent a lot of time hating him, too. I'd like to be able to say that in a different way, maybe just say that I feared him, which I did. But in the end, the truth is that I often hated him. When I was young, I found something written by a seventeenth-century clergyman. 'To be proud and inaccessible is to be timid and weak.' It was the first description, outside my own, that I had of my father. It was a confirmation of sorts; I clung to that for a number of years as a pointed insight to his character.

"I never knew where to step with him. It seemed he despised me, and I could never understand the reason. I don't think I'll ever understand it."

"Not everything can be understood or resolved," said Henry. "But it all has to be faced, I think."

"Maybe because my grandmother died when he was born, he never learned to love, never had a model for it. And my Grandfather Kavanagh was certainly not one to teach love or charity. As a believer, I still castigate myself for being unable to love my father unconditionally, with no looking back. It's the looking back that causes me to stumble.

"Coming out to Holly Springs has done what talking about Sam does for your mother—it makes it all fresh again."

"I also fought to love him," said Henry. "Just in a different way and for different reasons.

"After I learned the truth, I used to crawl up under the house to think about him, it was a very private, very fragile thing. I thought that if I hid somewhere, I had a better chance of finding him. I'd write his name on my school tablet, and try to draw his face from the descriptions Mama gave me. I'd take the drawings in the house and ask her, Is this him?

"Mama would say make th' nose a little longer or th' forehead a little higher, something like that, and I'd go at it again. It was mighty hard to try and spin the face of my father out of thin air.

"I remember sounding out his name, Mis-ter Matth-ew Kav-a-nagh, and sometimes, with great fear and trembling, I would whisper, Daddy. It was strange, and even scary, to think that a little black boy in the red dirt under an old house in Mississippi could call a prominent white man Daddy.

"The truth is always hard, but I'm glad Papa told me. Someone said, Out of every fresh cut springs new growth. It's helped me in a lot of ways to know the truth."

"I'd like you to know," he told Henry, "that I've forgiven him. Again and again. Once done, of course, back comes the Enemy to persecute and prosecute, and I must ante up to God and forgive yet again."

"There may be circumstances in this life," said Henry, "that God uses to keep bringing us back to him, looking for his grace."

"Yes." They were quiet for a while; bees browsed in the hot perfume of honeysuckle. "You never married?"

"I planned to. I was forty, an old bachelor. I met Eva on the train. She was wearing a black hat with a red rose. I thought she was the prettiest lady I'd ever seen. As I said coming out in the car, lives can be changed on a train."

"What happened?"

"Cancer. I wanted to marry her before she died, but she wouldn't allow it. She wanted me to go on, and find someone else. She was a wonderful woman. There won't be anyone else."

"I'm sorry," he said.

"And you?"

"Married when I was sixty-two. Adopted our son, Dooley, just a few months ago. If it weren't for Dooley, maybe I couldn't understand how your mother is going about this, and how urgently she wants your life to be spared. I would do the same for Dooley, of course. That's just the way it is. I have no idea where this will lead, but I admire Peggy for her courage and faith."

"Thank you for saying it."

He glanced at Henry, then turned on the bench and gazed full into his face. "I'm looking for my father," he explained.

"Yes." Henry looked back at him. "Me, too."

"You're tall like he was. And there's something about your eyes."

"Mama says he was a handsome man."

"Very. Your mother says you write poetry."

"I do. Packard taught us a lot through poetry. He liked Paul Laurence Dunbar, said to be America's first premier black poet, who wrote: 'Like sentinels, the pines stand in the park; And hither hastening, like rakes that roam, With lamps to light their wayward footsteps home, The fireflies come stagg'ring down the dark.' "

" 'Stagg'ring down the dark,' " he said. "I like it."

"I got a nickel for learning that; it was the first money I ever earned. Mama said you liked poetry as a boy."

"All my life, really. I'd like to read something you've written, take something with me, if that would be, I don't know, appropriate. I've never had a half brother before, so I hardly know what to do or say."

Henry's laughter was gentle, easy. "We're in that boat together, all right. There's a poem I'll send with you, but let me confess I'm not much of a poet in the long run, I just take down what comes."

"That will work," he said.

"I wrote it while Mama was praying, asking God what he wanted her to do about contacting you. I'd never written about my mother before. I'd always written about trains and how it feels to move through the night past towns and people and lives we can never know.

"Mama was sitting with her back to the window that looks out to the garden. She had her Bible open on her lap, but she was reciting the words from memory, as she often does. I happened to look up from my book and saw something so remarkable that the breath went out of me like a shot.

"I saw my mother's soul.

"I can't explain it. I thought that writing the poem would capture it, but nothing came of the struggle to say what really happened or what it did to the air in the room.

"As I said, I'm not much of a poet. What went on in that moment escaped me, though I tried hard to catch it."

"Poem or sermon," he said, "all one can ever really do is try and catch it."

They stood up from the bench. "She should be rested a little by now," said Henry. "Then I'll drive you back whenever you say."

Peggy's question burned in him as they went across the side yard and up the steps.

"Did you ever see the top of Mama's head?" Henry asked.

"Never. She would never take that blasted head rag off. I always wanted to see what was under there."

"I'll ask her to show you before you leave. As a man of God, or even as someone who cared about my mother all those years ago, you should see it."

They talked for a few minutes on the stoop. When they stepped inside, Henry went to his room and he found Peggy sitting in her chair.

"I could have slept 'til Judgment Day," she said. "But I aks Jesus to wake me up in fifteen minutes, an' he hit it right on th' dot. He's my alarm clock."

"I've used that alarm clock myself, more than once," he said, sitting on the footstool. "Peggy, I'm willing to talk to Henry's doctor."

She gazed at him for a moment as if in disbelief, then put her hand over her heart. "Thank you, Jesus," she whispered. "Thank you, Timothy." Tears pooled in her eyes.

"Henry's calling his doctor now, to work out an appointment for me. I need to leave Holly Springs day after tomorrow; I'll head up to Memphis and try to see him on the way home."

"Did Henry tell you what his doctor said today?"

"He didn't mention it."

"He says we have to hurry, Timothy, we have to hurry."

He took her hand and held it. "Please understand that I can't promise anything, Peggy."

"Yes. I know."

"You can trust me to do as God asks. Right now I'm too muddled even to hear his voice. Do you understand?"

"I do, I surely do."

"Remember when I used to ask you to take your head rag off?"

Her sudden smile was balm to him. "You was th' aggravatin'est little weasel," she said.

"I'm going to aggravate you some more. Would you let me see what's under there? Must be a pot of gold. Maybe the Holy Grail we've all been scrambling around to find."

She reached up at once and slid the scarf off and bowed her head to him.

Two long, ropy scars intersected at the top of her head to form a perfect cross.

"Dear God," he said, stunned.

"This longest one"—she ran her forefinger over it—"is where th' woods rider got me for bringin' Daddy a cup of water. An' this one's where th' Devil himself got me th' time you saved my life.

"But it's all in th' past," she said, consoling him. "All in th' past. It's been a reminder all these years of th' one who suffered for me."

He stood and leaned over and kissed the cross on top of her head. Then he placed his hand upon it and prayed for her, wordless.

When he sat again, she slipped the red scarf into place and adjusted the knot in the back. Her eyes were radiant. "All th' hurt an' all th' sorrow—even losin' Jack an' Sam—it's all covered by th' blood of Jesus."

EIGHTEEN

Butter.

He was halfway to Whitefield when he remembered.

He pulled off the road, turned around, and drove back to town, realizing he couldn't go to Whitefield, not yet.

At the convenience store, he bought bottled water and a pound of butter, and asked for a bag of ice. He dumped the butter into the bag and secured it with a twist tie. Then he drove west as if running late for an appointment.

Twelve miles out, he turned off the highway to the state road and followed it for two miles. Then he turned down a narrow road, now graveled, to the entrance of Indian Camp.

The cattle gate was closed. Only twenty minutes from the square, he had gone back in time fifty years. He got out of the car and walked along a rutted track to the gate and looked in.

The house was still there.

The top portion of the brick chimney lay scattered in the weeds, and the roof had caved in. Windowpanes were broken or missing. Porch timbers had sagged toward the middle and collapsed.

As wired as if he'd downed a blast of espresso, he unwound the

rusted chain, swung one gate open, then shut it behind him and re-
wound the chain.

People were shot for less than this.

His eyes searched the ground for fresh manure. Unbelievable
how some things never change. Right over there. And there and
there. Just like when he was a kid.

Where there were cows, there was very likely a bull. He'd had a
mild confrontation a few years back when he and Cynthia hied to
the country for a picnic. While lolling about on a quilt, he'd spied a
bull and urged her to run for cover, which she did. Looking the bull
in the eye and with no cape to unfurl, he had stood his ground until
she climbed over the fence. The bull had turned and lumbered off
down the hill, which he had found both a vast relief and an insult.

He looked across to the trees, where the Chickasaw princess had
convened her annual summer camp. He thought for a moment he
heard the drums, but it was the beating of his heart.

"Grandpa," he whispered. "I'm back."

He gazed toward the big meadow, where he'd run after Grandpa
told him the story of the cattle auction, and realized that, in his
mind, he was running, now, flat out across the broad avenue of fes-
cue cropped short by cattle. Yes.

He turned and sprinted back to the gate and opened it and went
to the car and unlocked the trunk and raised the lid and peeled off
his clothes. He laid his pants on the trunk floor as carefully as he
could, and followed with his jacket and shirt; he would need this
outfit for Memphis. Then he foraged for the running clothes he always kept in the car, and put on the pants and drew the string, and
pulled the top over his head and, standing on one foot and then the
other, shucked off his loafers, put on the socks, and stuck his feet in
the frayed running shoes. He tossed the loafers in the trunk and
shut the lid.

Closing the gate behind him, he broke into an easy lope—not

thinking, just moving. He didn't want to stop and stretch, he would
let his gait be the warm-up. Though he had jogged and run for years
since the diabetes diagnosis, he hadn't moved his limbs in weeks; he
was stiff as a cadaver.

He took it easy through the wide, rough yard and past the old
cornfield. Then he picked up speed as the ground leveled out to the
meadow and he was onto the plain of stubble and weeds and cow
pads and bugs simmering in the July inferno of northern Mississippi.

The sweat was already pouring.

He'd been a distance runner at Holly High, practicing five days a
week after school, and driving the eight-mile round-trip in his 1948
Chevy pickup. He'd been pretty fast in high school, but the real
thing broke through at Sewanee. Given a great coach and a great
team, his one-, two-, and three-mile runs all improved, but the two-
mile had been his best. He'd concentrated on it—literally eating,
sleeping, and dreaming it—and usually brought it off well under ten
minutes.

College was when he began running for his father. One afternoon on the track, the idea slid into his consciousness like the
moon appearing from behind a cloud: He would run as Matthew
Kavanagh might have run if he weren't handicapped—and he
would win.

The faster he ran, the more he'd been able to love his father
without the stain of pity, anger, or remorse. There were times when
his heart nearly burst with a fierce love that compelled him, drove
him, to be first at the finish line. On these runs which left him exhausted physically, but high as a kite emotionally, he called his father 'Dad.' Dad, Dad, Dad, Dad, Dad, he thought, in rhythm with
the pounding of his feet on the track. Allowing himself to think
this common appellation made him uneasy at first. As it grew more
familiar, it also became another way of loving the man who demanded to be called 'Father.' Indeed, it became a term of endear-

ment and even intimacy. By the end of his sophomore year, he was winning big time for his dad.

It was rough going across the fields of Indian Camp; he was drenched. He reached in his pocket and pulled out his sweatband and put it on as he spied the cow track to the spring.

His heart hammered as he switched to the smooth-worn track and picked up speed down the slope toward the spring.

There was a sense in which he was glad his father may have had a heart and soul, that his life had been more than bitterness and personal defeat. But it was also inconvenient to have his opinions altered—Emerson had remarked on that. Now he was charged to see his father as more than one-dimensional, perhaps even the man of feeling he'd proved to be the night they walked around the barn together. It was Christmas Eve . . .

He was scared to do it alone. Tommy thought he was nuts; no way was he slipping out of his house on Christmas Eve, he said, and stumbling around in the dark wearing a sheet.

But it was important to do this; he wanted to know how it felt to journey through the night, across the fields toward that bright star, to be one of the very first in the whole world to honor the Babe. When Matthew Kavanagh found his son sitting on the porch, tremulous and shivering in his shepherd getup, he hadn't offered to make the journey with him, but had looked at him curiously and gone in the house.

Somehow, he summoned the courage to do it alone, even knowing that cows were supposed to talk on Christmas Eve. The big drawback to this scheme was, if he heard their two old cows talking in the barn, he would die.

He reached the barn and touched its silvery, unpainted wood. More stars had come out, and he chose an especially big one to follow. Then he heard footsteps.

He whirled around, his heart racing, and in the twilight saw the figure of his father.

His father walked with him, then, neither of them speaking. When he stumbled over a castaway bucket and instinctively flung out his hand, his father caught it in his own and held it tight, and in the cold and velveteen darkness they continued around the silent barn, toward the house in which every window gleamed with light . . .

The track was hammered smooth as iron, though muddy in places from the late rain. He leaped the puddles and kept moving, his breath short but regular.

The peace was beginning to flow in, if only a little.

Thank you, Lord, for this inkling of what I hoped you'd give me. It's a mere drop, but as you showed Blake, there's an ocean in the drop, and I take it as your assurance.

Forgive my hard heart toward my dad. Forgive me for convicting him when he was innocent. And please help me love him not less, but all the more in everything I've learned this day.

I've got a lot to download on your mercy and grace. I've always rushed up to you and dumped whatever it was and hurried away, fascinated by my own busyness. I want to turn all this over to you slowly, carefully, examining every fragment as I pass it off, so there'll never be any question about it again. Every time I've dumped and run, I've nearly always run back and snatched it out of your hands. Help me in this. And please, Lord, supply wisdom and grace to Henry and Peggy, and to Cynthia and me in any uncertainty that lies ahead.

Right now, I'm absolutely certain of only one thing—that you love us, and that's where we all have to begin.

He saw Henry sitting exhausted behind the steering wheel as they said goodbye at Frank's place. 'You shouldn't have driven me,' he told Henry. 'It's all right,' said Henry. 'I wanted us to have time together.'

When he, Timothy, was sixty years old, no dog the size of a sofa had yet come into his life, no thrown-away boy with a galaxy of freckles, no good-looking next-door neighbor with legs that set the Main Street Grill on its head. He had been an old bachelor mired in his books, his armchair, and the fray of his parish. And look what had happened—his whole life had been changed forever.

There was no way in which he deserved to become the husband, indeed the soul mate, of a remarkable woman, and yet God Almighty had set her down in the yellow house across the hedge from the rectory, and there it was—a joy to be chosen or refused. He had almost refused.

And Dooley. When Dooley came to live with him, there had been no thought of refusing, though at the time he was completely clueless about the extraordinary rewards that lay ahead.

In like manner, Henry Winchester's best years might lie before him—if he was given the chance to choose.

There were the cows at rest in the deep shade of trees near the water, looking at him, curious.

He stopped in his tracks and crossed himself.

There were twenty or thirty of them, and no bull as far as he could see. Sunlight filtered through the canopy of trees, casting patterns onto the dark sheen of their hides and the surface of the water. He dropped to his haunches and gazed at them. It was among the loveliest sights he'd ever witnessed.

He leadeth me beside the still waters, he restoreth my soul.

For some time he listened to his heavy breathing and the strong, healthy pounding of his heart, then got up and walked back to the old house, mopping his face with the tail of his sweatshirt.

Indian Camp had stayed in the family well over a hundred years. At his grandfather's death, it had passed to his mother, Aunt Lily, and Uncle Clarence. At his mother's death, her share of the sale had come to him—a considerable sum for a young clergyman. He had held on to it as if it were his family personified in assets, and done a little investing with the help of a bishop who had a keen sense of those things.

After moving to Mitford, he'd given most of it to the Children's Hospital in Wesley, and used it freely as his priestly discretionary fund. He had bought the rectory with it, and done his bit to help remodel the yellow house. If anything should be left of it at his death, well, then, his wife didn't need it and neither did Dooley, so he'd leave it to the Children's Hospital, which would help toward adding a room or two, and updating the aging equipment.

He stood awhile, looking at the rotted stump of the tree where the snake once crawled from the attic to bask on a limb; at the porch where they'd sat talking, moon after moon . . .

'Can you see 'em comin', son?'

'Yes, sir!'

'Comin' in that big Buick town car, black as coal an' twice as shiny? Buy a black car, I always say, th' choice of presidents an' statesmen, an' a heap easier to keep clean. That's your daddy drivin' an' your mother, your beautiful mother, she's holdin' little Timmy on her lap. A year old, I'd say, right at a year, an' drivin' up Salem Avenue to Grandma and Grandpa Howard's house where th' little chap was born. Now they're pullin' in th' driveway an' your grandma and me, we're standin' on th' porch wavin' to beat th' band.'

'Granpa?'

'Yes, sir?'

'Are we happy?'

'Oh, yes. Yes, we are. We're all happy . . .'

As he approached the gate, he realized what had really happened since he'd come home to Holly Springs:

His own bear had lumbered up to the wagon.

He closed the gate and secured the chain without looking back at Indian Camp.

"Lord," he said, as he walked to the car, "you got to do this thing, amen."

NINETEEN

H ate to tell you this," said Ray. "Ol' Barnabas rolled in somethin'."

"Where is he?"

"Took hisself off to th' basement like a gentleman. There's
a drain in th' floor down there an' I hooked you up a hose. Smells
like skunk to me." Ray grinned. "Other'n that, he had a real good
time."

After an arduous bout of canine grooming, he took off the running clothes, which had their own wicked odor, and hosed himself
down, as well.

When had he been so exhausted? No wonder people waited
forty years to go home again.

He fed Barnabas, and fell across the bed in his clean shirt and
jeans and slept like the dead until someone knocked on the door.

T looked quizzical. "You okay?"

He hesitated, trying to find the answer, but couldn't.

"Supper's right around th' corner," said T. "Let your belt out,
Ray's puttin' on th' dog."

He had no idea how he could make it through supper. Everything he was feeling was on his face, hanging out there in plain
view, not to mention that he still smelled of skunk.

In the hall bathroom, he scrubbed his hands again and went downstairs. "How'd it go today?" Jovial, upbeat, that was the ticket. He could get through this.

"Basement steps done," said T, "gutterin' around back went up, an' fixed th' porch screen where I busted it out with a ladder."

"Had a good day," said Ray. "Caught enough to freeze some. You hungry?"

"Could gnaw a table leg."

He sensed their questions hanging in the air: *How did your day go? Did you talk to Henry Winchester? What was that all about?*

"I'm really sorry about the skunk odor," he said. "Thanks for your patience with us ol' North Carolina boys. I have a half brother." Belly flop, but he was in the water.

"Oh, yeah?" said T. "You hadn' said anything about a half brother."

"Didn't know about him 'til today." For the first time, he connected the dots. He could have a half brother from his father or his mother. "My dad," he said.

There was a thoughtful silence.

"You ought to have a beer," said T.

"If it was me, I'd have two," said Ray.

Supper passed in the kind of blur some people ascribe to their wedding ceremony. He said nothing more about what he'd learned, and they didn't ask—he concentrated on the meal, which was outstanding. How could he ever repay these good men who'd been sent by the Almighty as surely as manna had been sent for the tribes? Grace can't be repaid, his wife was known to remind him.

He cleaned up the kitchen as Ray left for a trip to the dentist and T walked over to his garage lab with Tater and Tot. Then, mildly sheepish about what he was doing, he went upstairs and collapsed on the bed and slept 'til nine o'clock, waking to the sound of a light rain.

What would they say in Mitford? He saw J. C. Hogan staring at him, mouth open—not a pretty sight. Mule would try to say the right thing, whatever that might be, and end up botching the job. Percy Mosely would think his new hearing aid had gone haywire, and, to put a fine point on it, the news would spread through town like a rogue fire.

Then again, why would anyone need to know?

He woke Barnabas from his sleep of contrition and, in the downstairs hall, snapped on the red leash.

But he'd never had a consuming secret, except for the brief time he'd stayed mum about his engagement to Cynthia. How did one contain so large and important a secret as the existence of a brother, black or white, half or otherwise?

One contained a consuming secret by denying its existence, of course—though as a priest, hadn't he seen enough acts of denial to last him a lifetime?

But all anyone wanted were his stem cells. Nobody had mentioned phoning on Sundays or getting together at family reunions. If he gave Henry what Henry needed, well, then, they were done, it was over—why even imagine what might be thought or said in Mitford, where none of this would ever be known unless he himself made it known?

In the rain, they walked to the edge of the woods, where Barnabas nosed a zoo of scents before giving in to the business at hand. They returned at last to the porch, his wet shirt a second skin.

In the end, what gored him like a knife was the betrayal of his mother. That's really what he'd been trying to get at—the fact of Henry's existence was primarily a shame to Madelaine Kavanagh.

Could he hold that against Henry? No. Could he hold it against Peggy? Yes, he could. But why? Did he want to add that baggage to his life in Christ, however imperfectly he may be living it? No. He did not. Well, then, he could hold it against his father, if he had to hold it against anyone at all; at this point, another stain on the memory of Matthew Kavanagh would hardly matter. But he didn't want that, either. He was seventy years old, and what he really wanted was to let God do the judging from here on. Period.

He sat in a rocking chair, steaming like a clam in his damp clothes.

In a nutshell, Peggy had loved his father; he had a half brother. Why worry about what to do with it? For reasons he couldn't completely understand, God was in this, and God would triumph. Period.

He liked putting periods where periods belonged.

Did he really need to be here through tomorrow night? He'd always thought the three-day rule for fish and guests should be amended to two-day.

He wondered if the Peabody would take dogs; he hadn't checked with the Peabody on his way out here.

He pulled his cell phone from his pocket and went through the rigmarole of being hooked up to the hotel. Dogs were definitely not allowed, and he was definitely not spending another night at the Silver something or other. Scratch Plan B.

So how should tomorrow fall out? Hill Crest, of course, then he'd take the photographs back to Mrs. Lewis. Jim Houck—he'd promised to have coffee with Jim Houck, and he'd want to say goodbye to Amy, and maybe Red. Then there were Rosie and Sylvie; he had to take the picture of Louis and Ol' Damn Mule to Rosie. As for Frank, maybe he'd stop by on the way out of town, plus, he'd just had a great idea.

So, no, he couldn't leave a day early. He rocked a little, realizing the truth: He didn't want to leave a day early.

He also didn't want to call his wife and tell her what was going on, but the cell phone was burning a hole in his pocket. He'd rather wait 'til he talked with the doctor, so he could give her the full story.

But talk with the doctor or no, he had to call his wife, he always called his wife.

Fine, but he wouldn't know what to say unless he spilled everything. It was against the rules to hide their feelings, and hadn't he paid his dues, big time, to work up to that life-changing agreement?

But she would be worried if she knew he might be considering what Peggy wanted him to do.

Then again, he wasn't really considering that, not until he knew more—much more.

Bottom line, he had to call his wife and tell her everything. Besides, she wasn't the worrier in the family—he was.

"Hail to thee, blithe spirit," he said.

"Hello, sweetheart. I was just going to call you."

"Cynthia . . ."

"You're going to tell me something," she said, "but you want me to sit down first. I can hear it in your voice."

She had the most remarkable propensity for this sort of thing.

" 'Are you sitting down?' is what you always asked before you told someone you were going to marry me." She laughed a little.

He could read her, as well—she was mildly uneasy.

"I have a half brother."

She drew in her breath.

"It's Henry Winchester, Peggy Lambert's son."

"Peggy!"

"She's alive and well, I've just spent the afternoon with them."

"Give me time, I'm . . ."

"So am I," he said.

"I mean, I'm just floored. I must say, though, since family is so darned hard to come by, it might be a very good thing."

His wife always won the medal for quick recovery. "I love you," he said.

"I love you back, with all that is in me. What is he like?"

"Tall. Well-spoken. Genuine. Writes poetry."

"Poetry!"

"Gentle. Nice-looking."

"Like you."

"Retired from the railroad; loved a woman named Eva who died of cancer."

"What's on your heart about this, Timothy?"

He told her the ruminating he'd done, the shock he'd felt and was still feeling.

"There's something else," he said. He told her that, too.

She had been holding her breath, and let it out. "I want to be with you when you talk to the doctor."

"And how will you do that, for Pete's sake? You can't drive."

"Not right now. But Dooley can."

It was completely unnecessary for her to come, but he was thrilled.

"Great," he said. "Wonderful. But you don't have to."

"I'll call Dooley as soon as we hang up. We'll be there. Where will we meet you?"

"I'm seeing the doctor Saturday morning at ten o'clock. That means you'll need to leave first thing tomorrow, it's a long drive—nine or ten hours with a break for lunch. Are you sure you want to do this?"

"I'm doing it."

"I'll call and make reservations for you and Dooley at the Peabody for Friday night, late arrival. Wish I could be there to meet you, but the Old Gentleman, you know, isn't allowed. I'll leave here early Saturday morning and see you at the hotel; we'll go to his office together. Thanks be to God you're coming."

"I should have gone with you in the first place."

"None of that guilt stuff," he said. "It's not allowed. What if Dooley can't do it?"

"Can't do it? Of course he can do it. He'll want to do it. And if he doesn't want to do it, I'll make him do it."

"In other words," he said, grinning, "he'll do it."

"I can't wait to see you," she said. There was always a note of music in her voice.

"I'll call him with directions—I think I came the quickest way."

Grace, and grace alone. After their talk, he sat listening to the rain as if newly released from incarceration.

It was convenient in any circumstance to have an opinion, a settled view of things. But he couldn't get at how he felt about what he'd learned today, or how it might change his life. 'The truth must dazzle gradually,' Emily Dickinson had written, 'or every man be blind.'

"Mind a little comp'ny?"

"Hey, T. I'd appreciate your company." He stood up. "Take the rocker."

"We done took it one time. You sit. We were ridin' by when some dude was off-loadin' his truck into th' dumpster. He dropped a sofa, two chairs, a table, this rocker, I don' know what all in there. We loaded up Ray's old truck an' furnished th' garage apartment."

They laughed.

"What goes around comes around," said T.

"There's no way I can ever thank you for your kindness to me. You're the balm in Gilead. What goes around does come around; one day, somehow, I hope to repay you."

"Don't mention it, we like havin' you. Looks like you're goin' through some pretty heavy stuff. To my way of thinkin', it helps to have somebody around when th' cheese gets bindin'. If I was doin' this job out here in th' boonies by myself, they'd have t' commit me."

"Ray's a great guy. You both got bingo. Where are th' boys?"

"Slung up on their bed at th' garage, with their feet in th' air."

Tree frogs. Rain shaking down among the leaves.

"I just had an idea," he said. "I'm a pretty dab hand in the kitchen. Let me cook tomorrow night. Steak—and my wife's scientifically tested oven fries. Got a grill?"

"Got a grill," said T. "Sounds great. Ol' Ray's gon' be over th' moon, he's had to eat his own cookin' for four years. I burn water, you might say."

"How's it going out at the lab?"

"It ain't goin'. See this place here?" T bent his head down and flicked his cigarette lighter. The small flame illumined a hairless spot the size of a jar lid on T's crown.

"I hadn't noticed it."

"I'm taller'n you, that's why. Three years I've messed with th' notion that kudzu could do th' job. I've used every formula in th' book, an' a couple dozen of my own. But it ain't workin'." T took a cigarette from behind his ear and lit it.

"Failure has been called the highway to success. When it starts working, count me your first customer."

"I know good as I'm sittin' here that kudzu is th' next big thing. It's gon' be like gettin' in on th' ground floor of Co-Cola. But personally, I'm about done with it."

"You're giving it up?"

"Tonight I am. Tomorrow might be different." T took a long drag off his cigarette.

"You ever talk to God about what you're trying to do?"

"I guess I believe in God, but can't say prayin' has any attraction—if you don't mind me sayin' so."

"Say on."

"Seems like God makes us, puts us down here, an' we're on our own. Like, Okay, buddy, I give you a brain and two hands, let's see what you can do with that. That's th' way I was raised by my old man, if you could call it raisin'.

"Look here, boy, he'd say, see that junk car I picked up for a hundred bucks? You make it run, now, you hear, but I ain't givin' you no money to do it with. One way or another, I'd get it runnin', he'd jump in it an' leave, come back a couple of weeks later, walkin', with some crazy woman hangin' on his arm.

"He was bad to drink, bad to fight, an' hell to live with. But no use goin' on about it.

"I finally got some sense an' left home at sixteen, in behind my brother who's two years older. He was a whole lot smarter than me, he's th' lawyer in Memphis who owns this place. Anyway, I hoboed out West an' got a job with a rodeo. Near about killed myself right out of th' box."

T laughed a little.

"Some sonofagun cowboy said he'd give me ten bucks to ride this ol' bull named Red. Said he was th' rodeo pet, gentle as a lamb."

"Uh-oh," he said.

"Ol' Red, he rode me around th' ring one time, then a second time, t' kind of show me off. Then he lit into savin' that cowboy ten bucks. Torpedoed me into th' stands an' busted my head wide open. It was a crowd-pleaser."

"Your father—is he still living?"

"If he is, he's in a ditch somewhere."

"Your mother?"

"Took off when I was ten. How 'bout your old man?"

"Deceased. He was a hard man, a broken man."

"Broke breeds broke," said T. "Try sayin' that after a couple shooters of Jack Daniel's."

"Thank God I never messed with alcohol," he said. "Not much, anyway. I got dog-drunk one night before a big track meet at Albany. Woke up in a pool of vomit—couldn't run, could barely walk. I was completely dysfunctional and completely humiliated. Truth is, I didn't have all the fun some people claim to have, or if I did, I couldn't remember it. Sick an' sorry, that was me. Right then, I knew one thing for sure. Alcohol wouldn't be my downfall. There might be a downfall in the cards, but it wouldn't be booze."

"I broke myself of booze."

He whistled. "Tough to get sober without help."

"Tough to get sober with help," said T. "Prob'ly ought to quit smokin', too, like Ray did a while back. Man. Quit drinkin', quit smokin', quit messin' with women. I might as well lay down an' die. Never expected t' end up some ol' dude out in th' sticks, playin' gin rummy an' watchin' th' History Channel."

T took a drag off the cigarette and exhaled. "So tell me somethin'. Goin' back to bein' broke, how come you ain't broke?"

"I am broke. What I've found in being a priest is that we're all broken. Fallen is perhaps a more scriptural concept, but usually what falls gets broken, so it's all the same.

"The upside is, he promises we'll be made whole in heaven. 'Til then, we keep seeking him, keep trusting him, keep letting him have his way with us. That's our job."

"Yeah, fine, but what's his job?"

"His job is to keep forgiving us and keep loving us. That's why, when he gives us something tough to do, he doesn't turn his back and walk away. He sticks with us, sees us through—but only if we ask him to. If we ask, he supplies everything we need to make our hundred-dollar car go like a scalded dog—to quote a friend of mine."

"I don't know about religion. It don't make sense t' me."

"Too complicated, that's why. I say, forget religion. What it's about, T, is the two of you, you and him. Nothing more, nothing less. A lot of people wonder why they were born. I believe what scripture says, that he made us for his pleasure. You might say he made us because he wants somebody around, somebody like you and somebody like me. Kind of what you said a while ago. Pretty amazing that he would want me around, I can tell you that."

T leaned his head against the back of the chair. "Too much for me, th' whole deal of livin'."

"I'm with you on that. Even with God in the picture, I still go through some hard stuff, and always will. But he's in it with me, which makes all the difference.

"The bottom line is, it's totally, fatally about surrender. That's what it takes—throwing out your agenda and trusting his. I was in my forties before I really got it. I was a priest before I got it."

"So how'd you get it?"

"One night, I came to the end of myself. I hit a wall and I couldn't go over it or under it or around it or through it. Dead end. I'd been reading a good deal, trying to figure it out.

"I thought a lot about something a young French mathematician wrote. He said, 'Let us weigh the gain and the loss, wagering that God is. Consider these alternatives—if you win, you win all. If you lose, you lose nothing. Do not hesitate, then, to wager that he is.'

"I'd been wagering a little here, a little there. That night, I wagered everything. I prayed a prayer that went something like this: Thank you, God, for loving me, and for sending your son to die for my sins. I sincerely repent of my sins and turn my entire life over to you. Amen."

"That's it?"

"That's it."

Barnabas growled as the headlights of a vehicle bounced along the gravel drive toward the house.

"Here comes ol' Ray with a head full of teeth. Wait'll you see these choppers, they'll scare you to death."

He smiled, oddly content. Considering tomorrow night's menu, Ray's timing was about as good as it could get.

TWENTY

She was waiting for him; he saw the curtains move.

Abandon hope, all ye who enter here. There would be no depositing of his delivery and running like a hare; no, indeed, this was life in the raw.

He checked his watch. Eight o'clock. He had five minutes, max, to endure fire from the Lewis cannons.

Fortunately, he'd met the florist having coffee on the square and she offered to open her shop. Bearing a dozen coral gladioli in one hand and the prints in the other, he rang the bell as directed.

Garbed in her wrapper and gown, Luola Dabney Randolph Lewis charged out the door on her cane, bearing a paper cone of coffee grounds. "I didn' sleep a wink last night, not one wink, so excuse my looks," she shouted. "Did you wash your hands first?"

"Yes, ma'am, I did."

"Do y'all use coffee grounds on your potted plants?"

"No, ma'am. But I hear it can produce a mass of blooms."

"A mess of *brooms*?"

"A mass of blooms!"

"Maxwell House," she said, dumping the contents of the cone into an urn filled with unidentifiable nursery stock. "French roast. I'll have begonias big as dinner plates. I don't like coffee anymore, th' medication makes my mouth taste like Reynolds Wrap; but I perk it anyhow, for the plants, then drink th' whole pot to keep from wastin' it. Waste not, want not, idn't that how Madelaine raised you?"

"Yes, ma'am." He proffered the flowers. "I brought you these as a token of my thanks."

She cupped a hand to her ear and shouted, "As a *what*?"

"As a *token of my thanks*!"

She stared at them as if they had wronged her.

"Glads," she muttered, snatching them from his hand. "I'll stick 'em in a jar in th' kitchen, comp'ny never goes back there. Do you think we can get a nice exhibit out of those eight-by-tens?"

"Absolutely. They're wonderful. I greatly appreciate seeing them. Thank you."

"I ought to give you one," she said, looking at him as if searching for a reason to do it.

"I wouldn't want to take—"

"Go on an' pick one. But I'll have to approve which one." She wagged the glads at a decrepit rocker. "Sit down right there, but watch it, it tips back if you're not careful. It threw a Baptist preacher on th' floor, he was fillin' in from Charleston."

He withdrew the prints from the envelope and paged through while she stood over him, breathing heavily. He knew exactly which one he wanted.

"There!" she shouted. "That one. That's th' one I might give you."

The statue in the pond grasses.

"That statue was never anything but trouble. When we did th' big garden in th' park, we had to plant a bush in front of it to keep th' town council happy."

"Aha."

"It wadn't our fault th' bush died in a hard freeze an' exposed th' whole business to th' good Lord an' everybody. It's stored in Sue Riley's basement. Do you want it back? I'm sure you could get it back, since it was you who gave it. It's a shame not to use it."

"No, thank you, I must get moving. I leave early tomorrow."

"Except for th' goat, I think it's a copy of David's Michelangelo. It's th' way God *made* th' opposite sex, for pity's sake. As far as I know, nobody in *Paris* ever planted a bush in front of th' real thing."

He laid the prints on the table and bolted from the rocker.

"Where's your dog?"

"In the car."

"Don't let 'im in my yard," she said.

"No, ma'am."

He was heading for the steps.

"They say dogs in New York do whatever they want to in people's yards and you have to scoop it up and carry it home in a ziplock bag."

"That's what they say. Well, goodbye, Mrs. Lewis, and—"

"Hold on!" she said, waving the photos at him. "You didn't pick one."

He wheeled around and took the prints and searched through quickly. "This one," he said. Please.

She squinted at it, then smoked him over, dubious. "Will you take care of it? You won't put it in a drawer, will you? Some people toss pictures in a drawer every whichaway, you ought to *see* some people's picture drawers."

"I'll take care of it. I promise."

"Well, go on an' take it, then, an' think of me when you look at it. I always believed your daddy was innocent."

"Thank you! Thank you very much, Mrs. Lewis, and God bless you. I'll never put it in a drawer, we have just the frame for it. Sterling. Hallmarked!" He was inspired to kiss her hand, but restrained himself. Too European for Holly Springs, much less clergy.

"Come back when you can stay longer!" she shouted.

He disappeared into the boxwood and raced to the car, slightly breathless.

Four minutes.

At Hill Crest, he roared through the entrance and up the hill as if pursued. He had rounds to make.

He parked beneath a sycamore at the edge of the lane and cranked the front windows down so his dog could get a breeze. Then he went around to the trunk and took out the bucket of tools which also contained a dozen roses, and headed for the blackjack oak.

Rain sparkled among the leaves and spangled the broad cushion of grass.

He had read in Second Timothy this morning, believing, as he had since a boy, that St. Paul had somehow directed the letter to him as well as to the earlier Timothy.

To Timothy, my dearly beloved son: Grace, mercy, and peace, from God the Father and Christ Jesus our Lord.

After years of delving the contents, he knew the epistle by heart.

For God hath not given us the spirit of fear; but of power, and of love, and of a sound mind.

He realized that each time he went to the letters, he possessed some looming apprehension of one sort or another to which this verse inevitably pointed.

There was no doubt in his heart or mind; it was very clear that he wanted to help Henry. But the thought of risking anything at all was tough to swallow.

He had stood at the window in his old room this morning and asked for the grace to let his fear go.

He checked his watch, wondering where Cynthia and Dooley might be—probably gaining on Johnson City, maybe even bound for Knoxville.

The roses had gone wild, waving their canes in the air like a choir of Pentecostals. He wouldn't do anything serious, it was the wrong season. "Just a little off the sides," he said, pulling on his pruning gloves.

He would begin at the left-hand corner of the fence, working his way to his mother's grave and then to his father's urn. He would pay his respects at last.

"Yoo-hoo!"

Jessica Raney loped toward him in a straw hat, waving a manila envelope.

"Look what I found!" She was slightly out of breath, and beaming. "I guess you think I live here."

He laughed. "Not yet, please."

"I was hopin' I'd find you, I was just thrilled when I saw your car parked out there. Abracadabra!" She pulled a photograph from the envelope and handed it to him.

His father. Standing in the foreground, talking to someone off-camera, and laughing. Behind him, and slightly out of focus, Peggy set a bowl on the picnic table as a woman with her back to the camera stood talking to someone wearing an apron.

"See how your daddy's hair photographed? Real silvery, almost like a platinum print. I thought th' way he was more dressed up than everybody made a nice contrast, an' look at th' composition of th' people behind him, I think that worked sort of well. That's your Peggy who ran away. That's Miz Floyd in th' apron, her husband worked in our dairy. An' I don't know who that is with her back to the camera."

"My mother." He remembered the dress. Light blue, with a pattern of pink hibiscus flowers, from Kennington's.

"Double bingo!" she said, elated. "It's all yours! An' guess what."

"I give up."

"Did anybody ever tell y'all your daddy's last words?"

He felt the beating of his heart. His mother had never made any reference to last words.

"Remember I was at th' hospital that day, an' th' nurse I went to take something to was your daddy's nurse. I called her last night to say you were in Holly Springs, and she remembered what your daddy said before he died. She said you left to go back to school, and a little bit later she went in to make him comfortable. She said your daddy stared at her a long time and then he said . . ."

A light perspiration broke onto his forehead. If he ever got out of Holly Springs alive and in his right mind, it would be a miracle.

". . . then he said, He was right. He was right."

He looked at the pruning gloves, at the wear on the fingertips, at the way the end of the right glove thumb allowed his own to poke through.

"I thought you should know that," she said, "in case nobody ever told you. People say stuff all th' time before they die, and a whole lot of it never gets back to th' family. When my grandmother died, th' last thing she said was, They're callin' my number, it's number eighty-six."

Tears streamed along her cheeks. "I loved my grandmother to pieces, she was so sweet and kind. I wasn't with her at the end. I was goin' th' next day, but she passed in th' night, th' nurse was holdin' her hand. She's buried over by th' dogwoods across th' lane."

He removed a glove and wiped his eyes with the heel of his hand. Would this never end?

He embraced her and patted her back, which somehow relieved the wrench in him, and stood away from her and saw the girl whose family owned the dairy with the silos visible from his back yard, the girl who sent him a card when his rabbits died.

"You're terrific," he said. "You're terrific."

"I brought th' picture in case you were here. I think God wanted you to be here."

"Absolutely. No doubt."

"I've got to run, my Nellie's in th' car. We're drivin' to Oxford to see my aunt today, she's th' last of my mother's side."

He had nothing to give her, no way to return the grace she had extended to him. "May I pray for you?" he asked.

"I would be honored," she said.

He took her hands in his and asked God to continue his watch over her, and to bless her for blessing her childhood friend and neighbor, and gave thanks for the gift of their old friendship and her generosity, and the long life of her aunt, and she kissed him on the cheek and walked toward the lane where her car was parked, and turned around and waved and called out, "I think I still have a crush on you!," and he lifted his hand and waved back, and she was gone.

TWENTY-ONE

Flags.

Bunting.

Traffic.

The town looked like a postcard that Tyson's could sell by the gross.

"Happy Fourth of July," he said to Amy. "Shouldn't you be getting ready for a barbecue somewhere?"

"I always work on the Fourth," she said, obviously proud of it. "But only 'til eleven."

"I'll take three postcards with the cotton wagons, three with the gazebos, and what else do you have of the courthouse?"

"We have a Fourth of July card, but they were fixin' the clock that year, and the hands are missin'."

"C'est la vie. I'll take a couple. Any handkerchiefs?"

"No handkerchiefs in ages. How about a little pack of Kleenex to stick in your pocket?"

He was through bawling—absolutely, completely done—but it might be handy for the glove compartment. "Barnabas and I are leaving in the morning; we wanted to say goodbye."

"I'll miss y'all." She came around the counter to scratch his dog behind the ears.

"We'll miss you, Amy. Thanks to you, I met Mrs. Lewis. When I stopped by this morning, she gave me a photograph of my parents."

"She *did*?"

"It's a great treasure. A wonderful gift."

"That is so nice of her. I know she has this really dark side, but she has a really bright side, too."

"Like the moon. And don't we all?"

"Did she sleep last night?"

"Not a wink, she said."

"Did she have any breakfast?"

"I don't know. Probably. She was putting coffee grounds on her begonias."

"That's great!" she said, clearly hopeful. "Will you ever come back?"

"Definitely. And I'll bring family next time. Thanks for your kindness; it means a lot. You've been one of the highlights of this trip."

She blushed. "What about your paper? Don't you need a paper this mornin'?"

"Believe I'll pass." He would see his family in the morning, and because of that, he didn't feel the need of anything, really. A small joy was stirring in him.

"I'll drop you a card," he said. "What would you like it on—the cotton wagons, the gazebos, or the Fourth of July number?"

"Oh, my gosh," she said. "How about all three? Kind of spaced out, over a period of time. I love to get mail."

"Consider it done. How about writing back with all the scandal?"

"Oh," she said, laughing, "we never have any of that in Holly Springs."

At Booker's, he found Red doing a window display—galvanized watering cans, galvanized tubs, galvanized troughs, galvanized buckets.

"My galvanized window," said Red.

"We're leaving early tomorrow, it was a pleasure to be at Booker's again. I smoked my first cigarette, earned my first wages, heard my first off-color joke right here."

"Ought t' put up a memorial plaque over th' seed bins. Speakin' of jokes, I got a priest joke for you if you wouldn't take it wrong. I only tell clean, but I can't say th' same for some of th' roughnecks we get in here."

"Fire away."

"This Irish priest is drivin' through Miss'ippi and gets stopped around Holly Springs for speedin'. Th' state trooper smells alcohol on his breath an' sees an empty wine bottle on th' floor of th' car.

"Trooper says, 'Sir, you been drinkin'?'

"Priest says, 'Just water.'

"Trooper says, 'How come I smell wine?'

"Priest looks down at th' bottle, says, 'I can't believe it. He's done it again!' "

He laughed.

"Hope that wadn't too sacrilegious."

"Actually, there's a very good sermon in that joke. I'll make a note."

"You ought t' come on home, it's th' goin' thing t' get back t' your roots. My wife's after me to sell th' business an' move to Kentucky, but I'm stayin' put. I wadn't more than six months old when my family pulled out of Louisville—no roots in that."

"I've had a good go at my roots this trip," he said. "The kind of hospitality I grew up with is still alive and kicking, that's for sure."

"You find anybody you were lookin' for?"

"I did. And some I wasn't looking for."

Red let Barnabas sniff the back of his hand. "My groundhoggers were askin' about you."

"Give those guys my best."

"Said they have somethin' for you. When you pullin' out?"

"In the morning. Seven o'clock sharp."

"I'll be in th' stockroom. Knock on th' back door; it'll be here."

"I don't suppose I could guess what it is?" Scary.

"Don't have a clue. But they been workin' on it a good bit."

What could he say? "I'll swing by."

He was headed for the door when he saw Will and threw up his hand.

"How those taps doin'?"

"You're talking to Fred Astaire. Take it easy, Will, I'll see you next trip."

He walked to Christ Church and followed the signs to the office, but couldn't locate anyone. Blast. July Fourth. He kept forgetting. Hanging on the knob of what he presumed to be the rector's office door, he found a needlepointed message:

SCOTLAND OR BUST

A vacuum cleaner roared somewhere in the building. He tore a scrap of paper from the notepad on the desk outside the office, wrote a signed promissory note, and placed it under a paperweight. That would keep him honest; he'd put a check in the mail as soon as he got home.

He went around to the Baptists, found the office, and pulled out his wallet.

"I'd like to make a gift in my grandfather's name," he told the church secretary, who was his age and then some.

"I'm not supposed to be here," she said.

"Where are you supposed to be?"

"Churnin' ice cream. I just came in to make copies of 'America the Beautiful,' we're havin' a sing-along before th' fireworks tonight."

"Will you take a credit card?"

She held out her hand, grinning. "Baptists take money in any form, and aren't ashamed to ask for it, either."

"That's the spirit," he said, giving her the card. "I'm making a gift in memory of my grandfather, who preached here for many years."

"Who was your grandfather?"

"Yancey Howard."

"Yancey Howard? Great day!"

"You knew him?"

"He baptized me in the creek at Walnut Grove, along with all my brothers and sisters. We loved him to death."

"My guess is, he loved you back."

"How much do you want to give? And how would you like us to designate it?"

He told her the amount and thought for a moment. "Ask your pastor to use it for those who're up against it."

"For . . . those . . . who . . . are . . . up . . . against . . . it," she said, writing it down. "Are you Miz Madelaine's boy?"

Boy. That was worth the ten-hour drive right there. "I am."

"I remember she had our Sunday School class to your house one time on a field trip. Your mother gave the lesson; it was about how God looks on his children as an orchard or a garden—how he has to prune us, sometimes, which really, really hurts, but that's what produces more flowers and more fruit. I never forgot that lesson about pruning."

He signed the card slip. "Did we know each other then?"

"I hate to say this."

"Say it," he said.

"I don't remember you at *all*."

That put a grin on his face all the way to Frank's parking lot.

He pulled out his phone and dialed.

"Hey, Dad."

"Hey, son." Maybe not his flesh-and-blood son, but his gut-and-heart-and-spleen son. "Where are you?"

"I-40 west out of Knoxville."

"You're making good time."

"Great time."

"Don't be usin' your lead foot on this trip."

"No way."

"Call me when you stop." He wasn't a fan of jabbering on a phone to someone who was driving.

"Yes, sir."

"Love you both," he said.

What had he heard in Dooley's voice? Relief? A good night's sleep? Whatever it was, he liked the sound of it.

He was right. He was right.

Did that mean what he wanted it to mean?

Did it mean he'd been given the grace to speak of God's love in a way his father could hear and believe? How could those particular words have meant anything else?

His father's soul delivered unto God. He mused on this miraculous possibility. Then again, how could he ever know the true meaning of that short but emphatic confession? Maybe it meant Timothy was right, maybe it meant Christ was right, or who knows, maybe it meant the doctor was right.

It would be revealed in heaven, of course, but he wanted to know now, wanted to believe his father's spirit was, as George Macdonald said, "in continuous touch with God."

He'd worked for decades to set up certain beliefs and rationales about his early years, shaping and molding the clay, as it were, until its form was, at least, tolerable. Perhaps what he'd heard from Jessica suggested more shaping and molding to be done. He couldn't say; time would tell.

Jim Houck was waiting in the front booth.

"How's it goin'?" asked Jim.

"Great," he said, sliding into the booth. "I'm headed out first thing tomorrow." He filled a mug with coffee from the beat-up carafe. "How about you?"

"Settled another piece of Daddy's dust yesterday."

"Glad to hear it."

"He left a good bit for me to settle if I want to keep livin' here. Seems like once I got over that big hump with you, it's easier goin'. How's comin' back been for you?"

He didn't have a pat answer; not yet, anyway. "To say the least, it's given me a new perspective. I've got a lot of sorting out to do. Think you'll stick here?"

"Have to stick somewhere. My old man left me a tract of land east of town, about twenty-five acres. Might build me a house, maybe set a trailer on it."

"I'd like to keep in touch," he said.

Jim reached in his jacket pocket and drew out a business card. "Call my cell phone anytime."

He looked at the card. "You sell Fords."

"Try to."

"Here's my home number," he said, pushing his own card across the table. "You're more likely to reach me there most days. I want to say again how much I appreciate knowing the truth."

"Felt better after tellin' it. It's been like tryin' to swallow somethin' that won't go down."

"Same here. One stone, two birds. I'll be praying for you, Jim."

"I can use it. Did I mention my old man went by th' hospital t' see your dad?"

"You didn't tell me."

"Couldn't remember if I did. I was pretty torn up, pretty nervous that day in church."

The doctor had felt reasonably positive about his patient's survival, though the recent stroke had been a setback. They might have to take him up to Memphis, but overall, the prospects for a certain level of recovery weren't bad.

Holding his father's hand, he'd delivered a passionate homily which he believed would change Matthew Kavanagh's heart for eternity. Though his father had turned his head away, he gripped his son's hand for a long time. No further words were spoken.

He waited, praying silently, then kissed his father on the forehead and left for Sewanee. He remembered the drive back as an agony of grief and self-doubt, and was devastated when the call came from his mother. Walking into his rented room near the seminary campus, he heard the phone ringing, and knew instinctively who it was, and why.

"They said your dad was in bad shape, so my ol' man went by to say he was sorry. Said it was layin' on him so heavy, he had to do it to get a minute's peace. Didn't want to, but had to. Said he told your daddy he still thought he was a s.o.b. th' way he handled his cotton dealin's, but he was sorry he put him an' his family through th' grinder. My old man was glad he went, said your dad passed that same day."

He was right.

So maybe that meant Martin Houck was right. He sat back in the booth, weary of knowing too much and understanding too little.

Jim set his coffee mug on the table. "I'd like to say it one more time. I'm sorry."

"Thank you. I forgive your father."

They shook hands, holding each other's gaze for a moment. He and Jim had come back seeking the same thing—connections. They had a shared past, and whether or not they ever saw each other again, they were bound together in some fraternal way that was more mysterious, if not deeper, than blood.

He was even further, now, from knowing the meaning of his father's last words. Nor could he really care anymore what Martin Houck had done to the Kavanagh family. It was history. It was all history.

On the way to Rosie's house, he sniffed vagrant smoke rising off grilling barbecue; passed cars and trucks flying the Stars and Stripes.

He knocked on the door, which set Zippy off, big time.

"Get in here," said Rosie, "we been lookin' fo' you. Where's that big dog?"

"In the car."

"Bring 'im on in."

Something was cooking in Sylvie's kitchen; the aroma made his knees weak. He fetched his dog, doing what Peggy had called a "skip dance" in his imagination.

"Butter beans," said Sylvie, "an' wilted lettuce an' onion with a little side meat fried out crisp an' crumbled on top."

"Don't forget th' cornbread you brownin' in th' oven." Rosie was smiling like Louis, proud and easy like Louis.

He sat with them at their kitchen table by a window that looked out to a bank of summer phlox. "Here's what must have happened," he said. "Coming from town, I was hit by a truck an' died and went to heaven." He was starving for butter beans and wilted lettuce and cornbread, starving for something deep and lost and rarely found.

Sylvie smiled a little. "Won't know 'til you taste it whether it's heaven or th' other place."

"I promise I didn't show up at lunchtime on purpose. I'm leaving tomorrow and on the run, and . . ." What could he say?

Rosie laughed. "You gon' have t' eat two helpin's to make up fo' comin' in on us."

It was three o'clock when Rosie and Sylvie walked with him to the car.

"We're still brothers?"

"Still brothers," said Rosie. "Always gon' be."

"I'll call you. I'll keep in touch. That's a promise."

"I'm gon' put Daddy an' Ol' Damn Mule on th' wall next to th' shotgun."

"Perfect," he said. "That reminds me." He took the yo-yo from the glove compartment and handed it to Rosie. "Remember this?"

"Looky here." Rosie was awed, reverent.

"Whip a new string on there and you're back in business."

"Been lost . . ."—Rosie calculated—"goin' on sixty years."

"Bet you can still make it sleep."

"Bet I'm gon' try. You comin' back to ol' Holly Springs?"

"I'm comin' back."

Rosie was suddenly crying. "You ain't got another forty years to stay gone." He embraced Rosie—and Louis and Sally and all the brothers, and all the good of all the past.

"You're always welcome," said Sylvie. "Welcome as th' flowers in May."

His grandmother used to say that.

There was no way he was ripping open the packet of tissues. He drove away, wiping his eyes on the back of his hand.

At the grocery store, he located the meat case and punched the bell.

"Three steaks," he said to the butcher. "Your best."

"That'd be Angus. Filet, T-bone, ribeye, or porterhouse?"

"That's a hard one."

"Grillin' or broilin'?"

"Grilling."

"Porterhouse. How thick?"

"Two inches."

It was payback time at Whitefield.

TWENTY-TWO

"Y ou're hired," said Ray.

T flicked his cigarette into the wheelbarrow. "All you got t' do is cook four nights a week an' put in a rose bed for m' brother's ol' lady. Th' pay ain't much, but you can keep your room."

"Sorry, boys, but I'm under long-term contract."

"Jus' as well," Ray told T. "He said he don't even play gin rummy."

"Jigsaw puzzles are about all the excitement I can stand—but thanks for the offer."

Barnabas snored at his feet; Tater and Tot nosed about the yard.

"Back at th' mansion," said Ray, "they used t' have entertainment after supper."

"We could do our joke," said T.

Ray grinned. "Ain't got but one joke we can tell a preacher." Ray cleared his throat. "An invisible man married an invisible woman."

"Yeah," said T, "an' their kids wadn't much to look at, either."

"T dug that up with th' leg bone of a dinosaur."

"Not bad," he said. Uncle Billy Watson would be turning over in his grave.

"That's our complete entertainment package," said T. "All she wrote. Good supper; we thank you."

"You nailed th' fries, that's f' sho."

"My wife worked on the recipe for months 'til she finally had a breakthrough. What did the trick was soaking the cut fries in cold water, and using a heavy bake sheet."

"Speakin' of breakthrough," said T, "I'm back on my hair cream. I had a killer idea last night. I'm gon' hit it again over th' weekend; it's gon' work."

"Glad to hear it. I'll start thinking about a name, maybe give it some thought on our way up the road."

"Better get over to Graceland while you're in Memphis," said T. "Th' Trophy Room'll bring tears to a glass eye an' I ain't kiddin' you. Awards from all over th' world, anywhere you can think of. Everybody loved Elvis."

"Three things you got to see fo' you pass," said Ray. "Th' Grand Canyon. Niagara Falls. An' Graceland."

"There's a lineup for you," he said.

Ray grinned. "Top three."

He couldn't get used to Ray with teeth.

"It sold a while back," said T. "Fifty-five million smackers. You never know what changes might go down."

He'd never paid much attention to Elvis, but he wouldn't want to say so—not here, anyway.

Ray removed a denture and stared at it. "Seem like he give me somebody else's uppers—this plate crowdin' m' mouth."

"Set 'em up there on th' rail awhile," said T. "Takes you a day or two to get used to havin' teeth again. He dropped his uppers off a twelve-foot ladder onto a concrete slab. Buckshot did somethin' to 'is lowers."

"Eatin' squirrel," said Ray. "I'm layin' off wild game an' stickin' to fish. Fish is good fo' th' brain."

"Don't get too smart on me, you'll be shuckin' this job an' goin' to live in th' islands."

Three men laughing on a porch in Mississippi. He could do worse. There was a lot to be said for sitting out here with the cicadas, talking about dentures, watching fireflies "stagg'ring down the dark." Shootin' the breeze, was what they used to call it.

"I'm flyin' up to roost," said Ray. "My back's botherin' me t'night."

"You gon' miss th' fireworks," said T.

"I'll catch 'em from my front window. Somebody jump in this rockin' chair, this is a good chair."

"Take your teeth. You don't want 'em settin' out here all night."

He would miss these guys. "Thanks for everything, Ray. See you in the morning at checkout time."

In the yard, Ray turned and threw up his hand. "Don't let th' bedbugs bite."

They watched as he vanished along the path, Tater and Tot at his heels.

T lit a cigarette. "Been good havin' you."

"Thanks. It was good being here. Very good."

"You comin' back?"

"I'm coming back."

"If my cream works out, I prob'ly won't be here when you get back. If it don't work out, my brother asked me to stay an' caretake th' place. But I don' know about that."

"Could be a good deal either way," he said.

T smoked. The rocker creaked.

He realized he wanted to talk about the extraordinary thing that had blindsided him. "The little house that fell in—"

A muffled boom, as of cannon, sounded across four flat miles. The western sky was a flame of orange.

"Yeah?"

"I told you about the woman who lived there—she's the mother of my half brother."

Boom. Saffron washed the sky.

"She's still alive. We had a long visit."

"How was it?" asked T.

"Good. His name is Henry Winchester." He was quiet for a time. "I always wanted a brother."

"My brother can be a pain in th' ass, but he's sure saved mine a few times."

"Henry needs a stem cell transplant. From a sibling."

"You bein' th' siblin'?"

"He has a sister, but her health isn't good."

"What about your di'betes?"

"My wife and son drove into Memphis around six this evening. We'll see the doctor tomorrow, try to get a grip on where this thing is going, how the diabetes figures in. Then we'll head home. Depending on the circumstances, I may come back to Memphis for . . . whatever needs to be done."

Cigarette ash burned against the milky twilight. "How you feelin' about th' whole deal?"

"Like I've been hit upside th' head."

"Pissed?"

"Maybe that'll come later. But I don't think so."

"How does knowin' God help you out in a case like this?"

"I believe he has a purpose for everything. I believe he'll bring good out of this, maybe even in a way I won't like very much. It's his call, not mine."

"Seems like any God a'tall would want you down here bustin' a gut, not leavin' it all up to him."

"Seems like. But it doesn't work that way. We've got to let him do the heavy lifting. We've got to grunt, that's for sure, but we've got to let him lift. The challenge is to trust him. Right now, I'm trusting him. Running a little scared, but trusting him."

"How do you take havin' a brother that's half black?"

"He's a good man. I like him. As for introducing him around back home, I'm not there yet."

"Ol' Ray an' me are kind of like brothers. Brothers without th' baggage, you might say."

"He'll die without a transplant." Sapphire and crimson bloomed in the sky above the distant courthouse. "On the other hand, he could die with a transplant."

They didn't talk for what seemed a long time.

He leaned his head against the back of the chair and closed his eyes. He would let this day, and those before it, go for now—he felt as if one shock and stupefaction after another had been wound onto a spool in the region of his heart; he wanted nothing more than to let it all wind off.

He surrendered himself to the loud, symphonic night, to the insistent cry of tree frogs, cicadas, and insects as exotic and unidentifiable as those of a rain forest—the sounds seemed to soak into his pores. How different this Mississippi night was from a mountain night. In the mountains, which he loved, the sounds of evening seemed to arrive from a great distance, razor-sharp and clean. Here, the night sounds were close, complex, many-layered, seductive.

A rivulet of sweat trickled along his spine; the stairs to his room seemed far away and steep, very steep.

"Nothin' to lose?" asked T.

He was startled by the question, then he remembered.

"Nothing," he said.

TWENTY-THREE

A single truth possessed many facets.

He realized that having a brother meant Cynthia had a brother-in-law. It meant Dooley had an uncle. And if he chose to give the name of his closest living relative when asked, it would not be Walter, but Henry. The domino factor would have a good run.

After a quick egg biscuit at Frank's, he knocked on Booker's stockroom door.

"Here you go," said Red, handing off a cooler.

Without lifting the lid, he knew. He was headed to Memphis with a groundhog.

"Cheer up," said Red. "You gon' like it. Have a good trip an' come on back, I'll put you t' work."

Was he going to keep the cooler cool or put the top down like he'd planned?

He put the top down and drove north, taking a shortcut through the country to the highway. He felt like a teenager headed for a heavy date.

"You're everything to me," he said when they talked last night. "Wife, sister, mother, sweetheart, friend." If there was anything more, she was that, too.

He had once called her brave, which puzzled her. "Brave in the face of life," he explained. And plenty brave, into the bargain, to marry Tim Kavanagh.

God had reserved for him a woman marked by suffering—as a child emotionally abandoned by her parents, and later as a woman cast aside by a philandering husband.

Her suffering had led her to a life in Christ, and in that fusion was created everything he'd ever hoped for in a mate—compassion, tenderness, honesty, depth, and nearly always, high good humor. She was the only woman he could have loved, though he never dreamed he might enjoy for his own such a composition of characteristics and a spirit marked by so many influences, including worldly success.

Indeed, he'd had no idea how to manage a woman like Cynthia Coppersmith, and so he stepped back from management, as did she, and somehow they had merged their lives.

He remembered the fight to hold on to his pitiable bachelorhood. Where would he turn, now, if not to her?

Chesterton had been wise to that sort of thing: 'There are no words to express the abyss between isolation and having one ally. It may be conceded to the mathematician that four is twice two. But two is not twice one; two is two thousand times one.'

At the side of the road, he saw a busted-open watermelon sitting on a stump in front of a hand-lettered sign:

FRESH PRODUCE
STOP IN

He slowed down, eyeing the cool flesh of the melon, flesh the color of crepe myrtle blooms. It was calling him, sure enough. He couldn't remember the last time he'd dived into a watermelon.

He passed the sign, drove a few hundred yards up the road, then hung a right into a driveway, turned around, and headed back.

As he pulled onto the gravel in front of the produce stand, a man appeared at the door of a house a few yards away. The screen door slapped behind him.

"Mornin' to you."

"Good morning. My mouth's waterin' for watermelon. That's a tempting promotion on your stump."

"Fresh-picked an' homegrown. We don't sell nothin' ain't grown local."

Cantaloupe. He chose one and sniffed the end born from the vine. It was redolent with the ripe scent of its seeded, peach-colored flesh. He was salivating.

"I'd like a cantaloupe to have tomorrow, and a ripe watermelon to get into tonight." He supposed they'd be driving straight from the meeting with the doctor, since Barnabas would have no place to lay his head in Memphis.

"This 'un right here's yo' watermelon." The man thumped a small, green-striped globe. "Listen at that."

No left thumb.

His mouth was hanging open. He closed it and took a deep breath.

"Would you mind if I guessed how you lost that thumb?"

"You guess how I lost this thumb, that melon don't cost you a red cent. Give you one guess."

"One guess," he said.

"Yessir, one guess." The man looked downright entertained by the prospect. "You get it right, you got you a sweet, ripe melon picked this mornin'."

"Deal." He was trembling a little. "You lost that thumb whacking the head off a chicken."

The man looked astonished. "Thass right. Sho did."

He also looked disappointed that the game was ending so abruptly.

"A cat got your thumb and ran off to the barn with it."

"You got it right ag'in. How you know that?"

"Let's see." He scratched his head. "When you were ten years old, you lived on Gholson Avenue in Holly Springs."

"Sho as you born, I did. How you do that?"

"There was a piano in Miss Lula's parlor."

"This some kind of magic trick?"

"I busted the vase an' you took th' whippin' for it."

"La-a-a-w have mercy. You th' little white boy I minded that time."

"It's me." They both guffawed. He pounded Willie on the back, Willie pounded him on the back.

"How many years?" asked Willie.

"A hundred," he said.

"This beat all."

"I've prayed ever since for the chance to thank you for what you did for me. It must have been a terrible whipping they gave you."

Willie grinned. "No whippin' a'tall. None *a'tall*. Miz Lula, she didn' let nobody whip me. If they was any whippin' t' do, she done it her ownself. My mama, she could put you in th' *bed* from a whippin', so one time Miz Lula said, From now on, I gon' be th' boss of whippin' this chile.

"Nossir, all I done was tell Miz Lula you didn't go t' do it. I said you was a good boy, an' yo' daddy was gon' tear yo' head off, I could see it in 'is face. So th' Lord give me th' notion t' say I done it."

"Thank you, Willie. Thank you." He was jubilant. "Thank you more than I can say. I've never forgotten that time; I was miserable about it. I went back to Miz Lula's after she died, trying to find out what happened to you."

"They sent me up here to my gran'maw, she lived in that ol' house in th' woods over yonder. She lef' me twelve acres of good land. I work a acre or two of melon an' cantaloupe every year, with a few squash an' tomatoes. Where you live at?"

"North Carolina. In the mountains."

"You get back to Holly Springs much?"

"First time in over thirty-eight years."

"How is it bein' back? I was fixin' t' leave a time or two, but never got aroun' to it."

"It's good," he said. "It's good to be back. And now it's even better."

"You ought t' go on an' eat that melon right here. Jus' set down at th' table, I'll cut it fo' you—an' there's th' salt."

"I'll have to go through it pretty quick, I'm meeting a good-lookin' woman in Memphis." He pulled a five from his wallet. "Can't let you give it to me, I cheated."

"Nossir, I'm givin' you that melon; it got yo' name on it."

"I'd like to pay."

"No way you gon' pay."

He sat down at the picnic table, enthralled.

"I've got an idea," he said to Willie. "Let's eat it together."

A few miles up the road, his hat blew off into a cornfield. Maybe he should stop and retrieve it; it was a perfectly good hat. But what was a hat when he'd found Willie after sixty-plus years? What was a hat when his wife and son were waiting? What was a hat when he had a brother whose life was on the line? The small things in his life were getting smaller by the minute.

He thought he heard a siren and glanced in the rearview mirror, then realized the sound was coming from the car.

He'd never been intimate with the inner workings of an automobile. He knew only that he didn't like the sound, which was like something winding up to fly apart.

He pulled off the road and sat for a moment, then checked his watch. Cynthia was expecting him at nine o'clock, a little more than an hour away.

He was innocent as a babe about what to do; he'd once given up automobiles for Lent, and for eight years had used his two feet, which had worked just fine.

Where was Lew Boyd's Exxon when he needed it? He had no idea what Lew's number was in Mitford, and lacked the patience to get it. Sweat stung his eyes. Barnabas looked doleful.

He took out his wallet, found Jim Houck's card, and punched the digits. Houck was a Ford man, he should know these things.

"What's it soundin' like?"

Feeling foolish, he duplicated the sound as best he could.

"Fan belt," said Jim.

"Or maybe it's more like this." He had another embarrassing go at vocalizing the problem.

"Could be your alternator or your water pump. Is your red light on?"

"No red light."

"What's th' temperature gauge read?"

"Let's see." He squinted at the dash. "Somewhere between one-eighty and two hundred."

"That's normal. Now start your engine. Hold th' phone to it an' let me listen."

He started the engine and popped the hood. Right there was the full extent of his skill with a car.

The sound was earsplitting. "What do you think?"

"I think it's your fan belt. If it's your alternator, it'll run for a little while on th' juice in your battery. If it's your water pump, it'll start throwin' steam an' you're not goin' anywhere t' speak of. On th' other hand, if it's your fan belt an' it breaks, th' amp gauge will drop back an' th' temperature will shoot up."

He got in the car and switched off the engine. "Can I get to Memphis?"

"How important is it to get there?"

"Urgent. Critical. Do or die."

"You might make it. Keep your eye on th' gauges—amp an' temperature. If it looks like trouble, I'm givin' you th' number of a dealership this side of Memphis. They're open Saturday mornin', they could bring you a belt or haul you in, whatever you need. I'll give 'em a jingle, say you'll be callin' or comin' in."

"Thanks, Jim. Thanks."

"I'd come ride with you, but I got a customer and he's got cash."

"I'll be fine."

"This guy's either gon' roll out of here in a loaded Crown Victoria or I'll never lay eyes on 'im again. Here's th' number of th' dealership if you need t' call. They're on your right about five miles south of town, next to a burger place. An', Tim, call me and let me know how it's goin'—I'll run up there if you need me."

Dooley was a college student, he'd still be dead to the world after the long haul from Mitford to Memphis. What could Dooley do, anyway? And why alarm Cynthia?

He looked at his dog, started the engine, and, over the clamor, shouted a petition. Given its focus and brevity, the prayer of his double-great-grandmother definitely had merits.

TWENTY-FOUR

He'd come up the road on a wing and a prayer, drenched with sweat and clenching his jaws 'til his molars ached.

Leon, the assistant service manager, gave him a thumbs-up. "All you need is a new fan belt. It'll take Eddie about forty-five minutes to slap it on, you'll be good to go."

"That's great, Leon. Terrific." He'd meet Cynthia in front of the hotel and they'd drive straight to the doctor's office.

Forty-five minutes later, he was paying the bill and marveling. He had no memory of any service to any of his cars ever being accomplished in the time predicted. This was history in the making.

He turned on the a/c and sat in the Mustang looking at a map of Memphis and the route to the hotel. He undid another shirt button and held his hand in front of the vent. Warm air. He'd fiddle with it later.

He was pulling out of the lot when the grinding and squealing began. He drove two blocks, firm in his belief that the noise would stop. It didn't. He recalled being mildly suspicious of "slapping on" a fan belt.

At a traffic light, the driver in the next car gave him a rude stare. The volume was deafening; his dog escaped from the front seat to the back.

He turned around and drove to the dealership, pulled into the service garage, and stood by his car until someone, anyone, made an appearance.

He called Cynthia's hotel room and told her to sit tight, then tried the cell phone number written on the back of the doctor's card and got a series of beeps. He vaguely remembered this as some kind of paging technology, and, feeling awkward, hung up.

Leon was clearly disappointed to see him.

"There's a new noise, something I never heard before. It started," he said with emphasis, "after you installed the fan belt." He reached in and switched on the ignition to demonstrate, then switched it off out of respect for his dog.

Leon looked mournful. "Eddie's stepped out for a sausage bis-cuit."

"Can't somebody else take a look?"

"Don't have anybody else. This is Saturday. We're open 'til noon as a courtesy to our customers—it's a new promotion deal we're tryin'."

"You're open as a courtesy to your customers, but there's nobody here to provide service?"

Leon pondered this.

"When is Eddie coming back?"

"Fifteen, maybe twenty minutes. Dependin' on traffic."

There was no balm in Gilead. None.

"Any idea what it could be?"

"Sounds to me like th' clutch on your air compressor."

"Can you look under the hood?"

"I'm not allowed t' do diagnostic."

"Can I drive it?"

"I wouldn't if I was you."

"If it's the compressor, what kind of time will it take to fix it?"

"Can't say 'til we look at it. It's an '84, we'll have to order the parts. I'd say two, maybe three days minimum to get you rollin'."

Two or three days minimum. If he was ever going to have a stroke, this would be the time.

"I've got to get out of here," he said. "Period."

"Come back Monday mornin' first thing, I'll work you in."

"You said I shouldn't drive it."

"You can leave it, we'll lock it up for you."

He studied the metal rafters, choosing his words. "This new promotional deal you're trying out?"

"Yeah?"

"It's not working."

He called Dooley's cell phone, got no answer, and left a message that he needed to be picked up and delivered to the doctor's office, ASAP. He sat in the Mustang, mopping his face with the tissues from Amy's travel pack. Thank heaven for Dooley's crew cab, there would be room for Barnabas. He rang Cynthia's room. Busy. He left a message

He dialed the doctor's number.

"Tim Kavanagh?"

"Yes, Doctor, I regret that I'll be late for our appointment this morning, I've had car trouble and I'm waiting for a ride to your office. My sincere apologies, I know how important this is."

"Don't think about it. I've got some catching up to do; I'll be here 'til noon. Ring the bell at the door, I'll give you the buzzer, straight down the hall."

He hadn't really looked at the doctor's card and didn't remember if Henry had mentioned him by name. He flipped the card over.

Jack R. Sutton, M.D.
Director, Stem Cell Transplant Program

He found Leon. "Where's Eddie?"

"Called in a minute ago. He's stuck in traffic."

"I need a taxi."

Leon removed his ball cap and scratched his head. "Guess I could give you our courtesy car service, if it's jus' one-way."

"It's just one-way."

"Car service is part of our new promotional deal," said Leon.

He kept his mouth shut, gave his dog water, counted the time.

Ten minutes. Fifteen. Twenty. When the black town car glided up, he and Barnabas clambered in. "Peabody Hotel," he said to the driver.

He had been perfectly happy sitting on the porch at Whitefield shooting the breeze. And now this piece of insanity, which made a busted compressor look trifling: The doctor who may be siphoning his bone marrow was the guy who once hated his guts for cruising around in a Thunderbird convertible with Peggy Cramer.

Jack Sutton, of all people. It was incredible. More than that, it was comedic. But he wasn't laughing.

"That's a dog and a half," said the driver.

"True." He heard this comment all the time; why couldn't people come up with something new, for crying out loud? The air in the car was flash-freezing the sweat on his forehead. Odd that Sutton had called him by name but clearly hadn't recognized or remembered who he was.

He fiddled with the vent.

"Too warm?" asked the driver. "Too cold?"

"Too cold." His whole system felt out of order, scrambled.

"I'll turn the temp up a couple of notches, how's that?"

He spoke to the rearview mirror, in which he could see the driver's eyes. "Good. Great." Blue. Squinty.

He tapped his foot, impatient. Nervous as a cat, his grandmother would have said. He kept forgetting that ardent, unrelenting prayer had brought him out here. He kept forgetting that God was in this.

"Car trouble?"

"First a fan belt, now maybe the clutch on the air compressor."

"That was your Mustang ragtop?"

"Yes."

"Sharp little ride."

"Thanks. My wife bought it for me."

"What year?"

"Eighty-four." He suddenly remembered the cooler sitting on the backseat. Two days in a locked car at ninety-five degrees and rising. What next?

The phone rang in his pocket. In the dark interior of the town car, he could read the lighted I.D.

"Hey, buddy."

"Hey, Dad. Got your message, I'm on my way."

"Have you left the hotel?"

"In the parking lot."

"Had to leave the car in the shop, they gave me a car service. I'm headed to the Peabody. I'll be there in . . ."

"Twenty minutes," said the driver.

"Twenty minutes. Cynthia's line was busy; ask her to meet me out front. Can you give us a lift to the doctor's office? Barnabas can ride in your crew cab."

There was awkward pause. "Sure."

"Thanks, son."

"See you in twenty."

"First time in Memphis?" asked the driver.

"First time in thirty-eight years." He had seen his father's Memphis lawyer about an issue in his mother's will before heading back to his parish duties.

"Memphis isn't the same town I knew as a kid," said the driver.

"How's the barbecue these days?"

"I'll write a couple of names down when we get to the hotel. Still the best, no contest. You been to Graceland?"

"Never."

"Ought to go."

"That's what I hear."

He thought about Dooley's hesitation to drive them to the doctor's office. Maybe he'd had something else to do.

"Nice dog."

"The best, no contest." He was talking to the driver's eyes in the rearview mirror.

"We have an old lab, she's a real sweetheart. She sticks with me an' th' cat sticks with my wife. Uppity creature; I never could get the hang of cats."

"A fellow named Robert Heinlein said, 'Women and cats will do as they please, and men and dogs should relax and get used to the idea.' Are you a Memphis native?"

"Holly Springs. Right down the road."

"Small world. Me, too."

"I've been back to Holly Springs a few times. When I was in Vietnam, I didn't know if I'd ever get back there or anywhere else. Die young an' make a good-lookin' corpse was my plan, but God had other plans."

As the driver braked for a traffic light, he sat forward to see more of the driver's face in the rearview mirror.

In what felt like slow motion, the driver turned around to look at his passenger. They stared at each other, wordless. The driver raised his right hand, and he raised his.

They pressed their thumbs together twice.

Hooked their little fingers for two beats.

Slapped their palms together two times.

Knocked their right fists together twice.

Spoke the secret word.

TWENTY-FIVE

Avery brisk walk, he thought as the doctor came along the hall. In fact, it looked as if Jack Sutton hadn't aged at all. Had the clock stood still for Jack Sutton, while racing ahead for Tim Kavanagh? Sutton must have had work done—a lot of work. As for himself, his jowls sagged, his chin bagged; he felt a hundred and two in the shade.

They were greeted with a handshake. "Jack Sutton, Father."

"My wife, Cynthia."

"Thank you," she said, "for taking time from your weekend."

"Glad to do it. Henry's one of my favorite patients. What's with the moon boot?"

"I missed a porch step," said Cynthia. "Two, actually."

"Did that myself once. In my case, however, I missed the entire porch, but it's a long story."

No way was this the Jack Sutton he'd known, who would be seventy if he was a day.

Holding hands, he and Cynthia followed Sutton along the hall to his office.

"Are you by any chance from Holly Springs?" he asked.

"My dad is from Holly Springs, I was born in Memphis."

"A junior, then."

"We have different middle names, actually. Dad's an Edward, I'm a Randolph."

Oncology had afforded the young Sutton an impressive view of downtown Memphis.

"I knew your dad," he said, "we were in high school together. How is he?" Somewhere, the elder Sutton's jowls were sagging like his own. A comforting thought.

"Not good. Cancer of the prostate."

"I'm sorry."

"So am I. He practiced here for more than thirty years. Retired only a few months ago. Please sit down."

"I remember your dad as the handsomest fellow at Holly High. You're his spittin' image, as they say."

"I take that as a compliment." The doctor sat in a chair opposite them and gazed at him intently. "So how does it feel to have a brother?"

He hadn't yet been able to put words to it. "It's a lot to take in. I . . . always wanted a brother."

"I always wanted a sister. Got two brothers instead. Good guys; a nephrologist and an architect. In any case, if you had to have a half brother come at you out of the blue, Henry would definitely get my vote."

"I'm diabetic," he said. "Type Two."

"You're managing it?"

"Yes. Pretty well."

"Most likely not a problem. Generally, there's nothing life-threatening in the donation of stem cells if you're in reasonably good shape. We'd give you a thorough donor workup and do blood and lab work, of course. What we'll need, bottom line, is an identical match of blood types. Without that, we go nowhere."

"I hear you drill into the bone, then siphon the marrow with a syringe." There it was; that's what he'd been skittish about.

"That's for a biopsy. We wouldn't take actual marrow from you, only blood. The older method is to remove bone marrow from the donor and transplant it to the recipient. Now we use a procedure called apheresis, which centrifugates the blood—spins it, actually, so the heavier particles, the red cells, fall to the bottom, and the lighter particles form a very thin layer on top—a layer of white blood cells including the stem cells—the gold, the cream. We siphon off the white layer, and that's the infusion we give to the recipient."

"What are the chances of an identical match?"

"With full brothers, the chance is only one in four. With half brothers, the chances are slim. Very slim. Maybe five percent."

"But worth moving ahead?"

"No question. To put it plainly, you're all we've got. If you find you're willing to do it, I can fast-track it. We could start doing blood work first thing Monday morning; we'll go from there, see what we have.

"If everything looks good, we'd get Henry up to Memphis and start the chemo immediately. Then we'd start mobilizing your white blood cells with a shot a day for five days. If it looks like we're getting what we need, we'd do your apheresis."

He and Cynthia looked at each other. The centrifugation had already begun—his head was spinning.

"Apheresis," said Cynthia. "Is that what you said?"

"Yes."

"Is it painful? Risky in any way?"

"Neither. The donor loses some red blood cells in the process, but only a few, and they're rapidly replenished. Apheresis is actually a pretty comfortable procedure. We insert a catheter in each arm—it's double-barreled to spin more blood, faster—and put the donor in a recliner for five or six hours. If you need it, we could give you a mild anesthesia, but that's rarely needed. Meanwhile, your family comes to visit, you read the newspaper, watch TV—there are worse ways to spend a few hours. We could have you on the road the following day."

"When would the infusion happen?"

"The same day. Soon after the apheresis."

Jack Sutton leaned forward. "I don't know if you can spare the time, Father, but between you and me, Henry doesn't have any time to spare."

The little boy under the house—as Henry talked, he'd been under there with him, both of them searching for their father.

Cynthia appeared skeptical. "From the donor's standpoint, it sounds too good to be true."

"The suffering," said Jack Sutton, "is done by the recipient."

"Tell us about that," he said.

"During the five days we're mobilizing your stem cells, Henry would receive chemo—perhaps even radiation therapy. He could have a high level of nausea and a good bit of vomiting. Plus myalgias, diarrhea, shaking chills—not to mention a terrific physical exhaustion.

"Later, there's always the risk of kidney or liver failure. I'm sorry to sound grim, but these are the facts.

"The point of the chemo, of course, is to do away with his immune system. We handcuff it, you might say, so the chemo can create space in his own bone marrow for your stem cells. Once your cells start circulating in Henry's system, we're on our way. Then we pray for them to engraft."

He realized he would want to be there as his cells flowed into the life stream of another human soul.

"Can anyone other than your team be in the room with him?"

"When we suppress his immune system, he'll have no way to fight infection, so we'll have to isolate him. The air in the room is filtered, and anyone who goes in wears gloves and a mask. He could have some visitation, yes, but limited and monitored. It's a delicate piece of business all around."

"The engrafting—how long does it take?"

"Ten to fourteen days."

"If all goes well, how much time before he can go home?"

"If he tolerates the transplant and his blood counts return, roughly four weeks."

Why was he hesitating? The issue was closed.

"Without your help," said Jack Sutton, "he'll always need chemo. When he grows resistant to it, as he inevitably will, the cancer cells will increase. I'd give him a year, maybe less."

"And with my help?"

"If you're a match, if your cells engraft in his marrow, it's very possible that he could lead a normal life."

"Consider it done," he said.

They were walking through the foyer after leaving Sutton's office, where he'd felt dim-witted, trapped in a dream. As Cynthia stepped into a patch of light from the windows, something sharp and new suddenly awakened in him.

He took her hand and pulled her to him. "You dazzle me," he said.

"Long time, no see, darling."

She folded her arms around his neck and touched his nose with hers. "Dooley has a surprise for you."

"You're all the surprise I need." He took her face in his hands and kissed her.

Home wasn't Holly Springs; home wasn't Mitford. Home was his wife.

TWENTY-SIX

W e've got it all worked out, Dad."
He and Cynthia and Dooley sat in the hotel dining
room with his surprise. Lace Harper was a great beauty, no doubt
about it. He looked at the two of them, his red-haired son and this
extraordinary young woman who had earned her early education
from the bookmobile. Merely to gaze upon this pair moved him
deeply.

"Are you completely in favor of Dooley's scheme?" he asked
Lace.

"Yes, sir. Completely. I slept for twelve hours last night."

"It might have been longer," said Cynthia, "but I snored and
woke her up."

"Fourteen hours for me," said Dooley. "I'm good to go. We'll finish lunch and head back with Barnabas; that'll put us at Meadowgate by eleven tonight. Which means I can help Hal castrate steers
at High Ridge Farm in the morning."

"That's something to hurry back for, all right."

Dooley grinned. "You got to do it all."

"I like your plan. Barnabas is always happy at Meadowgate.
How's the pool table working out?"

"Great. Thanks for letting us put it in the living room."

"You have Cynthia's generosity to thank for that."

"Lace shot a game, she was pretty good."

He liked looking at Lace and Dooley, who were looking at each other. "When we get home to Mitford, we'll all shoot pool 'til the cows come home. I'll bring barbecue."

"Chopped," said Dooley.

"Sliced," said Lace.

"Both," said his wife. "I love barbecue."

He dug out his wallet and handed over a bill. Dooley Kavanagh was worth big money since the inheritance from Miss Sadie, but it felt good to give his son a few bucks.

"You don't have to."

"I know. Get yourself a nice dinner, no fast food. There's a great Mexican place the other side of Knoxville. You can practice your Spanish."

"Muchas gracias, Papito. And at one o'clock"—Dooley glanced at his watch—"hasta la vista."

"I wondered," he said, "why you had to think twice about picking me up at the dealership."

"I knew Barn would take up most of the cab, and we couldn't all fit on the front seat. So we decided to save the surprise 'til after the doctor's visit."

"You can surprise me anytime with Lace Harper. Seeing you two together is a profound blessing."

"We love you both," said Cynthia, "and want the best for you in everything."

Dooley took Lace's hand. It was the most open display of affection he'd ever seen Dooley make toward the girl who once slammed him in the ribs for swiping her hat.

"I promise to pray for you and Henry," said Lace. "I think it's wonderful you have a brother."

Lace had a brother with the character traits of her malevolent father; there had been no contact in years. "You'll like him; he has fine sensibilities—and he writes poetry. Are you still writing?"

"Yes. But mostly just letters to Dooley." Her cheeks colored.

"Love each other," he said. "Whatever you decide to do with your lives, love each other.

"Loving can be hard. Sometimes we don't feel loving, but it isn't all about feeling. Very often it's about will. Practice that if you can." He thought he may have said too much, but he looked into their eyes, and knew he had not.

Under the hotel canopy, he prayed for their safe travel and gave the Old Gentleman a good scratch behind the ears. Watching the red truck pull away, he felt oddly bereft. His dog had been his right arm, his confessor, his soul mate on this trip.

Cynthia looked at him and smiled. "My turn now," she said, reading his mind.

They lay in bed on Sunday morning, watching the slow illumination of the sheers at the window.

"First light," he said. He'd read that Thomas Jefferson arose at first light, never deigning to wait until sunrise.

"I love first light."

"The ducks," he mused. The Peabody was famous for its twice-daily march of mallards from the elevator to the fountain in the lobby. "We must see the ducks."

"Absolutely. I love ducks."

He rolled onto his side and looked at her lying next to him. "What don't you love, Kavanagh?"

"Road food, magazine ink that comes off on my skirt, and lovers who can't find the courage to love."

"We'll be married eight years in September, and you're still ticked with me for taking so long to make up my mind."

Her smile was ironic. "No use crying over spilled milk. But it does help me understand their relationship. Dooley hasn't an ounce of your blood in his veins, yet his approach to love is very like yours."

"Fear, you mean?"

"Yes."

"With both parents abandoning him, why shouldn't he be fearful?"

"I didn't say he shouldn't be, I mean that he simply is. Just as you were. You were abandoned, too—by your father, by Peggy."

"And you, by your parents and then Elliott. So how did you know how to love in spite of that?"

"Perhaps because I had nothing to protect, nothing to lose by loving. You had your life as a bachelor to protect. It was a good life, you said, and I saw you living it and knew that it was good and deep and true. And of course you had your congregation to protect— after God, they came first, as they would with any shepherd worth his crust.

"But I didn't need to protect my calling, I find it improves with loving. And my heart—yes, it was broken as a child and then by Elliott, but God had healed it, and I knew it could never be truly broken again. So, if I had any fear when I found I was in love with you, it was only the fear of not measuring up to all you'd been protecting."

He never knew which way to step when they talked about these things. He lifted her hand and kissed it. "All we can do is watch and wait."

"What you said to them yesterday was perfect."

"It was you who taught me that."

She plumped the pillow and propped herself up on her elbows. "We could have breakfast in bed."

Seventy years old and still blushing at the thought of a waiter serving him breakfast in bed. "That would be great," he said, trying to mean it.

"Life is so full of the unknown, Timothy. Wouldn't it be lovely if we could absolutely count on Henry to grow strong and keep writing poetry and raising collards and beets?"

"Speaking of which." He threw the covers back and went to the closet and dug around in his duffel bag. He'd been eager to read it soon after Henry gave it to him, but the notion had escaped his befuddled mind.

"Look," he said, climbing back in bed. "It's one of Henry's poems. He wrote it while Peggy was praying about how to contact me and what to say. He says she often sits with the Bible open on her knees while she recites the text from memory."

"Read to us," she said.

He unfolded the handwritten pages and scanned the words; a chill ran along his spine. His brother's poetry.

> By the open window
> in April afternoon light,
> my mother's brown head—
> bald as a river rock
> beneath the scarred cross—
> bends over pages worn slick
> by the oil of years.
>
> Dignified and solemn,
> the supplications of the Prophet
> assemble themselves in
> the hall of her memory.
> She closes her eyes and
> summons them forth; they
> speak with power and might.
>
> *Bless the Lord O my soul*
> *and all that is within me*
> *bless His holy name.*

O Lord, I will praise Thee;
though You were angry with me,
Your anger was turned away,
and You comforted me.

God and God alone is my salvation;
I will trust and not be afraid:
for the Lord God Jehovah
is my strength and my song.

Stirred by a breeze from the garden,
the white curtain drifts onto her shoulder
like a mantle of snow.
Shadows quicken in darkened corners;
light trembles in the mirror of the floor.

Mighty God Jehovah,
blessed Lord Jesus,
I aks you—
let these old ears hear
a word behind me saying,
This is the way, Peggy, walk you in it.

There comes a scent
as of wash dried on the line
and hurried inside before
a summer storm.
I am at home in the long silence.

Then the old prophet speaks:
The Lord has written the letter.
She closes the Book
and sits small as a child
on the hardback chair.
I go to her

and kiss the graven cross
on the dome
of her brown head
and say, Amen, Mama,
and amen.

Somewhere an early church bell pealed.

He dropped the pages onto the blanket and took Cynthia's hand. They sat for a long time, their eyes closed, as the morning light increased.

TWENTY-SEVEN

Since his lab work and Henry's admission to the hospital, time had been one long siege, with few markers to distinguish the days.

That his blood had proved an identical match was "miraculous," according to Jack Sutton. But when he gave the news to Peggy by phone, she wasn't surprised or incredulous—it was, she said, the news she'd been expecting.

Masked and gloved and fervent in prayer, he visited Henry each morning and again in the early evening. Afterward, he had a walk and then dinner with Cynthia. Now allowed to drive, she had lost no time in renting a car and amusing herself at the library, a museum, and the bookstores. On Wednesday, Sutton initiated the series of shots that would mobilize his bone marrow to produce more cells. The days seemed vague as shadows, though punctuated by unexpected moments of clarity, and a heightened awareness of breathing, thinking, living.

His body felt the wallop of the shots. His bones ached as with flu; he maintained a low-grade fever and ate sparingly. He wanted only to be at his post in the recliner, getting the thing done. Henry Winchester was fighting for his life while Tim Kavanagh merely proffered his arm for a daily needle.

Sutton's comments on Henry's reaction to the chemo were mixed. "I've seen worse," he said. "But not much worse."

To hear the laundry list of side effects expected during Henry's chemo had been one thing; watching him suffer the effects was another. The chills were racking, and the nausea so severe that he, Timothy, unsnapped his tab collar and twice used the toilet for his own heaving. He begged God to give him a portion of the agony, then realized this petition had been fulfilled. Blood answered to blood—on some incalculable level of his being, there was an agony quite his own—it was an excruciating sense of helplessness in the face of suffering.

When he had left his father's bedside, he had in a sense let him go. Unless God Himself ordained it, he would not let Henry go.

He alerted his bishop to the need for petitions throughout the diocese.

"I'll tell you everything later. Right now, pray for Henry Winchester to accept a stem cell transplant and live a normal life. Henry Winchester, yes. Pray as if he were your brother."

He called Lord's Chapel in Mitford and talked with Father Talbot's version of Emma Newland.

"Get the word out," he said, "that someone close to me is in a struggle for his life. His name is Henry Winchester. Write his name down, please. Call the churches in town, especially Bill Sprouse at First Baptist, and thanks."

He rang his friends at Whitecap Island, then called the young curate serving Holy Trinity on the high ridge beyond Mitford.

"Especially ask Agnes and Clarence for prayer; devote time on Sunday to special petitions. Many thanks. And the preacher down at Green Valley Baptist—ask him, too, if you would; he's a prayerful fellow. Winchester, yes. Henry. Someone important to me. Please."

He was marshaling troops, he was calling up regiments; this was war.

TWENTY-EIGHT

His wife smoked him over, eyeing first the back of his head, then the front. "It isn't exactly your John the Baptist look."

"Good. Great."

"But it's definitely going there."

He remembered this pronouncement when, on a mission to the drugstore, he saw a shop advertising walk-in haircuts. Though he felt the several uneasy side effects of the shots, he couldn't lie around the hotel like a lizard. Getting a haircut would divert his mind.

Jolene was immediately available, and obviously glad to see him.

"My wife said to take a little off the sides and get it off my collar." He felt five years old relaying this message; he must learn to seize control of such matters himself.

"Has your wife ever cut your hair?"

"No. Maybe once. Not a good idea."

Jolene draped him with a cape. "It looks to me like your sides need thinnin', not cuttin'."

"Fine."

"They're a little poufy."

"So I've been told."

"I learned about hair from my grandma," said Jolene. "She cut my hair 'til I was out of high school."

"My grandma cut mine 'til I was twelve. Before I turned eight, it was on the house. After that, I had to mow her yard in exchange for barbering."

Jolene laughed. "I don't know what we'd do without grandmas."

"Amen to that."

"My grandma was so good-hearted, it's no wonder God picked her out for an Elvis experience."

"An Elvis experience?"

"It's th' greatest story of our whole family. I mean, none of my kin was ever cousin to Daniel Boone or kidnapped by Indians, or anything you could really talk about to people.

"I called my grandma Mam. When it happened, she was exactly my size: five-foot-two an' weighin' a hundred an' sixteen. She just loved Elvis an' wanted to express her love in—you know—a Christian way. So she baked him a cake."

"That'll do it."

"I don't know if caramel was his favorite, but that's what she baked—a caramel cake. It was two-layer, an' with th' pecans she put on top, it cost three dollars for th' makin's. I don't know if your family was ever like mine, but we didn't have three dollars to just fling around, you know?

"But anyway, Mam baked Elvis this cake, but she didn't have any way to take it up to Graceland. I mean, she didn't have a car. So she walked four miles to Graceland, an' the gate was closed. She was just devastated. She thought th' gate would prob'ly be open since it was broad daylight.

"She took it over there in a nice carrier that belonged to a neighbor, so it wouldn't get dust or car fumes or anything on it. Th' neighbor didn't want to let her use th' carrier, but since it was for Elvis, she said okay, but bring it back, it cost a ton of money.

"Well, she couldn't just stand at th' gate 'til th' cows came home. She saw there was enough room to push the cake under th' fence, but only if she took it out of th' carrier. So she took it out of th' carrier and pushed th' cake under on th' cardboard round, an' then she climbed over th' gate. She went over th' gate because it had better toeholds than th' fence, an', course, she had to take her shoes off to do it, they were high heels. Well, not exactly high anymore—Mam was so strapped, she'd walked th' heels off all her shoes, they were more like flats, you know?

"But when she got over to th' other side, she realized th' cake carrier was still settin' in th' grass on the front side. She didn't want to take a buck-naked cake up to the house, it wouldn't look right, so she crawled back over the gate and got th' carrier. That was not easy to do, you know? I mean, have you ever seen that gate?"

"I've never been to Graceland."

"You've never been to Graceland?"

"Not once."

"I can't believe it. Are you not from around here?"

"I'm from North Carolina."

"Well, that's no excuse, I can tell you that right now. You have got to go. Who'd want to die without goin' to Graceland?"

"I don't know," he said.

"I can just see my little Mam walkin' up that driveway in her flat heels an' knockin' on th' door. She said she was scared to death, she couldn't believe she'd got that far without runnin' back home like th' devil was chasin' 'er. An' who do you think opened th' door?"

She looked at him in the mirror, expectant, but he couldn't come up with anything.

"Elvis," she said. "Himself. He'd been out ridin' his horse in th' back yard an' thought it was maybe his, what do you call it, his, you know, person who shoes horses."

"Farrier."

"But it wadn't, it was Mam. He said, Who are you?

"She said, I brought you a cake.

"He said, What kind?

"She said, Caramel two-layer. From scratch.

"He said, Come in.

"Can you believe it? *Come in.* Elvis. Th' King. An' my little Mam right there in 'is house. He took her in th' livin' room, it had white shag carpet an' still does to this day. He showed her this glass-top table, said, Set it right there, I'll be back. She said he was wearin' a cowboy getup with a hat an' boots an' all. It was before he gained weight, which I personally think was fluid.

"He went off and came back with a knife and two paper napkins. He cut th' cake an' gave her a piece, then he took a piece an' they sat on th' sofa while they ate.

"An' you know what they talked about? They talked about her—my little Mam. He said, What do you do? She said, Wait tables. He said, Where at? She told him th' place, I forget th' name, they tore it down. He said, Where do you live at? She told him she lived with her grandma, told him exactly which corner an' everything, an' that it was a white house with blue shutters.

"He said, How'd you get over here?

"She said, Walked.

"He said, How'd you get in th' gate?

"She said, Climbed over—but pushed th' cake under th' fence.

"He said, This is really good cake.

"She said he ate another piece and offered her one, but she didn't take it, she had really nice manners. He gave her his autograph on a paper napkin an' walked her to the door an' said, Thank you for comin', an' goodbye, little darlin'.

"*Goodbye, little darlin'.* Can you feature that?"

His sides were definitely flatter. "That's a wonderful story," he said.

"But that's not all. Oh, no, that's just th' beginnin'.

"She hated she'd forgot th' cake carrier, because it was her neighbor's, but who could remember their cake carrier when you're up at Graceland hangin' around with Elvis? She figured she'd have to buy a replacement, though Lord knows, she shouldn't have to, bein' it was settin' up at Graceland—a fact which her neighbor could brag about for th' rest of her life.

"Two days later, she opened th' front door of my great-grandma's house, and what do you think was settin' in th' front yard?"

Her cheeks colored. "A baby-blue Eldorado Cadillac."

"Was Elvis in it?"

"Wadn't nobody in it. It had a big ol' red bow tied on th' hood, an' a big sign stuck under th' win'shield wipers sayin' LITTLE DARLIN. An' guess what was settin' on th' front seat."

"I give up."

"Th' cake carrier."

"I'll be darned."

"She was just thrilled; she said it was the best thing ever happened in her whole life, includin' marryin' my grandpaw when she was fifteen."

He shook his head, incredulous. "He just gave her a Cadillac?"

"Out of th' goodness of his heart. He had a heart as big as Texas, even Alaska. An' you know what?"

"What?"

"Mam couldn't drive a lick. She lived to be sixty-six and never did learn to drive a car."

"What did she do with the Cadillac?"

Jolene's eyes flashed with anger. "That's another story."

"Doesn't have a happy ending, then."

"No. Not one bit. I don't tell that part."

"Well, I certainly enjoyed the part you did tell. Thank you."

She removed the cape and whisked the hair from his collar.

"I tell it as a tribute to Mam for her thoughtful ways, and a tribute to Elvis for bein' a very kind man—a very *great* man. A lot of so-called intelligent people don't think he was a great man—but," she said, looking fierce, "they would be wrong."

"I believe you," he said.

"Are you comin' back to Memphis anytime soon?"

"Maybe."

"I'm here every day but Monday. You need somebody to give you a good conditioner. We rub in this really nice cream, then put a plastic bag over your head. All you do is lay back for five minutes an' take it easy."

"A bag over my head."

"Not your *whole* head."

"I'll remember that," he said.

TWENTY-NINE

What his wife dubbed Reclining Day, roughly in the tradition, say, of the church calendar's Rogation Day, had arrived at last, and thus he was reclining.

" 'With the knife the tree he girdled, just beneath its lowest branches.' " He hadn't meant to say that at all. *You look great in red*—that's what he meant to say. His wife never wore red; he liked red.

Cynthia raised one eyebrow. "We know who's going to have all the fun today."

"A little anxious?" the nurse had asked.

"A little, yes." A lot, actually. Though Sutton had called apheresis "a benign procedure," he had slept in quick, edgy doses and waked up anxious and off-kilter.

The nurse had requested a pill of some kind, and he didn't protest. "It'll settle you down," she said. "You're going to be just fine. Dr. Sutton usually puts a newspaper in the room; you can kick back, watch a game show—I'd be glad to swap places."

First thing this morning, he'd gone in to Henry. His color wasn't good, not at all, and he was too weak to talk. Yet he had looked up with evident pleasure, and smiled a little. "Tim," he whispered.

Henry's weight was dropping fast, the skin flattened against his cheekbones.

Henry whispered again, but he didn't catch it. He leaned closer. "May God watch over you."

"And you," he said. Touching Henry wasn't allowed; he felt as if his hands had been amputated.

Now, tethered to the machine in the exam room of a dialysis unit, he pondered Henry's spirit of surrender in this horrific circumstance. Henry was doing what the English clergyman Jeremy Taylor had promoted with great passion.

Nothing is intolerable that is necessary, Taylor had written. Now God has bound thy trouble upon thee, with a design to try thee, and with purposes to reward and crown thee. These cords thou canst not break; and therefore lie thou down gently, and suffer the hand of God to do what He pleases.

" 'With purposes to reward and crown thee,' " he said to his wife. "Very important to keep in mind."

Cynthia looked up from reading the newspaper and smiled. No, actually, it was a grin. "What was that pill they gave you?"

"Did they give me a pill?"

"I spoke with Leon about the car," she said. "He found a cooler on the backseat and took it home and put it in his freezer—to give you when we pick up the car."

No balm. No way, nohow.

"But his mother-in-law was visiting, and found the cooler in the freezer, and . . ." She looked at him oddly.

"And?"

"She roasted the groundhogs."

"Hallelujah." He would have applauded, but with a catheter in each arm and the mandate to keep his arms flat, he was limited.

"He said he's really sorry."

"Too late for sorry."

"He said they were the best he ever tasted. He'll put in new floor mats absolutely free."

"Deal."

"Is there something you haven't told me?"

"You won't believe it."

"I love things I won't believe."

"Later," he said. "As entertainment on the drive home. Which reminds me—I need something to write on."

She browsed through her carryall, which appeared to be living up to its name. She had been to a bookstore and bought whatever caught her fancy, including Wendell Berry, Graham Greene, Thomas Merton, and Annie Dillard. "How about a sheet from my sketchbook?"

"I was thinking a card, maybe. To say thanks to Smokey and the boys."

"Who?"

"You know—th' fellows in th' cammo."

"I've had a wonderful idea." She was clearly interested in changing the subject. "You said you wanted to come back in a couple of weeks to see Henry. How about letting Dooley drive you?"

"Oh, no. It's fine. I can do it."

"But he would love to do it; I know he would."

"He has his own life."

"He hasn't spent much time with his dad in years; and think how nice it would be for you. Besides, how long has it been since the two of you spent ten hours together in a truck?"

He laughed. "Never." It was an odd idea. But he liked it. Maybe he'd think about it.

A nurse flew into the room. A flying nurse. Well, not precisely flying, but moving quickly nonetheless, as nurses tend to do.

"You have visitors," she said. "Just checking to see if it's all right."

"Oh, yes," said Cynthia, "we love visitors."

He tried to sit up straight to see who was coming in, but he couldn't sit up straight. Blast. It was because the chair was reclining. Of course. He lay back and craned his neck toward the door and there was the red head rag. There was Peggy.

"Peggy," he said, unbelieving.

A nurse rolled her toward him in a wheelchair, her cane lay across her knees.

"I aks Brother Grant to bring me to Memphis to see how you doin'."

"Doing well, very well. My goodness—all the way to Memphis." His brain was churned butter; he wanted to stand up, but couldn't seem to manage it. "Have you seen Henry?"

"We're fixin' to go down there. First, we wanted to see th' one makes it all possible for Henry to get better."

"Peggy Winchester, my wife, Cynthia."

Cynthia was embracing Peggy and bawling like a kid. His wife would weep at the drop of a hat.

"It's mo' better to see you in th' flesh, you're a beautiful lady."

"It's wonderful to see you, Peggy, we thought we might have to wait until heaven."

"Feels like heaven right here, with what you all are doin' for us. God goin' to bless you for it, but Henry and I'll never be able to thank you enough. Never."

Please don't say that, he thought. It isn't done yet, it's just beginning.

"Is this the young man I found in my graveyard?"

A bass-baritone voice, offstage to the right. Then an elegant, elderly black man stood before him. A black man in a black suit, carrying a black book.

"This is our preacher, Brother Grant," said Peggy. "He says he met you as a little chap, when you were lookin' for me."

It was a wonderful life. To have a stage play right in this room, with real people acting real parts. And he'd thought the reward only a newspaper.

"I retired out where Peggy and Henry live, and took on a little church some years ago. Like Jacob, they won't let me go 'til I bless them." Brother Grant laughed. The sound of his laughter was a kind of nourishment.

"Brother Grant is older than me," said Peggy. "He's ninety-three."

"And still looking fit," he said, marveling.

Brother Grant smiled. "Psalm One-sixteen says, 'The Lord preserveth the simple.' Do you remember that day in the graveyard?"

"I remember it well. I bawled and you stood by me—you were a consolation. I thought you might be an angel, but the black suit threw me off."

"Been wearing black before th' Lord all these years. It was the best way I knew to keep away from flashy clothes and live out John three-thirty."

" 'He must increase,' " he quoted, " 'but I must decrease.' "

"That's it," said the old man.

"You all drove up here by yourselves?"

"Yessir, we did. We took it slow and easy."

"Brother Grant got what he calls pulled," said Peggy.

"Pulled? You mean . . ."

"Brother Grant got a warnin' for drivin' thirty-five miles in a fifty-five mile zone."

"Young policeman leaned in my window an' said, 'Do you know why I'm stopping you?' I said, 'Yessir, I'm th' only one you could catch.' "

Everybody in the play was laughing.

"It's a miracle," he said. "A miracle." Brother Grant, of all people. And Peggy.

"God stays busy with miracles," said Brother Grant. "Some people don't believe miracles still happen every day."

"They're missin' out," said Peggy.

"Amen," said Cynthia.

"Bless God!" said Brother Grant.

"If you let us," Peggy told him, "we'll come back in a little bit an' Brother Grant will lay hands on you."

"Thank you." He felt like a child, a very small child. "Please come back."

When they left, he closed his eyes for a time, incredulous and happy.

"I'm happy with you," said Cynthia. "We could be happy always if we always trusted God."

"There's the rub. Remember the quote from Elizabeth Goudge that stayed pinned over your drawing board for an eon?

" 'She had long accepted the fact that happiness is like swallows in spring. It may come and nest under your eaves or it may not. You cannot command it. When you expect to be happy, you are not . . .' "

She joined her voice with his. " '. . . and when you don't expect to be happy, there is suddenly Easter in your soul, though it be midwinter.' "

They smiled foolishly at one another.

"When you were in New York for such a long time," he said, "I'd go to your house to 'check on things,' as I called it. I really went to seek out your smell, and touch your paint boxes, and read the words that helped me realize again how happy you made me. You had given me the Easter I didn't deserve."

"Easter is never deserved," she said. "I'd never before given anyone Easter; if I gave it to you, it was by grace alone."

He studied his wife intently. He must tell her how terrific she was looking in red. General Henry . . . "General Henry E. Williamson!" he exclaimed.

More laughter. He was liking this machine with its double-barreled thingamajig.

"You're far too much fun, sweetheart. I'm going down for coffee, want some?"

"Not in Styrofoam, please." As a clergyman, he had paid his dues with coffee in Styrofoam.

"In Royal Worcester, then? Or Spode?"

"Meissen, if they've got it."

He heard his wife speaking to a nurse at the door. "I'll have what he's having."

He wondered if Jack Sutton knew he had a half sister and was an uncle to three children in Manhattan. Perhaps he knew, but never spoke about it.

It stood to reason that there were lots of half sisters and brothers out there. Miss Sadie had had two of her own, one from each parent, and both entirely unknown to her. By an extraordinary turn of events, her much younger paternal half sister now rented the rectory next door to him in Mitford. He remembered that Miss Sadie, who thought herself an only child, had longed for family, when all the while, family abounded.

He was examining the ceiling with some interest when the door pushed open. "You in here, Tim?"

"I'm in here."

"How's it goin'?"

"Couldn't be better. Glad to see you, buddy, thanks for coming. Pull up a chair."

Tommy moved a chair next to the recliner. Like everyone else in their age category, Tommy Noles was shrinking. And white-haired. And wrinkled, to boot. It was very odd to see Tommy with wrinkles.

"How fast will that thing go?" asked Tommy.

He mashed a button on the remote, and was suddenly sitting upright. "Goes like a scalded dog."

When Tommy grinned, his blue eyes disappeared, just like old times. "I can't believe this, Tim. My wife can't, either. She's heard all about you. This means a lot." Tears dimmed Tommy's eyes. "A lot."

Life was short; ask questions. "How come you ran out on us all those years ago?"

"Had to."

"I understand," he said. "I ran out on people, too."

"You probably know what happened to my mom and dad—they drank themselves to death. It was already pretty bad when we lived up the road from your place. By the time I went to college, they were goin' off the deep end—and so was I. I never talked about what went on at my house; I was always tryin' to protect them, and myself. I thought if you knew how things were, you wouldn't let me be your friend anymore."

"You were the best friend I had," he said. "Nothing could have changed that. Actually, we were both hiding something—you, because you knew what was going on with your parents, and I, because I had no idea what was going on with mine. Kids didn't know how to talk about such things back then, and probably still don't."

"I felt there was a kind of hell in me all those years," said Tommy, "and the only way to get it out was to get it scared out. I joined the Army and ended up a foot soldier in the ten-thousand-day war—Twenty-fifth Infantry Division."

He inevitably felt shame when talking with a Vietnam vet, as he had been openly opposed to the war.

"Military could get anything they wanted in 'Nam, and what I wanted was alcohol. I didn't mess with other drugs; alcohol was the familiar ease, it ran in my blood, it was milk for a cryin' baby. I figured I'd drink myself to death, it was the family way. But it seemed like a chicken way out in the face of all the suffering we saw.

"I was pretty cocky, I'd do most anything. 'Get Noles to do it,' they'd say. 'Noles'll do it.' Fed my ego.

"We started lookin' at what th' Vietcong did with tunnel systems. You wouldn't believe it—a lot of 'em were multi-level, constructed with wood an' clay, an' they ran all th' way to Saigon. Huge, some of 'em, hard to locate, an' so deep you couldn't destroy one with artillery or air strikes—a good many survived th' B-52 attacks. You should've seen what they had down there—hospitals, kitchens, sleepin' chambers, weapons storage, food bunkers, you name it. Some were like towns.

"A commander couldn't order a man into a tunnel, it was strictly volunteer, and out of th' volunteers he handpicked his teams. I'd heard plenty of stories from guys who went in—they called 'em tunnel rats—an' knew that a lot of 'em never came out. But I figured I could do it; I was th' right size for it—a hundred and twenty pounds drippin' wet—an' th' kind who didn't give a rat's ass.

"I knew there'd be pit vipers down there, scorpions, fire ants, spiders, bats—I hated th' bats, they'd fly right at you, get all over you. Man. I still dream about th' bats. But what scared us th' worst was gettin' buried alive in a cave-in. It happened a lot, and whoever made it out had to go in an' recover th' dead.

"But th' cave-ins were a maybe. What we knew for a fact was sooner or later we'd meet somebody down there; we'd see his eyes shinin' in th' dark an' hear th' pin bein' pulled out of his grenade.

"First thing I did was resign myself to th' fact I was goin' to die. I was older than th' rest of th' guys, but so what—they say the oldest soldier killed in 'Nam was sixty-two.

"One day, we located a trapdoor; th' commander wanted a team to investigate. I volunteered.

"It was like droppin' into hell. I knew if I could survive th' first one, I could probably make th' next one. I worked th' tunnels for two years with my buddy Rance Ortega. He was half Mexican, half Brit, an' a hundred percent gung ho. Rance was my rabbit's foot, th' best in th' division.

"Non gratum anus rodentum: Not worth a rat's ass. That's th' motto they gave the boys who worked th' tunnels, and that pretty much nailed it. If you thought too much of yourself, you'd better stay on solid ground. You had to go down th' hole as a nothin', a zero, or you'd never make it out.

"Course, what got a lot of th' guys wasn't snakes or grenades or th' VC, it was panic. We hauled 'em out screamin', sometimes totally gone, totally.

"I remember one of our rats crawlin' in to investigate a tunnel. We attached a rope to him. He got a little ways in, we felt the rope jerk, that meant he wanted to come out. When we pulled him out, he'd been decapitated."

Tommy's hand was shaking as he took a tissue from the box on the nightstand and wiped his eyes. "I don't talk about this, not to anybody. But I wanted you to know. It was important for me to tell you why I left an' you never heard from me. Thank God you climbed in my backseat th' other day. I thought I might have to die without tellin' you what went down.

"I knew the tunnels were where I'd been headed all my life. It was either goin' to scare hell out of me an' save my ass, or they'd be shippin' me home COD."

"What kind of protection were you going in with?"

"A knife, a standard-issue Army flashlight, and a Colt .45. Later, I traded up to a nine-millimeter German Luger. Big difference."

"That's it?"

"That's it. Most of the time I went in with Rance, but sometimes I worked alone, against th' rules. You know what I thought about a lot when I was workin' a tunnel? You."

"Me?"

"I was crawlin' horizontally, but it was like you an' me goin' up th' tank ladder. You were bustin' up that ladder like a monkey, not lookin' back. I stayed right behind you, but I was scared to death— th' wind was rattlin' us around like a couple of old socks. So I played this head game in th' tunnels, that I was followin' you up th' ladder, an' it made me feel safe—don't ask me why."

"Don't ask me why, either. I was scared out of my wits climbing that ladder."

"But you never seemed to be scared, you seemed to have it all together all th' time. I was always th' one haulin' my scattered parts around in a basket."

"I don't understand that," he said. "You were the best Indian fighter in the fort, you would do anything."

"I would do anything because I was a zero. You were a ten."

"No, I was never a ten. A four, maybe. Maybe."

"It probably won't surprise you to know that my whole life was turned around in a tunnel—in a rice bunker fifty feet below th' Iron Triangle. I'd gone in with Rance; I had a hunch that somethin' was goin' to happen that night—we pretty much went in at night because the VC occupied th' tunnels pretty heavy during the day. They'd made me a platoon leader, it was a big deal for me. Maybe I figured I didn't deserve it, that somehow I'd have to pay for it. Maybe it was my time to hit a booby trap, maybe trip the wire that opened the door on a crate of snakes, or hit a mine that would blow both of us to Saigon an' back. I could feel the panic comin' an' knew if I lost it, if I went mental, Rance would drag me out of there an' I'd never work a tunnel again. Nobody would ever say again, Send Noles, or Noles is th' best rat we got; they'd be sayin', Poor sonofagun, he's too old, he can't cut it anymore, send th' bugger home.

"That's when I called out to God. And he answered.

"Since I didn't know then that God is everywhere, I was pretty blown away that he was in th' tunnels, just like some guys found him in a foxhole back in the two big ones.

"In a way, it was kind of like a cave-in—this great big peace just kind of dumped in on me, washed in on me like a wave. It was powerful; it was like nothin' I'd ever known or felt in my life. Rance felt it, too. 'It's God,' I said. He said somethin' I won't repeat, he didn't want anything to do with God; ol' Rance was enough for Rance.

"That night I told God if he'd get me out of th' jungle alive, I'd straighten up. I got to tell you, I didn't know what I was talkin' about, I didn't know how to straighten up. It was foreign to me.

"When I came home from 'Nam, I was hookin' Johnny Walker hot an' heavy for about five years. Looked like I was gon' to kill myself, after all. In World War One, they called it shell shock. Second time around, they called it battle fatigue. After 'Nam, it was posttraumatic stress disorder. There was help back then, but it was hard to find—nobody wanted to mess with th' guys comin' home, and I wouldn't have taken help if they handed it to me on a silver platter.

"But no use runnin' on about it. What happened was, he hung on to me. I knew he wouldn't let me go. And he didn't.

"I go to AA every Wednesday," said Tommy, "an' meet once a week with four guys who served in 'Nam, one's a chaplain. It helps a lot.

"Things are pretty good now. But I've got to confess somethin', Tim. I'm th' one who told we climbed th' tank; I was about to bust, I couldn't hold it in. I leaked it to Jimmy Swanson an' he blabbed it all over town. I've always felt rotten that I broke my word to you and you took a really bad whippin' for it. I'm sorry."

"It's okay. I forgive you. But don't let it happen again."

He knew what laughter was: It was manna.

Tommy took a small box from his jacket pocket. "I wanted you to see this," he said, lifting the lid.

"The Bronze Star?"

"That's it."

He wiped his eyes with the heel of his hand. 'Or every man be blind,' he thought. "I'm proud of you, Tommy. Thank you." He couldn't find words. "Thank you."

"An' I've got somethin' for you." Tommy took an envelope from the breast pocket of his driver's uniform. "To you from me; no need to open it now. I want you to use it and give me a report." Tommy's blue eyes disappeared in the old Noles grin.

"Consider it done," he said.

"I talk to people sometimes when I'm drivin'; talk about God, what he can do for us if we let 'im. You made a whole career out of talkin' about God—except you get to talk to bigger numbers."

"Numbers don't matter. One soul at a time is enough. Is plenty."

"I've got to bust out of here, I'm pickin' up a rock band at the airport. They booked my stretch through Wednesday; I don't get a stretch job every day. If you get back to Memphis, I want you to meet my wife, Shirley, she's a lifesaver. An' my two kids an' grandkids. And what th' hey, I'd like you to meet my dog, too."

"We'll be back," he said. "We'll do it. We'll keep you faithfully in our prayers. God be with you, brother."

Tommy Noles. Lost and found. He didn't want to let him go.

At the door, Tommy turned and held up his thumb. "That's where I whacked myself with my knife, remember?"

He wiggled his thumb. "I remember."

They spoke the secret word.

THIRTY

He'd read the newspaper editorials, gotten hooked up to a calcium drip, called for the urinal, had his blood pressure taken, and eaten a cup of yogurt. There was only so much you could do on Reclining Day, especially if your wife had taken herself off to the Maternity Ward to gaze at infants.

"Maybe someday, but only maybe, I'll do a book about babies," she said before leaving. He saw the look in her eyes, and knew exactly what the look meant—she would definitely be doing such a book.

He tried to feel his blood running around in a circle, but he didn't feel anything different. He felt a nap coming on.

"Hey, Tim."

"T! Hey, yourself. What in the world are you doing in Memphis?" T's pompadour was looking good. Shiny.

"Had to come up for shutter hinges, a couple of light fixtures, this an' that. When you called an' said you'd be strapped in a chair a few hours, thought I'd drop by. What's goin' on?"

"Not much. They're just running my blood around in a circle, that's how they collect stem cells these days."

"How's Henry?"

"Have a seat, T. Struggling."

"Sorry to hear it. Keep us posted." T paused, respectful. "Ray's in th' hall."

"What's he doing in the hall?"

"Said he told you how he'd never come to Memphis again, no matter what; said he didn't want to give you a heart attack while you're hooked up to machinery."

"Ray!" he hollered. "Get in here!"

Ray walked in, grinning. "This my las' time in Memphis."

"Right. Good to see you, buddy, thanks for coming."

"We got to look out for our first big customer," said Ray.

T stooped over the chair and pointed to the top of his head. "Feel this," he said.

He raised his forefinger and felt it.

"Fuzzy."

"Dern right. Fuzzy as a peach. About a week, an' we got fuzzy. It's gon' work."

"Good timing. I might have a name for you." He'd finagled it out of his feeble brain one night at the hotel.

"Shoot," said T.

"But remember I'm a preacher. I'm no marketing maven."

"Yeah," said Ray, "but bein' a preacher puts you in sales, an' that's good enough for us."

"Let's start with packaging, so when I get to the name, you can, you know, imagine the way the name will look to the consumer."

"Good deal," said T.

"A white tube."

"We're with you," said T.

"Blue lettering. I read a study that said men like the color blue—has authority."

"What about women?" said Ray. "We don't want t' lose out on that demographic."

"I didn't get that far," he said. "But I'll keep it in mind. For the lettering, I'd use bold type. Sans serif." He'd done pew bulletins, he knew this stuff. "Sans serif is more contemporary, though I'm a serif man, myself. Okay. Here's the name . . ."

You could hear a pin drop.

"Mo' Hair."

"I don't get it," said Ray.

"Try again," said T. "If you don't mind."

"Okay. You'll like this. Hair to Spare."

"Man!" said T. "Hair to Spare. That's it. I like it. I really like it. What do you think, Ray?"

Ray's grin displayed the majority of his recent dental work. "Got your Kudzu King an' Marketin' Maven right here in one room."

"Ship me a case," he said.

"Hair to Spare," said T. "Right on th' money. Glad I asked you t' think about it."

"Cast yo' bread on th' water," said Ray, "an' some days it come back buttered toast."

"We need t' bust out of here, my brother's comin' tomorrow with a SUV full of lawyers and fishin' rods."

"There ought to be a joke in that."

"We got shutters to hang, light fixtures to put up—"

"But first, we got barbecue to eat," said Ray. "Right down th' street."

"Aw, man, I wadn't gon' tell 'im that," said T.

"You're breakin' my heart, boys."

"Chopped," said T.

"Baby backs," said Ray.

"Get out of here," he said.

A nurse flew in. "Grand Central Station," she said, none too pleased.

"No rest for th' wicked, an' th' righteous don't need none."

"You're chipper."

"How do I turn on the TV?"

She snatched the remote and hit a button; the screen displayed what appeared to be a tractor-pulling contest.

"No, wait," he said. "I don't want to watch TV, I never watch TV except for *60 Minutes*. How do you turn it off?"

She hit a button, the screen went black.

"How much longer?"

"Two hours," she said. "Forty-five minutes if you're lucky."

She jiggled something, plugged in something, hummed to herself.

"Is that 'Delta Dawn'?" he asked.

"Is what delta dawn?"

"What you're singing."

"I'm not singing."

"I mean, humming. Weren't you humming?"

"Not that I know of."

"Excuse me," he said.

He was exhausted. He opened his mouth to yawn, but couldn't get the job done. " 'First he built a lodge for fasting,' " he said, " 'Built a wigwam in the forest, By the shining Big-Sea-Water, In the blithe and pleasant Spring-time.' " He was on the water in a canoe. Very blithe and pleasant.

"Now look," said the nurse, "you've pulled your IV out."

"I didn't pull my IV out, did you pull my IV out?"

"Oh, good grief," she said.

"Is he misbehaving?" Now his wife was flying in.

"I don't know what they gave him," said the nurse.

"A cookie," he said.

"See what I mean?" The nurse jammed the needle in again.

"His doctor at home," said Cynthia, "claims he's sensitive to certain types of medication."

"They did give me a cookie; it was somebody's birthday, for Pete's sake." He wasn't going to take this anymore.

He seemed to remember that Peggy and the tall black man in a black suit had come in and read from the black book; he'd felt something warm on top of his head, he had tingled when he was touched. Then maybe he'd gone to sleep.

His eyes searched the small room for his wife and he remembered she'd left again, to sign papers. Had he told her how great she looked in red?

"Okay, sweetie."

This was definitely a nurse he hadn't seen before. She was unplugging, unhooking, very busy. He rather hated to get unplugged; sitting here had been blithe and pleasant, very blithe.

"You have family?" the nurse asked.

"Oh, yes. My wife. My son. My dog."

"Brothers and sisters?"

"Yes, yes."

"What do they do?"

What do they do? "Let's see. One is a retired railroad conductor; he had the northbound run on the *City of New Orleans*." He imagined the train racing along the track, people waving.

"I went on that train when I was little," she said. "My grandmother took me to New Orleans to see my aunt. She had fourteen cats."

"One is a Vietnam vet and owns his own car service. And one is retired from school sanitation."

"Um-hmmm," said the nurse.

"There's one who sells cars, I can't remember his name right now. He's trying to figure out where he fits in."

"A perfect description of my husband, bless 'is heart."

"And T, he can do it all, you name it—plumbing, electrical, dig for dinosaurs."

"Wow," said the nurse. Off came the IV bandages, hair and all.

"And there's Ray, of course." He wanted to complete the list; he was worn out. "He's cooked for presidents, movie stars, tycoons, you name it. You should taste his catfish."

"Yum, love catfish. Hush puppies, coleslaw, th' works."

"Billy. Billy. Willie runs a produce stand at the side of the road. His grandmother left him her farm; he's missing a thumb."

She held his wrist and looked at her watch.

"And my wife, she's my sister . . ."

"Oh, boy."

". . . in Christ, of course. Let's see. Peggy. Peggy's gaining on ninety, but she can still see a chigger crawling on a blackberry. Then there's Rosie . . ."

"Very interesting family." The nurse yanked something from the wall. "Large."

"Yes, ma'am," he said. Very large and interesting family.

THIRTY-ONE

"You've done it again, Tim."

Henry lay with his eyes closed, drowsy from the sedatives given to inhibit nausea during the infusion.

"What have I done?"

"Saved my life twice. By saving my mother's life, you made mine possible—and now, this. Somehow, I believe I'm going to make it."

I believe that with you, he wanted to say, but it was too soon; too much hard ground lay ahead.

The IV bag was currently emptying something vital of himself and their father into Henry's bloodstream. It was the end of a long journey; it was the beginning.

Henry turned his head on the pillow and looked at him. "Mama told me about the time you cut down the Christmas tree. She said you spent three nights at her house; you slept on a pallet by the fireplace."

The memory was vivid, it might have been yesterday. Cornbread and milk in a mason jar . . .

"She said that's when your mother miscarried your little brother—right here in this hospital."

Dear God. Of course. How was it he'd never guessed? In all the years since, no one had spoken a word to him about a matter of such great importance. 'It may not be the answer we're expecting,' his mother told him when he prayed for a brother, 'but God always answers.'

"I'm sorry if I said the wrong thing, Tim. I thought you knew."

"No, you said the right thing. It's okay." Sixty-four years between loss and gain. What goes around comes around.

"You've had a lot thrown at you in a mighty short time," said Henry. "The way you're able to handle the truth is something to see. It reminds me of a Dunbar poem that Papa taught us children— he called it a poem about attitude.

" 'A crust of bread and a corner to sleep in, A minute to smile and an hour to weep in, A pint of joy to a peck of trouble, And never a laugh but the moans come double. And that is life. A crust and a corner that love makes precious, With a smile to warm and tears to refresh us, And joy seems sweeter when cares come after, And a moan is the finest of foils for laughter. And that is life.' "

He adjusted the paper mask, which he loathed wearing.

"Which reminds me of something in turn. Samuel Rutherford wrote, 'Whenever I find myself in the cellar of affliction, I always look about for the wine.' "

"I'm certainly looking about for the wine."

"I'm looking for it with you, Henry." That he could say, that he could surely say. "How are you feeling?"

"My soul is easy."

"Nausea?"

"Not too bad right now."

"I have something to show you." He took the photograph from the manila envelope and held it up for Henry to see.

He noticed that his hand trembled, animating the women beneath the cherry tree.

"You'll never again have to try and spin his face from air."

Unable to speak, Henry fixed his gaze on the image of Matthew Kavanagh.

Afternoon light slanted through the window blind; illumined the face of the laughing man, the bowl in the brown woman's hand.

"A mole by his left eye—and looks like a gold tooth." Henry was reading the runes of their father's face.

"It was."

"That's a nice jacket."

"I remember that jacket," he said. "It was blue. Mother liked him to wear blue; she thought it looked good with his silver hair."

"Beautiful head of hair. Is that something on his lapel?"

He squinted at the lapel. It seemed he might touch it, feel the weave of the linen. "A daisy, perhaps. Mother sometimes put a flower in his buttonhole."

"He's wearing a tie," said Henry. "Yet this looks like they were in the country."

"We were at a dairy farm up the road. It was before the war ended; they invited the neighbors for a covered-dish. Dad always dressed up, he wasn't a fan of shirtsleeves unless he was working in the field with Louis."

"And there's Mama."

"Probably setting out a bowl of her good potato salad."

"So young," said Henry. "Everyone is so young."

"That's my mother in the dress with the hibiscus flowers." Her long, dark hair was caught up in a figure eight on the back of her head. She once looked at herself in the mirror before leaving the house in that dress and turned to him and asked, 'Timothy, do you think this dress is too exotic for Holly Springs?'

" 'No, ma'am,' he said. 'It's not too exotic for anything.' He'd been pleased to know she trusted him with a word like exotic.

Tears misted Henry's eyes. "They were beautiful, all of them."

"A dear lady I was in school with took that picture. She believes God charged her to give it to me, and I'm charged to give it to you."

"Thank you." Fatigued by the exertion, Henry closed his eyes. "Thank you."

"I'll put it back in the envelope," he said. "It'll be in this drawer when you're allowed to touch it. Try to sleep. I'll be sitting right here when you wake up."

As earnestly as he'd yearned for his father to love him, he had wanted to be able to love his father. Perhaps now he could love his father in Henry—and even in himself. Certainly he could love the man in the hosta grove who looked at his wife with such unguarded tenderness. He could love the man who paid a dear price to protect a young black boy from harm. He could love the man who had taken his son's hand and walked around the barn on the frozen eve of Christmas.

Feeling the weight of his own exertions, he sat in the chair by the window and dozed until the nurse came in and removed the empty IV bag.

Before the infusion, he'd been allowed to administer the sacraments, which had given them both an ineffable calm. Now that the infusion was complete, the sense of helplessness returned.

"I can only pray," he said, standing again by the bed.

"But that's enough. More than enough."

"Many people are lifting petitions for God's mercy and grace in the life of Henry Winchester. This prayer simply beseeches God to hear all of us who're praying, and grant answers according to his will."

He adjusted the mask again, and bowed his head and recited the old prayer he'd esteemed since seminary.

"Almighty God, who has promised to hear the petitions of those who ask in your son's name: we beseech you mercifully to incline your ear to us who have made our prayers and supplications unto you, and grant that those things which we have faithfully asked according to your will, may effectually be obtained to the relief of our necessity, and to the setting forth of your glory."

He made the sign of the cross over Henry. "In the name of the father and of the son and of the holy spirit." He pronounced the word in the Baptist manner, with the long *a*: "Amen."

"Amen," said Henry.

He was worn through utterly, there was nothing more to give or be gained.

"Even if we don't see each other again," said Henry, "I'd like you to know I will thank God for you the rest of my life."

"Not see each other again?" He tried to swallow the knot in his throat. "I guess I forgot to tell you: I'll be back in two weeks. You aren't shuckin' me off so easy."

"Brother Grant and some of the deacons will be driving up before long; Sister's coming every Sunday, and one of my old conductor buddies lives down at Ripley. I'll be fine. You don't have to come back if it's trouble."

"I ask you, Henry: What would the world be without trouble? Dunbar wouldn't have had a blasted thing to say. Besides, I'm hoping to bring your nephew to see you."

"A nephew." Henry smiled. "It hardly seems real. But Cynthia is mighty real; a remarkable lady—beautiful inside and out."

"Alis volat propiis."

Henry pondered this. "She flies with her own wings."

"Nailed it," he said, grinning. "She liked the Langston Hughes you recited—it was a striking contrast to the Longfellow I've been blabbing. Well. I'm on my way, then. We'll head out early tomorrow, but I'll call the nurses' station tonight—have them wake you up to ask how you're doing. They're fond of that sort of thing. By the way, I need to take some barbecue home. Do you happen to know where Elvis got his barbecue?"

"Everywhere he could, would be my guess."

He laughed. "I'll touch base every day. Remember that half of western North Carolina is praying for you."

"Don't worry about me," said Henry. "As long as I keep looking about for the wine, I'll be fine."

"You're a poet and don't know it."

"Deus te custodiat, Tim."

"Deus tecum fratercule," he said.

As he walked from the room, a nurse was standing at the open door with a plastic cup of pills. "Law help, what were y'all sayin'?"

"Henry said, 'May God watch over you.' I said, 'God be with you, my brother.' "

"What was that language?"

"Latin."

"Oh, phoo," she said, "I can speak Latin. Ere-whay are-yay ou-yay oin-gay?"

"To the lobby to pick up my wife, and off to North Carolina in the morning."

"O-gay afely-say."

"Ake-tay are-cay of-ay enry-Hay."

She laughed. "E-way ill-way. Ome-cay ack-bay."

He saluted. "Oon-say."

He met Jack Sutton in the hall.

"The technologist says it's going well."

"Yes," he said.

"I'm on my way to see him, I hear he's comfortable."

"I think so, yes. Again—when will we know if the cells are en-grafting?"

"Ten to fourteen days," said Sutton. "Then we'll find out whether we're going uphill both ways or headed for a breakthrough."

He'd like to think Jack knew he had a sister. Maybe he'd been in New York, say, for a medical convention; maybe he'd called her and they'd had lunch together, each searching the other's face for clues to the mystery of their father. There were a thousand ways it might have happened, or could happen yet.

"I'll be back in two weeks," he said.

"Good medicine."

"I'll stay in touch."

"You've been great, Tim. There was about a five percent chance your blood would be a match, and look what happened."

"Grace," he said.

"Plus you had enough cells to get the job done, which is no small feat for someone in your age category. We've all done everything we know to do; it's up to God. Travel safely, call me anytime."

"Thank you, Jack." They shook hands. "You're in our prayers. My regards to your dad."

"Sure thing."

In his imagination, he was already in his pajama bottoms in the bed at the hotel—the draperies closed, his wife reading in the chair with her feet on the hassock, the thermostat on seventy, the fan on auto.

He found her sitting in a corner of the waiting room, her nose in a book.

"Kavanagh! E're-way out-ay of-ay ere-hay."

She looked up at him and laughed; he saw the naked gladness in her eyes. "You definitely got your money's worth with that pill," she said.

THIRTY-TWO

It was as if he'd passed through a dark tunnel into a blaze of light. He knew what day it was; he noticed the weather; he realized he was ravenously hungry, and he was appalled at the condition of the clothes he'd been wearing for so many days, albeit with the extra shirt and pants Cynthia brought from home.

"Have poached eggs on unbuttered toast if you must," he said as they sat in the hotel dining room, "but I'm having a full-bore J. C. Hogan."

"What might that be, sweetheart?"

"Two scrambled eggs, a rasher of bacon, grits, biscuits, link sausage—and a bowl of fruit."

"I'll look the other way," she said. "But just this once."

"How 'bout those floor mats?"

" 'Go, Tigers'? Someone got the short end, and I don't think it was Leon."

While the valet service was bringing their car around and Cynthia was using the facilities, he called Walter.

"Walter, it's your cousin. Are you sitting down?"

"The last time you asked me this, you'd gotten engaged at the tender age of sixty-two. You can't top that."

"I'll let you be the judge." He paused a moment for effect. "You have another cousin."

There was a long silence in New Jersey as Walter examined reason and logic. "Another cousin? Come on. How in heaven's name could that happen?"

He told him.

"I called Walter," he said, as the Mustang arrived at the hotel entrance. "He's very keen on the idea of another cousin."

"Dominoes all over the place."

"By the way, before we leave Memphis, there's something important we must do."

She glanced at her watch. "You wanted to get out of town by eight-thirty."

"I've changed my mind. Vita brevis."

"Life . . . ?"

" . . . is short."

He checked his jacket pocket, which contained Tommy's envelope and the two tickets. Then, feeling an idiotic grin spreading over his face, he offered her his arm.

"The party's not over," he said. "We're going to Graceland."

Afterword

Henry Winchester was released from the hospital and returned home six weeks after the infusion of stem cells harvested from his half brother.

The current prognosis is good.

For more works by JAN KARON, look for the 🐧

At Home in Mitford
ISBN 978-0-14-025448-8

A Light in the Window
ISBN 978-0-14-025454-9

These High, Green Hills
ISBN 978-0-14-025793-9

Out to Canaan
ISBN 978-0-14-026568-2

A New Song
ISBN 978-0-14-027059-4

A Common Life:
The Wedding Story
ISBN 978-0-14-200034-2

In This Mountain
ISBN 978-0-14-200258-2

Shepherds Abiding
ISBN 978-0-14-200485-2

Light from Heaven
ISBN 978-0-14-303770-5

The Mitford Bedside
Companion
ISBN 978-0-14-311241-9

All of the Mitford books are also available in hardcover.

———————— ◈ ————————

JAN KARON books make perfect holiday gifts.

More Paperbacks from Penguin:

The Mitford Years Boxed Set
Volume 1–6: 978-0-14-771779-5

Patches of Godlight:
Father Tim's Favorite Quotes
978-0-14-200197-4

A Continual Feast
978-0-14-303656-2

Hardcover books from Viking:

Esther's Gift
978-0-670-03121-4

The Mitford Snowmen
978-0-670-03019-4

The Mitford Cookbook and Kitchen Reader
978-0-670-03239-6

———————— ◈ ————————

Also by Jan Karon from Puffin and Viking Children's Books:

Jeremy: The Tale of an Honest Bunny
978-0-670-88104-8 (hc);
978-0-14-250004-0 (pb)

Miss Fannie's Hat
978-0-14-056812-7

The Trellis and the Seed
978-0-670-89289-1 (hc)
978-0-14-240317-4 (pb)

Violet Comes to Stay
978-0-670-06073-3

Violet Goes to the Country
978-0-14-056812-7

In bookstores now from Penguin Group (USA)
All of the Mitford novels are also available from Penguin Audio.
Visit the Mitford Web site at www.mitfordbooks.com

To order books in the United States: Please visit www.penguin.com or write to
Consumer Sales, Penguin Group USA, P. O. Box 12289, Dept B, Newark, New Jersey 07101-5289.
VISA, MasterCard and American Express cardholders call (800) 788-6262 or (201) 933-9292.